THE ANOINTED

THE ANOINTED

THE ANOINTED

Michael Arditti

A

Arcadia Books Ltd
139 Highlever Road
London W10 6PH

www.arcadiabooks.co.uk

First published in the United Kingdom 2020
Copyright © Michael Arditti 2020

A catalogue record for this book is available from the British Library.

ISBN 978-1-911350-72-9

Typeset in Minion by MacGuru Ltd
Printed and bound by Printondemandworldwide.co.uk

ARCADIA BOOKS DISTRIBUTORS ARE AS FOLLOWS:

in the UK and elsewhere in Europe:
BookSource
50 Cambuslang Road
Cambuslang
Glasgow G32 8NB

in USA/Canada:
BookMasters
Baker & Taylor
30 Amberwood Parkway
Ashland, OH 44805
USA

in Australia/New Zealand:
NewSouth Books
University of New South Wales
Sydney NSW 2052

For Selina Hastings and Ginny Macbeth

AUTHOR'S NOTE

In rewriting the story of King David and placing the three women closest to him at its forefront, I have adhered strictly to the sequence of events in the Books of Samuel. I have, however, felt free to add and amplify characters, to reinterpret incidents and resolve inconsistencies, making a contemporary fiction out of an ancient myth.

THE HOUSE OF SAUL

Saul

Ahinoam, his wife

Jonathan
Abinadab ⎤
Malchishua ⎦ the twins — his sons
Ishbaal

Merab ⎤
Michal ⎦ his daughters

Hodiah, Jonathan's wife
Meribaal, Jonathan's son

Abner, Saul's cousin

Rizpah, Saul's concubine

Adriel, Merab's husband
Penuel ⎤
Hillel │
Malkiel ├ their sons
Shealtiel │
Adriel ⎦

Paltiel, Michal's second husband

THE HOUSE OF DAVID

David

Abigail	Ahinoam	Maacah	
Haggith	Abital	Eglah	— his wives
Huldath	Bithiah	Bathsheba	

Amnon	Absalom	Adonijah	
Shephatiah	Ithream	Ibhar	
Elishua	Elpelet	Nogah	
Nepheg	Japhia	Jerimoth	— his sons
Eliada	Eliphelet	Solomon	
Nathan	Shobab	Shammua	

Tamar	
Nechama	— his daughters

Jesse	
Nizebeth	— his parents

Eliab	
Shimea	— his brother

Serach, Shimea's wife

Joab	
Abishai	
Jonadab	— his nephews
Gamaliel	

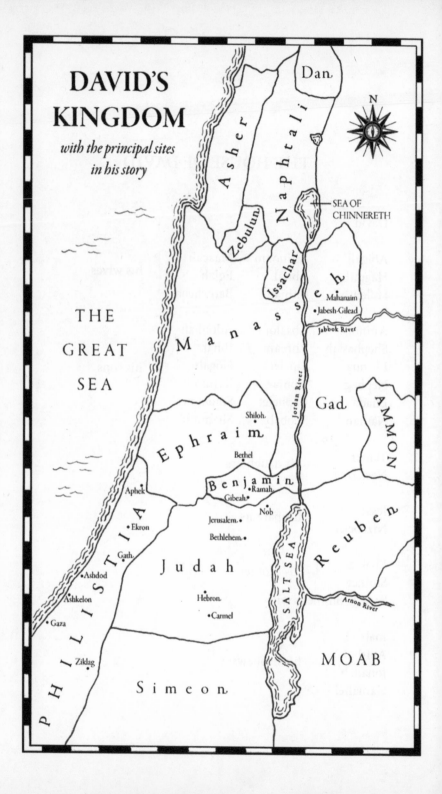

And when he had removed him, he raised up unto them
David to be their king; to whom also he gave testimony,
and said, I have found David the *son* of Jesse, a man
after mine own heart, which shall fulfil all my will.

Acts 13:22

ONE

Michal

I heard him before I saw him, strumming his lyre, the notes flowing through his fingers as smoothly as sand. Merab and I listened from the safety of the courtyard. Mother had forbidden us to enter Father's chamber when he was possessed by the evil spirit. Unsure what an evil spirit was, I pictured a Philistine god with a long, scaly tail, who could be caught as easily as a carp in the Sea of Chinnereth. So I waited until Mother's back was turned and crept up to the chamber, to find Father cowering in the corner, gnawing his hand, his eyes fixed on the empty air as if he could see something more dreadful than anyone had seen before. I was fourteen years old and terrified.

I ran downstairs, where Mother shook me as if I were the one possessed, before pressing me to her breast and assuring me that in time such spirits grew restless and moved on. But whereas ordinary men could afford to wait, a king had to resume his responsibilities. She did all that she could to hasten the process, wrapping bandages soaked in rose water round his brow and brewing him potions of hyssop, aloes and myrrh. She even sought out one of the sorceresses whom Father had outlawed, promising that, if she restored him to health, she would be free once again to practise her magic, but whether through incompetence or malice she failed. Then, as if to prove that he hadn't deserted him, the Lord showed a way forward. One morning while he was pacing his chamber, Father heard two Ammonite bondwomen singing a song of home. My brother Jonathan, who was with him, described him standing stock-still, his face relaxing as if he'd taken off a helmet. Jonathan immediately summoned the women and ordered them to repeat their song. At first Father listened calmly, but all at once his mood changed. He leapt up, throwing a footstool at one woman and taking a bite out of her companion's leg. They fled screaming. Jonathan forced them to return, but their agitation was transmitted to Father, and any virtue of their singing was lost.

With the tale of the bondwomen widely reported, Joab, my cousin Abner's armour-bearer, proposed to send for his uncle David, a shepherd of rare musical talent. No sheep-shearing, grape-gathering or New Moon festival in their home town of Bethlehem was complete without his songs. No one, Joab insisted, was better equipped to restore the balance of the king's mind. Abner was dubious that a simple shepherd could succeed where wiser men had failed. Merab and I were dubious of any claim made by such a boorish braggart as Joab. My mother and Jonathan, however, were ready to try anything and, to my relief, their faith was rewarded. David arrived and, according to Jonathan, showed no fear when Father bared his teeth at him. The moment he began to play, the colour returned to Father's cheeks like a sunburst after a storm. This time, moreover, the recovery lasted. After three days, he was deemed to be well enough to greet the household. Abner trimmed his beard, since he was not yet trusted with a razor. Jonathan and the twins bathed him. Mother brought him sweet fragrances and fresh linen. With Merab and our youngest brother, Ishbaal, I was one of the first to be allowed to see him. Sitting straight-backed on his couch and wearing his crown, he beckoned us forward. Merab and I moved to kiss him, but Ishbaal, who at ten was too old for such silliness, shrank back at the door. Jonathan took his hand and led him to Father, who patted his head as if he had returned from routing the Philistines rather than grappling with an evil spirit in a world known only to himself.

I stole a glance across the chamber at the musician, who stood, gaze lowered and clutching his lyre like a shield. To my astonishment, he was a young man, only two or three years older than me, although I brushed aside the comparison. For all the boyish purity of his voice, I had expected any uncle of Joab's to be middle-aged. As soon as we returned downstairs, I resolved to address the anomaly, seeking out Joab in the gatehouse, where he was regaling the guard with his role in David's triumph. He greeted me with a mockingly obsequious bow and asked how he might be of service in a tone that made the offer sound like a threat.

'I'm here on behalf of my mother,' I said, careful to conceal my interest. 'She wants to know more about the man who healed the king.'

'Ask anyone in Judah,' he replied pompously. 'We're one of the leading clans. David's father, my grandfather Jesse, is the grandson of Boaz, whose father fought alongside Joshua at the battle of Jericho.'

'Isn't he too young to be your uncle?' I asked, sounding as foolish as I felt.

'We're a large clan as well as a great one. Virile,' he added with a grin. 'David's one of ten. Eight boys and two girls. My mother was the eldest. She was twenty-three when he was born; I was three. As the youngest – and smallest – ' Joab said, drawing himself up to his full height, 'he was baited ruthlessly by his brothers.'

'And his nephew too, no doubt.'

'We were children. At six, he was sent to tend the flocks, freeing the others to work in the fields. I could never have endured the long summer days with only sheep for company. We used to joke that he preferred them to people. Though as he grew up, of course, there were compensations.' His leer lent his words a double meaning, although I couldn't work out what it was. 'I mean musical. He could play and sing to his heart's content without people shouting at him to stop.'

How anyone could object to such sublime music baffled me! I felt as deep a loathing for the entire family as for Joab himself. Leaving the gatehouse, I longed to find David to assure him that he wasn't alone: that there were kindred spirits in the world – in this very house. But although Father allowed me considerable licence to go about Gibeah, among men as well as women, he trusted me not to abuse it. It was one thing to have a private conversation with Joab, a soldier who was pledged to my protection, quite another to address a stranger, especially one so handsome.

It disturbed me to feel such an acute loss for someone I'd barely met. With Father's recovery, I had no chance even to eavesdrop on his playing, spinning fantasies as intricate as his songs. My sole ground for hope was that he hadn't returned home. As a mark of gratitude, Jonathan had invited David to stay with him and Hodiah. Knowing that Mother would welcome my visit to the sister-in-law she charged me with neglecting, I offered to take her a basket of figs. Pulling my veil across my face, both to pass unnoticed and to escape the dust, I wound my way through the airless streets to the east side of the hill. I was greeted by Menucha, our old nurse, as bent as a willow, who, trusting no one else with her favourite, had accompanied him on his marriage last year. She led me up to the roof where the two men were lying in the sun, their robes removed and tunics loosened. My arrival startled them but, while Jonathan swiftly regained his composure, David continued to look abashed as he fumbled with his belt. He stammered replies to my questions and I was struck that one so eloquent in song should be so shy in speech. When I praised his music, his face flushed red – although not as red as his hair, which glowed like fire, but a fire so gentle that I could plunge my fingers into it and not be burnt.

Jonathan watched our halting exchange in silence, but when David addressed me as 'My lady,' a title that for the first time felt apt, he intervened.

'My lady? Little Michal? She's not such a lady that she won't scream for mercy when she's tickled.' Without warning, he proceeded to prove it. I was outraged. If it had been the twins, who'd teased me since we were children, I might have understood, but Jonathan was the person I loved most in the world. Why should he wish to humiliate me in front of a stranger? Swallowing my tears, I joined in the game, but my pleas and protests were too brittle to fool my brother. Sensing my misery, he became all solicitude, smoothing my robe and calling to Menucha for mulberry juice. But with no sign of Hodiah and no explanation offered for her absence, I declared that I couldn't stay.

'Give me a kiss to show that I'm forgiven,' Jonathan said and took it without waiting for permission. But the kiss that I longed for languished on David's lips.

Jonathan insisted that he stay in Gibeah for the feast to celebrate Father's recovery. As ever, Father opposed any extravagant display. This was the man who, on the day of his election as king, had watched in mounting horror as the lot fell first on the tribe of Benjamin and then on the clan of Matri, even hiding among the baggage carts when the choice was narrowed to the family of Kish and, finally, to him. But with rumours of his indisposition circulating widely, he accepted the need to dispel them, not least for fear that the tribes would fail to respond to any future call to arms. He sent invitations to the elders across the land, with one to Samuel, the prophet and judge who had anointed him. Samuel declined, maintaining that he was too old to leave his home in Ramah, which came as a relief to me since his grim features and grizzled beard had cast a shadow over my childhood. Moreover, given Father's claim that it was the ever-vindictive prophet who had set the evil spirit on him, his presence would have been an affront. Mother undertook all the preparations, putting Merab and me to work, weaving garlands of rosemary and myrtle to adorn the house. Merab grumbled that there were servants and bondwomen enough for such drudgery, but I was glad of anything that kept me from thinking of David. I didn't mind thinking of him – quite the reverse – but it hurt to know that he wouldn't be thinking of me.

As the day dawned, even Merab was excited to wear one of the new chequered robes that Father thought fitting for his virgin daughters (Mother preferred *unmarried*). At midday we processed to the sanctuary, where a goat, a ram and a bull were sacrificed to the Lord for releasing Father from his torment – I couldn't help wondering why we didn't inveigh against his subjecting Father to it in the first place, but I knew better than to say so. The Levites sang, accompanying themselves on cymbals, pipes and horns, but the music, which I'd previously welcomed (not least for drowning out the terrified beasts' bleats and bellows), sounded crude after David's. If only he had been a Levite and allowed to join them, he could have remained in Gibeah forever. I revelled in the vision until, as if in rebuke, a billow of greasy smoke made me cough.

We returned home to find the feast laid out. Happily, only the elders from Gad and Asher had brought their wives and none had brought their daughters, so I was spared the feigned deference of girls from more exalted tribes, who felt that I'd usurped their position. Now that Samuel had renounced Father, they professed amazement that he had ever endorsed him. At the Festival of Reaping, I even heard one blame the Lord, suggesting that he had been beguiled by Father's height. 'Saul may look like a king,' she said, 'but isn't the Lord supposed to judge us by what's in our hearts?' I had promised Mother to ignore such provocation, but the effort was exhausting, so it was a relief to know that for now we were among our own clan, enjoying an easy intimacy that swiftly extended to our guests. Moreover, we shared an amused distaste for the roistering of the men, who sat across the courtyard, shouting, whistling, stamping and clattering bowls.

Midway through the meal, David stood up and moved to the centre of the courtyard. 'Like a hostage between opposing armies,' Merab whispered and, while I didn't care to think of the men as our enemies even in jest, I trembled for David as much as if the image were real. He, however, showed no fear as he sat and tightened the strings of his lyre before starting to play. He sang the old songs of Noah and the Flood, Enoch and the giants, and Jacob and his sons, making much of Benjamin in our honour. He sang new songs in praise of Father, likening his triumphs to those of Joshua and Gideon, and ending with a tribute to Jonathan's singlehanded raid on the Philistines at Micmash, during which Mother looked both distressed and proud and a cloud passed over Father's face – although it might have been the flickering of the fire. Then, when the cheers, from our side as well as the men's, died down, he sang a quiet song professing his faith in the Lord, which was unlike anything I had heard before. He showed no sign of tiring and I could have listened to him all night, but Mother caught my eye and, as if mistrusting its glow, dispatched me to bed.

I couldn't sleep, and not just because of the sounds that drifted up the stairs. It was more than a year since I had become a woman. But for all the monthly reminders that my body had changed, this was the first time that my heart had acknowledged it. Would I feel the same for every good-looking stranger? If so, how wonderful life was set to be! How enticing! How intense! Even after my restless night, I arose the next morning refreshed, alert and eager to find David. My plan was to congratulate him on his playing and then beg him to teach me. While I discovered music, he would discover Michal. Sitting by my side or, better still, directly behind me, scenting the cassia in my hair, sensing the softness of my fingers as together we plucked the strings, he would surely come to share my feelings. Despite my inexperience (so far I had scarcely even shaken a timbrel), I was confident that my deftness at the loom would translate to the lyre.

So, with another gift of fruit for Hodiah, which, had she not been busy preserving the leftovers from the feast, might have aroused Mother's suspicions, I made my way to Jonathan's house. I found Hodiah in the courtyard kneading dough, and, after the usual empty courtesies, which made me want to scream, I asked after David. To my dismay, she revealed that he'd returned home, travelling through the night to avoid the heat. For once she looked almost happy, and I felt an overwhelming urge to slap the fatuous smile from her face. My rage was so fierce that I feared that the evil spirit, having abandoned Father, had taken hold of me. I felt lost and bereft and sick and helpless. What made it worse was that, although he had come to mean as much to me as anyone in my family (with all the guilt that entailed), I knew that I was nothing to him but a silly girl who'd giggled and screamed when her brother tickled her. And, while I hated him for that indignity, Jonathan was the only person I could talk to about David without sounding false. When he finally came downstairs, eyes puffed and cheeks blotchy, dismissing Hodiah's proffered bowl of porridge with unwonted gruffness, I broached the subject, treading as carefully as a child on the edge of a well.

'Why has the musician gone home?'

'Father is himself again, thank the Lord.'

'But it's too soon. What if he has another attack?'

'We can send for David. Bethlehem's only a day's ride away. We gave him one of our best donkeys.'

In desperation, I pictured myself as a sorceress with the power to conjure evil spirits and so require David's recall. Then I remembered Father gibbering in the corner and blushed for shame.

Jonathan explained that, after his recovery, Father wanted no reminder of his affliction. As the first king of Israel, he felt a twofold obligation, to prove not only his own worth but that of the crown itself. The people's demand for a king had been contentious. Weary of warfare and the foreign armies garrisoned along their borders, they looked to other nations whose inhabitants tended their crops and their flocks and their children in peace. They wanted a ruler who would unite the factious tribes and drive out the invaders. Samuel, then the country's effective leader, objected. He denounced the call to be like other nations since, by a unique covenant, the Lord our God was also our king. He warned that he was a jealous God who would not brook an earthly rival. In the event, Samuel was the jealous one. Whereas the Lord acceded to the people's demand, he never accepted it. He presided over Father's election but lost no opportunity to take him to task, finally breaking with him on the slenderest pretext, which, even if the notion that he sent the evil spirit were discounted, had left Father prone to its attack.

News of that attack reached the Philistines. In the two years since their defeat at Micmash, they had kept to their coastal strongholds and, a few border raids apart, made no further incursions into our territory. Now, seeking to exploit Father's weakness, they marched into Judah, threatening to split the country in two. With his cousin Abner as his second-in-command, Father marshalled his troops and prepared to meet the enemy in the valley of Elah. This time he was accompanied by all three of my older brothers. Jonathan was already a seasoned soldier, but the twins, having just turned eighteen, were to fight their first campaign. Mother, too anxious even to watch them exercise, secured Abner's sacred oath to keep them from the thick of battle. Seeing them set off with faces as bright as their armour, I almost forgave them their taunts and prayed as ardently as Mother for their safe return. Ishbaal remained at home, puffed up by Father's parting words that he must be the man of the house, until his demand to take his meals separately from the 'females' earned him a rebuke from Mother and a ringing slap from Merab.

We didn't expect to endure his insolence for long. None of Father's recent campaigns had lasted more than a week. Even for one with my meagre interest in warfare, the pattern was predictable. The Philistines advanced; we rebuffed them; they retreated to their five unassailable cities. This time, however, things were different. Ten days passed without word from the field. Mother, fearing the worst, took regular peace offerings to the sanctuary. Finally, a messenger arrived for Ahitophel, Father's chief adviser, bringing news that the battle had been won – without one Israelite casualty. After days of deadlock when a monstrous Philistine champion goaded our forces, a young Judahite shepherd confronted him with nothing but a sling. He felled him with a single stone, whereupon their entire army took flight.

'All praise to the Lord,' Mother said. But, even with the Lord's help, the victory was awe-inspiring, not least when the messenger swore that the Philistine was six and a half cubits tall. Moreover his mention of the Judahite shepherd unsettled me. I told myself not to be fanciful: there were hundreds of shepherds in the hill country. Yet what were the chances of two from the same tribe coming to our aid within a year? I longed to ask the messenger to describe the youth more fully – starting with the colour of his hair – but I couldn't risk rousing Mother's and Merab's suspicions. Besides, what would it prove? Red hair might well be a Judahite trait. Such coincidences occurred daily; which was why there was a word for them. It would be wrong to let my regard for one Judahite shepherd blind me to the merits of the rest.

I turned back to the messenger, who was explaining that the Benjaminite troops would reach Gibeah in a matter of hours. With no time to spare, we went our separate ways: Mother to take a thanksgiving offering to the sanctuary; Ahitophel to proclaim the victory to the people; Merab and I to instruct the servants. Once preparations were in hand, I bathed, put on my chequered robe (now pleasingly tight around the chest), and joined Mother, Merab and Hodiah at the city gate. We stood in the dusty heat, while the women and children sang and danced, played pipes and shook timbrels, until a shout from the watchtower heralded the army's approach. At first I recognised only Father, or rather his mule, its white coat gleaming in the sun, but, as they drew nearer,

I made out Abner, with Joab bearing his shield; the twins, riding with a newfound swagger; and, finally, Jonathan, side by side with a man whom I'd never expected to meet again, let alone as the nation's saviour. His prominence in the procession left no doubt that the valiant shepherd was David.

Breathless, I watched the men dismount. The twins, forgetting that they were battle-scarred veterans, ran forward to hug Mother before recollecting themselves with lofty waves at Merab and me. The others greeted us warmly, except for Father, who gave us each a perfunctory kiss, and barely acknowledging the chants of 'Saul', headed straight to the house. Sensing the crowd's disappointment, Jonathan dragged a diffident David towards them and, without a word (which would in any case have been drowned by the cheers), clasped his hand in a victory salute, confirming even to those yet to hear the story that this was the hero of the hour. With his arm draped like a garland around David's neck, he presented him to us: first to Mother, who commended his courage, marvelling at his coupling of martial and musical skill; then to Hodiah, who echoed her sentiments, although, as she addressed David, her eyes strayed to Jonathan, her yearning to kiss him as palpable as her fear of a rebuff. Merab added her plaudits, while wrinkling her nose at the battlefield smell and bloodstains on David's tunic. At last it was my turn but, despite the sparkling speech on the tip of my tongue, I was struck as dumb as the serpent in Eden.

'Come on little sister, is this how you greet your country's champion?' Jonathan asked. All I could do was shake my head like a goose.

'Count yourself lucky,' Ishbaal interjected. 'She usually won't stop talking.'

Jonathan, indulgent even to Ishbaal, broke away from David, grabbed his impudent young brother and, feigning fury, wrestled him to the ground, releasing him unharmed to the regret of everyone except Mother. Deploring the impropriety, she sent Jonathan and David home to wash and rest before returning to eat with Father. Watching them go, I was surprised to see Jonathan lay his hand on David's shoulder as if to steer him through unfamiliar streets. Hodiah followed eagerly, but neither man looked round.

I blinked back the tears that unaccountably welled in my eyes and returned home. Struggling to make sense of both David's prodigious talents and his strange reappearance in our lives, I hoped for an explanation when Jonathan paid his usual visit to Merab's and my chamber before the meal. David hadn't joined him, although whether he considered that, as girls, we were beneath his notice or, as princesses, we were above his station, I couldn't say. Too wary of Jonathan's ridicule to ask, I urged him instead to tell us the story of the battle.

'It's really the story of David,' he said. And although it was another man's triumph, I had never seen my brother look happier. Ignoring her protests, he flung himself on Merab's bed and began. 'The Philistines were camped across the valley, close enough for us to hear them carousing at night and drilling in the morning, the clash of their swords a stark reminder that their weapons were iron and ours were only wood and bone. Neither side dared risk an attack. Without a priest to cast the sacred stones and determine the Lord's will, Father concentrated on securing our position. He seemed in command – of himself, I mean – but he'd lost the confidence that inspired us to victory over the Amalekites. Then, without warning, a man advanced from the Philistine tents. But what a man! I swear he was more than four cubits tall – '

'Not six?' Merab interjected.

'Are you mad? That's already a good hand taller than Father. He was magnificent. His armour gleamed. The purple plumes in his helmet rippled in the breeze. I was so dazzled that, for a moment, I forgot he was the enemy. Then he spoke, in a voice as deep as the valley itself.'

'And I'm the one who's mad!'

'I swear it,' Jonathan said, adopting a voice that might have been menacing had it not recalled the Nephilim giants with whom he'd peopled my childhood. '"Saul, Saul, why are you hiding up there on the hillside? Come down – " Oh, this is torture!' He resumed in his own voice. '"Come down and fight, Saul! Just you and me, man to man. Whoever wins, his side can claim victory. Fight in the name of your god! Or are you ashamed of the god you're not allowed to name?" Then he named him – repeatedly, mockingly, impiously – and Father bore it, grim-faced. We waited for him to accept the challenge. He's never shrunk from one before. He may be nearly fifty but he can crush an opponent half his age – me, for instance, during practice. But he hung back, as though the Philistine's mockery had unmanned him. Both Abner and I begged him to let us fight in his place, but he flatly refused. He was sure we'd be killed and the troops would lose heart and desert.'

'So what changed?' I asked, aching for David's arrival in the field.

'Nothing, for six whole days. Our forces marked time while the Philistine strutted and jeered. I warned Father that the men would be far more disheartened if no one took up the challenge than if one of us did and fell, but he wouldn't listen. It was as though the evil spirit still had a hold on him, making him doubt himself, his son, and even the Lord.'

'But what about David?' I asked, as insistently as I dared. 'Did you call him back to play for Father?'

'No need. He'd been sent with provisions for his three older brothers, who were among the Judahite contingent. By chance – that's to say, providence – he heard the Philistine's challenge and made up his mind to accept it.'

'But he's so small,' Merab said.

'Not tall, I grant,' Jonathan replied curtly. 'Which makes his success all the more remarkable. Joab brought him again to Abner – '

'I notice Joab didn't come forward himself,' I said.

'Fair's fair,' Jonathan replied, 'no one did. They were all too aware of Father's misgivings. But David was new to the camp. He entered our tent and, before he'd even spoken, it was as if a lamp had been lit.'

'You sound like one of his songs,' Merab said.

'Ignore her!' I said. 'What happened next?'

'I was astonished to see him, but still more astonished by Father, who showed no sign of recognising him. I worried that the evil spirit had lodged in his mind. Then I realised that for Father to acknowledge him would be to acknowledge his own infirmity. So I followed his lead. For his part, David took no offence, as though he'd never presume that a king or prince would remember him.'

'Unless he was also dissembling,' Merab said.

'You don't know him; he's far too modest, something you may find it hard to appreciate.'

'Stop interrupting!' I said to Merab. 'So what did David do next?'

'Begged Father to let him accept the challenge. When Father asked him if he wanted to die, he swore that he'd braved greater dangers guarding his sheep: killing marauding lions and bears with his bare hands.'

'Did you believe it?' I asked, over Merab's snort.

'I believed that he believed it,' he replied evasively. 'In the end, Father granted his request. I suspect that he thought him expendable.' I coughed to conceal a groan, as Jonathan stared at me in bemusement. 'There was a remote chance he'd succeed and, if he failed, the contest would have been too unequal to damage morale. He even offered him his armour, which was a nonsense, since it would have dwarfed me! Still, David insisted on trying it on.'

'More dissembling?' Merab asked.

'Why must you be so spiteful? As it turned out, he wore no armour of any sort and took no weapons except for a stick, a sling and a bag of stones. When he saw him, the Philistine was incensed, railing at our disrespect and threatening retribution. He pounded the ground, rocking from side to side, so blinded with rage that for the first time I thought that David might have a chance. He bellowed that he'd eat his flesh raw, which chilled me, but David was undaunted. I couldn't see his face, but I saw the contraction of his shoulders as he calmly appraised his target, took aim and hit him straight between the eyes. The Philistine stood stupefied, before toppling forward, less man than tree. A thunderous cheer rose up from our ranks while the enemy fell deathly silent. Then David surprised me again. No longer the noble warrior, he snatched the Philistine's sword and hacked at his neck until it snapped. He held the head aloft, letting blood drip over himself like rain.'

'Why the surprise?' Merab asked. 'Red-haired men are born to shed blood.'

'Then be grateful. If it weren't for him, the blood that was shed would have been ours. When they saw their fallen champion, the Philistines fled. Our men pursued them, slaughtering and plundering all the way to Gath and Ekron.'

'I am grateful,' Merab said. 'But you make too much of it. One well-aimed shot can't compare with all Father's campaigns or even your valour at Micmash.'

'It's a well-aimed shot that might win him a king's daughter.'

'What?' Merab said, as my heart leapt.

'Did I forget to mention it?' Jonathan asked slyly. 'The men maintain that Father promised his older daughter's hand to anyone who could vanquish the Philistine.'

'Don't be absurd!'

'I wasn't there, so I can't vouch for it. But you're eighteen, the same age as Mother when she had me.'

'Mother didn't marry a shepherd!'

'No, but Leah did and Rachel, when Jacob tended their father Laban's flock. There are honourable precedents.'

'In the past, perhaps. But the world has changed; we have

a king in Israel. And kings' daughters marry kings' sons: princes from Moab or Edom or Sidon.'

'Even so, there's no man I'd rather see married to my sister.'

What about me? I wanted to ask. Wasn't I also his sister? Wouldn't he like to see me married to David? I was fifteen years old, only three years younger than Merab. I was just as eligible as she was and far better suited to him. Even if for Father's sake, she were reconciled to the match, she would make David miserable. No matter how much he did for her, it would never be enough. Whereas I wanted nothing but to be near him. Yet, if by some miracle I were to win his love – and the Red Sea might as soon part again after my reticence this afternoon – I would have to win Father's consent. Not everything had changed since Jacob's time: an older daughter still took precedence. If, by a second miracle, Father agreed to our marriage, what was to stop him copying Laban's trick and substituting Merab for Michal?

To my profound relief, there was no further mention of Father's impetuous promise. Unlike last summer, David showed himself in no rush to go home, preferring to remain in Gibeah, hunting and sporting with Jonathan. At night they returned to Hodiah, whose woebegone air was even more exasperating now that she had a second hero living under her roof. I seized every excuse to visit them, running errands for Mother, whose pleasure at my compliance almost made me repent my subterfuge. From the smile that played on his lips when I brought another basket of cakes or cloth or a message I would have previously entrusted to a servant, I knew that Jonathan wasn't deceived. I prayed that he'd say nothing to David but, no matter the risk, I couldn't bear to keep away. Although never less than courteous, David behaved towards me with a reserve that Merab, still smarting at being treated as a trophy, insisted was inverted pride. I, more kindly disposed, ascribed it to shyness, which was something else that we shared.

Meanwhile, Father was visited by another evil spirit, unless it were the first grown more volatile and violent. Once again David was called upon to expel it, but his presence did more to provoke Father than his playing did to calm him. One moment he would hail him as the bulwark of his throne and, the next, accuse him of plotting with Samuel – whom David swore that he had never met – to usurp it. In a welter of recriminations, Jonathan denounced Father's delusions and Father Jonathan's ingratitude. It was a blessing to us all – even to me who dreaded the prospect of a day without seeing him – when Father sent David, in joint command with Jonathan, to drive back the Philistines, who had rallied and attacked border farms in Ephraim.

Taking leave of them at the city gate, Father seemed more settled but, on returning home, he sank back into despondency.

'I should be with them, leading them to victory.'

'You've led them to victory for the last fifteen years,' Mother replied. 'Over the Ammonites and the Amalekites and all the enemies who sought to rob us of our land. It's time to consign the fighting to younger men.'

He slapped her across the face. As she fell back, clasping her cheek, he held out his hand, studying it as if it were an unfamiliar vegetable he'd found in his bowl. I gasped, too shocked to scream. Merab moved to Mother, who shooed her away.

'It's nothing. Don't fuss. Your father's not himself.'

His confused expression confirmed it, but, if he weren't himself, who was he? I was tortured by the thought that he had become one with his evil spirit.

After a few days, Jonathan sent word that they'd repelled the invaders in a surprise attack, which, to my delight, he credited to David. Father dismissed the messenger so brusquely that I even wondered if he'd hoped for our defeat. He charged that only a brief account of the victory was to be issued but, as usual, the details leaked out and the widespread acclaim for David plunged him into deepening gloom. Any prospect of the men's swift return was dashed by Father's orders that they were to remain in Ephraim and bolster the defences. The following week he announced Merab's marriage to Adriel, the eldest son of the Manassehite chief. While not the foreign prince of her dreams, he was well-born and wealthy enough to content her. My dismay at her marrying a total stranger was not eased by Mother's assurance that the first time she'd met Father was on their wedding day. But, when Adriel arrived in Gibeah, his handsome face and sunny disposition endeared him to us all. So I said nothing to Merab, not least because her marriage removed a serious obstacle to mine.

I suspected that the match had been hastily arranged in order to quash the general assumption that, after this second triumph, Father would be duty-bound to offer Merab to David. My fear that Jonathan would be outraged was borne out. Summoned home for the ceremony, he rode side by side with David into the courtyard, where Father, attended by Abner and Ahitophel, was negotiating the bride-price with Adriel and his father. In honour of the occasion Mother served the guests herself, while Merab and I watched from the top of the stairs, my eyes darting to the new arrivals and hers remaining fixed on her betrothed. Ignoring the visitors, Jonathan leapt off his mule and, barely pausing to prostrate himself, upbraided Father.

'Does the king of Israel have no honour? How can he give his daughter to one man when he has pledged her to another?'

'Who? When? What fresh wickedness is this?' Father drummed his fingers ominously on his stool.

'On the battlefield at Elah, when the Philistine giant scoffed at us. You promised Merab to any man brave enough to confront him… strong enough to defeat him. This is that man.' He pointed to David. 'You Manassehites were there; you can bear witness.' Shrinking from the family quarrel, neither Adriel nor his father spoke. 'Abner?' Jonathan appealed in

vain to the one man guaranteed to put loyalty before truth.
'How can you allow this shame?'

'There is no shame.' David laid his hand on Jonathan's
shoulder. 'Who am I? A shepherd. No match for your sister. I
fought then, as I do now, for my God, my king and my land.
And my friend,' he added, with touching tenderness. 'That is
my true reward.'

'Thank you,' Father said coldly. 'You at least know better
than to seize on a promise made – if, indeed, it was made – in
the heat of battle. Now I suggest that you take my son to rest
and recover from – '

'No!' Jonathan shouted. 'If you won't give him his due,
I will.' He threw off his cloak and thrust it at David, who
accepted it uneasily. 'No, put it on. On!'

Mother hastened to intervene. 'Jonathan, you're tired.
You've ridden all day in the sun.'

'Put it on!' Jonathan ordered David, shrugging off Mother's hand as abruptly as her concern. When David hesitated,
Jonathan snatched the cloak from him and draped it over
his shoulders. He then unbuckled his sword-belt and, rather
than risk a rebuff, struggled to fasten it around David's waist.
David stood motionless, neither helping nor hindering him,
as though unsure which would cause the greater offence.

'Stop this now!' Father rose to his feet, while the rest of us
watched in alarm and Jonathan continued to fumble with the
belt. 'I gave you that sword, the first iron blade I won from the
Philistines.'

'There's no man who deserves it more. I'd give him the
whole kingdom if I could.'

'You may find that he steals it first.' Father's words sent a
chill through the courtyard. Trembling, Merab reached for
my hand, as Mother clasped Jonathan's elbow and led him up
the stairs. After a moment David followed, carrying the cloak
and sword as reverently as an armour-bearer. I slipped away
from Merab and joined them in Mother's chamber, for once

scarcely glancing at David in my anxiety for Jonathan, whose frenzy bore a frightening resemblance to Father's. Mother sat him on her bed but, rather than comforting him as I'd expected, she roundly chided him.

'What were you thinking? You of all people should know better than to provoke your father. And in front of the Manassehites!'

'He insulted my friend,' Jonathan replied, his dull voice almost as disturbing as his recent outburst.

'Your friend, your friend! I think he must have bewitched you.' She glared at David, who looked at his feet.

'He promised that Merab should be his wife.'

'It's time you thought a little less of his wife and a little more of your own.'

'What do you mean?' he asked sharply.

'Your father loves you very much. He loves all his children,' she added, as though recollecting my presence. 'But he rests his hopes on you. Everything he does is for you and your sons, to secure your succession. But where are those sons? You've been married for two years.'

'If he's so eager for me to succeed him, why did he threaten to put me to death at Bethel?'

'You forced his hand when you broke the fast. He'd made a rash vow.'

'Yes, he's given to those,' Jonathan said, looking up at her for the first time.

'Your father's a frightened man. Have you never wondered why he was so susceptible to the evil spirit? No, of course not. To you, he's the big man who held you as a child, the strong man who led you into battle. But when he wears his crown, he's neither big nor strong but frightened: frightened of failing himself, his people and, most of all, the Lord. You know as well as I – as well as anyone – that he never wanted to be king. But it was the Lord's will and he submitted to it. He had a right to expect that the Lord's prophet would support him. Samuel!' She curled her lip as if the name were a curse. 'Instead, he undermined him at every turn. Remember when the Philistines mustered at Gilgal? He charged Father to wait for him for seven days before giving battle. The days went by and he still hadn't come. The men were growing restive and threatening to desert. Father had to act fast to prevent disaster. With no priest at hand to divine the Lord's will, he ordered a sacrifice to entreat his blessing before the attack. No sooner was it made than Samuel arrived and denounced him for disobedience, warning him that his house – that's you, Jonathan – wouldn't survive. It's as if he had been waiting for that moment, willing him to fall short.'

'Samuel was hard on me too,' Jonathan said, and I recalled the cries of pain, which had almost reconciled me to my exclusion, when the prophet came to teach him and the twins the stories of our ancestors.

'You were a boy; Father was a man – although Samuel made him feel like a boy again. What happened at Gilgal was not unique. You were there when Father defeated the Amalekites and spared the king, after Samuel had ordered a wholesale slaughter.'

'He said it was the Lord who ordered it.'

'He always did,' Mother said bitterly, 'when there was no one to contradict him.'

'I had nightmares for weeks. I'd seen my share of carnage but nothing to compare with Samuel's savagery. He made the king kneel before him and bare his neck. He picked up Father's sword, but it was too heavy for him and it took five or six strokes before the bones split. Blood poured on to him as he held up the severed head.' To my dismay, I was reminded of David's decapitation of the Philistine but, when I looked at the man himself, he was listening impassively. '"Thus perish all the Lord's enemies," he said. And, though he was speaking of the Amalekite, he was staring at Father.'

'Ever since then, despite all your father's attempts at

conciliation, he's refused to see him. How about you, young man, who've set father and son at odds, what do you think the king should have done?'

'Obeyed the Lord's command,' David replied, without a pause.

'I wonder if you'd be so sure of yourself if you were in his place, determining the fate of a fellow ruler... But then that's what he's afraid of finding out.'

'What do you mean, Mother?' Jonathan asked.

'Probably nothing. Your father's dearest hope when he became king was that the Lord would speak to him. But he did so only through Samuel. Now Samuel no longer speaks to him, he feels abandoned by them both. Given how brutally he condemned Father, you might think that Samuel would blame himself for anointing him or even...' Mother stopped short as though afraid of implicating a higher authority. 'But no, it's always wilful Saul... wicked Saul. And even you, his eldest son, who should be his greatest support, turn against him.'

'Thank you,' Jonathan said, his voice filled with remorse, 'for helping me – for helping us both – to understand him.' Mother frowned at the coupling. 'But there's still no excuse for his spurning David.'

'No?' Mother asked. 'In their last ever conversation – though, from what he told me, Father uttered no more than two or three words – Samuel informed him that the Lord had rejected him in favour of a worthier man. He hoped it was you – I think he could have borne that – but then that would have validated the very house that Samuel reviled. So Father is on guard against any possible claimant: someone known or unknown to him, a prophet or a soldier... or a musician.'

'Me?' David asked, betraying his confusion. 'I've explained before; nothing could be further from my mind.'

'Maybe,' Mother said, 'but minds change. Now I should go to the king.' She turned to Jonathan. 'You should go to your wife.' She turned to David. 'And you should go.'

I watched the two men hurry down the stairs and steal through the courtyard, avoiding any further confrontation with Father. Rash as it might sound, I was convinced that I – a mere girl – was the only one who could make peace between them, but my intervention would have to wait until after Merab's wedding. The contract was signed later that afternoon and the celebrations set to begin on the morrow. At daybreak, Mother led Merab to the hillside spring where she was to purify herself. It wasn't just my resentment of another rite from which I was excluded that made me question its purpose. If anything were to purify her, it was love. But on her return, rather than shivering from the water, which was freezing even in summer, she glowed more brightly than ever. To cap her delight, Father gave her some of the precious stones that Adriel's father had brought and Mother and I adorned her in them for the first of the feasts that evening. Glittering in the torchlight, she walked through the courtyard to join our aunts and cousins and Adriel's mother and sisters. With her pendants tinkling, she leant towards me and whispered that Adriel's mother had more whiskers on her chin than her son. Although too far away to hear, her new mother-in-law was close enough to smell mischief. Deflecting her scowl, I prayed that she would treat Merab kindly when she took her back to Manasseh.

David was called upon to play, but what would have been an honour for the shepherd who arrived from Bethlehem a year ago felt like a humiliation for the soldier who had twice vanquished the Philistines. To make matters worse, he was accompanied by the Ammonite bondwomen. I longed to tell him that there was one person present who suffered on his behalf. Yet, he showed no rancour as he sang a song in praise of Merab, who gave him the same curt nod that she did the servants. His was not the only humiliation, since among the company was Rizpah, the harlot whom Father kept in a house outside the city. The one virtue of his infirmity had been to prevent his visiting her. Although the twins took a perverse pleasure in pointing her out to me in the street and I liked to think that her deep bow was a reflection less of my status than of her shame, I wasn't supposed to know of her existence, so I could do no more than shoot sympathetic glances at Mother, whose pain at losing her daughter was compounded by the presence of such an unwelcome guest.

Midway through the meal, Father signalled to Mother that it was time to escort Merab to Adriel. Straightening her robe and jewellery, Mother led her through the courtyard, which rang with whoops and roars reminiscent of the soldiers' homecoming. Merab's face flushed, with excitement or embarrassment or wine or maybe all three, as she walked unsteadily between Father and Mother up to the chamber from which, for the next seven nights, I was to be banished. I imagined our positions reversed and I was the one being taken to join my bridegroom. I speculated on what lay in store. From all that I'd gleaned, I pictured darkness and nakedness, blood and seed, pain and pleasure, but I had no idea in what order or to what degree. It offended me that, unless he were bragging, even Ishbaal knew more about what transpired on a wedding night than I did. Men made fun among themselves of something that women held sacred. I looked at David and gave thanks that there was one man I could trust to show respect.

I watched as, waving Father's sword to ward off the evil spirits, Merab made her way to the chamber, where Adriel and his brother Jotham waited to greet her. Father, Mother and Jotham then returned downstairs, affording the bride and groom their first taste of privacy, although the twins, seemingly licensed by Father, twice ran up and hammered on the door, to the cheers of the men below. With their banter growing coarse, Mother sent me with my cousin Keziah to my aunt's, where I was to stay during my week of exile. Keziah's prattle made me realise how much I already missed Merab. First thing the next morning, I hurried home, eager to talk to her, only to find our chamber door shut and what I took to be the wedding sheet strung from the lintel. In the middle were several red spots, like the blood sprinkled in a sacrifice. Mother, seeing me stare, came up and hugged me more warmly than usual. 'Look, there's barely a speck. It's nothing to be afraid of,' she said, as if I would know instinctively what she meant.

When at last she emerged, Merab looked so joyful that, for all Mother's obliqueness, I felt reassured. Was I ascribing my own hopes to her or was there a new light in her eyes, such as I'd seen in Jonathan's when he and David returned from Ephraim? Had she found the fulfilment in love that he had in battle? I needed to know what to expect or at least what to wish for. But when I questioned her, she prevaricated, claiming first that what she'd felt couldn't be put into words, which was patently untrue since the Lord gave us a word for everything, and then that she didn't want to spoil the surprise, when she knew full well that I loathed surprises. It was as if, overnight, she'd crossed a river whose current flowed too fast for me to follow.

Given her newfound happiness, it seemed cruel that she was able to see Adriel only at night. He spent the day hunting and hawking with his brothers and mine, while she entertained Adriel's mother and sisters, taking them up to the hills or to meet old friends, leaving me at home. Even when we were together, she favoured them, setting her loom beside theirs and chatting so volubly that she dropped her shuttle, a fault that would have earned me a severe rebuke but for which she was excused. Her older sister-in-law made a reference to Adriel's shuttle, which I failed to understand but, from Merab's blush and Mother's frown, was sure must be ribald. On an ordinary day, Mother would have noticed my wretchedness and consoled me, but she was preoccupied with the welfare of her guests and the week of feasting. Even so, I suspected that she would have preferred to provide meals for another month than to bid farewell to her daughter who, as soon as the celebrations were over, left for Manasseh with her new family (hateful phrase!). Fighting back her tears, she kissed us all again and again, even Ishbaal, who recoiled as though stung. She made me promise to visit her in the spring, although I planned for her to return long beforehand for my wedding.

If the plan were to succeed, my first step was to speak to Jonathan, who called on us more often after Father lodged David in the gatehouse. 'You can do what you please during the day, but at night you're to go home to your wife,' he'd told Jonathan, which was unfair since he had always gone home to Hodiah, whether David were there or not. I intercepted him as he left a meeting with a Hittite emissary. My innocent 'Is something wrong?' sparked a tirade against Father's tyranny, which ignored the fact that he and the twins had enjoyed far greater freedom than Merab and I, who were subject alternately to strict discipline and stifling affection. Nevertheless, I knew better than to challenge him when I needed his help.

'It's not as if Father has forbidden you and David to see each other or sent one of you to Asher and the other to Simeon. You can exercise together, explore together, hunt together,' I said, increasingly aware that I had no idea how they occupied their time.

'You don't understand.'

'Because I'm a girl? Because I'm fifteen? Or because I'm your sister?'

'Forgive me! I feel as if I'm splitting in two. Father may not have sent David away, but I will... I must.'

'Why?' I struggled to keep my balance.

'There's no other way. His very presence enrages Father. Even the music that cured him last year threatens to revive his evil spirit. I'm sure that he'd concoct some pretext to have him killed if he weren't afraid of provoking the people.'

'Then you're right; he must go. At once! But it will be so hard for you.'

'You do understand. I'd never dreamt that anyone else – let alone another man – could bring me such pleasure, such peace, such contentment. He's more than my friend; he's myself. He's more myself than I am. I'm sorry; I know that that makes no sense.'

It made perfect sense since I felt the same. Yet our two loves could not have been more different. Jonathan's was the daytime love of a friend, whereas mine was the night-time love of a future wife. For all that I cherished the uniqueness of my feelings, I envied my brother the easy expression of his. I'd watched him rest his hand on David's shoulder and the small of his back; I'd watched him wrestle him to the ground and punch him on the arm, his playfulness compounding my pain. Despite my wealth of fantasies – passing him his bowl or his lyre, dropping my mantle in his path and even fainting at his feet and reviving, slowly, as he carried me to my bed – I had never so much as brushed David's skin.

'If only Father had allowed him to marry Merab,' I said, marvelling at my insincerity.

'He promised… if not in so many words.'

'He wouldn't mistrust him if he were allied to our clan.'

'You're not making things any easier.'

'Not yet, but maybe I could.'

'How? She's married to Adriel.'

'What about me?'

'What about you?'

'As a bride for David.' I gulped.

'You?' He laughed. 'I'm sorry, but you… little Michal!'

'Why little? I'm almost as tall as him.'

'Yes, but – '

'And I'm fifteen years old. Fifteen. Plenty of girls my age are married.'

He looked me up and down as if seeing me afresh after years in captivity. 'True.'

'Then David could stay here with us… with you.'

'You'd do that for me?'

'Of course. And for Father – to ease his mind. And the kingdom – to preserve its best general… second-best.'

'You were right the first time,' he said with a smile. 'But are you sure it's what you want?'

'I've felt so alone since Merab left. Mother's forever finding fault with me. I'm ready for my own household.'

'And it helps that David's good-looking.'

'Like Adriel,' I said casually. 'Besides, I don't want to move away. David's living here. Or will he have to return to Bethlehem?'

'No, he has enough brothers.' Jonathan's face shone. 'Who knew that I had such a clever sister? But we must take care not to arouse Father's suspicions. Merab's open disdain for David was what made it safe to endorse the match.'

He hurried away to find David. I felt excited but also exposed. Although he swore to present the scheme as his own, what if David saw through it? I had been so absorbed in my own desires that I'd given no thought to his. Was it too much to hope that he felt as drawn to me as I did to him but, afraid that I'd prove as haughty as Merab, he'd feigned indifference? Or did I disgust him, with my callow mind and, worse, my scrawny body? Would he reject the scheme outright, regarding marriage to me as too high a price even for closeness to Jonathan and kinship with the king?

I saw him in the evening when he and Jonathan came for their regular meal with Father and Abner. As they passed through the courtyard, Jonathan winked at me but David gave me no more than a respectful nod. Desperate, I mined it for meaning. Was it a grateful acknowledgement or a gentle rebuff? Or was I worrying unduly before Jonathan had had a chance to talk to him? Feeling sick, I excused myself from the table and escaped to bed, longing to be alone with my thoughts. But I'd reckoned without Mother and her bowl of restorative soup, her concern even more cloying than Keziah's chatter.

My deception threatened to rebound on me the next morning when Jonathan asked Mother's permission to take me to the river where he and David were practising archery. She insisted that I stay and rest, whereupon he picked her up and, ignoring her protests, refused to put her down until she agreed. Both appreciative and jealous of his ability to influence her, I promised to keep out of the sun and not to tire myself. Giggling like five-year-olds, we raced to the gatehouse where David was waiting. Just the sight of him made my heart spin. My rush of sensations made no sense as, all at once, I found myself rising to the firmament and sinking into Sheol.

'I'm glad you've come,' he said, and my confusion redoubled as I longed both to leap into his arms and run back to hide in my chamber.

We made our way through the streets, and for the first time I felt that the looks of respect, admiration and even envy I attracted were less on my own account than that of my companion. Although part of me was grateful that they acknowledged his worth, another part was frightened of their intruding on my happiness. I was relieved when we reached the meadow, where the only distraction was a flock of sheep. 'Friends of yours?' Jonathan asked David, who laughed, while I bristled.

Invoking my promise to Mother, Jonathan made me sit in the shade of a giant cypress, while he and David took aim at a target they'd carved on an oak. I was heartened to see that, despite their rivalry, they were proud of each other's prowess. With new loyalties pitted against old, my hope that their scores would tally was fulfilled unexpectedly when David's arrow hit Jonathan's and, rather than knocking it off the trunk, split it in two, the one's arrowhead lodging in the other's shaft in what felt like the perfect expression of their friendship. Awestruck, they broke off and joined me to eat a simple meal of almonds, figs and bread.

All of a sudden, Jonathan jumped up, claiming to have

glimpsed a distant roe. He grabbed his bow and ran off in pursuit, leaving me alone with David. This was the opportunity for which I'd prayed but, as the silence between us grew thunderous, my one desire was to flee.

'You must love your brother very much,' he said at last.

'More than anyone else in the world,' I replied mechanically.

'Me too,' he said. And I loved him for his discernment, while wondering what it would take for it to be extended to me.

'Joab said that you have seven brothers.'

'You asked him about me?'

'I... I...'

'I'm sorry, that wasn't fair. Yes. I'm the youngest. That's why I was put in charge of the flock. Not – whatever Jonathan might say – because of my affinity with sheep.'

'I'm sure he doesn't mean it.'

'No, I don't think he does.'

He gazed at the copse as if willing Jonathan to reappear. I hurriedly bit an almond, which stuck in my teeth. 'When Jonathan attacked Father for forbidding you to marry Merab,' I said, in an effort to draw him out, 'you declared that you were just a shepherd and no match for her.'

'I would never want to marry a woman who didn't want to marry me.'

'What about one who did?'

He looked at me so gravely that I thought I'd burst, but then a smile spread across his face. 'You're as fearless as your brother,' he said, and I returned the smile. 'Our clan has always placed worth above wealth. My father's grandfather, Boaz, married Ruth, a Moabite woman so poor that she gleaned the grain from his fields. He couldn't have chosen better.'

'Our clan was unremarkable until Father was elected king. We still live in the house where he was born. The people wanted to build him something larger, but he refused. He was afraid of breeding resentment. I loved him for his modesty.'

'Where would you like to live?'

'In a shepherd's hut... in a cave... in the desert like our ancestors. Anywhere, so long as it's with you.'

There! I'd said it and it could never be unsaid. He looked at me again and I willed him to kiss me. It seemed so natural and right that I failed to see why he held back. For a moment I closed my eyes and felt his lips on mine, only to open them and find that it was the breeze. His one move was to clasp my arm and, although I reminded myself that shyness had been among his first attractions, I was unable to shake off a sense of disappointment. Why didn't he kiss me? We sat in a welter of unformed, unfulfilled desires, until Jonathan, his arms as empty as expected, strolled back into view.

Despite my disappointment, it felt as if something had been settled between us, but it wasn't until Jonathan took me aside on our return that I could be sure. He explained that for David himself to propose the match would be disastrous, so once again he'd have to intercede. Blind to my impatience, he added that he had to wait for the right moment, which came sooner than I feared, with the news that Nasib, King of Ekron and Father's lifelong adversary, had died. Summoned to his chamber the next morning, I saw at once from Jonathan's face that Father had consented. Not since the sacrificial ram broke its bonds and butted the priest at Nob had I struggled so hard to suppress a smile.

'How old are you?' Father asked me.

'Fifteen... nearly sixteen.' Since I was born the month after he became king, I would have expected him to remember.

'How would you like a husband?'

'If it pleases you, Father.'

'Nothing pleases me; but it suits me. You may be surprised to hear that Jonathan has picked one out for you – or maybe not in this new world where sons know better than their fathers.'

Seeing the telltale vein throbbing on Jonathan's brow, I

replied quickly. 'I'm sure that he was only trying to anticipate your wishes.'

Father grunted. 'What do you say to David?'

Yes, yes, yes! was what I said in my head. *Yes, yes, yes, yes!* was what I said with every fibre of my being. 'I'd be happy with him, Father,' was what I said out loud.

'Why?'

There were so many reasons, but I knew better than to cite his smile or his charm or his valour or his victories, all of which might be taken as a threat. 'I think I'd like a husband who sings.' When Father laughed and Jonathan sighed, I knew that it was the right answer.

'How much would you say you're worth?' Father asked.

'What do you mean?'

'David can't expect to have you for nothing. You saw the treasure that Adriel gave for Merab.'

'He's not rich,' I said, alarmed by this new obstacle.

'Then we'll have to find something else.'

It wasn't until later when Jonathan, ashen with anger, sought me out that I learnt that the something else was the slaughter of a hundred Philistines. I was horrified. If he succeeded, our marriage would be built on blood, and if he failed, there would be another corpse to add to the pile: mine.

'Don't worry,' Jonathan said. 'He won't fail; he enjoys the Lord's favour.'

'So did Father.'

'Then he forfeited it. Now you know why. It's despicable. He pretends that he's testing David's strength, when it's patently obvious he wants him to perish in the attempt.'

'Will you go with him?' I asked, so concerned for his safety that I was even willing to imperil Jonathan.

'No, he's to go alone. With Joab as his armour-bearer.'

I was somewhat reassured since, despite my dislike of him, Joab was far too shrewd to follow anyone – even a kinsman – to certain death.

'Must he bring back a hundred heads?' I asked, still haunted by the decapitation of the Philistine giant.

'Of course not,' Jonathan said. 'Their swords and helmets will be more useful – and less putrid.'

David set off the following dawn with a terse farewell that attested to his impatience to complete the task and claim the prize. Weeks passed without word from him. For all his assurances, I could see that Jonathan was anxious, but I was afraid to rouse his suspicions by expressing my own fears. I wished more than ever that Merab were here or, at the very least, we had been taught to write. In her absence, I had nobody to confide in but Mother, whose response to my dejection was to fill my days with chores. Then one morning when I was in the olive grove, a bondwoman brought news that David had been sighted in the valley. My hands were stained and my hair tangled but my only thought was to see him – alive – and I ran to the city gate where Father, with Ahitophel at his side, was hearing petitions. Brooking no interruption, he ordered the suppliants to speak even though, like everyone else, they had turned towards the path. Moments later, David appeared, followed by Joab. To my dismay, the packs on their donkeys were too small for the stipulated swords or helmets, yet David showed no unease as he prostrated himself in the dust.

'My lord and king, I have done as you asked, killing not one but two hundred Philistines.'

'I don't doubt it,' Father said, with a thin smile. 'Just as you killed the lions and bears that threatened your flock. But we require proof.'

I looked again at the unladen donkey and, setting aside my own hopes, longed for David to leap on its back and ride off, sparing himself the inevitable humiliation. Instead, he beckoned to Joab, who pulled down a pack, untied it and emptied it at Father's feet.

My surprise turned to revulsion at the stench, redolent of fish that had been inadequately smoked. Drawing my veil over my nose, I stared at the pink and grey shrivelled matter, which resembled the crawling creatures that we were forbidden to eat. I presumed that David wished to shame Father for his cruelty but, while applauding the intent, I dreaded the consequence.

'See,' he said, 'I have circumcised the uncircumcised ones. Two hundred Philistine foreskins.' The gasps from the spectators were replaced by cheers, which faded when Father sprang up, his face grey. 'Let anyone who doubts me count them.'

'That won't be necessary.' Father said coldly. 'You have done what we asked.'

'Twice what you asked, my lord.'

'Come!'

With a brief bow to me, David followed Father, Ahitophel and the guard. Alone, I gazed at the grisly payment. Although I had attended Ishbaal's circumcision, I'd been too young to understand what it entailed. When Father raised his knife, I'd thought that he was sacrificing the baby and screamed, provoking Mother's scolding and Merab's scorn. Since then I'd learnt that, at eight days old, a boy shed his blood for the covenant. I knew that the rite was performed on the most private part of his body, the part that would be revealed only to his bride on their wedding night, and that, unlike the Ammonites, the Moabites, the Hittites and us, the Philistines observed no such rite. Now David had performed it for them and on full-grown men. Had they been dead or alive? Was it the ultimate degradation? Why couldn't he have chopped off their fingers?

My reflections were cut short by Joab who, chasing away two drooling curs, plucked the foetid foreskins from the ground and threw them into the sack. Meeting his smile of derision with one of defiance, I returned home. Later that day Father informed me that I was betrothed to David. Nothing could have made me happier – unless, of course, he had come in person, but he'd ridden straight to Bethlehem to tell his family and bring them back for the feasts. With her mind on the storeroom, Mother was relieved that only three of his brothers accompanied him, along with his parents, Jesse and Nizebeth, and Jonadab, his eight-year-old nephew, the most enthusiastic member of the group, whose youthful gallantry was at once endearing and sinister. My only regret was that Merab, now pregnant, was forbidden to undertake the journey.

Mother led me to the spring for the rite of purification. I stood numbly in the water as she explained that I must come back every month to preserve a stainless marriage bed. But the icy immersion would be a small price to pay for the joy of lying with David. We returned home, where Mother and Hodiah helped me to dress for the first feast. I wore a robe dyed from the pinkest hyacinths and a scarlet mantle embroidered with gold and silver stars that Mother had worked in secret during the weeks that David was pursuing the Philistines and which pleased me as much for her faith in him as her love for me. Dismissing Hodiah, whose unconcealed delight in my marriage moved me, she brushed my hair, running it through her fingers as if feeling my childhood slip away.

'You're happy today,' she said, 'and I'm happy for you. But remember that from now on your happiness must be your husband's happiness. Your body is no longer your own.' Startled, I turned to face her and she instantly pushed me back, making me wonder when my body had ever been my own. 'David will break you open like a seal. You understand?' I nodded, forgetting that she was braiding my hair. 'You'll feel pain and humiliation but it will be transformed by love, just as when the Lord blesses you with children, the pain of childbirth will be transformed to joy.'

Her evident discomfort made her remarks hard to follow. I presumed that the seal was the one on the marriage contract but, far from feeling any loss, I couldn't wait for David to break it and turn me from a single person into half – or, if that were too much to ask, a quarter or even an eighth – of a pair.

Mother completed the braid and concluded the conversation, unlocking her coffer and taking out jewellery for me to wear. Putting on the earrings and nose-ring, the bracelets and anklets and necklaces, which Father had once given her, I felt a renewed repugnance at the payment he'd demanded of David. Unlike Merab, decked out in Adriel's gems, I would have to return these to Mother at the end of the week. As resentment rose up in me, a servant announced that the guests had assembled and the prospect of my noble bridegroom banished the memory of my sordid bride-price.

I saw him the moment I entered the courtyard, wearing a brilliant white robe and a garland of lilies and roses. The depth of my desire for him shocked and even frightened me. What had once been a dispassionate love, happy just to know that such a man existed, was now a desperate longing not only to see and to hear but to smell, touch and taste him. 'Keep your eyes straight ahead,' Mother whispered, as she led me first to Father and then to Jesse. I kissed their beards, after which Father kissed me distractedly on the brow and Jesse respectfully on each palm. Circumventing the younger men, we moved to the women, where I sat between Mother and Nizebeth. Despite the richness of the stewed sheep's tail and the beauty of the Ammonite singing, I had never been so eager for a meal to end, not even when, as a girl, I'd had to sit through the revelry at the Festivals of Reaping and Gathering. I sustained myself by surreptitious glances at David, alternately relieved and disappointed that our eyes never met. Then, looking up from a dish of honeyed dates and sesame cakes, I saw that he and Jonathan had left and knew that I wouldn't have long to wait.

At last Father rose from his stool and signalled to Mother that we should join him. Preceded by four guards and followed by a group of boisterous kinsmen, we processed through the streets to the house that was my wedding gift from Father. Never had I felt so well disposed towards the waiting crowds, especially the girls whose cheers were coloured by their own dreams and desires. As we approached the gate, Father gave me his sword to ward off the evil spirits but, jolted by its weight, I let it fall. Mother gasped, ever ready to discern an ill omen, but silencing her with a frown, Father picked up the sword and returned it to me. Clasping it in both hands, I sliced the air before bringing it down on a pomegranate, which Mother had placed on the threshold.

'May your children be as numerous as the seeds of this fruit,' she said, pointing at the pulp.

'It doesn't always follow,' Father said, glowering at Jonathan.

After relinquishing the sword to Father and kissing Mother, I stepped over the burst fruit and entered the house. Father, Mother and Jonathan left with the guard, but the rest of my escort remained, their hoots and howls dashing any hope that I would be spared the cacophony that had marked Merab's wedding night. While I resented the intrusion, David seemed to welcome it. Then, as if rallying himself, he led the way to our chamber.

'You look very like your brother,' he said, studying me in the lamplight.

'Is that good?'

'I thought so once.' He turned away. 'You must be tired. You'll want to go to bed. I'll leave you.'

'What?'

'To change,' he said and went out.

I took off my jewellery and my robe and unpinned my hair but kept on my under-tunic in case it was a husband's right – or duty – to remove it. David returned, wearing only his tunic and, with a sidelong glance at me, slipped into bed. After a moment of doubt I followed. He put out the lamp in a misplaced courtesy, plunging the room into darkness. I feared that he would take the heaviness of my breath for dread. He shrugged off his tunic and the moonlight seeping through the window disclosed whorls of hair on a chest hard as a shield.

He gripped my under-tunic and drew it up to my thighs. I tried to wriggle out of it without appearing forward but, when it caught beneath my hips, I gave in and pulled it off. For the first time in my life, I was naked in bed beside someone other than Merab. I wondered if it were the same for him. I had heard guards boasting of the captive women they'd ravished, but that was punishment not love. I had even heard of women who devoted themselves to pleasuring men: not one man, like Rizpah, but many men like Rahab, who had hidden Joshua's spies in Jericho. But as he traced the line of my hips with trembling fingers, he seemed as unsure of my body as I was of his.

The diffidence that had once enchanted me now felt like a betrayal. He edged towards me and cupped my breasts, as if they intrigued rather than enticed him. I longed to caress his chest, now glistening a silvery white, but, mindful of Mother's words that my body belonged to him, not his to me, I lay inert. Suddenly – shockingly – he rolled on top of me and, giving me no time to recover, pulled apart my legs, which instinctively resisted. The challenge appeared to excite him and he prised me open, although it felt more like tearing the meat from a bone than breaking a seal. I felt a sharp cramp and then nothing as, with a cry like a wounded animal, he rolled off me and banged his head three times on the wall.

Lonely and bewildered, I wondered what had happened. Was this all that there was to be between us? If so, Mother had made too much of the pain and Merab of the pleasure. I peered at David, who sat with his head in his hands. He picked up a knife from the floor.

'No!' I screamed.

'Are you mad?' he asked, with a note of contempt. 'Do you think I mean to murder you?'

'No… I don't know… I don't know what I know.'

'They need to see blood. Or do you want to humiliate me twice over?' Leaving me none the wiser, he stabbed his palm and let the blood drip on the sheet. 'It will be dry by morning.

You'll say nothing to your mother or the other women, understand?' I nodded as if it were daytime. 'Understand?'

'Yes.'

I lay awake, trying to silence my breathing, an effort compounded by the knowledge that he was doing the same. It was as if the least sound might force us to recognize our separateness when we had expected to celebrate our union. At first light he leapt out of bed, threw on his tunic and left the chamber without a word. I slipped on my robe and dithered at the door, unsure whether to follow him and tell Hamdan, the Ammonite bondwoman, to prepare food and drink. He returned while I was still undecided and examined the sheet. Satisfied, he pulled it off the bed.

'Things will be better, I promise,' he said, with surprising tenderness. He left the room and I listened as he went outside to hang up the sheet. It drew a smattering of applause from passers-by or, for all I knew, people who had waited there all night. Shortly afterwards, our newly allied brothers arrived to take him hunting. While his brothers greeted me respectfully and the twins made comments that as usual were intelligible only to themselves, Jonathan folded up the sheet to keep as evidence should David ever decide to divorce me, a prospect that he laughed off as loudly as the rest but which no longer felt so remote to me.

The hunters returned for the evening feast, after which David led me home. Once again, he put out the lamp, peeled off his tunic and slipped into bed. Once again, he thrust open my thighs with a roughness that quickened his passion. Once again, he had barely entered me when he broke off. Bruised in mind and body, I had no chance to talk to him since he left with his companions at break of day. I knew that I mustn't complain since it'd been the same for Merab, although I doubted that she had lain awake all night, desperate for Adriel's embrace. To add to my misery, the rings under my eyes were taken by one and all as evidence of his ardour.

Even the bondwomen, severed from their husbands, smiled as they served my food and joked to each other in their own language, which for once Mother let pass. My loneliness grew so acute that, on the fourth night, heedless of the immodesty, I confronted him.

'Do you have another woman?'

'What?'

'In Bethlehem or even here. Father has Rizpah. I'm not supposed to know about her but I do.'

'No, not at all! You mustn't think that. You're the only one. My first.' As he stumbled over the words, I stifled a cry of relief. So I hadn't disappointed him. This warrior, who had killed a multitude of Philistines, hadn't known a single woman. His admission emboldened me and I leant across and kissed him, first on the lips, then on the neck, and then on the chest. He lay unmoving, as I let my hand slide down his steely stomach to the softness between his legs. Then that too hardened, and I felt a mixture of excitement and dread. With a sound between a whoop and a yelp, he sprang on top of me. He took hold of my hair and spread it over my face like a veil. He clasped both my wrists in his left hand and opened my legs with his right. I bit my lip, desperate not to deter him. He entered me and at last I understood Mother's warning about the pain. He bore into me as if he were dispatching an enemy, but I willed him on. Suddenly I felt all his muscles tense, including the one inside me. He fell back with a shout of 'Yes,' although I hadn't spoken. I became aware of a strange odour, both metallic and salty, and a dampness between my thighs. As I tested it with my finger, I saw that it was blood. I couldn't tell if it were my blood or his blood or the seeds that were in his blood, but I didn't care since I knew that it was a balm, not a threat.

Hamdan perceived my delight at once when she brought in my morning basin of water. She beamed, as though recalling her own wedding night, and I was touched that this Ammonite woman, who had seen her own husband ripped from her arms, should set aside her grief and resentment to rejoice with me. Jonathan was less gracious when he came to fetch David for another day's sport, only to find him lingering over a cup of buttermilk.

'I'm so sorry if I'm disturbing you,' he said, in response to a revealing yawn. 'No doubt you'd prefer to loll in bed supping from the bridal bowl.'

Blushing, David jumped up and followed him out with barely a glance at me, but I wasn't offended. Something had changed between us, which couldn't be undone. The rest of the festivities passed in a blur, my senses honed solely at night when we were alone together. At the end of the week, his family returned to Bethlehem. Given the constant tension between Father and David, their prompt departure was understandable. Only Jonadab appeared to think that his uncle's discomfort mattered less than his own proximity to the king. He begged to stay, even proposing himself as armour-bearer to Ishbaal, who had yet to draw a sword, but he had to be satisfied with his father's promise to bring him back in the spring. I was relieved that David's duty to Father kept us in Gibeah, since a week of Nizebeth's chilly composure had cured me of any desire to live under her roof. More than once she seemed ready to confide in me (doubtless about some childhood feat of David's), only to think again. However much I enjoyed hearing his virtues extolled, I preferred to discover them for myself.

Married life soon established its own rhythm, one too rich to be called a routine. Apart from a brief foray into Gad to crush an Ammonite incursion, David remained in Gibeah, passing his days either in the countryside with Jonathan or at his lyre. I relished the music, as perfect and pure as birdsong, but knew better than to say so after my compliments distressed him so much that he threatened to give up playing. Since we took our evening meal with my parents, I had little food to prepare and, when not at my loom, I was at a loss how to fill my time. So I paid regular visits to Hodiah, who had mellowed since falling pregnant. She even maintained that it was me she had to thank for it.

'How?' I asked in bemusement.

'When you're with David, Jonathan comes home to me. I waited so long: I never thought it would happen. I pray to the Lord that it will be easier for you.'

The imminent birth served to reconcile Father and Jonathan. It heartened me that a woman's belly should be the bridge between two such headstrong men, and I hoped that mine would be the same for Father and David. The desire for a child consumed me. It would be the testament to my love for David. It would perpetuate the bond that dissolved as soon as he spent his seed. His vehemence was not in doubt. After the first desolate days, he lay with me every night that I was clean. I learnt the distinction between happiness and pleasure as he pushed himself (and me) as hard as if he were wrestling with Jonathan. Like Hodiah, I prayed to the Lord to make me fruitful but, on Mother's advice, I also prayed to Ashtoreth, the goddess of conception, placing her grandmother's idol in my chamber. David objected that its presence was an affront to the Lord, but for once I stood firm. So we compromised by setting it behind a curtain.

My hope that Father would relent towards his new son-in-law wasn't realised. He made a show of friendship, seating him at his table with Jonathan and Abner, but no one, least of all David himself, was deceived. 'Every time he looks at me, I feel as if he's searching for a hidden weapon,' he said, as we returned home one night. In the event, it was Father who used a weapon against him. I was with Mother, two of my aunts and Hodiah, trying to lull the newborn Meribaal, when Jonathan, red with fury, and David, white with fear, burst into the chamber.

'Father isn't possessed of one evil spirit but an army,' Jonathan said, ignoring his mewling son. 'We were listening to

David play – beautifully,' he added, as though that alone should have mollified Father. 'Then, without warning, Father grabbed a spear from one of the guards and aimed it at David. If he hadn't recoiled – '

'I didn't,' David interposed. 'A mouse ran across the floor. It distracted me.' I vowed never again to disparage vermin. 'We should go home,' he said to me. 'Who knows what your father's capable of in this state?'

'No,' I said, surprising myself by my resolve. 'I shall go to him. You're my husband. I must put an end to this wickedness and convince him that you're not a threat.'

'Don't interfere!' Mother said. 'You'll make things worse.'

'What do you suppose you can do that I've not already tried?' Jonathan asked.

'No, Michal's right,' David said. 'The king isn't thinking clearly. So maybe he'll listen to her.'

Fortified by his words, I entered Father's chamber, to find him sprawled on the floor, face and hair soaked in sweat, with Abner leaning over him, trying to coax him up. I approached him warily, reminding myself that wounded lions could still pounce.

'Father, it hurts me so much to see you like this.'

'Michal, little Michal, you're the only one who loves me.'

'That's not true. We all love you: Jonathan; Merab; the twins; David.'

Abner's grimace showed me that it was too soon to have mentioned David; Father's shriek confirmed it.

'No! He deceives you as he deceives your brother, as he deceives Abner. I alone see him for what he is.'

'Believe me, Father, David loves you.'

'No, he loves only this.' He scrambled across the floor and grabbed the crown from his bed, pressing it so tightly on his head that it bit into his flesh.

'That's not true.'

'I say it is! I'm your father. The only man you should trust.'

'He's my husband. I love him.'

'Not for much longer.'

'What do you mean?'

'I should never have permitted him to marry you. It's your brother who's to blame. But don't worry, I'll set you free.'

'I don't want to be free. I am free!'

'You should go now, Michal,' Abner interjected.

'No, stay! Here, with the father who loves you. Before the night's out, you'll be rid of him forever.'

'Then I must return home at once,' I replied, appalled by words that required no explanation. 'Or David will suspect. He'll foil your plans.'

'Of course. Clever girl! Go, go now! What are you waiting for? Go!'

Needing no encouragement, I fled from both the chamber and the house. I trusted that the gathering darkness would shroud me as I ran like a fugitive through the streets, arriving to find David waiting in the courtyard. Before I could utter a word, he launched a bitter attack on my family.

'What do you want from me? It's not enough to vanquish his enemies, but I have to prove to your father that I love him. It's not enough that we've made a sacred vow, but I have to prove to your brother that I love him. It's not enough that I've married you, but I have to prove to you night after night that I love you.'

'I thought you were proving that to yourself,' I said, in a voice as small as I felt.

'What do you mean?'

'There's no time. You must escape. Father intends to take your life. I don't know how, but from what he said, the guards may be coming for you tonight.'

'Where can I go? There's no way out. The main gate's locked and bolted.'

'But not our chamber window.' I gave thanks that the house was built against the city wall. 'You can jump out.'

'On to the dunghill?'

'It will break your fall.'

'It's eight cubits high.'

'Quick! Go upstairs and tie the bedsheets together. I'll lower you.'

'You'll never bear my weight.'

'Hamdan will help.' I called into the storeroom. The bond-woman appeared, her usual blank expression augmented by her bleary eyes. 'Come upstairs please!'

She followed us to the chamber where, with David wavering, I set her to knotting the sheets.

'What's the use?' David asked. 'Even if I hit the ground without breaking my neck, the guards will soon catch up with me.'

Each demurral made me more determined. 'I'll put Hamdan in the bed – under the cover. If the guards come, I'll say she's – you're – sick. I'll warn them not to get too close. They won't return till morning. By then you'll be far away.'

'Are you mad? Look at her!'

I gazed at the vast woman with thighs the size of his chest and was seized by panic. At which point, inspiration struck. 'Of course,' I said, pulling back the curtain. 'We'll use the idol. Then if the guards come, Hamdan can let them in. Now go! Go on, go!' Suddenly, my pain at our separation swamped my relief at his escape. 'Promise to send for me as soon as you're safe. I'll join you wherever you are. No matter where.'

David stood on Hamdan's shoulders and hauled himself up to the window. Hamdan and I clung to the sheet as he edged himself out. I suppressed the stabbing pain in my back, content to know that each tug brought him a step nearer to freedom. All at once the sheet sagged and I heard a dull splash. I climbed on to the bondwoman's shoulders, less deftly than David, and, taking hold of the window ledge, looked out to see him emerge unscathed from the dunghill. I seemed to scent his disgust as he shook and scraped the muck from his face and hands. Assured of his safety, I asked Hamdan to help me down and we set about untying the sheets. Together, we laid the idol in the bed, turning it on its front where the hips looked narrowest and the breasts were hidden. In a flash of inspiration, I plucked some of the stuffing from a pillow and arranged it on the stone head. Although red rather than black, David's hair was as thick and wild as the goat's, which, as long as no one held a lamp too close, would enhance the likeness. How gratifying that the goddess he'd scorned should have come to his rescue! My fear that she might object to my appropriation of her image vanished when I realised that, since I would be unable to conceive if David were dead, I was also honouring her.

We had barely restored the room when an urgent knocking at the gate confirmed my suspicions. We hurried downstairs, where Hamdan, more bewildered than ever, let in a troop of eight guards. His bluster accentuating his unease, the captain demanded to see David.

'He's ill in bed and can't be disturbed. I've given him a draught of henbane to help him sleep.'

'My orders are to take him to the king.'

'I am the king's daughter and will answer for any offence.'

After a moment's hesitation, he gathered his men and left. I led Hamdan up to my chamber where, staggering under its weight, which appeared to have doubled during its brief removal, we returned the idol to its niche. Exhausted, I collapsed on to the bed, only to be woken at first light by renewed banging at the gate. This time I opened it myself, to be confronted by Father.

'Where is this man who's so sick that he disregards a summons from his king?'

'He's gone.'

'Gone?'

'Left. Run away. Escaped your wrath.'

His face was so menacing that I didn't need to feign my

sobs. Grabbing my arm and ordering his men to follow, he dragged me up the stairs. I narrowly escaped tripping over my robe as we entered the empty chamber. He tore down the curtain as though expecting to find a tremulous David, but what he found instead inflamed his fury.

'What's this?'

'It's from Mother. The goddess Ash – '

'I know what it is! So you pray to this worthless idol. What are you and your mother trying to do to me? Do you want the Lord to abandon me forever?'

I saw that, whatever else might divide them, Father and David were as one in their fear of the Lord. 'But if the Lord has no time for women's concerns…'

'Then they must renounce them.' With the strength that both impressed and terrified me, Father grabbed the idol and, his back and knees barely buckling, tipped it over the balustrade into the courtyard. As it shattered, I felt my hopes of conception shatter with it.

Father lurched forward and, for a moment, I was afraid that he'd throw me after it.

'Why?' he asked, the anger in his voice replaced by pain. 'Why did you lie to the soldiers?'

'He threatened to kill me.'

'They would have protected you.'

'I couldn't be sure. The men love him so much. I was frightened that they'd revolt and follow him. I was thinking of you.'

He looked at me as if he wanted to believe me, which hurt more than if he'd struck me. Then his face became flint and his voice venom. 'No. You were thinking only of him. But you'll pay for it. You are not to leave this house, do you hear? No one is to come or go without my permission. I'll teach you to disobey me!'

The full nature of the lesson became clear over the following weeks. Cut off from the world, I paced the courtyard as if it were a cell. I wove a cover for my bed and a robe that I feared

I should never have occasion to wear. Hamdan borrowed
David's lyre and taught me some Ammonite songs, but my
voice was so much weaker than hers that I lost heart. From
time to time I heard a ruckus in the streets, but the walls were
too thick for me to ascertain the cause. Hamdan went back
and forth to the well but, although her language resembled
ours, she claimed not to understand a word that the women
said. It was her revenge for years of servitude and I had no
redress. Then at last I received a visitor and, barring one,
nobody could have been more welcome. Bribing the guards,
Jonathan entered the house and brought me news of David.

'So he's safe? Thank the Lord!'

'He's with Samuel at Ramah.'

'I thought that he didn't know him.'

'He doesn't. He has taken refuge there. He reckons that
Father won't dare to act against the prophet.'

'So what happens now?'

'I'll plead David's case again to Father.'

'You're the last person he'll listen to.'

'I've no choice. We've sworn to defend each other with our
lives.'

'You'll take up arms against Father?' I asked, aghast.

'No, never. But I'm ready to die for David.'

I feared that the distinction would be less precise in
practice.

'Father claims that he plans to seize the throne from you.'

'There's no need; I would willingly surrender it to him. Not
since Gideon... not since Joshua has there been such a leader.
He'll make a far better king than me.'

'Not true!' I said, my loyalties split. 'Who else would have
braved the precipice to attack the Philistines at Micmash?'

'That was reckless, not brave. But the Lord was with me that
day, as he is with David now. I'm happy to swear allegiance to
him. His friendship – his love – has been the greatest blessing
of my life.'

I had never felt so proud of my brother. His noble spirit shone through his every word. I wondered uneasily whether David would be so generous about him.

Confined to the house, I wasn't privy to Jonathan's stratagems but, three days after his visit, he sent word that he had prevailed on Father to pardon David and welcome him back for the Festival of the New Moon. The pardon extended to me, and relief at my release from captivity mixed with excitement at my reunion with David. On the morning of the Festival, I attended the sacrifices in the sanctuary, making a deep obeisance to Father, who gazed at me distractedly, and to Mother, whose kiss was cold. I returned home, donned my newly woven robe, scented myself with aloes and cassia, put ornaments in my hair and waited for David. By the early evening, when the guard arrived to escort me to the feast, he had yet to appear. Terrified that he'd been ambushed on the way, I strove to stay calm as I entered the courtyard and took my place alongside Mother, Hodiah, my aunt and cousin. While the others greeted me warmly, Mother kept aloof, blind to the injustice of blaming me for being as faithful to my husband as she was to hers.

The food was the richest I'd had in weeks, but it tasted as bland as the lentils and buttermilk that Hodiah mashed up for Meribaal. He'd grown so fast during my detention that I felt an added pang for what I'd missed. I glanced across the courtyard where Father sat with Abner, Ahitophel, and his four sons, a place left empty for David, and longed to speak privately to Jonathan. In the event, it was Hodiah who set my mind at rest – and my heart racing.

'Don't worry, David is here,' Hodiah whispered.

'Where?' I looked around rapidly.

'No, not here. At our house. Jonathan did all he could to persuade him to join us. He said that the king was expecting him and would be furious – insulted – if he didn't appear. But David didn't trust him – '

'Jonathan?'

'No, the king. Though who knows? He's started to mistrust everyone. So Jonathan promised to gauge the king's mood.'

'But why hasn't he come home?' I asked. 'The guards were removed yesterday.'

Hodiah dipped her finger in the paste and slipped it into the baby's mouth. As he sucked contentedly, she searched for a reply. 'Isn't it obvious? If the king were planning to arrest him, your house would be the first place he'd look.'

At once reassured and fearful, I entered into the general chatter as Keziah, ignoring her mother's rebuke, quizzed me on my part in David's escape. 'Is it true you dressed him in your robe and veil and led him through a secret passage in the city wall?' A commotion across the courtyard saved me from responding. Father shouted; Jonathan jumped up, sweeping his cup and bowl to the ground, and strode towards us. As he did so, Father snatched a spear from the guard, who stood as still as a basking lizard, and hurled it at Jonathan, narrowly missing him and hitting the heel of a bondwoman kneeling at the hearth. Her screams were answered by two of her fellow servants, while the rest of us stared in horror at Father.

'Wife, you've betrayed me,' he shouted at Mother, who paled. 'Who could believe that this unworthy cur, this deceitful scoundrel, who puts fidelity to his so-called friend, a man who wants to tear the crown from his head, the head from his neck, the…' He struggled to compound his charge. 'Who could believe that he's any son of mine?'

Mother wept on my aunt's shoulder, as Jonathan turned back to Father. 'It's you who's unworthy of David, a man who has shown you unstinting devotion. No wonder Samuel condemned you. If anyone has torn the crown from my head, it's you!'

Father pounced as if trying to rip Jonathan's throat, even though he was several paces away. Abner restrained him, as Jonathan turned to his wife. 'Come!' he said, holding out his hand. Clasping her howling baby to her breast, Hodiah accompanied him out. Abner and the twins led Father up to his chamber; Mother made to follow, but my aunt insisted that she go with her until Father recovered. A bevy of wailing servants surrounded the stricken bondwoman, while one of their number fetched honey to salve her wound. Eluding the guard assigned to escort me, I walked home alone.

Hours went by as I waited for David to appear, confident that the conqueror of the Philistines would be able to evade a search party. When dawn brought no more relief than dusk, I determined to seek him out and, borrowing Hamdan's mantle, made my way across the city. I entered Jonathan's courtyard to find Hodiah rocking Meribaal in her arms but, drawing nearer, I saw that it was the mother and not the baby who was crying.

'What's wrong?' I asked, fighting for breath. 'Did Father send his men? Where's Jonathan? Where's David?'

'No, no one's been. They're on the roof. Safe in each other's arms.'

'Thank the Lord!'

'If you say so.'

'I must go up to them.'

'No, you don't want... really. They'll be sleeping.'

'While I've lain awake all night, waiting for my husband to return!'

'You'll grow used to it.'

'I'll creep up. I promise not to disturb them. I just want... need to see him for myself.'

'Wait, Michal!'

'Not another moment. He's my husband!'

Furious with Hodiah for obstructing me, I climbed the stairs to the upper floor and the ladder to the roof. Poised on the middle rung, I peered at David and Jonathan huddled together like soldiers on the eve of battle. They looked so beautiful in the milky light, David's pink arm resting on

Jonathan's tawny shoulder, that I wanted to run up and kiss them both, but I was afraid of startling them and, while it pained me to admit it, of embarrassing David, who was clearly more at ease naked before his friend than before his wife. All at once, he stirred and ran his arm lazily down Jonathan's back, lower than was necessary to rouse him. I knew that I should announce my presence but a curious unease prevented me. Jonathan woke and, laughing, kissed David on the lips, not dutifully or amicably but with passion. I longed to look away, but I was stuck fast as when the twins tied me to a tree. Then, Jonathan had rescued me; now, he was the one who tortured me, as he slid his tongue down David's chest and lapped it like a dog. Next, David took the lead, pinning Jonathan's arms behind his neck, which felt like a double betrayal since it was a grip that I hated but I'd borne it, thinking it unique to us. Yet, far from looking discomfited, Jonathan grinned as David pushed him on to his stomach and entered him as he had... almost as he had done me.

I wanted to scream; I wanted to run; but my voice and my legs were frozen. Was this how men behaved on their own? Was it something else that I should have been taught to expect? No, I knew without knowing that what they were doing was wrong. Yet they looked so right together that it felt like a greater wrong to intrude. Whereas I had endured David's brutishness, Jonathan embraced it. From his smiles – from his sighs – it was clear that for him happiness and pleasure were the same. At once everything fell into place, from my previous sight of them together on this very roof to Jonathan's fervent advocacy of my marriage. Rather than my concealing my true feelings from him, he had concealed his from me. I wanted to punish them and shame them. I wanted to tell Father where to find David and the whole city how I'd found him. But, even as I envisioned my revenge, I knew that I could never exact it. In spite of my hurt and humiliation, I cared for them both too much. For the first time in my life, I wished that I were a man: not so that I'd know how to read and write; not so that I'd be free to roam where I pleased; not even so that my husband would look at me the way that he looked at my brother; but so that I could be heartless and faithless and selfish and vicious and base, without a qualm.

Breaking away, I returned to the courtyard to find Hodiah waiting, as if to make common cause. 'You were right,' I said, gaining some consolation from thwarting her. 'They were asleep. They looked so peaceful that I didn't want to wake them.'

Jonathan called on me later in the morning. My first impulse was to instruct Hamdan to tell him that I was sick, but curiosity to hear what he had to say won out. When he addressed me with the composure of the practised deceiver, my despair was complete.

'David left at daybreak as soon as the gate was opened. He wanted to see you but he was afraid that there'd be guards.'

'I understand,' I said, draining my voice of emotion.

'He asked me to give you this ring,' he said, handing me a gold and amber band, engraved with a Philistine dove.

'Really?' I asked, wondering if he had done so of his own accord or at Jonathan's instigation or even if it were a gift to Jonathan, which guilt had impelled him to pass on to me. 'It's beautiful. But you must have it.'

'What? Why?'

'See, it's too big for me.' I twisted it around my middle finger. 'It will fit you perfectly.'

'Nonsense,' Jonathan said, putting it on his little finger, where it stuck.

'What did I say? Besides I'm sure that David would rather you wore it.'

'It's a woman's ring.'

'Even so.'

Jonathan was wearing the ring whenever I saw him over

the next few weeks. In spite of my newly restored liberty, I rarely left the house. The city was rife with rumours of David's flight, some saying that he'd joined the Sidonians or even the Philistines, some that he was raising a rebel army to fight the king, with Joab as his first recruit. The most credible, that he had sought refuge with the priests of Nob, was confirmed when Father summoned Ahimelech, the high priest, to appear before him. I too was summoned, expressly to witness my husband's disgrace. Ahimelech, quivering like a beast at the slaughter, explained that David had claimed to be on official business and entreated him for food. They had none except for the sacred bread in the sanctuary, which they gave him when he swore that, having known no women for three days, he and his men were ritually pure. I laughed out loud to learn that, yet again, he had been true to the letter of the Law and false to it in every other respect. But I couldn't laugh at the aftermath when Father sent an Edomite captain with a troop of guards to kill the priests. Some said that as many as eighty died, along with all the men, women and even children who had served them in the town.

Father's next move was to divorce me summarily from David and arrange my marriage to Paltiel, a Manassehite elder. It was not until he arrived in Gibeah, accompanied by Merab and Adriel, that I discovered he was sixty years old, bald, with pitted cheeks and a carbuncle on his chin the size of his nose. The one person from whom I hoped for sympathy withheld it. Merab, nursing her first child and expecting her second, was more dismissive than ever of my concerns. Having never hidden her contempt for David, she gave it free rein, denouncing him for defying Father and me for abetting his escape. Jonathan, true to form, was outraged by the divorce, warning Father that it was against the Law for any man, regardless of rank, to give his daughter to a second husband while the first was living. Father retorted that David was a traitor and therefore as good as dead – indeed, he soon would be dead – before banishing Jonathan from his presence, prompting my brother to condole with me on an insult that I had barely registered.

'It's an outrage,' he said. 'That relic is no match for a king's daughter.'

'You thought a shepherd a match for a king's daughter.'

'He was a hero, young and handsome. Have you seen Paltiel? How can you bear to take him to your bed?'

'At least I can be sure that he won't take anyone else to my bed.'

'What do you mean?'

'I saw you with him, Jonathan.'

'With whom?' he asked, lowering his gaze.

'David.'

'Of course you have. Everyone has. He's my friend.'

'I saw you with him on the roof at the last New Moon.'

'You were there?' he asked, gulping so deeply that his cheeks appeared to meet.

'To my unending regret.'

'I am so sorry.'

'For what you did or for what I saw?'

'I wish that I could say "both", but I can't. But what you saw… what David and I were doing… you did see what David and I were doing?' I nodded. 'Believe me, that had nothing to do with David and you, or me and you, or anyone else besides us.'

'Really? You exist in your own private world, like Adam and Eve in the Garden of Eden? What about Hodiah? What about Meribaal?'

'It's hard to explain.'

'Then don't! But perhaps you'll understand why an old man, an ugly man with a face like a rockfall, is all that I want and all I deserve.'

TWO

Abigail

Nabal's mother hangs the chain around my throat. As ever, she holds it for a moment too long as though she pictures the beads as blades. As ever, I thank her for her kindness in lending me the jewellery, which, as we both know, is not for Abigail but for Nabal's wife, the richness of my adornment as sure a sign of her son's prestige as the richness of the feast. The gold and amber beads were a part of her bride-price from Nabal's father. Nabal gave no bride-price for me, but then there was no father or brother or even uncle or cousin to whom he might have paid it, since my entire clan was massacred in an Amalekite raid. Some would say that the thrift of the match was part of its attraction and, after twenty-five years of marriage, I might agree. But back then I believed him when he praised my youth and beauty and the fortitude with which I bore my loss. He claimed that his sole desire was to protect me; and, short of betrothal to the king himself, what greater protection could I have wished than the hand of the Calebite chief? True, he had a protuberant lower jaw that gathered drool, a belly like a woman bearing twins, and a scraggy beard like a sheep with scab. But his plainness made me feel secure. I thought that it would compensate for my poverty. I was wrong.

His whole clan opposed the match, his mother suggesting that, since I had no menfolk to avenge my shame, he should take me as his concubine. But he was stubborn and, moreover, he had convinced himself that he'd been elected chief by dint of his discernment. We married and I made every effort to be a good wife, not least at night, when even the bondwomen, who lived lives of unrelenting toil, looked at me with pity. I yearned for a child, to have someone in my life whom I could love without strain or obligation; I yearned for a son to consolidate my position in the household. I conceived quickly

– I conceived quickly eleven times – but the longest I ever carried a child was three months. On the two occasions that there was a body in the blood, it resembled a crab more than a person. But I believe that I could have even loved a monster if it were mine. Now it's too late. My cycle of blood, once as regular as the moon, is erratic. I find myself sweating at night even when Nabal is nowhere near. I feel my breasts smart even when he's not clawing them. His mother urges him to renounce me in favour of a younger, more fruitful wife but, so far, he has ignored her, although less from love or sympathy or even force of habit than indolence.

Nabal's mother – I must give her her name, Shirah, although to me she's purely a function – leaves me and goes to dress. She is intent on outshining all three of her sons' wives, not, as one might expect, to elicit compliments but, rather, to disparage them. She takes more pleasure in upbraiding people for their insincerity than in thanking them for their kindness. 'I suppose I can trust you to see that all is in order,' she says, as though I hadn't spent every waking hour for the past three days drilling the servants, cleaning the chambers and preparing the food. However much she maintains that she runs the household, she knows full well that, without me, it would fall apart. I am the one who keeps the peace between the brothers; I am the one who feeds the bondmen, pays the servants and hires the labourers; I am the one who advises Nabal on what produce should be kept and what traded, always careful to credit my opinions to him. I break into a rare smile at the thought that, no matter how different its objects, Shirah and I have one thing in common: our contempt.

I go downstairs to speak to the servants. With three days of feasting, the sheep-shearing festival makes heavy demands of them, which I am determined that they should fulfil. I must remind them once again which meats are to be served on which day, which wines are to be served to which guests and which guests are to eat in which place: the dignitaries and elders in Nabal's chamber, the lesser clan members in the courtyard, and the shepherds and labourers in the field. I approach to find that, instead of the anticipated bustle, they are deep in discussion. They break out and stare at me with a mixture of indignation and alarm that I think it wise to ignore.

'Is everything ready?' I ask, with a polished smile. 'People will be arriving soon. I've heard some children outside.'

'We're ruined, Mistress,' Oren, the head servant, replies. 'You should escape.'

'Why, what's wrong?' I ask, envisioning Nabal's fury should weevils have infested the storeroom or last year's wine have soured.

'It's not for me to say.'

'Nonsense! You just have.'

'Ten men came to see the master this afternoon.'

'I heard. Weren't they labourers from the river field?'

'No, they were bandits from the camp at Maon.'

I know all about the camp, which is barely an hour's ride away and a concern throughout Carmel. David, the great general who married the king's daughter, fell from favour and fled into the wilderness, where followers have flocked to him, some equally disaffected and others, among them the youngest son of one of our clansmen, lured by his legend. The elders urged Nabal to make overtures to him, but Nabal, eager to avoid taking action of any sort, let alone the clash that might result if his approaches were rejected, temporized. As weeks passed with no news from the camp, he boasted that David was too in awe of his eminence and power to confront him. I, having climbed to the roof and seen the distant camp swell like a festering boil, was less convinced. The fact that ten men have come, in a show of strength as much as a neighbourly visit, confirms my fears.

'You shouldn't call them bandits. After all, no one was hurt; nothing was stolen.'

'So far.'

'What did they want? Did any of you hear?'

'All of us. They knew about the sheep-shearing. They begged the master for a share of the feast.'

'And he refused?' I ask, already knowing the answer.

'He rounded on them,' Oren replies. 'They were respectful – at least their voices were soft. But the master raged that he hadn't sweated and strained all his life to squander food on a pack of bandits.'

'That was his word,' Oren's wife, Helah, interjects.

'Only you can save us,' Oren says.

'How? What you are to me, I am to the master.'

They gaze at me in reproach. Chastened, I make my way to Nabal's chamber to find him drinking with his brothers, Achim and Yimnah. I pray that I've come at a good moment, when the wine has rendered him docile but not yet bellicose or insensible.

'My lord,' I say, showing him the subservience that he demands in company. 'The servants – misinformed as ever – claim that you've refused alms to our new neighbours in Maon. I rebuked them soundly. "How dare you?" I said, "when your master's munificence is renowned throughout Judah. Besides – "' I add, turning my rebuke into a reminder – '"it's the custom at sheep-shearing to share our feast with everyone: beggar, bandit or king."'

'That's enough!' he says, draining a cup of wine, not all of it down his throat. 'Of course I refused them and would do so again. Neighbours, you call them? They're brigands. Traitors to the king and to the land. Their leader – this David of whom there's so much talk – offered his services to the Philistines. He sought shelter in Gath but, terrified that they'd kill him, he pretended to be mad, since the Philistines revere madmen as we do prophets.' His brothers laugh politely. 'But King Achish was cunning. He knew that David would do more damage to us here than at the head of a Philistine army, so he sent him back, where he's gathered a rabble of outcasts and murderers.'

I listen to him in bewilderment. I've heard whispers that King Saul is possessed and has turned against his own son as well as David, but they remain whispers since no one dares repeat them out loud. I've heard too that David plotted to seize the throne, using the princess to further his ambitions. Who knows what to believe? The truth is like a traveller growing dustier with each step away from home. What's certain is that people no longer hold David in the same regard that they did when he slew the Philistine champion eight years ago.

Nabal's voice, dripping with scorn, rouses me from my reverie. 'This David is a scoundrel. He saved the people of Keilah from the Philistines yet, a month later, they were ready to yield him up to the king, preferring to risk another enemy attack than to have him and his men plundering the town. So he went on to Ziph, but no honest man would have any dealings with him. Would you have me be the first? When his mob came this afternoon, they had the gall to claim that, if it weren't for them, there would be no feast: that it was their presence in the hills that had prevented raids on our flocks. I told them that they were the only raiders I needed protecting from and turned them away.'

'Of course you're right, my lord,' I reply, but, while I acknowledge the justice of his argument, I am dubious of its wisdom. 'And yet, to keep the peace, wouldn't it be prudent to give them what they ask?' I look to his brothers for support, but they would rather see me chastened.

'And have every blackguard in Judah knocking at my gate? I may as well hand over the keys to my storeroom! And why not my strongbox for good measure? You forget that I have responsibilities to my clan,' he says, in his most sententious tone.

'Didn't the elders ask you to negotiate with David?'

'At the time of the barley harvest, yes. Now they've urged

me not to submit. First, he will take our wealth; then, the king will take our lives.'

'Remember his reprisal against the priests of Nob last year?' Achim says.

'And they were priests,' Yimnah adds.

I have no doubt that the elders are keen for Nabal to make a stand, since it will be his house that is razed to the ground, his stores that are pillaged, and his women that are violated if David wreaks revenge. But I know better than to argue since it's only the wine that has saved my cheeks – and even my teeth – from punishment. I go down to greet our guests, whose voices, high and low, soon fill the courtyard. I am grateful for the women's chatter, which, while as trivial as that of my sisters-in-law, is at least different. After the usual round of illnesses, deaths and marriages (with pregnancies and births skipped over in deference to me), the talk turns to David. As elsewhere, some think him a villain and some a victim and it amuses me to hear them speak with such authority of a man they have never met. I pay more heed to a cousin from Juttah who saw him pass through Kain. Although the lack of detail is frustrating, I am intrigued by her account of his appearance: 'as splendid in his mud-stained tunic as Joseph in his many-coloured cloak.'

As the meal wears on and melons and pomegranates replace pigeons and geese, I learn that David's men have visited most of the women's husbands, none of whom has refused their requests. It's clear that, in encouraging Nabal to hold out, they have deliberately deceived him, either in the hope that he'll prevail and David will withdraw from the region or, more sinisterly, that he'll fail and David will attack him. Jealous of his wealth and authority (and forgetting that they or their fathers acclaimed him chief), they long for David to humble him. Despite myself, I feel a pang of sympathy for his plight.

The guests leave, to return tomorrow, their resentment of Nabal not preventing their accepting his hospitality. Making my way upstairs, I look into his chamber to find him supine in a puddle, which I suspect isn't wine. On other nights I would have tried to clean him but, tonight, my revulsion is too acute and I retreat to the chamber that I share with my maidservant, Ahinoam. The snores, loud and soft, that usually lull me to sleep now compound my agitation. I lie restless, brooding on Nabal's folly in rebuffing David. Convinced that I alone can avert his impending revenge and save the household from ruin, I conceive a plan, which, for once, doesn't dissolve at dawn. Before Shirah, Nabal or any of the family wake, I rouse the servants and tell them to join me in the storeroom. Assuming that David sent so many messengers not just as a threat but to indicate the size of gift that he anticipated, I inspect the food for tonight and tomorrow's feasts in a kind of frenzy, instructing Oren and the others to take one... no, two... no, all five of the roasted sheep, two sacks of beans and peas, three sacks of sesame seeds, three sacks of barley, and as many loaves of bread, lentil and fig cakes, gourds of grape and date syrup, and skins of wine, that can be loaded on to our dozen donkeys. I'm exhilarated by the prospect not just of appeasing David but of thwarting Nabal and Shirah who, with no call to check on the provisions, will welcome their guests this evening to a meal of empty bowls. I shall be beaten, locked up and perhaps even cast out, but it will be worth it. After twenty-five years of coercion, the one thing that they haven't destroyed is my will.

The donkeys protest at their burdens, sparking my fear of discovery, but even Shirah, alive to every transgression, sleeps through their telltale brays. I lower my veil and, with each servant driving two beasts, we make our cumbersome journey to Maon. Approaching the ridge, I find that we're too late as three or four hundred men pour out of the camp and head towards us. The servants panic and urge retreat but I overrule them. Even if we abandon the donkeys and reach home, the house will never withstand such an onslaught. Besides, if David is the brute that Nabal claims, he will slaughter us all, masters and servants alike. Our one hope is to throw ourselves on his mercy so, with a show of confidence, I press ahead. A terrifying roar rises up from the bandits, who sweep down on us like a rockfall. I await the inevitable but, just when they're poised to attack, David raises his hand and they draw back. I dismount from the donkey, as glad of my veil as a soldier of his helmet, and walk towards him. Although my vision is clouded, I am dazzled by his presence. He's a slight man, poorly dressed, riding a donkey that Nabal would have spurned, and yet he lights up the landscape. The trees and boulders, the clefts and mounds, the very earth and sky, seem to frame him like the setting of a jewel. It makes no sense; he's twenty paces away and yet I feel as if he is standing next to me, his eyes... his hands wandering over me, evoking sensations I have only ever known in my dreams. All my life I've envied Rebecca, who fell so in love on seeing Isaac that she almost slipped off her camel. She was set to marry him, whereas I may be about to be killed by David. Nevertheless, I find to my consternation that even death at his hand seems preferable to life with Nabal.

I fall at his feet and the dust in my mouth and nostrils seems fitting. I raise my head, clear my throat and speak.

'My lord, your servant begs a hearing.'

'And what servant is this?'

'Abigail, wife of Nabal.'

'Well met! My men and I are about to pay your husband a visit. You are wise to have left home.'

'Will you hear me, my lord? I will not rise from this spot until you do.'

'You think that I am to be bargained with?'

'No, but I trust to be reasoned with.'

'Ha! You're bold to venture out here. Did your husband send you?'

'No, my lord. Not him nor anyone of his house. I came of my own accord to redress the wrong done to you yesterday.'

'And I come to avenge it.'

'Then avenge it on me, for I alone am to blame.'

'Was it you who refused aid to a "base shepherd"? Was it you who described my men as "ragged sheep"? He will learn that they can be ravening wolves.'

'No, but it was me who failed in my duty. Had I been free to greet your men, I would have granted their request. But I can make amends.' I point to the donkeys, who alone are oblivious of the danger. 'Here is every morsel of food prepared for this evening's feast. The boards will be as bare as on the Day of Atonement.'

'You make amends for your husband's negligence, but what of his insult?'

'Surely that is of no consequence? He is of no consequence. A braggart! A buffoon! He spouts bile when he's sober and spews it when he's drunk. He is unworthy of my lord's wrath. You kill him and you kill a fool. You kill his household and you kill those whose only offence is to serve a fool. We aren't all blessed to serve a man like my lord.' He frowns and I fear that I have spoken out of turn. 'What's more, the beasts that you'd need as sin offerings would exceed all Nabal's flocks and herds.'

'Your words are as sweet as your husband's were bitter.'

'And true, my lord. Our lives are paltry but yours is of great worth. Don't lay it open to reproach.'

'Too late! I am an outcast in the wilderness living on what I can extort from honest men.'

'But the Lord favours you.'

'What?' He looks shocked.

'I see you wearing a crown.' A sunbeam turns the blaze of his hair to gold. 'And your son and your son's son.' I don't know what possesses me – the Lord doesn't speak through women – but I am as sure of what I see ahead of him as I am of what lies before me now.

His intense stare frightens me. Whatever else, he is still the king's son-in-law and I have spoken treason.

'How do you know?' he asks, in a voice that is gentler than his gaze.

'I don't know; I see.'

'Won't you raise your veil?'

'Would my lord open his gate to his enemies?'

'Am I your enemy?'

'Isn't every man the enemy of a defenceless woman?'

'Defenceless, you?' He laughs. 'Your words have blunted my sword. Tell your men to bring over the donkeys. They won't be harmed. Then go home. Your husband; your household; your whole clan owe you their lives. I trust that they will honour the debt.'

The transfer effected, David tugs on his donkey's reins and turns round. His men appear to waver, as if weighing the richness of the provisions against the thrill of bloodshed, but after a minute they follow him. As I watch them leave, I'm riven by conflicting emotions: joy that I – and I alone – have saved a score of innocent lives; desolation that I shall never see David again. I have no words for what I feel or why I feel it, but for a few heart-stopping moments I have encountered the only man who would give my life meaning... that is, he would if I weren't married and he at least a dozen years my junior. True, there was a flicker of interest in his eyes, but it was my judgement that he praised, a quality men admire more in other men's wives than their own. Nevertheless, it's a flicker for which I would be ready to risk everything, riding after him and removing not just my veil but my robe and my tunic... Appalled by my recklessness, I seize on the servants' congratulations to laugh at myself under the guise of general relief.

In my preoccupation, I barely register that we have arrived home until roused by Shirah's rasp.

'Where have you been? And why the attendants? These dolts' – she indicates Helah and the servants who have stayed behind – 'purport to know nothing.'

'No more they do.' I see that my plan of shaming Nabal in

front of his guests is not to be and describe my encounter with David. 'There's no need to thank me,' I say, when, screeching like a hawk, she clambers up to Nabal's chamber. Feeling the gaze of the household upon me, I follow, only to stop at the door. Nabal lies where he did last night, although the stench of sweat, wine and wastes now seems to have penetrated the walls. Even Shirah can't hide her disgust as she skirts a puddle and, with grim relish, shakes him awake. He opens first one eye and then the other, his arms flailing as if to waft away the swarm of bees that he slowly identifies as his mother's voice. Allowing him no respite, she shrieks: 'We're undone! Your wife – that woman – has taken everything we set aside for tonight's feast – the mutton, the bread, the barley, the wine, the seeds – and given them to the bandits.' While he struggles to make sense of her charge, she repeats it with fervour, as though the prospect of my punishment offsets the loss. He totters to his feet, fixing me with a glare that empowers me to speak.

'No, your mother hasn't told you everything. She's left out the beans, the syrups, the lentil and fig cakes.' He staggers towards me, aiming a blow so clumsy that I make no attempt to duck. 'She also omitted to tell you that I've saved you and her and the whole clan from the consequence of your avarice. On the way to Maon, I met four hundred men coming to raze the house to the ground and butcher its inhabitants.'

'She's lying! Hit her!' Shirah shouts.

'I've saved you both but I don't expect thanks, any more than for the twenty-five years I've grubbed and toiled for you.'

'Hit her!' Shirah repeats.

'Yes, hit me,' I say, and I'm shocked to discover that it's what I want. Why? To consolidate my hatred for him? To punish myself for my desire for David? To affirm my strength: that, after this morning's encounter, no hand nor stick nor whip will hurt me again?

He stumbles forward, right arm raised and foaming at the

mouth, but, just when he's poised to strike, he collapses gibbering at my feet. He gasps and clutches at his chest, then all at once falls still. The colour seeps from his cheeks like water from a sieve. I should feel elation or, at the very least, relief, but all I feel is a gaping lethargy. Shirah crouches and cradles his head. 'He isn't dead; he isn't dead!' she exclaims, and what I take for a vain hope turns out to be true. 'Help me lift him on to the bed,' she says. Then, either assessing his weight or reluctant to let me touch him, she pushes me away. 'No, run for help. Now!'

I obey blindly, fetching two servants who haul him on to the bed. He's not only heavy but stiff and I am taken back twenty-five years to when I found the corpses of my mother, my father, my sisters, my brothers, my aunts, uncles and cousins scattered across the courtyard, covered in flies, with no one to help me bury them. Whereas their flesh had hardened in several hours, Nabal's has taken a matter of minutes. Moreover, he is not dead. He may be impervious to word or touch, but he's still breathing, like a snake that sleeps through winter. Shirah sits by his side, sponging his face, although for once it isn't soaked in sweat. I shuffle like a bird with one wing, unable to fly away and unwilling to draw near.

'I'll mix a potion to revive him. Aloes, cinnamon, cumin and anise, if we have any left.'

'If you didn't give it away to the bandits!' she says savagely.

'No, we used it when Machia had the fever.'

'So now you'll try to poison him?'

'Why? So I can be married off to Achim or Yimnah?' Even she can see that that would be escaping a trap to fall into a snare. She urges me to go and, when I return with the potion (minus the anise seeds), I find my two prospective husbands, along with their wives, occupying the chamber. They lower their voices at my approach and turn towards me in harsh reproof. Yimnah accuses me of goading Nabal and provoking his seizure. Although one glance at his bloated body is enough to refute the charge, I say nothing but, rather, hand Shirah the potion, which, prising open his jaws, she spoons down his throat only to watch it dribble back. Achim proposes to set out at once for the sanctuary at Hebron to sacrifice a sheep for his recovery. I long to tell him that it's pointless; I have seen the man whom the Lord favours and it's not Nabal. The others find reasons to leave, as if to conceal the only valid one: their helplessness.

For the next ten days they return sporadically while Shirah and I watch over the living corpse. I too sink into a kind of stupor, which is neither restful nor troubling but as devoid of sensations as his. I revive only when I retire to my chamber at night, leaving Shirah exultant in her solitary vigil. Then on the tenth day, Nabal dies. I put on my widow's robe, the chafing goat's hair an added incentive to remarry. I may not have long to wait, for Nabal has scarcely been entombed when Achim, as his oldest surviving brother, stakes his claim. Yimnah sets aside their rivalry to ensure that Nabal's wealth remains in the clan. Machia, however, is less sanguine. All the rancour she felt towards me when I was her brother-in-law's wife is doubled now that I am to be her husband's, taking precedence over her not just in the household but in his bed. Yimnah's wife, Zillah, obliged to defer to us both, is sure to fuel her malice. I'm amused that, having sneered at my barrenness, they are now prepared to concede, however tacitly, that the fault may have been Nabal's, trusting Achim to prove more potent. I contemplate refusing him but, although Ahinoam offers me a refuge with her parents, I prefer to remain in the one place I know as home.

Achim must wait ninety days before we marry in case a son to inherit Nabal's name is already growing in my belly. I say nothing to disabuse him and relish this interval when I have no prescribed place in the household and am treated with neither respect nor resentment but indifference. It is as if the law against touching a corpse has been extended to the widow. I feel an anonymity which is the closest I come to freedom. Then, sitting one morning in my chamber, I hear a commotion in the courtyard. Looking out, I see at least fifty armed men confronting Achim, Yimnah and a group of cowering servants. I strain to listen as their leader strides forward, but his voice is so loud that I recoil, bumping into Shirah.

'I am Joab, kinsman to great David, son-in-law of King Saul. My general has heard of your chief's death and sends me to grant you his protection.'

'We thank you for your general's concern,' Achim replies, 'but we have already paid dearly for his protection. Besides, the clan has a new chief. I am to lead the Calebites. My strong arm stretches over all their lands.'

'You misunderstand me,' Joab speaks as if to a simpleton. 'My general is willing to relieve you of that burden. In return, he requests the hand of Abigail, the chief's widow.'

I gasp. Shirah grabs my wrist and tries to drag me back into the chamber. I push her off with a strength that springs directly from David's proposal. She falls against the wall with a moan that I barely register as I fix my attention on Joab.

'What impudence!' Achim says. 'Do you think us so ignoble that we'd swear allegiance to a bandit? I myself am to marry Abigail as soon as the Law permits.'

'Is that your last word?'

'It is.'

'It is indeed,' Joab says, drawing his sword and skewering him in the stomach. Achim drops to the ground. A deathly hush descends, broken by a single scream. I turn to see Machia and Zillah together at the rail. But it's Zillah who screams, while Machia stands as still as Lot's wife, turned into salt. I'm shocked, as much by my own composure as Joab's savagery. 'I trust that that answers your objections,' he adds. 'But my general has no wish to force anyone.' He leisurely sheathes the sword that belies his claim. 'It is for the woman herself to decide. Where is she?'

'Here,' I say, walking slowly down the passage, conscious that everyone except Machia and Zillah, who weep in each other's arms, is staring at me. Even Yimnah looks up from his dead brother. I descend the stairs at a steady pace as if pondering my decision, although I made it the moment I heard the proposal. For the first time, my life will have a purpose beyond the everyday. I may finally find an answer to the question that has gnawed at me ever since the Amalekite raid: why was I the only member of my clan to be spared?

'Your general does me too much honour,' I say, on reaching the ground. 'I am happy to accept.' Ahinoam, facing me, claps her hand over her mouth. I have scandalised her; I have scandalised the whole household, and no one more so than myself, but I don't care. David is an outcast, a royal outcast but an outcast nonetheless; the king will hunt him down and, if he finds him, he will no more spare the women who are with him than he did the priests of Nob, but I don't care. David is married already, to a princess who's young and by all accounts beautiful, but I don't care. I have had forty years of behaving prudently; now I'm doing the opposite, and I don't care. 'Tell your general that I long to serve him. I am ready to give him many sons,' I say, hoping that Joab is standing too far away to demur.

'I thank you, lady.' Joab walks forward and kisses my hand. His lips are fleshy and cold. 'I shall return with him in three days.'

'But the Law – ' Yimnah interjects.

'My general's ardour brooks no delay. I trust that will give you time to prepare the wedding feast. We have seen how richly you celebrate the sheep-shearing,' he adds, with the trace of a smile. 'I almost forgot; it's customary for the bridegroom to bring gifts. So I'll leave you with a dozen men to guard the household.'

'They are a gift?' Yimnah asks, outraged.

'They will be when they're removed.'

Joab and the majority of his men depart. I gaze warily at those who remain but, apart from their pressing demands for food and drink, they show commendable respect for a household in shock. I am grateful for their presence the next morning when I follow the body to the tomb. We make a sorry band since, afraid of further violence, few of the clan attend. Those that do regard me with undisguised malice. The heat is so punishing that I am sure I'm not alone in praying as much for a swift end to the lamentations as for Achim's smooth passage into Sheol. Then, when the sepulchre stone is removed, the stench of Nabal's recently interred corpse makes even Shirah cut short her keening. We return home and I shun the burial feast, retiring with Ahinoam to my chamber where we weave a wedding robe of finest linen to replace my widow's garments. At dusk Helah brings us a soup, which she vows she has made herself, dispelling my fear that Shirah has administered the poison she accused me of intending for Nabal. I have no desire to eat but I know that I must since I'm as light-headed as if I had drunk ten bowls of wine.

The men Joab has left to guard the household guard me from its wrath, nevertheless I keep to my chamber, fashioning my robe and envisaging my future. After the meagre attendance at the burial, the men are determined to avoid a similar slight to their chief and comb the countryside rounding up the clan, who arrive on the wedding morning looking daunted. From my vantage point on the upper floor, I watch David ride into the courtyard, crowned with a garland of blood-red anemones. Leaping from his donkey, he stands two palms shorter than Joab. He glances up at me, and I'm seized by the fear that he glimpsed my surprise through my veil. Yimnah greets him stiffly and I retreat behind a rail as they come upstairs to sign the marriage contract, which makes David master of all the land and goods that passed to me on Nabal's death. I suspect that they are the main attraction, but

Yimnah's summons prevents me from brooding. Ahinoam adjusts my veil a final time and I enter what I still think of as Nabal's chamber. I kneel before David, who kisses my hand, draws me up and uncovers my face. My cheeks sting as he stares at me. I wonder what Joab has told him to expect but read nothing in his gaze but its intensity.

'Do I displease you, my lord? Did you expect Rachel only to discover Leah?'

'Didn't Jacob love and honour Leah?'

'He did, my lord.'

'Didn't she bear him six sons?'

'She did.'

'No, you don't displease me.'

He takes my arm and leads me downstairs, where the servants have laid out the feast. We're no sooner united than we must part, he to his place with Yimnah, Joab and the elders and me to mine with Shirah, Machia and Zillah, to whom my presence, let alone my marriage, is an affront. Scarcely a word passes between us and I linger over every mouthful to fill the silence. I envy the merriment across the courtyard, but a hurried look reveals that it stems entirely from David and his companions. The Calebites sit grim-faced, only raising a cheer to order.

'Is this David now to be our chief?' Zillah asks, as I chew a date. I resolve to answer in a way that shows my commitment to him is free and absolute. Calling for a bowl of water, I cross the courtyard. All eyes are on me but, whereas the others are uneasy or perplexed, David's are smiling. Head bowed, I kneel before him, untie his sandals and slowly – lovingly – wash his feet before drying them with the tips of my veil. I make to return to my place but he clasps my hand.

'Have you finished eating?' he asks. 'Shall we go upstairs?'

With no mother or father to escort me to my bridegroom, I was afraid that Shirah and Yimnah would arrogate the right. 'Whatever my lord wishes,' I reply, relishing the murmurs at another breach with tradition. He leads me up to Nabal's chamber, which he has taken as his own. Although Ahinoam has filled it with sweet-scented herbs, I fancy that I still detect Nabal's stale flesh and step closer to David, who smells like a freshly tilled field. He grins at my approach and throws off his mantle. I marvel at his rugged arms and sturdy chest. Nabal was soft-bellied even when we met, but David is as taut as a timbrel... I wish that he had chosen a chamber empty of ghosts.

'You're shaking,' David says, as he steers me towards the bed. 'Are you afraid of me?'

'No, my lord.' Although I say the words routinely, I find that they're true. 'Not of you, but of others.'

'Who, the Calebites? Don't worry, my men can control them.'

'No, the king.' He knits his brow, but I am determined to speak. 'I told myself that, far away in Benjamin, he was no threat.'

'No more he is.'

'He's sure to pursue you more relentlessly than ever. By marrying me, you've insulted his daughter.'

'On the contrary, he insulted me by marrying his daughter to another man.'

'The princess has married again?'

'Yes. Her brother risked everything to bring me the news.'

'But how, while you're still living? It's against the Law.'

'The king sets himself above the Law.'

'But it's the word of the Lord.'

'Then he's surprised when the Lord abandons him!'

'Do you know her new husband?'

'Only that he's a Manassehite and old.'

'Poor lady! It's no joy being married to an old man.'

'The young one didn't bring her much joy either.'

'I can't believe that,' I say, as the lamplight gilds his skin.

'I treated her unjustly.'

I wonder if he's trying to impress me with his honesty or prepare me for pain. 'Then maybe she'll be happy with him,' I reply quickly.

'I doubt that she will ever be happy with anyone.'

I long to talk of more cheerful matters – or, better still, not to talk at all – but his frankness inspires mine and there is something I must mention or else our lying together will be a lie. He is twenty-six; I am fifteen or so years older (I'm not being coy; I don't know my exact age. My parents are dead and no one thought to record the birth of a girl).

'You spoke of Leah, my lord.'

'What?'

'And her sons. I won't be able to give you six. I may not be able to give you one.' I screw up my eyes to staunch the tears. 'A man like you deserves many sons. For that you need a younger wife.'

'I shall have one. I shall have many. Sons and wives.' I bite back my sense of betrayal. 'But for now, all I want is you. Are you tired?'

'Not at all.' His sigh shows that I've misunderstood the question. 'But I would like to lie down.'

'Shall I put out the lamp?' he asks, with a smile.

'Not on my account.' I am more intent on admiring his body than concealing my own. Turning away, I take off my mantle and tunic and unbind my breasts. I leave my loins covered and, turning back, I see that he has done the same. He follows me to the bed, lying at my side, although I yearn to feel his weight upon me as much as I longed to escape from Nabal's... I must cease these comparisons! He takes my hand and I feel him tremble. 'Are you cold, my lord?'

'Not at all.'

'Then ill?' I ask, as the trembling quickens.

'I've disappointed one woman; I'm afraid of disappointing another.' He speaks as if spitting out nails.

'You could never disappoint me.'

'Michal felt the same. We were young, shy of each other. Her brother is my greatest friend. I thought that would help. I was wrong.'

'I'm not young. I'm not even shy, although I was certain that I would be.'

'Thank you. I knew at once you'd understand.'

I have no idea what he means but I'm determined to reassure him. 'Of course,' I say, squeezing his fingers.

'I began to fear that I wouldn't be at ease with any woman.'

'Is she... was she?' I want to ask about his other women but feel constrained.

'Yes,' he says. 'I've slept among many men – in camps, on campaigns – but only with one woman.'

I am starting to see that his very strength makes him afraid of hurting me. At the risk of appearing wanton, I know that I must take the lead. I lean over him, kiss his face and neck, stroke his chest and stomach, loosen his loincloth and slip my hand beneath its folds. In response, he rolls on to his side and grabs my breasts. Struggling not to wince, I arch my back and press my hips against his before removing my under-tunic and guiding him inside me. I find myself whispering instructions. 'Put your hand here... no, not so fast.' He laughs. 'Is anything wrong?'

'Not at all. But you remind me of my father teaching me how to ride.'

'I don't mean to offend you.'

'You haven't. On the contrary. Please, teach me everything you know!'

He proves a quick study, promptly adding intricacies of his own. I never knew that a man could have such vigour. Nabal was no sooner pleasured than he fell back in a daze, but David barely catches his breath, indeed, each spasm seems to revitalize him. At first modesty impels me to muffle my cries, but I rapidly abandon all restraint and shriek with delight, even after the guests have left and the household is still. Let the whole clan know that I now have a husband worthy of the name! Shortly before dawn, he flags and, after a final kiss, studies the wedding sheet with as much care as Nabal did, finding proof not of my purity but his own potency. He asks for wine and, slipping on my mantle, I step outside where the faithful Ahinoam has kept watch. She smiles either at what she sees or what she has heard and I embrace her without a blush. She brings in a wineskin and pours two cups, looking first shocked and then beguiled by David's nakedness. She leaves, flashing me a sly smile, and I return to bed, snuggling up to David, savouring the salty sheen of his skin.

'Not too weary?' he asks.

'Not in the least,' I reply. I want to banish sleep forever and share every waking moment with him. I don't even want to dream of him, unless I can be certain that he's dreaming of me. Married to Nabal, I sought love only from children and, blessed with none of my own, looked to my nephews and nieces, pressing almonds or figs into their eager hands for which they paid in hugs and kisses. But David has shown me that love can be mutual and unconstrained.

'What drew you to me,' I ask, 'making you send Joab when you heard of Nabal's death? Was it the three thousand sheep and thousand goats, the fields of wheat and barley, the olive groves and vineyards?'

'Why do you say that? I'd want you even if you were your own maidservant.' He glances at the door through which Ahinoam has just left. I am not sure that I believe him but I can see that he believes himself, which is enough.

'But why?'

'Everything about you. Your courage in coming to confront us alone – ' I make to protest. 'Very well, with a handful of servants. Your resolve to save your household when I doubt that many of them would have done as much for you. Your bearing. Your beauty.'

'I was veiled.'

'It shone through… it's true! The warmth of your voice; its sweetness. Shall I go on?'

'Yes please,' I say. Until now no one has named even one of my charms.

'But most of all, it was when you acknowledged me as king.'

'It wasn't a ploy. I don't know how but I saw it with utter clarity.'

'There's no need to apologise. You said you weren't weary. May I tell you a story?'

'Of course.'

'One I've never told anyone, not even my dearest friend – especially not my dearest friend.' It is hard to be sure in the half-light but his face seems to crumple. 'I was very young. Ten or eleven. The prophet Samuel came to Bethlehem, my home town. People were honoured but alarmed.'

'No wonder. I've heard that the Lord spoke to him more often than to anyone since Moses.'

'I've heard the same. Nobody could work out why he'd come. As a judge he confined his activities to Ephraim and Benjamin and rarely ventured into Judah. I still remember the turmoil as brother denounced brother and clan denounced clan for the hidden transgressions that they expected him to expose. In the event, he hadn't come to punish us but to offer a sacrifice. My father and all the elders prepared for the ceremony, and Samuel gave specific instructions that my brothers and I should attend. He summoned us one by one and sprinkled us with holy water, looking increasingly disappointed in my brothers (I have seven), his face finally lighting up when he came to me. After the sprinkling, he took a horn of oil from his mantle and anointed me. He spoke a long blessing, but I was too conscious of the stickiness on my forehead to pay much heed. Besides, I was steeling myself for the inevitable mockery – and worse – from my brothers. We had barely finished the ritual meal when Samuel asked if I would take him to see my sheep. I was horrified, but my father gave me a look that made the cost of refusing painfully clear. Samuel kept his hand on my shoulder the whole way – except when he moved to ruffle my curls. I was young and personable – '

'I can imagine.'

'As I feared, my brothers made crude jokes – even the older ones, who were married with sons of their own – about why Samuel had favoured me. Jokes which I barely understood and have no wish to repeat. But his intentions were entirely innocent. Once we reached the flock, he scarcely gave it a second glance. Instead, he revealed that the Lord had commanded him to visit my father and anoint one of his sons as king. "Which one?" I asked, presuming that he wanted my help – although I had no idea why. "You," he replied. "The moment I purified you, I knew for certain."' I long to tell him that it was the same for me when I hailed him as king, but I'm afraid to interrupt. 'I was confused. We had a king, our first king, and although I'd heard my father complain that Saul was capricious, he looked to the day when Jonathan, whom everybody admired, ascended the throne. But Samuel insisted that I was the one who would succeed, rule over my people and lead them to glory.'

'He spoke for the Lord,' I say, with both pride and apprehension.

'He made me promise to tell no one, not my father or mother and especially not my brothers. He reminded me of the story of Joseph.'

'The part where his brothers throw him into the well?'

'Yes. When I first heard it, I took their side. Joseph was so vain, boasting that they'd all have to bow down before him. And who's to say that, as a boy, I wouldn't have been as bad? Samuel was adamant that I run no risks. So I kept his prophecy to myself. My only subjects were my sheep, to whom I issued regular edicts. From then on, I waited for word from Samuel but it never came. Over time the memory faded. I even wondered if I'd made it up, the way I make up songs. Then five or six years later, my kinsman Joab, who was armour-bearer to the great general Abner, summoned me to Gibeah, where the king was possessed by an evil spirit. Music alone had the power to relieve him, so Joab thought I could help.'

'You're also a musician?'

'I'm *the* musician,' he replies, with a laugh. 'At any rate I enabled Saul to recover. I began to suspect that I'd misheard or misunderstood Samuel and what he'd said wasn't that I was to be a king but to heal one. I certainly couldn't envisage a worthier king than Jonathan, who honoured me with his friendship. But with Saul himself again, there was no reason for me to remain in Gibeah and I returned to my sheep.'

'Until you joined the army.'

'What makes you say that?'

'Because you defeated the Philistine giant.'

'It was my brothers who joined the army. Three of them... the three oldest. My father wanted to send them provisions and, mistrusting anyone outside the clan, he dispatched me to ensure that they weren't purloined along the way or in the camp. As soon as I arrived, I heard about the Philistine who'd struck terror into our troops. He'd issued a challenge to settle the battle by single combat, which Saul – and whatever else he may be, he's no coward – refused. Moreover he ordered all his officers to do the same. I knew at once, with the same absolute certainty Samuel had described, that I was the one who must fight him. I'm not a tall man.' I start, amazed he should think that I might not have noticed. 'But the Lord guided my hand and... well, you know the rest.'

'Everybody knows the rest.'

'The king acclaimed me as the saviour of the land and rewarded me richly. But, once we returned to Gibeah, he changed... or, rather, chopped and changed. Half the time he praised me and wanted me by his side and the other half he reviled me and wanted me out of his sight. Jonathan, ever the peacemaker, explained that, some years earlier, Samuel told

Saul that the Lord had abandoned him and chosen his successor. The king – and the queen as well – were increasingly convinced that I was the one. I don't know – I doubt he does himself – whether he finally allowed me to marry Michal so as to ensure my loyalty or to render me harmless. Of course I didn't breathe a word of what Samuel had told me. I even swore that I'd never met him, which fills me with shame.'

'Why? He might have killed you.'

'Not on account of Saul – I owe him nothing – but of Jonathan. I lied to the man to whom I swore always to speak the truth.'

'But your ultimate loyalty is to the Lord and you had to protect that.'

'He would never have betrayed me. He would gladly have given up the throne for me. I know he's the better man.'

'But would he be the better king?'

'Maybe. Who can tell?'

'The Lord.'

'The Lord, yes.' He breaks into a smile. 'The Lord. When Saul's jealousy grew murderous, Jonathan helped me flee. Although it was Michal who brought me the warning. Without her, I'd be dead... I'm sorry.'

'Don't be. I commend anyone who saved you.'

'I wish I could have spoken to her as I speak to you. I wish I could have felt for her what I feel for you.'

'That makes me happier than I can say.'

'For the past two years I've lived like a hunted animal. Saul has scoured the land to find me and kill me. And he came so close. Though not as close as I came to killing him.'

'What? When?'

'In a cave at the spring of Ein Gedi. My scouts spied him leading an army of three thousand men against us. Our force amounted to a mere tenth of their number, so we took refuge in the caves. I was hiding near the mouth of one when Saul came in to piss... relieve himself.'

'Wasn't it dark? How did you know it was him?'

'By his height; it's unmistakable. And the glint of his helmet. With one thrust of my sword I might have put paid to his persecution forever.'

'What stopped you?'

'That's what I've asked myself. And what my men asked me – far less politely. It's no small matter to strike down the Lord's anointed, even for one whom the Lord has anointed in his place. I can only assume that the Lord himself stayed my hand, keeping me from taking on the guilt of Saul's death, just as he sent you to keep me from taking on the guilt of Nabal's.'

'You think that he sent me?' I ask, seeing myself in a new light.

'I'm sure of it… Sparing Saul's life cost me another year and a half in the wilderness, even moving down into Sinai.'

'And across into Philistia?'

'So you've heard about that? I was desperate. Caught up in a kind of madness – and not only the madness I feigned. But through it all, the one thing that sustained me was my visit to Samuel at Ramah. I was worried about putting him in danger, but I doubted that even Saul would raise his hand against the prophet, and I needed to know the truth. I arrived just in time. He was lying in bed, his hoary beard and milky eyes reminding me of the ancients who lived for hundreds of years. He wanted to get up, but his wife forbade it. Once again he laid his hands on my head, although now it was because he was blind. He admitted that he was dying full of regrets, and I thought: If Samuel dies full of regrets, where does that leave the rest of us? One regret was his sons, whom he'd trained to carry on his work but who'd turned out to be corrupt. He begged me to beware of loving my sons too much, which perplexed me since I had none. But his greatest regret lay in choosing Saul.'

'It was the Lord who chose him. Samuel was merely his voice.'

'That's just what I said. "At times the Lord gives a man more than he merits in the hope that he'll prove worthy of it." But he refused to be consoled. He repeated what he'd prophesied all those years ago and told me that the hour was fast approaching. I left him to sleep and, when I returned, he was dead. His wife insisted that he'd kept death at bay until I arrived.'

'Had you sent word that you were coming?'

'Not at all. I had no one to send.'

'Then how?' He looks at me knowingly, and I see what it means to be favoured by the Lord.

'In the absence of his sons, I laid him to rest. I left, reassured that the words I'd carried inside me all these years were true. But, with his death, I can only prove them by the sword.'

I yawn and apologise; he laughs and kisses me. The next thing I know, I'm waking up with my arm stuck to his chest in the sultry afternoon heat. I study his face in repose, but, alert to the gentlest glance, he opens his eyes, grabs my shoulders and pulls me on top of him in a prelude to further coupling. Our sighs and moans mingle with the indistinct voices of the servants preparing the evening's feast, and the freedom I feel in his arms is enhanced by my release from drudgery. As the sun goes down, we slough off our sluggishness and start to dress. To my amazement, I'm not ashamed to stand naked in front of him, even when washing off his seed. Decked in Shirah's sequestered jewels, I go downstairs to take my place among the women, relishing the resentment, envy, prurience and rage that play on the various faces. With icy courtesy, Shirah asks if David had everything he needed and Zillah giggles, receiving a glare from Machia as though she'd broken a pact. I affect not to notice and, knowing that nothing will anger them more, prattle on about David's plans for the clan of which he is now chief.

We suffer one another's company for a further five evenings, since David has decreed that, despite the truncated betrothal, we are to observe the full week of feasting. In-between, he and

I keep to our chamber, turning day into night and night into day, measuring time solely by pleasure. We share intimacies of the past as well as the present. He asks about my family, as though charting his future sons' lineage, and I admit that, although I was fourteen or fifteen when Nabal's men rescued me, I recall nothing of life before the Amalekite raid.

'For years I sought a remedy, making regular offerings in the sanctuary and even secretly visiting the wise woman of Beth-Anoth, until Shirah found out and Nabal beat me. In the end, I decided that my parents, my sisters and brothers, had taken my memories with them to Sheol, in order that I might live on in the world, free from regret.'

'So, the first thing you remember is what?'

'Terror, as the Amalekites swept into the courtyard. Somehow I managed to scramble, unobserved, into the cistern, biting my lip as scaly creatures scurried about my feet. The next is hearing voices – Israelite voices – and being hauled up into a world that was at once familiar and monstrously new. I gazed at the ground strewn with butchered bodies, uncomprehending... numb, until I saw a hand, which I recognised at once as my brother Sagiv's, without the little finger he'd lost chopping wood. The sight of that hand... the lack of that finger tore at my heart and I screamed. I'm told that I didn't stop until several days after they'd brought me here. Shirah took care of me, more kindly than at any time since, although I later learnt that, denied Amalekite captives, she intended to keep me as a servant. But she reckoned without Nabal, who decided that the time had finally come to take a wife. Perhaps he thought that my gratitude would outweigh my revulsion – and for a while it did.'

David comforts me, first with kisses and caresses and then with promises that no one, friend or foe, will hurt me ever again.

At the end of the week the daylight world reasserts itself. Spies report that, having driven the Philistines out of

Ephraim, Saul is preparing to march against us. Any hope that we might win over Nabal's clan and live here in peace has to be set aside. Joab urges David to escape to the hills, arguing that, while well-supplied, Carmel lacks viable defences, and that the Calebites are sure to prove treacherous, delivering him to the king in return for Nabal's land. To Joab's undisguised irritation, David refuses to decide without casting the sacred stones and summons Abiathar, the priest from the camp at Maon.

'Why didn't you invite him to the wedding?' I ask David, pained to learn that, despite his proximity, he failed to attend. 'Or did he have scruples?'

'Of course not. What about?'

'My remarrying so soon; your marrying someone much older.'

'Not at all,' he says, with a sigh at my mention of age. 'He's utterly loyal. But he was the last man I wanted there. He's Ahimelech's son.' I look blank. 'The high priest Saul slaughtered at Nob. Abiathar was the only one to escape alive. I can never see him without remembering that I'm to blame for the deaths of his father and eighty-four of his fellows.'

'Not even one of them! The blame rests entirely with Saul.'

'It was me who put them in danger. Moreover I lied, claiming I was on the king's business so that they'd feed me.'

'You were desperate; you had to eat.'

'There's worse. The only food they had were the twelve sacred loaves laid out in the sanctuary. So I told them that my men and I were ritually pure. We'd known no women for three days.'

'Was that another lie?' I ask, striving to sound dispassionate.

'No, it was the truth. At least for the men. But for me it concealed a graver lie.'

'I don't understand.'

'Nor should you.'

His grim expression deters further questions. It softens

when Abiathar approaches, resplendent in a gold-embroidered tunic and jewelled breastplate, which I'm awestruck to learn were worn by Aaron in Sinai. David introduces us and I discern a warmth in Abiathar's eyes, as if he senses that I too have endured indescribable horrors, even though he knows nothing of my past. At David's bidding, he takes out the Urim and Thummim, the sacred stones that he rescued from Nob and entrusted to David's safekeeping. It's David's fondest wish that the Lord should speak to him as he did to Samuel; but, while he may be the Lord's anointed, he is not his prophet and, like Joshua and Gideon before him, he must ascertain his will from the stones. I watch, eager to discover whether the white or the black stone prevails when the priest asks if David should remain in Carmel (black), if he should remain in the land (black), if he should seek refuge in Zobah (black), Moab (black), Edom (black) and Ammon (black). It's only when, almost as an afterthought, David proposes Philistia that the white stone falls face up.

Joab objects that David is no more likely to be welcomed there than on his previous visit, but David overrules him, saying that only a fool would dispute the will of the Lord. I am grateful that he didn't think to ask the stones whether I should accompany him, since the sole will I must dispute is his when, as I anticipate, he charges me to remain in Carmel. He maintains that travelling so far from home is too arduous for a woman. I remind him of his own great-grandmother, Ruth, whose story has been transmitted from tribe to tribe. When she abandoned her clan in Moab for the sake of her mother-in-law, how much more should I do so for the sake of my husband? 'Women's arguments,' he says peremptorily, although I can't tell if he means the women in the story or the woman who has invoked it. So I remind him of Joab's warning that the Calebites will align themselves with the king and demand Nabal's land in exchange. What's to stop Saul defying the Law again and marrying me to Yimnah?

Indeed, what's to stop him rebuffing the clan and marrying me himself to establish a foothold in Judah?

'How would I live without your foresight… your acumen… your wisdom?' he asks, granting my request.

'And how would I live without your honour and courage?' I reply, although, in truth, it's not his virtues that I would miss most.

Before we leave, he must attend to his parents. Ever since fleeing Gibeah, he has been fearful that Saul will punish them. The man who spared the Amalekite king has been replaced by the man who showed unconscionable cruelty to the priests at Nob. When we're away in Philistia, who's to say that he won't wreak revenge on Jesse and Nizebeth? David initially plans to take them with us but, after consulting Joab who, with a pointed glance at me, declares that we're already overburdened, he resolves to place them under the protection of the king of Moab. Not only will he esteem any enemy of Saul, who routed his army twenty years ago, but Ruth's clan will be keen to claim her descendants.

Escorted by ten of David's men, we travel north to make the arrangements, riding through a landscape that shifts imperceptibly from dusty slopes dotted with olives and vines to lush wheat fields and verdant meadows. Approaching Bethlehem, our retinue swells as villagers of all ages come to cheer Jesse's celebrated son, some running up to clasp his hand or touch his robe, others simply standing at the wayside, gaping. Two of his brothers emerge from a copse and greet him awkwardly before conducting us to the house, where, after kneeling for their blessings, David presents me to his parents. Stung by their reserve, I'm convinced of their preference for the younger, prettier and more noble Michal, but, when I put it to David, he insists that their only quarrel is with him.

Although astounded that they could find fault with one who has brought such renown to their clan, I see it for myself when, joined by three more of his brothers and various wives, sisters and children whose names I struggle to retain, we sit down for the meal. Wasting no time, David spells out the danger posed by Saul. He states bluntly that his brothers can take care of themselves but, as a dutiful son (Jesse crumbles a crust), he intends to take his parents to the safety of Moab. His brothers endorse the scheme but, far from thanking him, Jesse rails that, by betraying the king and plundering the land, David has brought shame on his grey hair, a hank of which he plucks out for emphasis. He pleads to be allowed to die among his ancestors, whereupon David, losing patience, replies that he won't have any choice if Saul marches on Bethlehem. He swears that the exile is temporary and, if not, his father can die among his Moabite ancestors, a proposal that fails to placate him.

Frustrated by his father, he appeals to his mother, who is equally loath to leave, although, for her, the sticking point is her cooking pots.

'There are cooking pots in Moab, Mother,' David says in exasperation.

'I fed him every day for fifteen years and this is how he repays me!'

Eventually they're persuaded to go, without the cooking pots but with so many mats, cloths, lamps and utensils that we have to take two extra donkeys. Shimea agrees to accompany his parents, together with his wife, Serach, and sons, Jonadab and Gamaliel. Once again night becomes day as we travel after dark, to avoid both the heat and any spies who might report our progress to Saul. At dawn we set up camp in a sheltered gully. Since water is too precious to boil, Serach and I prepare a meal of bread, cheese, dried chickpeas and fig cakes, after which we spread out our mats and mantles and try to sleep. With too little flesh to protect her from the gravel, Nizebeth squirms, muttering a stream of prayers and lamentations. Serach and I comfort her as best we can before lying down ourselves. No sooner have I shut my eyes than David moves across to sit beside me. He takes me in his arms and, while I long to show everyone watching (and everyone is), how much he desires me, I am conscious that it's not just the water for cooking that's restricted.

'I smell like my donkey,' I whisper.

'My favourite perfume,' he says, nuzzling my neck.

His chest may be as solid as the ground but it's far more congenial, and I wake a few hours later refreshed and ready for the evening's ride. We make our way into the wilderness, where, with no further risk of detection but an ever-present one of losing our footing on the loose stones and crumbling paths, the steep scarps and narrow ridges, we brave the broiling sun and travel by day. The following afternoon we reach the caves of Ein Gedi, where David spared Saul. After the constraints of the past three days, we drink our fill at the spring before washing both ourselves and our clothes in the pools. Bathed and refreshed, the men pick mallow, from which Serach and I make a soup. After the meal, David and Shimea climb an adjacent crag to determine the best course through the hostile terrain. They return with a path mapped out and, for the first time since quitting Carmel, David and I spend a night alone, among the scrapes, whoops, splutters (and, for him, bittersweet memories) of a cave. The next morning I leave him to sleep and, with no one in sight but the two watchmen, walk to the edge of the ridge and admire the pale sunlight shimmering on the blue-black sea. To my surprise, Nizebeth, who has hitherto kept her distance, approaches me.

'I only met the princess once, at their wedding,' she says abruptly. 'She was too young and trusting for David. You're far better suited.'

'Thank you,' I say, taken aback.

'He's not an easy man. No one knows that better than me. He was born with a full head of hair. Flame-coloured. I used to say that he burnt his way out of my womb. He was so much smaller than the others. They teased him mercilessly. His father was no help. He believed in letting the boys fight among themselves to prepare them for manhood. So it was left to me to keep the peace. David was fearless, seizing every opportunity to provoke his brothers – even the eldest. Then I'd have to protect him when they retaliated: two, three, four against one. Which only made them hit him even harder when my back was turned. The more he needed my protection, the more he resented it. He blamed me for their lack of respect. Respect? He was six years old! So he pushed me away. As if he couldn't be both my boy and his own man. The others did the same but, as always, he went further, spending days – sometimes weeks – alone in the hills, no doubt to show that his sheep were better company than us. Now he's twenty-six and I scarcely recognise him. This rebellion against the king: nothing good can come of it. It's only – '

She breaks off quickly and I turn to see David behind us.

'Talking about me?' he asks, with a dangerous smile.

'Men are so vain,' I say lightly.

'The word is *shrewd*. So what's she been telling you?' he asks Nizebeth.

'It might be the other way round,' I say.

'In which case it will be nothing but good.' He gives Nizebeth a quick kiss. 'Have you forgiven me for taking you away from your cooking pots?'

'I always forgive you, David; I'm your mother. But don't expect other women to do the same.'

'I'm too old for platitudes,' he says gruffly. 'Now if you can tear yourselves away from your chitchat, it's time to leave.'

Choked by dust and bitten by flies, we make a tortuous descent through the ravine. Jonadab, whose sharp eyes David envies, raises his hand and points to a lion poised on a nearby ridge. Serach and Gamaliel scream and Nizebeth stutters a prayer but, to my amazement, I'm more excited than frightened. I'm so sure that, were it to attack, David would repeat his boyhood feat and strangle it barehanded, that I'm almost disappointed when, with a toss of its mane, it pads away. We ride on until, alerted once more by Jonadab, we shield our gaze from the shimmering sun and follow his hand to a remote peak. Our delight at seeing the towering ramparts of Mizpah is tempered by the realisation of how far we have still to travel. Three days later, after a wary trek through treacherous marshlands and a vertiginous ascent that makes even Nizebeth grateful that the struggling donkeys weren't further encumbered, we arrive at the city gate. Apprised by his sentinels, the Moabite king is waiting to greet us. Following a lengthy exchange of compliments, he instructs his servants to take us to chambers where we can wash and rest before returning downstairs to eat. The meal is lavish and flavourful, the rich array of meats especially pleasing after our meagre diet. Moreover, the queen affirms that they have been cooked according to our laws, much to David's relief given Nizebeth's assertion that she would rather offend our hosts than risk pollution. Despite the warmth of the welcome and the excellence of the fare, conversation falters since, although theirs is not a tongue severed from ours by Babel, their foreign inflections are hard to follow.

In a speech clogged with courtesies, the king professes himself honoured that David should see fit to entrust his parents to his charge and pledges to defend them to the death. Not only is he bound by blood since the queen and Jesse are distant cousins, but he exempts the Judahites from his execration of the Benjaminite Saul. Far from harbouring an equal hatred of all our twelve tribes, the Moabites reserve their particular loathing for the Benjaminites. Long before Saul vanquished them on the battlefield, the Benjaminite judge, Ehud, bringing the annual tribute to their king, tricked him into granting him a private audience in this very chamber. He strapped a dagger to his thigh and drew it unnoticed, stabbing the king to death. After escaping, he rallied the Israelites to attack the demoralized enemy, killing another ten thousand men on the banks of the Jordan. The king's face hardens as he describes the slaughter and I fear that he is about to repent of his pledge. Then, with a smile, he declares that he knows that Saul is as faithless as Ehud, slandering David and seeking his life.

Assured of both the king's friendship and his parents' safety, David is eager to depart. He bids his family a perfunctory farewell and I am puzzled that, having known them for barely two weeks, I feel or, at least, express more regret at leaving them than one who has known them all his life. I can't tell whether he is afraid of betraying his emotions or of having none to betray. 'Look after him,' Nizebeth whispers, as she clasps me to her thin bosom. 'Sometimes the strongest men need the most care.'

The return to Maon is long and wearing but eased by familiar paths and lighter loads. We reach the camp, where Joab and his brother Abishai greet us with bad news. No sooner had we left for Bethlehem than rumours spread that David had made peace with Saul. Joab strove to rebut them, first by argument, and then by executing two of the instigators, but the damage was done and several men deserted. Morale, already low, sank still further with reports of Saul's advance on Carmel. As predicted, the Calebites surrendered to the king, who slew the dozen guards that David had placed there (a loss Joab shrugs off as if they were beads on a counting stone). Saul then marched on the camp, and, with no time to regroup, Joab was left to defend it against a force ten times larger, better equipped and more disciplined than his own. Just as he was bracing himself for an assault, the enemy sounded the retreat. He suspected a trap but later learnt that Saul had withdrawn to tackle the more urgent threat from the Arameans, who'd seized on his absence to invade Manasseh.

David's immediate response is to seek revenge on the Calebites. Scarcely has he paraded through the camp, putting an end to talk of defection, than he calls for twenty warriors – men for whom carnage is its own reward – to accompany him in a raid on Nabal's house. I refrain from pointing out that the house is now his or pleading on behalf of my former kinsmen, preferring to save my entreaties for the servants, who were compelled to obey their masters. He promises to spare them for my sake and to welcome any who are willing to join us. Watching anxiously for his return, I am overjoyed to find that Ahinoam is among those who have accepted his offer. She spots me and runs forward to prostrate herself, swallowing her shock at the callouses as she kisses my feet. I lead her to my tent where she recounts how David's men stormed the house and killed Nabal's entire clan.

'Machia too?'

'Yes.'

'And Zillah?'

'Yes.'

'And Shirah?' I hardly dare breathe the name. Ahinoam nods. I try to determine what I would feel could I feel anything but shock. Do I retain a shred of affection for the woman who once gave me a future, or, over the years, has my heart grown as hard as hers? I am distracted by Ahinoam's sobs.

'The children too,' she stammers.

'Dead?' I ask. She nods again. 'All of them?' She wails and I press her to my breast, both to comfort her and steady myself as my body contorts with pain. They were the closest I came to having children of my own. When they were babies and too young to understand what was said, let alone to repeat it, I cradled them in my arms and chucked them under the chin and called myself Mother. What sort of mother fails to plead for her children's lives? But I never dreamt that David would punish those who were innocent of everything but their parentage. I feel a germ of hatred for him in my heart and tear it out before it sprouts. He is the servant of the Lord and I am that servant's servant. This is the Lord who struck down the firstborn sons in Egypt: the Lord who commanded Moses to kill the Midianite women and children and Joshua the Canaanites. This is not a Lord who perceives guilt through a man's – much less a woman's – eyes. And I blink away the tears from mine.

Having dealt with the Calebites, I expect David to announce our departure for Philistia but, instead, he lingers in Maon. Aimless and restive, the men quarrel among themselves and murmur against their leaders. Some have brought their wives – or so I choose to think of them – and some their children, sparking resentment in those who are single. With David's blessing, I set out to make improvements to the camp. I begin by taking charge of the provisions – both foraged and plundered – checking that they are safely stored and fairly distributed. I secure a stretch of river where the women are able to cleanse themselves according to the Law and away from the men. For everyday washing, I dispense soap made from olive oil and plant ash. Even so, my skin is sore and scurfy and David's kisses are tinged with remorse. Although I can do nothing with the men's tents, which reek like goat pens, I make certain that our own is kept fresh. I persuade Joab to bring back a bed from a ransacked homestead and install it as a surprise for David. But, far from thanking me, he complains that the men will think him womanish. 'Not at all,' I say, chastened, 'they'll regard it as fit for their future king.'

Although I alone have knowledge of Samuel's prophecy, the men trust in David's protection as implicitly as in the amulets they strap to their arms when they pray. Then one winter morning a disaster strikes, which threatens that trust. Joab is leading a raiding party through the wilderness when half a hillside, loosened by torrential rain, sweeps down and swallows fourteen of his men. With the rubble too heavy to move, they leave the dead to rest in the unhallowed tomb, their bones like veins in the rock. A pall hangs over the camp and Joab insists that nothing but David's playing will lift it. David protests, declaring that he hasn't picked up his lyre since leaving Gibeah, but Joab laughs off his excuses. While respecting David's reluctance, I echo Joab's demand: the music that drove the evil spirit from the king must surely restore harmony to the camp.

I marvel that he took his lyre with him when he fled, but he explains that it was Jonathan who, knowing that it was as precious to him as his sword, brought it to him in secret. The men are eager to appraise his artistry, which is almost as fabled as his valour. As they troop beneath the drizzle into a clearing, I feel a tinge of apprehension at seeing so many men in one place, and not just any men but thieves, bandits, rebels against their clans and their king. But they fall silent the moment that David begins to play. He sings songs about the heroes of old that I feel sure I've heard before, which can only have been in my childhood: a memory of a time before memory. He sings songs about his victories over the Philistines and such is the purity of his voice and the delicacy of his touch that they don't sound boastful. He sings a plaintive song addressed to the Lord, asking why he has forsaken him. This moves me most of all, but the men start to fidget and, when he embarks on a second in a similar vein, Joab interrupts, pointing to the rain, which has been teeming down, unheeded. His sombre expression makes clear, however, that it's the despair, not the downpour, which worries him.

I withdraw to our tent, leaving David to drink with his men. I fall asleep and wake at dawn, expecting to find him lying beside me, elated by wine and adulation, but, instead, he is slumped on the ground as though too befuddled to clamber into bed. Savouring a moment when I share him with no one else (not even himself), I lean forward to discover that, unless he has grown an extra set of limbs in the night, he is not alone. I stifle a scream as I glimpse Ahinoam sprawled beneath him. She starts and pulls a mantle around herself, as if her nakedness alone constituted her shame. David, usually so alert, stretches and slips a languid arm over her breasts. I wonder if he is genuinely asleep or giving me time to recover. How I wish that I were Shirah, ready to beat my maidservant for the slightest fault! But then she's no longer my maidservant... So what is she? My rival? My successor? I sink down and Ahinoam moves to comfort me as she used to do for some cruelty of Nabal's, only to shrink back in the knowledge that the cruelty is David's. Why did he bring her here? Surely he could have found another tent? Joab would have relished keeping his secret, especially from me. Unless he doesn't want to keep it secret, least of all from me.

He springs up, naked, still betraying the excitement of the night, and stoops over the bed to kiss me.

'Good morning,' he says. I nod, mistrusting speech. 'Did you sleep well?'

'Too well,' I say, wondering if, by staying awake, I might have stopped them. 'And you, my Lord?' I ask, forced into a new formality.

'Like a bear. I dreamt that I was lying with a beautiful young girl.' He turns towards Ahinoam, his eyes opening wide. 'A miracle!'

His feint is so obvious that I can't help laughing and my laughter frees him. He kisses me with a passion that makes me forget not only Ahinoam but the world. When I look up, I see that she is staring at us, terrified. I long to reassure her but that must wait until we are alone, without the man who both unites and divides us.

'It was you who told me she was beautiful,' he says.

'That's true. I also told you that your nephew Gamaliel was beautiful,' I reply, my courage returning.

'I warned you I would have many women,' he says, 'and I will. But you are the first.' He pauses as though recalling Michal. 'The first to teach me how to love a woman. And I shall always put you first.' I gaze at Ahinoam, her trim waist peeking through the mantle, and wonder how long that will last.

David smiles as though he can soothe my pain as easily as rubbing oil on an injured sheep. Throwing on his tunic, he hurries out, leaving Ahinoam and me as wary of one another as strangers. She falls to her knees, begging my forgiveness for sharing where she should have served. Even if I didn't love her, I wouldn't blame her. When giants and generals bend to his will, what chance has one young woman? Over the following days, I surprise myself by drawing closer to her. She feels more like the sisters I once had than my maidservant. I beg David, for all our sakes, to clarify her position: is she to be his wife or simply his concubine? But he refuses to say, as if it would threaten our fragile accord. Ahinoam and I do all that we can to avoid friction, as sensitive to each other's feelings as to David's needs. Except on those days when one or other of us is proscribed from intimacy, there is no rule as to which nights he spends with her and which with me; he makes his choice at the end of the evening meal. The one time I rebelled was when he summoned us together. I explained that I was willing to share him but not at the same time. Ahinoam was more acquiescent, although she assured me later that it was from deference rather than desire. So, with a feeble pretence at joking, he withdrew his request. I can't deny that I feel pain when I see or, worse, hear them together, yet his pleasure remains my pleasure even if he takes it without me. When he summons me after spending one, two or, sometimes, three nights with her, I sense a new tenderness in him as if he knows how much I've missed him and wants to make amends.

The winter storms soak the ground, protecting us from enemy attack but further delaying our journey to Philistia. Then, with the first spring shoots, come reports that Saul has mustered a force of twenty thousand men to march against us. One of Jonathan's servants, braving much on his own account as well as his master's, arrives from Gibeah to warn us. David is avid for news of his friend, the adopted brother whom he loves more dearly than any of his clan.

'The king trusts no one,' the servant says. 'He accuses the prince of plotting with you to depose him.'

'Why didn't I kill him when I had the chance? If he harms one hair on Jonathan's head, I shall never forgive myself.'

'He's overwrought,' I say, perturbed by David's passion. 'He wouldn't raise his hand against his own son.'

'He raised his spear against him. It was only the tremors of rage that sent it astray.'

Word of Saul's preparations animates the men who, after months of idling, are aching for a fight. Although encouraged by their resolve, David fears that they will betray their inexperience when confronted by a superior force led by an expert strategist such as Saul. They, meanwhile, express total faith in his ability to vanquish any enemy, no matter the odds. In the event, that faith remains untested since the Philistines advance into Ephraim, and Saul is once again obliged to deploy his troops against the invaders. David instructs Abiathar to cast the Urim and Thummim to divine how to proceed now that the immediate threat has been lifted, but the priest refuses, saying that the stones have already ordered him to journey to Philistia. David vacillates: anxious to obey the Lord, and yet to avoid a move that will outrage his fellow countrymen and leave him open to charges of treason.

'Will the Lord still be with me if I leave the land?' he asks me.

'Of course. Wasn't he with Abraham and Moses in Egypt? Didn't he send plagues on the Philistine cities when they stole the sacred Ark?'

'Yes, and how has Saul marked its return? By leaving it to moulder. No wonder that the Lord has rejected him! When I come back to the land – '

'When you ascend the throne.'

'I mean to restore the Ark to its place of honour, so that the Lord has a home among us and our sons and grandsons forever.'

With that vision before him, David sets off once again to seek refuge with King Achish of Gath, although this time with his wits intact and six hundred followers. To judge by their bluster, rape, theft and murder are never far from the men's minds, and I pity the villagers whose fields we trample and storerooms we denude, our errant crew even more intimidating than Saul's army. After four days we reach Gath, more citadel than city, its walls as mighty as mountainsides, its turrets spiked by soldiers with spears. Stopping some fifty paces from its gates, David orders the entire troop to lay down its weapons and kneel. Sweat pools in the crease of my neck, which, as the soldiers raise their spears, is exposed. I have a cramp in my right leg and a mutinous urge to pass water. The silence feels as sinister as it did inside the cistern all those years ago. Without warning, the great gates scrape open to reveal a man so resplendent that I take him for the king. David disabuses me and bows to the palace steward, before charging Joab to fetch the Philistine sword, which he has brought as a peace offering. Even in Joab's brawny arms, it looks unwieldy and, when David holds it aloft like a priest's slaughter-knife, I suspect that rather than capturing it on the battlefield, he looted it from one of their temples. Instructing Ahinoam and me to accompany him and everyone else to wait, he walks into the city.

I feel as if I have entered a new world. The streets are unlike any that I've ever seen: wide, paved with stones, and lined not just with houses of two and even three floors, but stalls displaying richly embroidered cloths, red-and-black patterned pots, fruits as bright as jewels and vegetables with buds like flowers. The people are equally striking: men who shave their chins and gather their hair in knots; women who paint and parade their faces. Brooking no delay, the steward steers us towards the palace. David described Saul's house as little larger than Nabal's, but this is as vast as the sanctuary at Hebron. The king receives us not in the courtyard but in a chamber that seems to be set aside for the purpose. He sits on a golden throne, flanked by his wife and son, the picture of embellished indifference. I draw my veil across my face and wish that I'd thought to sprinkle myself with balsam. Awestruck, I gaze at the walls, as lavishly adorned as the people, with patterns of birds and fishes in the same colours as the pots. David walks slowly up to the king and lays the sword at his feet, which, paying obeisance so unexpected that I gasp, he kisses. He steps back as the king, barely lowering his gaze, orders a slave to hand him the sword. After examining it closely, he turns to us with an expression I cannot decipher and addresses us in a language I cannot comprehend. I pray that a smile is a fitting response to what may be a sentence of death.

David, who mastered the language during campaigns that it's wiser not to mention, replies, and the king continues the conversation, although it takes me a moment to realise that he's speaking heavily accented Israelite.

'The general tells me that his women are unfamiliar with our tongue, so I shall speak in yours. I speak it perfectly.'

'You do, indeed, my lord,' I say, as Ahinoam simpers. 'But will the queen understand?'

'Her understanding is of no importance.' He looks at her with such benign condescension that I wonder whether she's deaf. 'I trust that you have recovered your reason, General?' he asks David, before turning back to me. 'The last time he entreated our protection, he had lost it entirely.'

'A temporary affliction, caused by King Saul's tyranny,' David says.

'Yes, we've heard how he banished you, sought your life and demeaned you by marrying your wife to an old man of no standing.' I sense the strain behind David's fixed smile. 'I regret that we were unable to assist you, but we have too many madmen in Gath already. My people believe that the gods favour them as beings halfway between our world and theirs.'

'I understand, my lord. And I am once again fully of

this world. So I come to you in friendship and homage, still cruelly persecuted by my king, to place the six hundred men and women I command at your service.'

'Your women too?' Achish asks with a smile as dangerous as David's is deferential. 'No need to be afraid,' he says to Ahinoam and me, 'I have women enough.' He glances at the queen, who stares straight ahead like a child in a game of dare. 'I prefer to take my pleasures elsewhere.' He leans over and fondles the boy, who is patently not his son. 'We know that you remain in conflict with Saul. Indeed, it's the absence of his greatest general that has prompted my brother kings of Gaza and Ekron to resume their attack on Judah.' I refuse to look at David as he hears himself cited as the agent of his country's plight. 'A general, moreover, who has inflicted such damage – such wanton savagery – on us in the past! But that is the past. We accept your homage and welcome you to our kingdom. We shall require – '

His requirements are drowned in an uproar at the door. The largest man I have ever seen, his head grazing the lintel, his arms spanning the portal, pushes past the guards to enter. He prostrates himself before the king but, although his body is humble, his voice bristles with threat. After listening to a series of snarled interjections, Achish orders the slave to hand the man the newly restored sword, which, given his size and pugnacity, strikes me as reckless, but, far from brandishing it, he clasps it to his chest.

'Your wife looks perplexed,' Achish says to David. 'Perhaps you'll explain to her what's happening.'

'This man – Lahmi – is the brother of the Philistine I killed,' David says, turning to me with ill-suppressed irritation.

'Which one?' I blurt out, mindful of the many hundreds he is reputed to have killed in battle, not to mention Michal's bride-price.

'You may well ask,' Achish says, and I wish that I hadn't as I catch David's glare.

'His name was Goliath – a great warrior, who had been taunting our troops for days. I felled him with a single stone. It was a lucky shot.' He directs the last remark to the king and, as ever, it's impossible to tell how much of what he says he believes and how much he shapes to suit his audience. I doubt that he knows himself.

'Now Lahmi demands that I hand David over to him in retribution for his brother,' Achish says, picking up the thread. 'Blood for blood. It's a tempting proposition.' He appears to weigh it up. 'But also unjust. After all, it was Goliath who issued the challenge. And David has returned his sword.' Suddenly, its size makes sense.

'I retrieved it from our sanctuary at Nob,' David says, 'and offer it to you, my lord, as a token of my loyalty and respect.'

'And I accept it in like manner,' Achish says. 'We welcome you and your people to Gath.' He speaks to the steward, who quits the chamber. 'I've given orders that they be brought into the city. Any Philistine who harms a Judahite will be put to death. But I trust that you'll understand if, as a precaution, I insist that you leave all your weapons at the gate.'

The king beckons another official for a private exchange. It is as if, in dismissing us from his mind, he has dismissed us from his presence. As we linger uneasily, I glance at Lahmi, who sneers and fingers the blade of his sword. The steward returns and escorts us out, explaining that, while the rest of the company are to be lodged in the gatehouse and the palace precincts, we are to stay in the palace itself, although not together. David and his chief men – Joab, Abishai and Abiathar – are to reside with the king, while Ahinoam and I are taken to a part of the palace reserved for women.

I've never heard of such an arrangement, which calls to mind male animals being kept apart for sin offerings in the sanctuary. But, when he shows us to our chamber, all my unease disappears. It leads off an inner courtyard, furnished with trees, a pond and flocks of birds – not the owls, doves, swallows and sparrows familiar from the woods near Carmel, but exotic birds with extended beaks and tails, shimmering plumage and pouting pouches, as if the Lord created them purely for our enchantment. Several women, closer to Ahinoam's age than mine, stand up at our approach. We have no common language other than signs and smiles, but it is enough for us to greet one another as friends.

The days pass slowly. The perfumed indolence almost makes me homesick for the foetid bustle of the camp. Only the queen enjoys the freedom of the palace; the other women are as confined as the birds with their clipped wings. At first it is hard to distinguish the wives from the concubines but, in time, I learn that twelve of them are married to the king, most having borne him children. Several, coming from the distant lands with which the Philistines trade, are as unintelligible to one another as they are to us. It seems odd that a man with a marked preference for his boy should have such a superfluity of wives, while David has only two; but the women express no resentment. They make up for his neglect by the tenderness they show each other: washing and plaiting each other's hair; painting each other's faces; dressing each other in elaborate robes. Although Ahinoam is charmed, I find their attentions intrusive and have to remind them that there are parts of my body that I prefer to soap myself. The queen alone remains aloof, less from pride than languor, for which she displays an extraordinary capacity. As her honoured guest, I sit beside her for hours, listening to the trilling and squawking of the birds, dabbling my feet in the pond, eating honeyed fruits and fretting about growing fat.

Although inside the palace all is calm, outside there is mounting discord. David has ordered us to respect Philistine customs while never forsaking our duty to the Lord. It is a delicate line to tread. Rather than offend my hosts, I eat meat red with blood, but I baulk at pork. Some of our men are less scrupulous and, urged by the local women, attend the temple of Dagon, even, it's rumoured, making offerings. But one custom they refuse to countenance, let alone respect, is that of two men sharing intimacies that are reserved for husband and wife. The king is not alone in his preferences. The Philistines sailed here from the land of Meshech and Tubal, where such intimacies are rife. At their feasts they sing of their ancestors who sent companies of loving couples into battle, believing that they would fight all the harder for each other's sake. In translating, David describes them as 'brothers', as if to shield Ahinoam and me from the full meaning, but Joab's grimace makes it clear.

'I have known such brothers,' David says.

'Not among our own people,' Joab replies darkly.

Despite sharing Joab's repugnance, I say nothing. Let their gods lead them astray! If the queen connives at Achish's fawning on his boy, who am I to condemn it? My country-men are less indulgent and, when a Philistine lewdly accosts a young Judahite in the street, a brawl breaks out in which two of our men and three of theirs are killed. The elders, egged on by friends of Lahmi, exhort Achish to expel us. David, insist-ing that a king must never yield to pressure, is confident that he will allow us to stay. Unconvinced, I propose a solution that I hope will satisfy all parties

'You admitted yourself that you're marking time here,' I say to David. 'Your people are losing heart; they're losing disci-pline and they're losing the Lord. Achish trusts you. Why not ask him to set you and your men to work... send you to patrol the countryside or defend the borderlands?'

'He'll laugh in my face. It's one thing to grant me his pro-tection, quite another to offer me a command.'

'Surely it's worth trying?'

David moves away, mocking my ignorance of government. But the seed, once planted, is hard for him to uproot. He puts the scheme to Achish who, to his surprise (although not to mine), consents. That night, David reports their conversation, repeating my words to me as though he were showing me my face in a mirror. I have no objections. Since everything that I have – body, land and goods – belongs to him, why not my words?

Achish's next problem is where to send us. It is evident that his trust in David is qualified, since he names several towns that are close enough for him to keep us under scrutiny but not too close for six hundred armed men to descend on him unawares. After lengthy consultation with the king of Gaza, in whose territory it lies, he settles on Ziklag, an outlying garrison that has lain abandoned for several years. Lately, the region has been subject to regular raids from the neighbouring Simeonites. He orders David to drive them back and shore up the country's southern borders. We take abundant supplies of grain, oil and dried fruits, as well as sheep, goats and chickens, although, to Achish's amusement, David declines a drove of pigs. I bid farewell to the royal women, to whom I've grown as close as our speechless communication permits, but I'm shrewd enough to realise that their tears are prompted as much by my liberty as my leaving. Our number is swelled by thirty or so Philistine women who, shunned by their own people for their relations with Judahite men, have little choice but to accompany us.

We set off at dusk and seem to travel through time itself, since the countryside is so barren that the only marker is the moon. Barely stopping to rest, we reach Ziklag by daybreak. The fortress exudes an eerie silence, broken by a sporadic hiss or screech. For all the dung and the debris and the foliage poking through the walls, the buildings are solid and, at David's request, I allocate chambers, first to families, then to couples, and finally to single men. Although space is scarce, I reserve a house for David. He has commanded camps, both of soldiers and rebels, but never before a town. One day he will rule a country, and his quarters must reflect that.

After two weeks spent restoring the garrison, we receive messengers from Achish reporting a Simeonite assault on the city of Avim and ordering David to retaliate. I fear that, in averting a conflict between our men and the Philistines, I have provoked a more serious one between David and Achish. The king knows that, if David attacks Judah, he will be reviled forever by his countrymen yet, if he holds back, he will forfeit Philistine protection. But David assures me that he has a plan. He will lead his men against the Geshurites and Gizrites, who threaten both Philistia and Judah, and claim that the booty he presents to Achish has been pillaged from the Judahites. To my relief, the plan succeeds and, month after month, he sends or delivers cattle and oxen, sheep and goats, cloth and pots, to Gath. Only once is he almost undone by the Gizrite markings on supposedly Judahite shields, but, quick as fire, he declares that the Judahites captured them first.

While pleased with the plunder, Achish is suspicious of the lack of slaves. David alleges that the Judahites are so ashamed of being taken prisoner that they prefer to kill themselves, their wives and their children. Achish, inclined to regard our people as savages, is easily persuaded. In fact, the only savagery is David's. I rein in my revulsion when he returns from forays against the enemy tribes with tales of having left no one – man, woman or child – alive. I understand the need for such wholesale slaughter, since a single survivor might alert Achish to David's deception, but I am disturbed to detect the same excitement in David as in Yimnah and Achim after a day's hunting.

Three seasons pass and, while buoyed by his successful stratagem, David is dejected at his deference to one so easily duped. He repeatedly enjoins Abiathar to cast the sacred stones in the hope that the Lord will instruct him to rebel but, no matter how the priest frames the question, the answer is the same: David must serve Achish and stay in Ziklag. Despite Abiathar's warning that he risks trying the Lord's patience, David persists in his demands, arguing that, since the Lord refuses to speak to him in person, as he did to Abraham and

Moses, or in dreams and visions, as he did to Samuel, he has no other means to discern his will. Although we all – Abiathar, Joab, Abishai, myself, (even Ahinoam, who echoes my words) – do our best to reassure him, he remains wretched, fearing that Moses's *jealous* God would be better described as *fickle*, and that he will renounce him just as he did Saul. Trusting that his songs will prove more effective than his prayers, he withdraws to his chamber and opens his heart to the Lord; but for every song praising his mercy, glory, righteousness and grace, there are two asking why he has abandoned him and pleading to be restored to his favour.

The songs grow even bleaker with the news of the Philistine advance into Judah. After successive defeats, they have mustered their largest ever force, pitching camp in the plain of Sharon, and Saul has marched north to meet them. Achish orders David to bring his men and join him at the town of Aphek. David, more despondent than ever, no longer asks why the Lord has turned against him, but, in songs as pitiful as a midwife's wail, asserts that he has condemned him to a living death.

On the night of his departure, which, to my delight, he spends with me rather than Ahinoam, he wakes from a dream, screaming in terror. I quieten him, fearful that his voice will carry into the streets where the men are starting to gather. He shrugs off my concern as brusquely as my caress. 'I was on the battlefield, slaughtering our men – ' I don't need to ask *whose* – 'when I found myself face to face with Jonathan. As I raised my sword, he flung his to the ground. I tried to wake myself up – somehow I knew that I was dreaming – but I was rooted to the spot and, before I could stop myself, I brought my sword down on his head. His body split in two, like a log, half on either side of me.'

'It was a dream.'

'But doesn't the Lord speak to us in dreams? Didn't I ask him to speak to me as he did to Samuel?'

I lull him to sleep in my arms, until Joab comes to collect him at dawn. Like the rest of the men, whose loyalty is first to themselves, then to David, and lastly to their comrades, he has no qualms about fighting his fellow countrymen. After years of skirmishes, he declares himself spoiling for a full-scale battle, flaunting his enthusiasm at David like a goad.

We women play our age-old part, crowding the gate to wave the men off with cheers and chants. As the footsteps fade, I walk back into the garrison that I am to command until David returns. Believing the enemy tribes to have been subdued, he has left a mere handful of men to guard us, an error that is exposed later in the day, when we are attacked by an Amalekite horde. The guards, either resentful of their charge or reckless of our safety, are caught unprepared and hacked to pieces by brutes for whom butchery is sport. I run to the rooftop and watch as, unimpeded, the Amalekites swarm through the town, seizing women and children. To my amazement, they don't kill us – even a woman who bites her aggressor's wrist has her head cracked with an axe-handle rather than slashed with the blade – but my relief turns to horror at the prospect of protracted torment. I search desperately for a refuge and, with none in sight, my only recourse is death. I walk to the edge and am about to jump, when I see Ahinoam dragged screaming from a doorway and know that I cannot abandon her. The next moment, an Amalekite climbs the ladder and ogles me. As I gaze at his snarl of hair and the blue markings on his arms, I am thrust back to my girlhood. Sweat streams down my neck and breasts, seeping through my robe. I register the mixture of disgust and arousal on my enemy's face and, for an instant, I become David, leaping forward and kicking him off the ladder before he can gain a foothold on the roof. He falls back with a resounding howl, and I pass out.

I wake to find myself lying outside the garrison walls, my head in Ahinoam's lap. As she holds a damp rag to my cheek,

I realise that I am bleeding even before I feel the smart. It is swiftly compounded by a stab in my calf as an Amalekite orders me up. Ahinoam protests and is punched in the shoulder. I struggle to rise, although my legs feel as if they are made of broken pots. Despite the open terrain, the Amalekites force us into a knot and prowl around us with bestial relish. Children scream and their mothers stop their mouths as the men grab at our mantles, signalling that we should throw them off. Next, they reach for our robes, tugging them over our heads and beating us if we falter. When they pluck at our tunics, several women resist and a young boy runs to their aid, butting a brute in the groin. While his cronies laugh, the man unsheathes his sword and is poised to strike but, at a shout from the headman, he replaces it and contents himself with kicking his assailant in the chest. The boy lands at our feet, and, to prevent a recurrence, we hasten to obey the command. Stripped to our under-tunics, we cross our arms bashfully over our breasts. Conscious that I must show myself worthy of David's trust – and banishing the fear that I'll never see him again – I address my fellow captives.

'Don't be ashamed! These men are no more than rats that have crept into our chamber. They're beneath our contempt... unworthy of notice.'

A stinging slap gives the lie to my words. My one solace is that the men have allowed us to undress ourselves. If they intended to ravish us, they would have done so where we stood, tearing our clothes as a prelude to mauling our flesh. Instead, their aim appears to be to degrade us, with only a casual pawing and poking at our breasts – swiftly curtailed by the headman – to slake their lusts.

Yoked together like cattle, we march through the night into the desert. The Egyptian slaves, impassive witnesses to our ordeal, bring us water at intervals too irregular to anticipate, but they – or, rather, their masters – refuse to let us stop to drink, so that as much slips down our chins as into our mouths. With no breaks, we are forced to ease nature on the move, while the Amalekites laugh like children watching terrified goats foul themselves in the sanctuary. Three women faint, pulling down their companions as in a game of pins. Their mild beatings are further confirmation that our captors wish to keep us unharmed.

The headman calls a halt at dawn. Overcome by hunger, I gulp the porridge a slave pours into my hands, like a donkey with a feedbag. As the chill air penetrates my bones, I huddle up to the five women to whom I'm bound and wait in dread for the morning sun to burn my skin and inflame my blisters. Staggering up with the others, I beckon the headman, who must have some idea of my rank from the rings he tore off my fingers. I shudder violently and blow on my hands to simulate cold. Then, ignoring his leer at my quivering breasts, I point to the insect bites on my arms and thighs and shade my eyes from the rising sun as if its watery rays were blinding. He watches indifferently before shrieking orders to his men who fetch our robes from the carts. Unable to pull them over the ropes, we are forced to step into them, further amusing our tormentors as we squat in concert to ease them on to our shoulders. The return of the clothes is no simple act of kindness, as I discover in the afternoon when I snatch a few words with one of the slaves. I ask if he knows where we are heading. He looks bemused and I fear that I've mistaken either his language or his race. Then, taking pity on me, he whispers that we are to be sold as concubines to the king of Midian. His voice isn't soft enough to escape the headman, who drags him away by his hair, relishing the women's screams as if they were cheers. After beating him ferociously, he calls two of his men who lift the lifeless body between them and toss it aside like refuse.

I must now add guilt to the pain, fear and exhaustion that assail me as we resume our trek through a landscape so unchanging that only our torn feet and aching bodies attest to our progress. When we stop to rest at daybreak, the women's resentment is no longer confined to the Amalekites but extends to our own men and, above all, to David for leaving us unprotected. From time to time one relents and expresses the hope, however faint, that he'll rescue us.

'Never doubt it!' I say. 'When has he failed us? As soon as he returns to Ziklag and discovers that we're gone, he'll come after us.'

'How, in this desert?' someone asks. 'Our footprints are buried in the sand.'

'The Lord will guide him.'

'The Lord has abandoned us,' she replies. 'We are no longer in his realm but subject to foreign gods.'

'He is mightier than all of them,' I say. 'Remember how he delivered our forefathers from Egypt!'

'Our *forefathers*, quite!' another says. 'He won't raise his hand for a group of women.'

I can find no answer that won't ring hollow, to myself as much as to them. So, urging her to sleep, I lie down beside my fellow captives like a bead on a chain. I have just closed my eyes when Ahinoam leans over me and murmurs: 'You say that David will save us... that the Lord favours him above all men.'

'I do,' I reply. 'Look how he vanquished the Philistine – you saw the size of his brother! Look how he escaped from Saul!'

'Then how can he deny him the chance to see his son?'

I try to hold her but she recoils. 'Ahinoam, I've reached an age when it's hard – perhaps even impossible – for me to give him children.'

'Not you,' she says, and her anguished expression makes me wish that it were still night. 'Me! I'm bearing his child. It has been four months since I bled.'

'Why didn't you tell me?'

'I'm sorry,' she says, sobbing. 'I was afraid you'd be jealous.' Shock and confusion, fear for Ahinoam and her child, together with doubt that he or she – but surely he – will ever know David, tussle in my mind, but I don't feel a tinge of jealousy. To be jealous of her youth and fecundity would be to be jealous of time itself. 'It should have been you. You wanted it. David would have wanted it. Nabal's wife, a great lady.'

'Greater by far for being David's wife, as you will be too.' I picture their child, graced with his nobility and strength, her sweetness and innocence, and their combined beauty. 'I'm happy for you. You've given him what he wants more than anything else.' I forbear to add *after the crown*. 'And you've given me hope. Now I know that the Lord will guide him to us so that he can save his unborn son.'

After eight days my faith is rewarded: days in which only the sight of Ahinoam's belly has kept it alive. At dawn we arrive at the mouth of a canyon, where the Amalekites set about carousing, their clamour joining with the chafing ropes, blistered skin and blazing sun to stop all but the youngest and weariest of us from sleeping. By mid-afternoon they finally tire, leaving only their snores and the odd youthful whimper to break the silence. Suddenly, the air is thick with dust as an armed band sweeps over the rock, their wild roars filling me with terror until I realise that they are aimed at the Amalekites. I grab Ahinoam and pull her as close to me as our tethers allow. Swords clatter; flesh rips; men, women and children scream; donkeys stamp and bray. Gradually, the cries of fear and pain give way to laughter, cheers and a cacophony of voices calling our names. I hear David calling mine and shout back with the force of twenty Abigails. Moments later, he's beside me, taking me in his arms, while Ahinoam clings to us both. All around us, men are untying the women and children, but David, impetuous as ever, slices the rope that binds each of us to the other. I untwist the loop from my neck and cup his face in my hands, as much in wonder as in gratitude, and give thanks to the Lord for guiding him through the vastness of the desert.

'How did you get here?' I ask, eager for a human as well as a divine explanation.

'We returned to Ziklag to find the garrison sacked, the men slaughtered and all of you gone. We set out at once, and the next day came across this slave, lying bleeding, dying of hunger and thirst.' He points to the Egyptian standing behind him, his face livid, his chest and arms crudely bandaged. 'He told us that the Amalekites were taking you to Midian. So here we are.'

'Thank you, my friend. You shall have a place in my household,' I say to the Egyptian, who falls to his knees, his reply lost in the ticklish kisses he plants on my toes.

All my guilt at his punishment dissolves, for, if I hadn't questioned him, he wouldn't have been cast out and, if he hadn't been cast out, David would never have found us. To crown our blessings, every Amalekite has been killed and not one of our men suffered more than a flesh wound. Joy abounds but, while sanctioning the celebration, David fears that the men are making too free with the looted wine to start the return journey at nightfall. He orders them to gather the remaining supplies and load them on the carts. I take the opportunity of a moment alone to walk through the canyon, gazing down at the carpet of corpses. I contemplate the faces, some twisted in agony and others strangely peaceful, as if the swords had swept down on them like feathers. Now and then I see a twitch and hear the empty, eerie sound of a dying breath. I turn away, not wishing to intrude, since even my mortal enemies deserve dignity in death. I recall the corpses strewn across my family's courtyard but draw little comfort from the reversal. If this is vengeance, it feels hollow.

'This is no place for you,' David says, pulling me away. I hear the disapproval in his voice, as if I've chanced upon a mystery concealed from every Israelite woman except for Deborah. 'I've reorganised the baggage so that there's a donkey for you.'

'Just one?'

'The carts are crammed. The men won't be happy if we abandon any of the spoils.'

'Then you should give it to Ahinoam. She needs it more than I do.'

'Why? She's young... healthy. What are you trying to say?' The moment he asks, he knows the answer. Without waiting for me to speak, he rushes to find her and a happiness that I can never share. My woman's blood has been dry for three months; I rage at the least inconvenience; and even before the abduction, I ached with fatigue. I wait beside the donkeys, just another encumbrance on the journey, until David and Ahinoam arrive, rejoicing in an event that appears as miraculous to them as the rescue. He lifts her on to the one untethered donkey, tenderly spreading the blanket beneath her, and starts out, keeping hold of the reins, negotiating every bump in the rock and shift in the sands with the utmost care. He sets a slower pace than usual, as though an extra day's journey matters nothing compared to the comfort of his wife and unborn child. Night falls, and as Ahinoam dozes, he turns to me, tramping beside him, and relates his unexpected return to Ziklag.

'We met up with Achish at Aphek. But the other Philistine kings refused to fight alongside us. They berated Achish for summoning us, convinced that in the heat of battle we'd defect.'

'Maybe they were right?'

'Maybe. But now I need never find out. With four voices to one, Achish was obliged to back down. He apologised abjectly, declaring that I'd proved my loyalty time and again and that his fellow kings were fools. I protested so violently that, for a moment, I feared I'd convinced him to defy them. But he bowed to their demands and sent me back to Ziklag. How can I ever have doubted the Lord? He – and he alone – saved me from having to choose between an alliance that would have damned me forever in the eyes of my people and a betrayal that would have left us exposed to Philistine revenge. What's more, if we had stayed a week longer, who knows if we would have ever caught up with you?'

We return to Ziklag and the third of David's force who have remained to repair the damage. Their delight at seeing their comrades back with their women and children is tempered by the suspicion that the family reunions will be coupled with material reward. But David surprises everyone by announcing that the plunder is to be divided equally among all his men, irrespective of whether they accompanied him into the desert. 'We are brothers, and those who've laboured to prepare for our homecoming deserve recompense just as much as those who took part in the rescue. Are not your wives and children more valuable to you than any amount of riches?' he asks, silencing the rumble of discontent from the returning fighters. 'I know mine are. Which is why I shall send my share of the spoils to the towns and villages where we camped on our march through Judah. For they too are my brothers.'

The men applaud his generosity and I applaud his acumen, since I know that he is looking to the day when they are no longer his brothers but his subjects. How soon that day comes may depend on the course of the current battle. Banished from the field, he can do nothing but wait for news and sends Joab to Gath to report back the moment that he hears any. Each day's silence leaves him more uneasy. Despite – or because of – Ahinoam's condition, he spends most of his nights with me, although his listless embraces make it clear that his mind is elsewhere. My sleep is as broken as his and, after a dream in which I am trapped in a blood-filled cave, I wake to find him staring out of the window, as if the sky's darkness were an expression of his own.

'Who do you want to win?' I ask. 'The Philistines or Saul?'

'It's in the Lord's hands; he will decide,' he replies, cloaking his equivocation in piety.

After two more days in which his agitation reduces me to silence and Ahinoam to tears, a sentry brings news of a solitary rider heading towards us. I follow David to the gate where, as the rider dismounts, I see that he's an Amalekite in Achish's service. Croaking with thirst, he grabs a goat-skin and pours water down his throat. Seemingly unaware of David's impatience, he moves without a word to his camel and takes a crown from his bag.

'King Achish sends you this, my lord,' he says, kneeling and presenting the crown to David.

'Achish sends you his crown?' I ask. 'Why? Has he been defeated?'

'No, the crown is Saul's. I remember it well.'

'We have won a great victory,' the Amalekite says. 'The Israelites are routed. Saul is dead. Your sovereign lord, King Achish, appoints you to rule your people in his name.'

'And Saul's son... sons?'

'I know nothing. But surely they must perish alongside all the king's enemies.'

'And all of mine,' David replies, drawing his dagger and stabbing him in the chest. Then, holding the crown as solemnly as if it had been given to him by Samuel himself, he walks into the garrison. I remain staring at the corpse, my lifelong loathing of the Amalekites buried in the shock of David's rashness. I understand that he was horrified by the death of an anointed king; I understand that he was anxious about his dearest friend. Nonetheless, I fear Achish's fury at the murder of his servant.

I follow David to his chamber, where he stands, gazing at the crown as though it were a scroll in which to read his future.

'Whatever possessed you?'

'What?'

'Why did you kill him?'

'A slave!'

'But Achish's slave! He'll be enraged. We must find a plausible excuse. What if you said that he boasted he'd killed the king and brought you the crown of his own accord?'

'Woman, you know nothing!' I recoil, from both the tone and the epithet. 'Why do you suppose Achish sent that slave rather than one of his own men? Because he knew that if I am to secure the loyalty of my people, I must show that I played no part in Saul's death – indeed, that I was so appalled by the news that I slew the bearer. Yet, if I had slain a Philistine, he would have been forced to retaliate. Now leave me.'

I obey, no longer Abigail but *woman*. Never, not even as the target of Nabal's most withering scorn, have I felt so remote from my husband. Yet to my wonderment, the Lord has given me the means to draw David closer. It appears that I have been wrong these last few months; I am no shrivelled wineskin but a fruitful vine. I shall say nothing until I am certain, not least because any announcement is bound to be coloured by the report that Joab brings back from Gath. David's worst fears have been realised: not only Saul but his sons – the young princes, Abinadab and Malchishua, and the eldest, Jonathan – have been killed. He betrays no emotion, not even when Joab describes the degradation of their bodies: their heads cut off and paraded through Philistia; their armour exhibited in the temple of Dagon; their corpses hung from the battlements of Beth-shan. He orders one of his men to bring him sackcloth and ashes, and ink and papyrus, and locks himself in his chamber, refusing all food and drink. Joab walks away in disgust, denouncing such grief as womanish. Ahinoam and I linger by the door, listening as his prayers and sobs are interspersed with fragmentary chants and gentle strumming. At nightfall, I venture to knock and, to my surprise, he lets me in, his ashen face lit by a doleful smile.

'I've written a lament for them all.'

'Even Saul?' I ask.

'He was our first king, a great king… at first. And the twins.

No two brothers were ever so close. I once had a sheep who gave birth to a lamb with two heads. As close as that.'

'Surely it died?'

'So have they. Too young to fulfil their promise: too young even to show it. And Jonathan... Jonathan. Never has there been a finer man! He was my sun, my moon, my stars, my everything.'

'We'll do our best to console you,' I say, wondering if Joab were right and sorrow has unmanned him.

'It can never be enough. My first love.'

'Michal?' I ask, perplexed.

'No. No woman's love could compare with his. He was my other self, my better self. He made me my better self.'

He sings me his lament. Although misery leaves him fumbling for both the words and the strings, it is the most heartfelt tribute I have ever heard. But when he repeats his assertion that Jonathan's love surpassed that of any woman, the image of Achish and his boy springs into my head, making me wish that he had phrased it better.

The following morning he assembles the entire company in the forecourt. 'Tomorrow we leave for Gath and then for Judah,' he announces, to a chorus of cheers. 'Saul is dead, but, although he was our enemy, he was our king. Jonathan is dead, and he was our friend throughout our adversity. I should have buried them both, but their bodies have been left, with those of the two young princes, as carrion on Philistine walls. So, instead, I honour them in song.' He takes up his lyre and plays the lament exactly as he did for me. The ensuing silence suggests that the rest of his audience share my misgivings, until a loud burst of applause affirms their approval. He yields to their demands to sing it again and, by the fifth repetition, everyone, even the children lagging a phrase behind their parents, accompanies him. Their fervent endorsement of the brotherly love he extols puts my carnal imaginings to shame. 'Let us never forget!' he says, finally laying down his lyre. 'Let us never forget!' And I don't know – I don't know that he does himself – whether he's referring to the dead heroes or to the song.

We spend the remainder of the day preparing for our departure, first to Gath to pledge allegiance to Achish, and then home. Joab, for whom a broken oath is of no more import than a broken bowl, itches to rebel as soon as we cross the border, but David is more circumspect. Abner, the great general, who survived the battle, has crowned Saul's youngest son, Ishbaal, king at Gibeah, setting up his capital at Mahanaim, east of the Jordan. According to David, Ishbaal is as unlike his brothers as a hyena to a pride of lions, but the Israelites have accepted him, thereby splitting the kingdom. Alone, the Judahites are too weak to fight the Philistines – not least after the loss of their finest soldiers – so David insists that we submit to them, until he either joins with Abner or else defeats him and claims the Israelite throne. The same messenger who brought the news of Abner informs us that a group of men from Jabesh in Gilead, a town which, in his youth, Saul saved from the Ammonites, has repaid the debt in an audacious raid on Beth-shan, rescuing the remains of the king and princes, burning them and burying the ashes in the sacred grove.

'Burning them?' David asks. 'Then how will they rest with the bones of their ancestors?'

'The Jabeshites feared that the Philistines would pursue them and break into the tomb, my lord,' the messenger replies.

Conceding that it's the lesser outrage, David sends Abishai to Jabesh to honour the men's valour. The rest of us make our way to Gath, where David kneels in homage to Achish, who proclaims him as his vassal king. When we take our leave after a week of feasting, the queen draws me aside and without a word – not even one that I've taught her – hands me a tiny amulet of a baby astride a bull. She is the first to divine my secret and I am overwhelmed with gratitude, as much for the recognition as for the gift. Banishing the thought of our imminent revolt, I hug her before mounting one of the camels that Achish has provided for the journey. David's hope that they will transport us back to Judah twice as fast as the donkeys is confounded by my frequent need to rest. As he struggles to curb his impatience, I blame my frailty on the heat.

The closer we draw to home, the more David worries about his reception. Although their recent defeat has removed the threat of armed confrontation, there will doubtless be Judahites who, oblivious of the Lord's plan, regard him as a traitor. Joab urges him to base himself in Bethlehem, in the bosom of his clan, but David, loath to appear partisan, favours Hebron, the burial place of Abraham, and the kingdom's holiest site since the sacking of Shiloh.

'Hebron is a Calebite city,' Joab says.

'You forget that I'm the widow of the Calebite chief,' I reply exultantly.

The people of Hebron haven't forgotten, waving palm fronds to greet me at the city gate and lining the streets, cheering my name. David, walking beside me, clasps my wrist as though angered by his subordination. When I try to break free, he tightens his grip, giving me the same strained smile that he does the crowd. He commandeers the largest house but, after the friction in Gath, he lodges only a few of his men within the city walls, dispatching the rest to neighbouring towns and villages. Losing no time, he summons the elders of every Judahite clan, feasting them royally for two days. On the third, he assembles them in the sanctuary, where, after Abiathar makes thanksgiving offerings for our safe return, he takes a horn of oil from the fold of his robe and holds it aloft.

'This oil was given to me by the prophet Samuel who, seventeen years ago, anointed me king in my father's house.' His brother Eliab, representing the absent Jesse, looks as shocked as everyone else. 'Years later, I visited Samuel at Ramah, where he reaffirmed his – that's to say, the Lord's – choice. He was hoping for the chance to do so before you all, but he died that same day in my arms.' I gasp, as his misty eyes attest to the power of his self-deception. 'Just as Moses anointed Aaron and Samuel anointed Saul, so I take this sacred oil and anoint myself in the Lord's name.'

I study the stunned faces of the elders, who assumed that they had been summoned to acclaim him king, only to find that, unlike Saul, he is dependent on no one's voice but the Lord's. It is his moment of triumph and, when he comes to me that night, I cap it with the news that I am bearing his child. He is dumbstruck, even when I add that I am in my fourth or fifth month, just one month later than Ahinoam. At first I suspect that he's aggrieved at being kept in ignorance, but his eyes well with tears, more legitimate than those in the sanctuary, when I explain that I have said nothing until now because of my past disappointments. I have never been able to carry a child for more than three months, but this one is different; this one is his. He plants a line of kisses across my belly as if to ease the child's passage into the world. I feel a fluttering inside me like a bird in flight. Every limb, every bone, every muscle, every sinew, tingles with new life, as though I too am anointed by the Lord.

THREE

Michal

Like any household slave, I had my price. David demanded that I return to him: not for love or in gratitude that I had betrayed my father to save his life, but because he'd won me with two hundred foreskins, the filthiest part of our enemy. I wasn't married; I was bought. The tips of two hundred penises! Although perhaps I should have considered myself fortunate? Most women were not deemed to be worth one.

I received a message from Abner stating that, after six years of bitter fighting – fighting which in Manasseh we had been largely spared – he had negotiated a truce with David, whose principal demand was that I should be restored to him. Neither man wasted time ascribing it to sentiment, with Abner simply reporting David's claim to the woman for whom he had paid the brutal bride-price. As Paltiel read out his words, I was plunged into the world of intrigue, duplicity and coercion that I'd hoped I had escaped forever. I had supposed myself forgotten: that I had slipped into obscurity like the unnamed women in the ancestral stories that Samuel drummed into my brothers: Cain's wife and Noah's wife and Seth's and Enoch's daughters. Even if David, surrounded by his new wives and concubines, were to remember me, I never dreamt that he would want me back, since the prohibition against a man's remarrying his wife once she had been married to somebody else was greater still than that against a wife's remarrying while her husband lived. Yet, despite his professions of piety, he showed no more qualms about breaking the Law than my father. And Abner, to whom my feelings were as trifling as an enemy's pleas, endorsed his demand, ordering me to settle my affairs and prepare to leave for Hebron within the week.

It was twelve years since I'd last seen David and seven since my father died on Mount Gilboa. We'd received conflicting reports of his death, but the one point on which all agreed was that he had fought valiantly in the thick of the battle, even after my three brothers perished. Towards dusk he was shot by a Philistine archer, after which the reports diverged, with some saying that the arrow lodged in his chest and others that it was a mere flesh-wound in his thigh. Likewise, some said that knowing the day was lost, he begged his armour-bearer to take his sword and stab him, and when he refused, he fell on it himself; others said that when he refused, Father appealed to the watching soldiers but only an Amalekite slave was willing to kill the anointed king. That same slave then took word of his death, along with his crown, to David who, according to further reports, slew him on the spot. Why? Was it from horror at my father's death or guilt at his own defection? Or was it, as some whispered, from fear that the Amalekite would reveal the truth: that Father had simply sought help to bind his wound and the slave, in David's service, had seized the opportunity to kill him?

The fulsome elegy David composed for my father and Jonathan was a clever ploy to distance himself from the murder. It was recited the length and breadth of the land, even reaching us here in the far north. Stumbling on Paltiel's great-nephew, Jeriah, teaching it to Merab's son, Penuel, I ordered him to stop, shocking him by my vehemence, until Paltiel explained my relationship to the dead warriors, shocking him still more by the glimpse into my past. But it wasn't grief at my father's and brother's deaths or even disgust at David's deviousness that roused me, so much as the evidence of his abiding love for Jonathan: that the pleasure I had seen them take in each other's body was no mere extension of the pleasure that they'd taken in each other's valour or swordsmanship but the expression of a passion far deeper than David had ever felt for me. Moreover, I was sickened by his attempt to portray it as a martial ideal: a love of comrades from which, unlike the love of women, they weren't required to abstain on the eve of battle. I wondered what his men would have thought, as they performed their rites of purification, had they known that their generals were defiling themselves in their tent.

Either the elegy, or the memory of his youthful victories, or the band of ruffians at his command, or his new wife Abigail's influence over the Calebites, or a combination of all four served to win round the Judahite elders and he was crowned at Hebron. Meanwhile, Abner crowned Ishbaal at Mahanaim so that, after their brief unity under my father, the tribes were once again divided. Without the Urim and Thummim, which were in David's possession, or any prophet to impart the will of the Lord, many Israelites expected Abner to claim the throne for himself. Not only was he our greatest general but, given Ishbaal's waywardness, he was by far the worthiest candidate from the house of Saul. He won further esteem by his readiness to place loyalty to his cousin above personal glory. I, however, knew him to be as cunning as David. By rejecting the trappings of power while enjoying its substance, he showed that his authority didn't derive from kinship or election or even divine favour but rather from his own strength and sword.

That strength had waned and that sword had buckled during the lengthy war with Judah. David, eager to unite the kingdom that he himself had sundered, launched repeated raids against the northern tribes, at times leading his men in person but more often ceding command to Joab, once Abner's armour-bearer and now his fiercest foe. After six years, the conflict remained inconclusive, but it was clear, even to those of us far from the field of battle, that the Judahites had the upper hand. As ever, David attributed his success to the Lord, but he might equally have cited Dagon, since his Philistine allies had invaded Ephraim, forcing Abner to fight on two fronts. In his message to me, Abner claimed that both he and his army were exhausted by the relentless bloodshed, and I realised with a start that the man who, from my earliest childhood, had seemed as ageless as the hills of Judah, must now be seventy-five. Paltiel, who had seen him at the council of elders, maintained that he was as robust as ever and the real reason he wanted peace was his breach with Ishbaal. With touching if misplaced gallantry, he refused to elaborate, so, when he retired to bed, even more distressed by Abner's message than I was, I sought out his nephew, Teman, who had accompanied him to the council and was happy to tell me what he knew.

'We were summoned to discuss the conduct of the war. Some voices, especially from Benjamin and Ephraim urged the king to sue for peace.'

'So Ishbaal couldn't even count on the backing of his own tribe?'

'They'd borne the brunt of the fighting. At that point – only a few months ago – Abner was keen to prolong the hostilities. He insisted that our forces were larger, stronger and better equipped.'

'And Ishbaal?'

'He barely seemed to follow the arguments. When he was called on to speak, he looked as if he were about to be chastised. He mumbled a few words of support for Abner and dried up.'

'That's my brother!'

'Abner's scorn for him was palpable. But, while he deferred to him in public, we heard that things were very different when they were alone. Matters came to a head over a woman… Rizpah.'

'Who?'

'I'm sorry. I thought you'd know.' He floundered. 'Ishbaal brought her with him from Gibeah.'

'The concubine?'

'Yes.'

'My father's concubine?'

'I think so.' He blushed.

I hadn't spared her a thought in years: Rizpah, whose sole purpose in life was to sow discord. The knowledge that Ishbaal had taken her with him was doubly painful when he'd fled so quickly that he'd had to leave Mother behind: Mother, whom he had vowed to defend; Mother, who had defended him throughout his childhood when the rest of us – here, I had to plead guilty – derided him.

'She and her two sons live with the king.'

'She has sons? What about their father?'

'I understood... I may have misunderstood.' His embarrassment spread to his feet, which he shuffled. 'I understood that they were your father's sons.'

I started to gasp and struggled to still my breath. Did this explain Ishbaal's silence? We hadn't seen each other since I married Paltiel and, while a part of me was grateful for his neglect, another part was offended that, with our brothers and sister dead, he had made no attempt to reach out to me. But then why contact a sister who would revive memories of his boyhood humiliation, when he had two half-brothers whose tainted blood made them consummate flatterers?

'How old are they?'

'I don't know; I only saw them briefly. At a guess about nineteen and twenty. They weren't at the council.'

'I should hope not!'

'But when Abner's on campaign, they're the king's chief advisers.'

'Don't you mean lackeys?'

'They seemed pleasant enough... not at all conceited. Some of the household say that, without them, the king would never attend to any business at all.'

'It's all for show,' I replied, irritated by Teman's fairmindedness and unwilling to allow Rizpah's sons a shred of integrity. Even if I were wrong and they were worthy sons of my father, there was no excuse for their mother's behaviour. Whatever his faults, Father had been a great king, whereas Ishbaal was as spineless as the slimy creatures that the twins used to slip inside his loincloth. To have transferred her affections to him so readily exposed not only her innate immodesty but that her sole concern was the dubious honour of sharing a king's bed.

'So Abner demanded that Ishbaal send Rizpah away?' I asked, relieved that, despite his overtures to David, he respected the proprieties. 'Was he trying to erase the stain on my father's memory?'

'I think he wanted her for himself.'

'Abner?'

'Rumours ran rife at the council, and I've heard more since we returned.'

I was stunned. I knew that he'd had a wife who'd died long before I was born. He was such a thickset man that Merab and I used to speculate – wickedly – that he'd crushed her to death in bed. He had never displayed any interest in remarrying. Unlike so many of the elders and captains who visited us in Gibeah, he never hugged us too closely or pressed his peppery kisses on our cheeks. He was happiest in the company of his men, in the gatehouse and on the training ground. In the agonizing days after learning the truth about David and Jonathan, when I'd looked at every man I knew with fresh eyes, I'd wondered whether Abner was of a similar stamp, but, even before I realised that theirs was a unique aberration, I had absolved him. I presumed that now that he wished to lay down his sword, he was looking for a new wife. Given that he must have known her in Gibeah, his choice of Rizpah seemed less perverse. Maybe he had taken messages to her from Father, which had enabled him to discover qualities in her that were hidden from the rest of us? Although a man of his renown might have hoped for a young, fecund woman, maybe Rizpah's age was part of her appeal? Maybe at seventy-five, any desire to perpetuate his house was overshadowed by the fear of leaving his children defenceless at his death?

'I understand. He wants – he deserves – a companion in his final years.'

'Possibly. But that's not how the king sees it. He fears that Abner is using her to stake a claim to the throne.'

'What nonsense! Ishbaal is as muddle-headed as ever. You say that the woman's two sons are his most trusted advisers. They should have instructed him better.'

'It's not that simple. Your father was our first king so we have no precedent, but in Moab and Ammon when the king dies or, more to the point, is overthrown, the new king establishes his right by seizing his wives and concubines.'

Choking back a wave of biliousness, I felt unexpected sympathy for Rizpah, which I strove to expunge. She and I had more in common than I had supposed. We were both the instruments of ambitious men. It was Ishbaal's seizure of her that had led to David's demand for my return. Teman's account dashed any lingering hope that he wanted me for myself rather than my name. I would bring him by birth what he must otherwise take by blood. As aghast at the prospect of returning to David as of leaving Paltiel, I thanked Teman and went up to our chamber, to find Paltiel hunched on the bed, his knobbly face streaked with tears. I sat down and held him, my own fears forgotten in the need to allay his.

Abner's summons and Teman's disclosure made me realise as never before how generously Paltiel had treated me when Father bound me to him. Had he been younger and more confident, he might have pressed his advantage; instead, he was full of contrition for taking me to this remote territory and even more for taking me to his bed. His first wife had died young, and he shared the house with her elderly mother, his widowed aunt, two sisters and their families. Leading me up to the roof, he announced that all the land as far as the eye could see belonged to his brothers, nephews and cousins. 'We're a close-knit clan,' he said, with pride that felt like a threat. Every one of them treated me with kindness and respect, which I repaid with arrogance and contempt. I brought winter into their lives. I played the princess far more determinedly than I had done in Gibeah. I outdid Merab in my airs. My every other word was a command or a complaint, both of which they sought to answer. Their very solicitude enraged me further. I wanted them to punish me the way I was punishing myself. Yet little by little their affection disarmed me. After declaring that I was a stranger to menial tasks (a claim that Mother would have refuted with either a laugh or a slap), I was never required to so much as fetch a pot from the hearth. My initial sense of superiority turned first to worthlessness and then to shame. I longed to share in both the work and the companionship but, like a prisoner who clung to her chains, I was frightened of the freedom I craved.

Then one day I rose before dawn, leaving the bed I divided with Paltiel, and came downstairs to find his sisters, Hodesh and Tirzah, making the bread for the men to take into the fields. They looked at me in surprise but said nothing as though afraid of being shouted down. I also said nothing but watched them mill the flour and tip it into the trough, adding the water and leaven. Silently, I took the trough from Tirzah's hands and over to a bench, where I placed it at my feet and started to knead the dough. Although I enjoyed their confusion, I knew that I had to speak or risk being regarded as even more disdainful, turning their labour into my sport.

'You may prefer to use your hands,' I said, 'but the Ammonite women in my father's house taught my sister and I to do it this way.'

'It looks quicker,' Tirzah said tentatively.

'And easier on the back,' Hodesh added.

Conversation faltered, but by the time that the dough was made, shaped and placed on the hot stones to bake, we had touched on their families, the coming harvest, and the swarms of locusts that descended the previous summer, turning the noon sky as black as midnight, and which preyed on their minds since they had no prophet to explain what it meant. At daybreak, the men and boys arrived to eat their bowls of buttermilk and collect the bread and fig cakes. Ithai, Hodesh's youngest grandson, less shy of me than the rest, asked if I wanted to see the sheep. Hodesh, horrified, rebuked him, but I assured her that there was nothing I would like more. Smiling, as if he had answered a question that baffled his elders, he took my hand and led me to the fold, where the flock gathered around him. I was amazed that, with only the slightest distinctions of face and fleece, he knew each sheep by name, insisting that they answered to it when called. But after a duly compliant Grey Ear and Stripy, half a dozen responded to Brown Leg, whereupon his roar of frustration sent them scattering.

Fighting back the memory of that other shepherd boy who had blighted my life, I watched attentively when Ithai showed me how he drove the sheep up the hillside, even pretending to run away so that they would gambol after him. When one wandered off on her own, I expected him to follow, but instead he aimed his sling with formidable accuracy, landing the stone a few palms from her head, prompting her to scamper back to the flock. This time I couldn't banish the thought of David honing the skill that had enabled him to fell the Philistine giant.

I spent many mornings on the slopes with Ithai, although, try as I might, I never managed to identify any sheep other than the leading ewe. Then, when he was needed to help with the almond harvest, climbing trees to dislodge the fruit that the men couldn't reach with their sticks, he asked if I would tend the flock. Nervous of the responsibility yet eager to earn his trust, I agreed, setting off at dawn with a bag of bread and date cakes but without his sling since I was more likely to hit any errant sheep than to rescue her. The day passed quietly: not a single sheep slipped or strayed and I counted every last one back into the fold. I returned to a stream of compliments for what I realised, to my dismay, had been the greatest accomplishment of my life.

In time, I took on other tasks, not just in the fields and orchards but in the house. I swept floors, mended clothes, beat rugs and emptied the grate, all of which I had previously left to bondwomen. The one task to which I was never reconciled was milling flour. Every second morning, Hodesh, Tirzah and I spent three or four hours on our knees at the grindstones. But even that brought some satisfaction, since a simple soup at the end of a gruelling day tasted better than the richest feast eaten in indolence. Then, when with limbs so heavy that I dragged them up the stairs, I made my way to bed, I knew the unique joy of being revived by a man who loved me: not a young man, not a strong man, not a man at whom anyone would look twice unless it were in surprise or mockery, but equally, not a man with his mind fixed on my father's crown or my brother's flesh.

Paltiel lay with me as a suppliant rather than an overlord. Yet it didn't make him shy. He enveloped me in his desire and his touch made me whole again. The revulsion I'd felt when I first saw him was transformed not just to tenderness but to passion. Even the carbuncle of which he was so ashamed no longer reminded me of mould on a tree trunk but of a plant in bud. My one regret was that I had failed to give him a child. I no longer prayed to Ashtoreth, who was either deaf or powerless, but addressed myself to the Lord. In time, he answered my prayers, although not in the way that I would have chosen. It was as if, unable to forgive my past disloyalty yet wishing to reward my newfound devotion, he refused to give me a family of my own but made me mother to my dead sister's sons.

Merab and I had been estranged ever since she'd sided with Father over my marriage to Paltiel. My hope that, once I'd moved to Manasseh, we would be able to repair relations was dashed by the discovery that the territory was divided and she lived on the far side of the Jordan. We saw each other less often than if I'd stayed in Gibeah, where she took her growing family every summer until Father's death and Mother's capture by Joab. I even suspected that she resented my wedded happiness, believing, like Father, that my exile should be a punishment. When Adriel succeeded his father as Manassehite chief, she grew more distant still. I accompanied Paltiel to several councils but it was clear that she found her unprepossessing brother-in-law an embarrassment. Then Adriel was killed fighting against David. Merab, pregnant with her fifth child, gave birth prematurely, dying when her women failed to staunch her blood. With the children of his own dead brothers to support, Adriel's cousin, newly elected tribal chief, wrote to Ishbaal, suggesting that he would be better placed to raise his nephews. Ishbaal, true to form, ordered instead that they be brought to Paltiel and me.

At a stroke we had the family for which we'd yearned: Penuel aged seven, Hillel aged six, Malkiel aged four, and two-year-old Shealtiel, as well as a baby I was able to name myself; although Paltiel insisted that we call him Adriel after his father. The first few months following their arrival were hard. They refused to settle, grumbling about the food, the beds, the flies, even the lingering smell of the donkeys who had recently vacated their chamber. I realised that they were distressed and confused by the death of their parents but failed to see why they chose to punish the very people who sought to help them. At my wits' end, I accused them of ingratitude, reminding them that they might have been sent to live with their Uncle Ishbaal. Hillel retorted that at least he wasn't married to another man's wife, and I slapped him. He whimpered; the others were shocked; I was ashamed. He had obviously picked up the phrase from Merab or Adriel with little idea of what it meant. No wonder the Lord had sealed up my womb when that was how I treated children! I apologised, but it was too late. After weeks of moaning and yelling, the three older boys refused to speak to me (Shealtiel had just learnt to talk and, despite his brothers' remonstrances, nothing could curb his babble). I reasoned, pleaded and, finally, threatened them, but to no avail. Paltiel, ever-patient, insisted that the protest would peter out, which it did, when first Malkiel, then Hillel, and finally Penuel, as angry with his brothers as he was with me, backed down. It was Penuel who moved me most, when, fighting back the tears, he revealed that, as the eldest, he felt a responsibility to take his father's place. I held him in my arms, breathing in the summery smell of his hair, and explained that his first responsibility was to himself.

I promised that I would be their mother in all but name, yet in time they gave me that too. My happiness was tinged with guilt at dispossessing Merab, although I told myself that only the three oldest boys remembered her and Malkiel's memory was fading fast. I would have liked a niece to call my daughter but, when I confessed as much to Paltiel, he laughed and asked me which of the boys I would be willing to give up in exchange. 'None!' I protested, since I valued each distinctive character, even Adriel who, I maintained to Paltiel's amusement, had a unique way of rubbing his ear when he slept. Although if forced to surrender one, it would have been him, at least until he were weaned and I no longer had to watch the wet nurse press him to her breast.

Paltiel who, according to his sisters, had been the most diligent of uncles, took to fatherhood as a matter of course. He threw off as many years as his shortness of breath and swollen ankles would allow in order to lead the boys on expeditions through the countryside. He objected as loudly as they did, albeit with less conviction, when I insisted that he combine the play with lessons in reading and writing. I joined them, finally acquiring the skills that I had been denied in childhood, but my participation came to an end when Paltiel engaged an itinerant Levite to instruct the boys in the laws and traditions of the tribes. He refused to let me attend, even as an observer, although I never discovered if this were because I was a woman, for whom learning was redundant, or the daughter of the man who had ordered the massacre at Nob.

David was sure to have spies in Ishbaal's household. Had they told him of my adopted family? If so, how could he ask me to leave it? I'd heard that he'd had six sons from as many wives since settling in Hebron; would he tear any of them from their mothers? Trusting to the fondness – if not love – he had once felt for me, I asked Paltiel to write to him but, against my advice, he chose to appeal to Ishbaal, convinced that, if nothing else, pride would prevent his allowing Abner to surrender his sister to the Judahites. He was wrong. In a letter that reeked of revenge for his boyhood slights, Ishbaal declared that Saul's daughter must sacrifice her own concerns for the sake of the kingdom. I pictured him gloating as he dictated the message or rather, as a scribe embellished it, since its cadences were far too measured to be his.

Seeking to clear my head, I walked to the river, where I chanced on Hillel and Malkiel fighting. They looked perturbed when, having pulled them apart, I made no attempt to rebuke them or to discover who was at fault but clasped them to me, eliciting their bewildered oaths to love and protect each other all their lives.

Two days after the messenger brought Ishbaal's demand, Abner reiterated it in person. In the eleven years since I'd seen him, he had scarcely changed. His thick hair and close-cropped beard had grizzled, heightening the contrast with skin as dark as an Egyptian's. His hooded eyes remained watchful as a hawk's. He stood straight-backed and sturdy, his legs as ever straddled a cubit apart. He exuded the acrid smell of a sheep or goat being led to sacrifice but, unlike them, he was fearless.

He greeted me with a curt bow, brushed my hand with his lips and addressed me as 'My lady', his gruff tone making it plain that it was we who should be honouring him: a view with which, to my chagrin, Paltiel concurred, welcoming him with a warmth that Abner inevitably construed as weakness. I seethed as I saw the contempt in which Abner, the broad-shouldered man of action, held Paltiel, the soft-bellied man of peace, but I reserved my keenest resentment for myself when, after eleven years in which I had come to treasure my husband's qualities of courtesy, consideration and fair-mindedness, I saw him through Abner's eyes as a gnarled nonentity. I was relieved when, after a meal that he devoured as heedlessly as if he were heading for battle, Abner sent him away.

'I shall be in my chamber if you need me,' Paltiel said.

'We won't,' Abner replied shortly. I gazed at the ground as Paltiel shuffled up the stairs.

'I'm here to escort you to David,' Abner said, even before Paltiel was out of earshot.

'That's quite impossible.'

'You needn't fret. I have twenty men outside to help load any necessaries.'

'That's not what I meant.'

'But it's what will happen. I wrote to you a week ago. You've had time enough to make ready.'

My only recourse was to throw myself on his mercy, but tears and pleas would betray weakness, abhorrent to a man like Abner. An appeal to his better nature would be self-defeating. So I chose to address him as my kinsman. 'You were my father's right arm.'

'With the scars to prove it.'

'Do ties of blood count for nothing?'

'Why else would I have put your father's son on the throne and propped him up for six years, when he has proved to be incapable, corrupt and, worst of all, ungrateful? But no longer! We must stop tearing ourselves apart and unite under a strong king if we're to preserve our integrity.'

'Under David?'

'Yes.'

'Even though he has sworn allegiance to the King of Gath?'

'He has broken vows before.' Abner smiled. 'Judah is suffering from famine. The people blame it on the alliance with the Philistines. They say that the Lord is angered by their subservience to a land ruled by foreign gods. David is discovering what your father discovered too late: that the people are less dutiful in peacetime than in war.'

'Then why not incite them to abandon him?'

'Even if we had the power – and our troops are worn out – it would be futile. Who would we propose in his place? Ishbaal? David needs peace so that he can break with the Philistines and regain his peoples' trust. We need peace because we lack the resources to fight against both the Judahites and the Philistines. But several of the northern tribes remain hostile to him. That's why he needs you – Saul's daughter – to bolster his support.'

'Surely the fate of the kingdom doesn't depend on one weak woman?'

'You underestimate yourself,' he said, disregarding my tone.

'Besides, he already has my mother in his household, endorsing his claim to Judah over that of her own son.'

'You are his wife; Ahinoam is his concubine.'

'What?' I gulped back the horror in the hope that I had misheard.

'His concubine. I raced to her rescue as soon as I learnt of Ishbaal's flight, but Joab and his men reached her first.'

I'd heard nothing of her since her capture as, unlike David and Jonathan, we had no chain of messengers. I'd comforted myself with the thought that, had she been taken ill or died, I would have been told. But who else besides Abner would have brought me news of her shame? 'He made her his concubine?' The words fogged my brain.

'Haven't I said so twice?' he replied tetchily. 'He's laid claim to your father's harem.'

'My father didn't have a harem. He had a wife of forty years

– my mother – and a concubine, Rizpah, whom my brother took for himself and now you've taken from him.'

'And delivered to David.'

'What?'

'What do I want with her? David has to show himself your father's undisputed successor.'

'By abducting – by violating – a woman as old as his mother, a woman who has borne six children, including Jonathan, whose household he'd sworn to defend?' I tried to black out the image of my mother, a woman so devoted to my father as to seem aloof even from her children. How had David treated her? Had he coupled with her once to prove his kingship to his people or many times to prove it to himself? 'Did you see her while you were in Hebron?'

'No, the women don't come and go as freely as in your father's house. They appear for foreign embassies, feasts and sacrifices, but otherwise remain apart.'

However much the prospect of such seclusion appalled me, it would at least ensure that my mother's ignominy was concealed. For the first time I saw a virtue in my summons to Hebron: not to unite the country, let alone to resume relations with David but, rather, to take my revenge. I pictured myself as Jael, the brave Kenite woman who had killed the Canaanite commander, Sisera, when he sheltered in her tent. Like her, I would seize a mallet and drive a peg into my enemy's head. Both repelled and exhilarated by the image, I turned back to Abner.

'So David wants to lie with me after lying with my mother? What sort of man is he?'

'He's a king.'

I begged Abner to give me a week – or even two or three days – in which to prepare for the journey. As I spoke, I weighed the possibility of fleeing into the wilderness. If David could hide for four years from my father, why shouldn't I do the same from him? Or else I could cross the border, seeking refuge with the Ammonites. Would they welcome me as a fugitive from David or rebuff me as Saul's daughter? And what if David, jealous of his honour, marched against them? Would they harbour me or surrender me to him? I was given no chance to find out, since Abner insisted that we leave within the hour, threatening to strap me to the donkey himself if I refused to go willingly.

I summoned all the women of the house and any men at work in the nearby fields and announced that my brother Ishbaal was sending me on an embassy to David, in the hope that, as his former wife, I could convince him to disband his troops and make peace between the two kingdoms. I feared that a word – or worse, a laugh – from Abner would expose my subterfuge, but he kept silent, not, I felt sure, from respect for me and still less from concern for the others but to avoid any display of emotion. A greater peril came from Paltiel, who watched from the top of the stairs, his torrent of tears not those of a man about to wave his wife off on an official mission but of one who feared that she would never return.

He made no move to descend and I made none to comfort him. Instead, I called for the children, whom I had sent out of sight during Abner's visit.

'You've been busy, my lady,' Abner said. 'Five sons!'

'They're not mine. They're the grandsons of my husband's sister, Hodesh,' I replied, trembling.

'I know whose children they are,' Abner said with a sigh. 'Be quick and say your farewells,' he added, stepping outside.

'Why did you say we were Aunt Hodesh's grandsons?' Penuel asked.

'Then I'd be Jeriah's brother and Ithai's brother,' Shealtiel said, frowning.

'It was just a precaution... more of a game, but one that I'd like you to play when I'm not here. If anyone asks, you must say that you're Uncle Teman's sons. What's wrong with being Jeriah's and Ithai's brothers? You're all friends.' Life, even in the far north, no longer seemed safe for Saul's fatherless grandsons. Ishbaal, who'd handed over his sister to his more powerful rival, would have no compunction in handing over his nephews if David perceived them to be a threat.

'No,' Penuel said, 'I'm King Saul's grandson and I shan't ever deny it.'

'It's who you are, not who your grandfather was, that counts,' I said, fearful that the newly sprouted hair on his upper lip and chin would embolden him. 'I'm relying on you to take care of the others.'

'I can take care of myself,' Hillel said.

'Of course you can. You all can,' I said, floundering as I gazed at five-year-old Adriel. 'But you don't have to; you have each other. I've told you before: brothers look after brothers.' I kissed them casually, to preserve the pretence of my imminent return, and hurried upstairs before despair overtook me. Paltiel stood by the rail as if he were melting. I hugged him and he crumpled like a child. His whole body shook as if each tear were a convulsion. Tightening my grip, I urged him to be strong, not just for the children's sake but for mine, since all that would sustain me in Hebron was the knowledge that he and the boys were going about their daily pursuits, missing but not mourning me.

His unconvincing nod was the most I could expect. I entered my chamber where my bondwoman was packing my chest. At the bottom, reeking of cedar oil, were the robes I'd brought from Gibeah. I preferred to take the ones I'd woven here, even if they were only woollen. But, for my journey, I knew that I must wear the sackcloth I had last worn at Merab's death. I sent the woman to the courtyard to gather ashes, which I smeared on my face and hands. Then, casting a final glance at the chamber where I had been so happy, I made my way downstairs. With my head already halfway to Hebron, I was less concerned with the impression I made on those I left behind than on the man I was soon to re-encounter. Malkiel's scream alerted me to my mistake. Of all the boys, he had been the most affected by his parents' death: old enough to recognise his loss but too young to understand it. Now, as he clung to his eldest brother's waist, tears and mucus streaming down his face, I berated myself for evoking his bitterest memories.

I was afraid that Abner would force me to change, ripping off the robe that made a mockery of his charge; instead, he smiled, as if there were a part of him that rebelled against yielding to David and was grateful that I'd embodied it. But, when I moved to console Malkiel, his smile faded and, with a snarl of contempt, he upbraided me for keeping the donkeys waiting. Enjoining the boys to remain in the courtyard, I walked to the gate to say my most painful, most private farewell. For all my resolve, I couldn't look Paltiel in the eye. I had seen his expression of anguish and incredulity once before, on a labourer who'd chopped off his hand on a woodpile.

'Take me with you,' he said. 'I'll petition the king to make me his lowliest servant – anything, so long as we can be together.'

'He'd never agree,' I replied, knowing that, while some men might enjoy the sight of a rival's self-abasement, David would regard Paltiel's passion as a rebuke to his own indifference. 'You're needed here. You must raise our children. You must teach them to grow up like you.'

'A man who stands idly by while his wife is snatched away?'

'No more, Paltiel, please!'

'I can't live without you.'

'Die then!' He stared at me, aghast. 'Do you think I want you there? A feeble old man who reminds me of my disgrace. I'm going back to my true husband: the first... the only man I've ever loved. I'm going back to be a queen.'

'In sackcloth and ashes?' he asked, and my attempt to make him hate me was over before it began.

'If you love me, you'll do as I say. If you love me, you'll promise me that everything will go on here as before, a good life led by good people, a life I can dream of even if I can no longer share it.'

'Enough!' Abner interjected, reminding us that we weren't alone. 'That's slave talk. It's time to leave.'

'I'll walk with you,' Paltiel said.

'No!' I begged him. 'It'll be easier for us both to part here.'

'Am I allowed to accompany you?' he asked Abner, who stared at him as if he'd lost his wits.

'The way is open for all,' he replied. Then he led me to the donkey, heaving me on to the saddle so roughly that I almost slid off. We set out: Abner and myself riding; the soldiers marching at our side; Paltiel doggedly trying to keep up. I fixed my gaze ahead, horrified by the spectacle of my sweating, sobbing, stumbling husband. The men's laughter forced me to look down. 'Go home. Please go home,' I pleaded, but Paltiel either could not or would not hear. I was humiliated for him and also, to my shame, for myself. As he struggled on, slipping behind and staggering forward, I felt my love for him falter in turn. I knew then that, even if by some miracle, he were to persuade Abner to betray both his kings, we would never be the same to one another again.

Having laughed along with the rest, Abner lost patience, ordering the men to double their pace and goading the donkeys to trot. The soldiers jeered as Paltiel, his face red as a pomegranate, lurched on. All at once, the taunts ceased. I swung round, tugging the reins so hard that the donkey brayed in protest. Blinking away an ash, I watched Paltiel, his limp more pronounced than ever, lagging further and further behind yet refusing to give up. As he receded into both the distance and the past, I turned away, vowing never to look back again.

Four days later, we arrived in Hebron, a city that had never favoured the house of Saul. I had been there once before, accompanying my father to make a thanksgiving offering in the sanctuary. Not even victory over the Moabites had endeared him to the inhabitants and we had walked through the streets in silence, broken only by a few lonely cheers and muttered curses. I stifled a shudder lest any onlooker should attribute it to anxiety about my second visit rather than remembrance of my first.

Abner had sent two of his men ahead to announce our arrival, but the figure waiting at the gate was not the one I was expecting.

'Greetings, my lady.' With a brisk bow, Ahitophel, my father's former counsellor, helped me to dismount. He frowned at my appearance before wiping his hands on his robe.

'You serve David now?' I asked sharply.

'I serve the kingdom.'

'Aren't they one and the same? It's been many years.'

'They haven't changed you.'

'Oh but they have,' I replied. 'I hope they have... I know they have. Far more than you can ever imagine.'

With an uneasy smile, he turned to Abner. 'Judah welcomes you, General.' Abner grunted.

'Where is David?' I asked. 'Why isn't he here?'

'The king has been called away. He apologises for his absence and promises to return directly.'

'He does me too much honour.'

'Not at all,' he replied, wincing. 'But you must want to wash and change after your journey.' Now it was my turn to ignore the barb. 'I'll take you to the palace.'

'What palace?' I asked, startled by a word I knew only from stories. Abraham and Joseph and Moses attended Pharaoh in his palace, but I had never heard of one in Judah.

'The king built it soon after he arrived. Come!'

We made our way through the crowded streets, the sackcloth saving me from scrutiny. We arrived at a heavy gate, crowned with a lion's head and guarded by two armed soldiers, that was in sharp contrast to the modest house from which my father had ruled. Ahitophel escorted us into a large courtyard. Asking Abner to wait, he then led me through a side gate into a second courtyard, adjacent to the first.

'These are the women's quarters,' Ahitophel said, as I marvelled at the unique construction. 'Here you can be free among yourselves.'

'Why can't we be free among the whole household?'

'You'll find that you prefer it.'

A gangling young man, his cheeks shaved and chin bearded, scurried out to greet me. With a flicker of unease, he bent to kiss my hand.

'A pleasure to see you again, my lady... Jonadab,' he added, sensing my bemusement. 'I was at your wedding to my uncle.' Unearthing a long-buried memory, I found an unctuous boy, desperate to be noticed. That at least explained the singular beard. 'Exactly,' he said, misreading my expression. 'Such a glorious day.'

'Now I remember you. You were great friends with my brother Ishbaal.'

He blanched, as though I had accused him of treason sixteen years on. 'I was very young,' he said coldly.

'The princess is tired,' Ahitophel interposed. 'We must acquaint her with her new companions.'

'Of course,' Jonadab said, beckoning a bondwoman. Although my overwhelming desire was to see my mother, I was obliged to wait as six women, accompanied by children and servants, processed into the courtyard. Gazing at the sumptuous robes, I wished that I had found a more graceful way to convey my grief. For four days, I had endured the chafing cloth on my back and thighs, while my face and hands itched with grime, but the man whom I had planned to confront wasn't here. Instead, I was subject to the ill-concealed dismay of five of the women and the open disgust of the sixth, whose dark skin marked her out as a foreigner. Ignorant of our ways, she must have assumed that sackcloth was all I possessed.

Jonadab introduced the first woman: Abigail of Carmel, whom David had married while in hiding from my father. She was tall and slender with a long nose, deep-set eyes and freckles. Her tightly combed hair was strewn with jewels as if to distract from its streaks of grey. She had a kindly face, but looks could be deceptive and it was rumoured that she had poisoned her first husband to gain both her freedom and his wealth. Given her age, she must have employed exceptional wiles to attract such a vain man as David. Apart from myself, she was the only woman here not to be clutching a child. With gratifying deference, she stepped forward, pressed her forehead to my hand, and fell back.

Next in line was Ahinoam of Jezreel. I started at the name and, for one blessed moment, I wondered if Abner might have been confused and the Ahinoam Joab had abducted – the Ahinoam David had defiled – was her. Then she spoke, explaining that her father had served under mine and she had been named for my mother, and the moment vanished. She was young (no more than twenty-five), notably pretty, with lips that appeared to be permanently smiling, which, however provoking to most husbands, must have been reassuring to a king. She was not as bejewelled as Abigail, although, as she thrust her son forwards, it was clear that she needed no ornament to affirm her status. 'This is Amnon, the king's firstborn,' she said with pride. I studied the boy but, apart from the russet tinge to his hair, saw nothing in him of David. Instead, I felt my heart tear at the thought of Adriel, my own five-year-old, left behind in Manasseh. I smiled tentatively at Amnon, who stuck out his tongue. Abigail rebuked him, while his doting mother laughed.

The third wife was Maacah, daughter of Talmai, king of Geshur. Jonadab pronounced her full title as though to emphasize that I wasn't the only princess present. It was Maacah who had sneered at my clothes. Either from a sense of her own dignity or repugnance at the ash, she didn't defer to me like the others but simply inclined her head. She was the only woman to have brought two children: the first, a girl asleep in her arms, Tamar; the second, a boy of three or four, Absalom. Lighter-skinned than his mother and with a strong suggestion of David in his high forehead and square jaw, he seemed precociously aware of his good looks, sauntering towards me and tossing his curls, like Merab when she'd played at being a bride. In contrast to his truculent half-brother, he hugged my legs, resting his head on my thigh, until summoned back by Maacah, evidently a stricter disciplinarian than Ahinoam. Even on first meeting, I discerned an enmity between the two women that I was keen to exploit.

The remaining three wives were Haggith, Abital and Eglah, each with an infant son. I'd understood that David had six sons but the tally must have included Tamar. Nonetheless, I felt sure that he prided himself on the preponderance of boys. I tried to memorize the last three children's names but my brain was tired and I yearned to see my mother. Her absence from the conjugal muster was both a comfort and a concern. Did she rank above the others as a former queen or below them as a captive? Determined to find out, I ordered Jonadab to take me to her without delay. Grimacing at my tone, he obeyed, leading me into a cool, dark chamber at the back of the courtyard. After a moment I distinguished two women who, with eyes more accustomed to the shadows than mine, had knelt as soon as we entered. One, Rizpah, had every reason to do so: indeed, she would have done well to stoop lower, crawling in the dust like the condemned serpent in Eden. The other should not have knelt to anyone, least of all her own daughter, and I ran forward to raise her up.

'No, leave me!' she said, pushing away my hands.

'It's Michal, Mother,' I said, squatting beside her.

'I know,' she said. 'Be kind. Go now! I can't bear you to see me.'

I flung my arms around her wizened shoulders. 'Be still, Mother!' I said, as she squirmed from my grasp.

'Close your eyes! Please close your eyes and let me look at you. Then I won't ever look at anyone again.' I did as she asked and felt her cup my face like Paltiel's blind aunt. 'You're in mourning,' she said, as she stroked my grimy cheeks, now streaked with tears.

'For me. For you. For us all.'

She let out a low wail. 'All I've wanted – all I've prayed for – since they brought me here was to see you again. "Then I can die at peace," I told the Lord. But I was wrong. I can't bear you to see me – not like this.'

'I'm here now. We'll never be parted.'

'No! What sort of daughter are you? If you loved me, you'd go. If you honoured me, you'd gouge out your eyes rather than see me like this.'

'You're frightening me.'

'The shame, the shame, the shame!' She pounded her chest so hard that I feared for her ribs.

'Not you! You have nothing to be ashamed of,' I said, fighting for control of her hands.

'No? A mother who takes her daughter's place in her husband's bed?'

'Not by choice! You're no willing concubine.' Mindful of Rizpah, I looked up to find her hovering behind us. 'All the blame… all the shame is David's. May he be cursed forever!'

'I never trusted him. But your father and your brother brought him into our house. "Reward him for what he has done for us," I said to Saul. "But not with your daughter." Your wedding feast was wormwood in my mouth.'

'Did he hurt you, Mother? Please tell me he was gentle!'

'His every touch was like the stone that he flung at the Philistine, but I couldn't die.'

'Tell me it was just the once: that he lay with you to assert his claim to the throne.'

'Is a man who paid double your bride-price a man who'd stop at *once*?'

'No!'

'I am the scroll on which he sought to rewrite your father's reign.'

'Stand up, Mother. You must stand up!' I hauled her to her feet. 'It's I who should kneel to you. I should have let Father kill him instead of aiding his escape. I should have killed him myself. But I'll make up for it now. It's not too late. If he calls for me at night, I'll slip a knife under my robe. I've changed, Mother. The little girl who retched at the blood on the altar has slaughtered chickens and ducks and even sheep and goats. And David is an animal... nothing more.'

'Nonsense!' Deaf to my sobs and pleas, she was roused by my outrage, scolding me as if I were ten. 'It was just such a foolish notion that made you want to marry him in the first place. What can mere women do?'

'If that's what other mothers tell their daughters, we'll always be *mere women*. Who can we look to if not ourselves? There's no man coming to rescue us. Ishbaal? The brother who handed me over to David without a second thought; the son who abandoned you when Joab's armies approached Gibeah and fled with Rizpah?' I was again alerted to the alien presence. 'What exactly are you doing here?' I asked her, before turning back to my mother. 'What is she doing here?'

'Be gentle, Michal,' she replied. 'As she has been to me. After six years alone, I have a friend.'

'Forgive me, my lady.' Rizpah sank back on her knees. 'I never meant to harm you or your house.'

'But you did.'

'She had no more choice than I did,' Mother interjected.

'Not with David, perhaps. But with Father? She could have carved ugliness into her cheeks.'

'I was young. Flattered by the king's favour.'

'Well, you've paid for it now.'

'Yes. I was led up to the palace roof like a heifer into the sanctuary. The king – '

'Father?'

'No, David.'

'Then give him his rightful name: the usurper… the tyrant.'

'He'd had a canopy erected. All around it stood men. Soldiers? Elders? It was too dark to tell. Flaming torches lit up a bed where the… David lay naked. He didn't stand or acknowledge me in any way but, with a flick of his fingers, he ordered his servants to remove my robe and my tunic and… and everything.'

'There's no need to go on,' Mother said.

'Is this what happened to you?' I turned to her in horror.

'No, I was wrong. Go on,' she said grimly to Rizpah, giving me my answer.

'The servants threw me on the bed and the king – David – took me with equal ferocity.'

'You must be used to that.'

'Michal!'

'No. Your father was a kind man; he treated me with respect. Even Ishbaal, for all his coarseness, showed me some consideration. But David was brutal. He attacked me like a boy who'd cornered a rat. Stabbing it again and again and again long after it was dead.' I sneaked a glance at Mother and prayed that she was trembling from sympathy for Rizpah and not anguish at her own recollections. 'When it was over, he walked out to a chorus of cheers not just from the rooftop but from the street below. As if he were returning home after a great victory – except that the voices were all male. That was when I realised that the torches had thrown our shadows on to the ramparts for everyone to see.'

'And tonight – or whenever he returns from Hormah – that will be me.'

'No, my lady – '

'No, Michal. You're his wife. You are his by law not conquest. He won't dishonour you.'

The mention of the Law, broken first by my father and now by David himself, brought little comfort, but I kept silent since, whatever the pain and humiliation in store for me, it was nothing to what my mother had suffered. I longed to be alone with her, to mend her spirit, but Rizpah, ever the interloper, remained.

'I beg you to help me, my lady,' she said. 'Not for my sake but for your father's... your brothers'.'

'They're dead.'

'Your half-brothers,' Mother said. 'Rizpah's sons.'

'David demanded that Abner bring them with us,' Rizpah said softly. 'But, as soon as we arrived, he imprisoned them in the gatehouse. I haven't seen them since.'

'Why? Because they were Ishbaal's advisers?'

'No,' Mother said. 'Because they're your father's sons.'

'I'll deny it,' Rizpah said. 'I'll swear that I lay with half the army – that I'm no cleaner than the ground we lay on – if it helps my sons. I'll send them far away, to be slaves in Moab or Amnon. I don't care if I never see them again so long as I know that they're safe.'

For all my resolve to hate her, I was moved by her misery, not least because it reflected my own. 'David never took intercession kindly, but I'll do whatever I can.'

'Thank you.' She kissed my hand, wetting it with her tears as well as her lips.

'Stop that!' I said, pulling away. 'I'm not a man, to be so easily won.'

'I'm sorry, I – '

'Enough!' I said, shrinking from my own rectitude as much as her servility. I turned back to Mother. 'What of Father's grandsons? Will David feel equally threatened by them?'

'He's threatened by everything. He who was once so fearless now sees danger in every shadow.'

'He knows what it's like to be Father.'

'He knows what it's like to be king.' For the first time she held my gaze, as if there were more at issue than her own remorse. 'You've brought up Merab's children.'

'They call me Mother.'

'It's seven years since I saw them, and then only Penuel, Hillel and Malkiel. A lifetime... two lifetimes for Malkiel. I think of them every day, wondering if they take after their uncles – whether my dead sons live on in them – or if they're more like Adriel's clan.'

'They're themselves.'

'Do they know about me?'

'As little as possible. No, don't look hurt! They know as little as possible about all of this: Father, Samuel, David, the crown. I want them to grow up to be men of peace, working the land. Whenever I caught them whittling swords, I snatched them away. Yet they always contrived to make more.'

'They're boys.'

'So it seems.' I wondered whether Paltiel would be equally vigilant. His indulgence, so pleasing in the past, now worried me. How would the boys fare without me? Would they adjust to my disappearance as easily as they had to Merab's? I reminded myself that they still had Paltiel. But he was crushed by grief. How else could he have followed me along the way, an act as irresponsible as it was demeaning when the boys needed him at home? I trusted that he had waited until nightfall to return, sparing them the horror of his limping, wheezing weariness, swollen eyes and soiled robe. Yet, even as I tried to resent him, I knew that it was a ploy to protect myself. Whatever transpired, he would be a loving father. My one fear was his age. For the first time in years, I wished him other than he was, a younger man who would live until Adriel, the last of his sons, was full-grown. And they were his sons, no matter who had sired them: Penuel ben Paltiel, Hillel ben Paltiel, Malkiel ben Paltiel, Shealtiel ben Paltiel, Adriel ben Paltiel. I repeated the names like a prayer: names that would preserve both the memory of the best man I had ever known and, by obscuring their royal lineage, the lives of the boys who bore them.

I would convince David to allow me to go to the sanctuary, flattering his vanity by professing to take a thanksgiving offering for our reconciliation, instead offering the Lord one of the beasts for which he displayed such insatiable hunger, in supplication for Paltiel's health and our sons' protection.

'You have a sixth nephew,' Mother said, puncturing the vision. 'Meribaal.'

'He's alive?'

'Of course.' Her surprise turned to alarm. 'Why? Have you heard otherwise?'

'No... yes... I'm confused. Wasn't Hodiah captured by Amorites?'

'Yes. Your father and brothers had marched against the Philistines. Hodiah left for Asher to visit her ailing father. He recovered, but she was seized by raiders on the way home. Then we heard the news from Mount Gilboa. Menucha panicked and, with no word to anyone, fled with the boy to her brother in Lodebar.'

'So he's safe?'

'He's alive. You must remember how clumsy Menucha was?'

'She was old.' I also remembered Mother's jealousy of the nurse who rivalled her in her children's affections.

'She fell and dropped him, breaking both his legs. Too terrified to return for help, she bound his legs to sticks and carried on to Lodebar.'

'He must have been in agony!'

'I can't bear to think of it! By the time she arrived, the bones had started to mend but badly, with his feet turned inwards. He can't walk any more but crawls like a sea creature.'

Tears welled in my eyes, less for Meribaal, whom I scarcely

recalled, than for Jonathan, his straight-limbed father. 'Have you seen him?' I asked.

'How? That villain Joab dragged me here. But there's a former servant of your father's, Ziba – do you remember him?' I shook my head. 'You will when you meet him. Menucha is long dead, as is her brother, but her nephew has charge of Meribaal.'

'And David knows nothing of it?'

'It seems not. Ziba has the occasional word from Lodebar and brings it to me when he can. But it's hard. Men are forbidden the harem.'

As if to belie her words, or rather to assert his privilege, Jonadab entered the chamber to inform me of David's return. Proclaiming his excitement at being the one person to attend both our wedding and our reunion, he led me back into the courtyard where my mother's namesake was sitting with two of her fellow wives and their children, although the focus of everyone's attention was Amnon, who stomped up and down, squashing ants.

'Do you wish to prepare? Shall I call for water?' asked Jonadab, who appeared to have given up hope that I might change my clothes.

'No. All I need is here.' I walked to the hearth, raked up a handful of ash and rubbed it on my face, repairing the ravages of the journey. While the three women watched in silence, Amnon, furious at being ignored, picked up an ant and pressed it into his younger brother's mouth.

Jonadab studied me with a mixture of fascination and disquiet, before leading me back into the first courtyard and through an archway into a third. Dazzled by the building's immensity, I walked up the stairs and entered a long, sombre chamber. A cluster of lamps at the far end lit up a golden throne on which David sat, as rigid as the wood. I was shocked by the contrast with my father who, even in the council of elders, had occupied an ordinary chair. The only throne in his kingdom had been the Ark in faraway Kiriath-Jearim, set apart for the Lord. Despite his grievance, Father had been careful to maintain the distinction that David blurred.

As we approached the throne, Jonadab fell to his knees. Brushing his hand from my sleeve, I remained standing while lowering my eyes, not in homage but in dread of what I might see – what I might feel – when I looked up at him. My heart was stone, but I feared its treacherous quiver. I wanted to ease myself into his presence: first, hearing his voice; next, seeing his face; and finally, touching his hand or his lips. I recalled the hold he had once exerted over me. His was the evil spirit that had possessed me and, unlike my father, I couldn't look to his music to set me free.

'I've brought the Princess Michal, my lord,' Jonadab said, breaking the silence.

'I see that the way was dusty,' David said, after a brief appraisal of my appearance.

I baulked. Was this all he could find to say to his wife – his beloved's sister… his predecessor's daughter… or whatever I was to him – after thirteen years. 'I'm in mourning,' I replied.

'Who for?'

'My husband.'

'I am your husband,' he said, and the muffled fury in his voice, once so familiar, emboldened me to look up. He had changed. His neck had thickened until only his bushy beard, a deeper russet than his hair, distinguished it from his jaw. His hair remained luxuriant but his hairline appeared to have edged up his forehead like a cover that had slid down a bed. His right cheek was badly scarred, which surprised me since it was widely believed that none of his enemies came close enough to strike a blow. His chest and shoulders looked broader than ever, which might have owed something to his richly embroidered mantle; but he was no taller – a thought that would not have occurred to me had I not been living in a house of growing boys. Having feared that I might feel a tinge of desire – however slight, however residual – on seeing him, I was dismayed to feel a twinge of regret at its absence. He was my youth and, while it would be as futile to weep over the passing of time as over the sun's setting in the evening, a part of me hoped that seeing him would restore the hope, the joy, the innocence, the excitement and whatever else I had felt back then. I wondered if he were hoping for as much from me.

'He was my husband,' I insisted. 'Paltiel ben Laish.'

'I knew that he was a weak old man. I didn't know that he'd died.'

'He hasn't. Not yet. But I'm afraid that his heart will break at our parting.'

'A man who breaks his heart over a woman is no better than a woman himself.'

'So speaks a man who plucks a woman from her family like a wolf snatching a ewe from her lambs.'

'What lambs? Did the old man give you children?'

'No.' I blacked out the image of the five motherless boys for fear he should see it reflected in my eyes.

'I have given my wives six sons. One died.'

'And daughters?'

'Two or three. Wouldn't you want a child with me? You're thirty-six years old,' he said with habitual precision. 'There's still time.'

'Since when have you been so familiar with the ways of women?'

'Since I built them a harem.'

'Them or yourself?'

'What's theirs is mine. I am their king.' He rose from the throne and thrust his face a palm's breadth from mine. 'Your voice has grown hard but your skin has stayed soft... as soft as the first time I touched it.' He touched it again; I flinched; he smiled. 'I'd forgotten how beautiful you are.'

'As beautiful as my brother?'

It was his turn to flinch. 'What do you mean?'

'The lament you wrote on his death. "Surpassing the love of women."'

'It was a different sort of love.'

'Is there a scale? The Lord at the top. Next Jonathan. Then all the women you take to your bed: wives, concubines, slave girls.'

'Wait and see. Tonight, it will be you.' He drew back. 'Don't fight me, Michal; you'll only lose. It may take a week... a month... a year, but you'll lose. Everyone does. See how the Lord smiles on me.' He gestured expansively at the chamber without taking his eyes off me. 'The king of Gath himself has nothing finer. You can share it with me.'

'Along with the rest of the ewes in your fold?'

'I warn you; don't fight me.' He snapped his fingers and Jonadab emerged from the shadows. I was shocked to discover that he had been present all along. Were even a king's most private moments public, or did David require a witness for them to feel real? 'Jonadab will take you to your chamber. You'll find everything you want. Clean yourself and change your linen. Your husband lives.'

As we walked out, I couldn't stop shaking. Jonadab nodded approvingly as if it were the only appropriate response to meeting the king. In truth I was horrified by David's presumption. In the past, his wanton self-confidence had been tempered by moments of self-doubt. Now, with the palace, the throne, even the harem, attesting to the Lord's favour, he had abandoned all vestige of modesty: 'Don't fight me, Michal; you'll only lose... Everyone does.' He had betrayed my father; he had violated my mother; he had torn me from my home: yet he was convinced that I would yield to his will, as eager for his calloused caresses as when I was a girl and knew no better. But he was wrong. I vowed to keep my hatred burning like a lamp at the bedside of a frightened child. I vowed to keep my body as cold and unyielding as a hidden blade.

Jonadab led me to my chamber, which was perfumed with

jasmine and henna. Either from the heavy smell of the herbs, the strain of seeing David or the exertion of the journey, no sooner had he left than I crawled on to the bed and fell fast asleep. I dreamt that I was on the seashore waiting for a ship to transport me to a distant land. Merab appeared at my side, although she was only seventeen while I was twenty years older. I had no time to ponder the incongruity, since the ship docked, with our five children on board. After a moment of relief, I was seized by terror that, in the joy of the reunion, they would set sail again without me. I waded into the water, but what I thought were waves lashing my legs was Abigail shaking me awake, announcing that she had come to help me prepare for my night with David.

Ahinoam and Eglah followed her, the one carrying a fine white linen robe and the other a bowl of oil of aloes. Three bondwomen brought in basins of water, soap and towels. Much as I wished to prolong my defiance, I was grateful to wash off the ash that had inflamed my skin. Ahinoam soaped and sponged me with a tenderness that I felt moved to praise. 'I learnt from the kindest of mistresses,' she replied, and I discovered, to my amazement, that she had been Abigail's maidservant. David had lain with her within weeks of his marriage, but they hadn't let it drive them apart. Abigail and Ahinoam were equally affectionate with Eglah. She was David's latest wife, the daughter of the Reubenite chief, and, of all her manifest attractions, I felt sure that the greatest for David had been her father's amity. She sang an ancient song of the Lord's sacred rainbow as she dried me and rubbed my body with oil. I was reminded of Mother and Hodiah dressing me for my wedding feast to David. Then I had gone to his bed full of love and hope and excitement, mixed with a touch of foreboding. My only emotions now were revulsion and contempt.

Jonadab came to collect me. Too obtuse to realise that the death I brought David went deeper than the goatskin and grime, he cast a satisfied glance at my fresh robe and clean face. 'You are truly blessed. The king has been impatient to welcome you back. This whole week he has taken no other woman to his bed.' I scorned to reply and he smiled at my gratitude. Even in a world where one king lay with his father's concubine and another with his wife's mother, there was something uniquely squalid in Jonadab's abetment of his uncle's nightwork. We entered David's fusty chamber. Jonadab announced my arrival, bowed and shuffled out backwards, as though loath to forfeit a single glimpse of his royal master. David raised his hand to silence me and studied a scroll, an obvious contrivance, since I was left with nowhere to sit but the bed, which I immediately rejected. Finally, he set down the scroll and approached me.

Every movement released a memory. As he touched my arm, I was taken back to our wedding night when, more nervous of me than of the Philistine giant, he'd had no notion of how to proceed. Now, with the women in his harem lining up for him as docilely as the donkeys in his stable, he undressed me with consummate ease. I gave thanks for the lamplight, kind to both my blistered skin and my flushed cheeks, as he examined me with chilling intensity. Was he looking past the sad, sour woman for the sweet-faced girl he'd once known? Was he comparing me with his younger, meeker wives, on whom even motherhood had left no scars? Or was he yet again chipping away my breasts and hips and chopping off my hair to find my brother (a practice that I could now view with equanimity)? On reflection, I decided that it was none of these, since the only person David could appraise with such fervour was David. It wasn't my youth that he was looking to recover but his own.

His lips shackled my neck, while his hands roamed my flesh as if reclaiming his homeland. He shrugged off his loincloth, drew me on to the bed and climbed on top of me. I gasped beneath his weight. As he nipped and tongued, and

— 164 —

squeezed and crushed, and fingered and pawed, I longed for the diffidence that had once dismayed me. Whereas Paltiel's sole aim had been to please me, David would no more have asked if I enjoyed his embraces than if a bondman enjoyed his blows. I panicked that, notwithstanding my resolve, my body would betray its excitement, and, the more he threatened to inflame my desire, the more I sought to douse it. I reminded myself that he had molested my mother, conjuring up images of their coupling that I'd struggled to suppress.

His passion spent, he slid out of me, while pressing his hand between my legs. I tried to break free but he held me fast. It was as if he had anointed me with a precious unguent and was determined not to waste a drop. Was he so sure of his potency as to suppose that I would conceive at the first encounter? For years I had prayed that the Lord would open my womb; now I prayed with equal ardour that he'd seal it.

'I've missed you,' David said.

'How fortunate that you had my mother to take my place!'

He laughed, as though my jibe explained my hostility. 'I lay with the queen for the sake of the kingdom.'

'But it didn't succeed – not with everyone – so now you need me.'

'You're too proud, Michal: prouder than any woman has a right to be. You've started to sound like your dead sister. I should hate you for it. But I don't; I almost admire you. And I shall win you back.'

'I'm already here.'

'No, not your body, that's easy. Your heart.'

He told me to dress. I had barely finished when he called Jonadab to take me back to the harem. I was grateful at least that he didn't require me to stay, extending the ordeal until dawn. Paltiel and I had found peace in one another's arms: peace that plainly eluded David. I suspected that he was prone to bad dreams and reluctant for anyone – even a woman – to witness his weakness. The thought made me smile, which

Jonadab misconstrued. 'Yes, the king is an incomparable lover,' he said, with a reverence that made me shudder. Although in the bloom of youth, he was the one man with access to the harem. Was it kinship that made David trust him? Or did he know him to be no threat: happier furnishing other men's beds than his own?

Over the following weeks, I grew accustomed to the harem. As if to ensure his own pre-eminence, David allowed us few diversions. The harem door had no lock, yet none of the women opened it. Refusing to be confined, I ventured into the main courtyard, but there was no one to be seen except servants and soldiers, and, despite my defiance, I hesitated to enter the great chamber, where David heard the petitions that my father had heard at the city gate. My temerity did not go unremarked, and Ahitophel, with only mild embarrassment at our reversed roles, informed me that David would rather that I didn't rove the palace.

'Does he forbid it?'

'Of course not,' he said smoothly, 'he knows that he has no need.'

I spent much of my time with my mother, although I was forced not just to give up any hope of reviving our former closeness but to acknowledge that it existed largely in my head. She sought solace in her memories and, while I was willing to join in her praise of Jonathan and the twins, I declined to endorse her veneration of Father. To hear her talk, he was a man without faults, perfect as both husband and king, whose misfortune had been to provoke Samuel's jealousy. More than once I had to stop myself reminding her of the occasions when he had hit her for suggesting that he step aside for younger men and publicly accused her of infidelity. Painful as it was to admit, she was happier with Rizpah, who colluded in her revision of the past. Despite her abiding anxiety for her sons, she cared for my mother with a devotion that even I couldn't attribute to guilt.

Civilities apart, I was determined to keep my distance from the other women who, emulating Abigail, honoured me as both Saul's daughter and David's first wife. In ordinary circumstances, I might have befriended Abigail, who exuded contentment – even serenity – despite the death of her only child. Her companions regularly called on her to resolve their disputes, the bitterest of which were between Ahinoam and Maacah. Ahinoam jealously guarded her position as mother of the king's eldest son. At times when extolling Amnon's virtues, she showed so little sensitivity to Abigail's loss that I wanted to strike her. Maacah, a Geshurite princess, made no secret of her contempt for those of lower rank, above all Ahinoam, a maidservant who'd had the effrontery to give birth before her. Their hostility, so overt that I had perceived it on first meeting, was transmitted to their sons, Amnon and Absalom, fighting now for their father's affection as I suspected that one day they would for his crown. Each had his adherents in the harem: Amnon wooing them with swagger and tenacity, Absalom with coquetry and charm. Moreover, Amnon displayed a disturbing fondness for Absalom's sister Tamar. Even Ahinoam failed to protest when Maacah gave him a hearty slap on finding him lifting the two-year-old's robe.

Fiercer even than the women's advancement of their sons was their rivalry for David's attention. Each evening Jonadab arrived, all ogles and smirks, to lead one of us to his chamber. I tried to work out what governed the choice. Was there a pattern – a schedule – or did it depend on his mood? Ahinoam when he felt passionate? Haggith when he felt tender? Maacah when he wanted a challenge? Michal when he wanted a son? I had assumed that, unlike lesser men, he never had to lie alone during his wife's impurity, but Abigail explained that, by a quirk of the palace, the women's cycles concurred. At those times, Jonadab summoned someone older – such as herself, she said quickly, although I had already pictured my mother.

For now, I was his favourite. I hadn't aroused so much envy since the elders brought their daughters to Gibeah. Yet every encounter widened the gulf between us. He was intent on my bearing his child, wearing me down as he would an enemy garrison: by stealth, by siege and, finally, by direct assault. 'Our son will be king after me,' he declared, 'the heir to the house of David and the house of Saul.' But the prospect of spiting Ahinoam and Maacah was nothing to that of spiting David.

Month after month I suffered his desire and relished his disappointment. His hope of uniting the houses grew more urgent after Abner reneged on his promise to deliver the Israelite tribes. They remained loyal to Ishbaal who, for all his failings, was the son of the Lord's anointed, the king whom Samuel, the last of the prophets, had exhorted them to elect. Then one afternoon when I was making a floral crown for Tamar, who evinced a touching attachment to me, I heard a hubbub from the main courtyard, in which one name was audible: Abner. I hurried outside, where Jonadab informed me that he was dead.

'My cousin Joab killed him,' he said, stressing their incongruous kinship. 'He and his men ambushed him at the well of Sirah.'

'Wasn't he under David's protection?'

'You may not remember, but Abner killed Asahel, Joab's brother... he was also my cousin,' he added redundantly.

'Of course I remember,' I said, bridling. 'But that was years ago, on the battlefield. There was no blood guilt.' I had seen them together several times since then, most recently engaging in one of the drinking bouts to which idling soldiers were partial, the veteran general more than a match for his former armour-bearer. Had Joab been toying with him, feigning friendship to spin out his revenge? No. He was a man who drew his sword as fast as he drew breath: a man for whom discretion was another word for cowardice. Such an ambush bore the mark of a man who weighed up every outcome, a man who had concluded that Abner either enjoyed less influence with the Israelites than he claimed or, in the last resort, couldn't bring himself to betray his own clan. There was only one man to fit that description.

My suspicions must have been widely shared or else David would not have taken such pains to dispel them. He summoned the entire household, men and women, together with all the Judahite elders, to the great chamber and, with Joab prostrate before him, professed his innocence of the crime and abhorrence of the perpetrator. Rising from the throne, he moved to Joab and raised his foot a few digits above his head as if about to stamp on it, like Amnon on the ants. I heard a gasp to my right and turned to Jonadab, whose face oozed excitement. Just when I thought retribution inevitable, David stepped away, brushing his sandal on Joab's ear.

'You jackal, you serpent!' he said. 'May you be accursed forever! May the water that you drink poison your veins! May the food that you eat rot in your belly! May your riches be scattered like seeds in the wind! May every boy in your house be born crippled and womanish! I call upon all here to bear witness that Joab and Joab alone is to blame for this wickedness. I and the whole kingdom will mourn for Abner, a great prince and a great general.'

I put on the sackcloth and ashes, as David decreed, but I didn't grieve. Once, I would have shed bitter tears for the mighty uncle of my childhood, who carried me on his shoulders until I touched the sky, and wedged me in the fork of a willow, waving goodbye and filling me with the safest sort of terror. But ever since he handed me back to David, like a cow that had strayed into his neighbour's field, I'd felt nothing but loathing for him. I'd even rejected his offer to seek out news of Paltiel and the boys on his return to Manasseh since, for all that I longed to hear it, I refused to assuage his guilt.

David's curse had no noticeable effect on Joab, who didn't

fall ill or lose his wealth or see his sons grow maimed or unmanly. He wasn't even banished from the palace and, on the rare occasions that our paths crossed, he gave me a knowing smile as if somehow my fathoming the plot made me complicit. The question that exercised everyone was whether, now that Ishbaal had lost his foremost general, David would march against him, or whether he was afraid of antagonising the Israelite tribes. I learnt the answer from Abigail, the one woman in whom he confided.

'I bring sorrowful news,' she said. 'Your brother Ishbaal is dead.'

'How?' I asked, more surprised than saddened. 'There's been no battle. Did he have a fever? Was he drunk and missed his footing? Did he gorge himself until his heart gave out?' If she recognised the allusion to Nabal's suspicious death, she hid it well.

'He was murdered.'

'By whom? Joab?'

'No! Why? Two captains of his guard. Brothers: Benjaminites, from your own tribe.'

'When did it happen?'

'Two days ago. He was in bed asleep.'

'Defenceless!'

'So he wouldn't have suffered. The men told us themselves.'

'The murderers? They came here?'

'They brought his head.'

'Only his head? What about the rest of him?'

'I don't know. David sent me away.'

'Only his head? Is that how they killed him? Or did they cut it off for the journey? Less weight for the donkey. Quicker to give David the good news.'

'Not at all! He was incensed. He ordered them to be straightaway put to death. He has had their hands and feet strung up by the city well.'

'Just as with my father.'

'When the Philistines hung his corpse from the battlements of Beth-shan?'

'No, when David killed the Amalekite who brought word of his death. You were there then too, weren't you?'

'Yes,' she replied uneasily, as though reluctant to make the connection. 'He couldn't help himself. He was so outraged.'

'Or was it – then as now – an attempt to stop them exposing his collusion? Who is it that gains most from Ishbaal's death?'

'Us… all of us, if the wars between the tribes cease and we unite under one king.'

'We were united under one king. But David robbed him, first of his son, then of his daughter, and finally of his crown.'

'Everything he does is in the name of the Lord who anointed him.'

'Really? What evidence do you have of that? When Samuel anointed my father, he did so before the elders of all the tribes. When he anointed David, he didn't even do so before his own clan. There was no one present but David.'

'Samuel confirmed it when David went to visit him in Ramah the very day he died.'

'So again there were no witnesses!'

'There was Samuel's wife.'

'What was she like? I've often wondered.'

'I never met her. She died not long afterwards.'

'How opportune!'

'I know what you're implying, but you're wrong. David is a good man, blessed by the Lord.'

'Maybe when he was young, performing those miraculous feats. But what about now, when even with Abner's endorsement, even with Ishbaal's weakness, he hasn't secured the support of the Israelite tribes? What about now when, despite all his prayers, my belly remains flat? What about now when the harvest has failed for the second year running and the people see it as the Lord's punishment?'

'But on the nation, not on him.'

'If only they made that distinction! Like my father, he's counting the cost of wearing the crown. Please excuse me, I have to tell my mother that the last of her sons is dead.'

As I walked away, I wondered at the emptiness I felt. Was it shock or indifference? I tried to invoke the love I'd felt for Ishbaal as a baby when I'd dandled him on my knee, teaching him to clap hands that clutched emptily at the air and dance on legs that had yet to stand. But then he grew up, boastful, petulant and snide: the kind of boy whom, according to my aunt, only a mother could love. And she had loved him. I suspected that she'd loved him all the more to make up for how deeply the rest of us despised him, and certainly more than she'd loved me. Now I had to break the news of his death. For once I hoped that the confusion she'd suffered in recent weeks, and which had so frustrated me when I tried to tell her of Abner's death, had become permanent and she would suppose that I was announcing his victory or even his marriage. But, as the Lord would have it, her mind was clear and, with a face drained of colour and a voice of hope, she asked me to describe the circumstances of his death, which I did, as sparingly as I could.

'Where is he now?' she asked.

'The murderers brought him to David,' I said, glossing over the beheading.

'I want to see him.'

'Are you sure? Wouldn't you rather remember him as he was?'

'He's my son! I have the right, or is even that to be taken from me?'

'No, of course not, but – '

'So shall I entreat the king myself or will you?'

Eager to save her a further encounter with David, I made my way to his quarters, where Ahitophel informed me that he'd already left for Mahanaim. Before setting out, he had given orders for Ishbaal's remains to be buried in Abner's tomb. I asked whether my mother might see them first, to which he had no objection, while reminding me that the head had been hacked off in haste and endured a hot and dusty journey. Recalling my long-ago trick with the idol, I suggested that, before my mother entered, we should place the head on a bed and fabricate the body under the blankets, but he refused to sanction it without David's approval. So I returned to the harem and tried to prepare my mother for the shock, but hearing only 'Ishbaal' and 'here', she clasped my hand and hurried through the courtyard as if to welcome him home from battle.

The guards at the chamber door stepped back more discreetly than usual as I followed her inside, where my dead brother's head had been covered and laid on a chest like a salted goose in a storeroom. Mother moved uncertainly towards it and lifted the cloth, letting out a gasp, which turned into a wail, which turned into a burst of pitiful yelps.

'That's enough! You must go,' Ahitophel said anxiously.

'No!' Mother said, picking up the head. For a moment I feared that she was going to kiss the lips, which had turned the bloodless grey of earthworms, but instead she pressed it to her breast, rocking gently. I watched in silence, unwilling to intrude for fear of what I might release in her, but when a few moments later she stood stock-still, I walked up and slowly prised Ishbaal's head from her grasp. I stared at it, mocked by the resemblance to the man he once was: the dried blood like soup he'd dribbled on his beard; the stench from his gaping mouth like foetid breath. Most lifelike of all were his eyes, frozen in dread as if at the very instant he'd recognised his killers. I placed the head back on the chest more heavily than I had intended and the thud caused Mother to scream. I ushered her away, allowing her a few hours to recover before, in the late afternoon, we accompanied Ahitophel, Rizpah and Abiathar to bury the former king with far less ceremony than we had his general. As Abiathar led the lamentations, I prayed that, despite their recent rift, Abner would protect my brother in death as he had in life.

David returned three days later but, when he summoned me to his bed the following night, he made no mention of Ishbaal's death nor of the traces of ash on my skin and hair. He barely acknowledged me at all, even at the height of our coupling, except to boast that he had secured the prize for which he'd striven so long. The Israelite tribes had acclaimed him king and would confirm his election at the next new moon. 'My kingdom will extend further than your father's,' he said. 'I shall renounce my pledge to the Philistines and drive them back into the sea.'

The elders arrived in Hebron and, in spite of the worsening famine, David feasted them royally. On the third and final day, we gathered in the sanctuary, Mother and I wearing new crimson-edged robes woven by Rizpah. Abigail had recounted with awe how, when elected king of Judah, David had anointed himself. She had counselled him this time to defer to the high priest and, when Abiathar stepped forward with the sacred oil, I caught her expression of relief. At the same moment, Nechama, Maacah's newborn daughter began to howl. As if not to be left out, Tamar joined her, swiftly followed by several of their half-brothers and sisters. David's murderous glare at his children greatly enlivened the ceremony.

'I don't care for these new songs,' Mother whispered to me, loudly enough to amuse those women who weren't trying to quell the din. 'Is it time to dance yet?' she added, and I realised that she was back with her sisters at Shiloh, preparing to venerate the Ark. For all the pain it caused me, I knew that I should be grateful that Ishbaal's death had blunted the last of her wits.

The ceremony concluded, we processed back through the streets. The raucous cheers of the soldiers served to emphasise the silence of the townspeople, whose storerooms had been plundered to furnish our feasts. At the palace, we were shepherded into the great chamber, where the elders lined up to pay homage to their newly crowned king. As Eglah's father, first in order of precedence, knelt before the throne, David thrust out his foot, causing him to recoil. 'Kiss it,' hissed Joab, not only restored to David's favour but promoted to Abner's old command. Grey-faced, the Reubenite chief complied, setting an example that the others followed.

Returning to the harem, I remarked that my father had required men only to kneel at his feet, not to kiss them. Abigail sprang to David's defence, explaining that he had adopted the practice from the Philistines. Yet, even as he introduced their practices, he was shaking off their yoke. Achish, mistrustful of David's loyalty now that he was king of all Israel, summoned him to Gath. David defied him, trusting his spies' reports that dissension within the Philistine ranks would delay the inevitable reprisals. In the meantime, he addressed himself to matters at home. According to Abigail, as ever our principal informant, his overriding ambition was to found a new capital. Spurning the Israelite sites that he might have procured peaceably, he had settled on the ancient Jebusite city of Jerusalem. Although it was only a few hours away from Gibeah, I had never been there. Faced with its impregnable ramparts, my father had maintained an uneasy truce with the king. David, true to form, set out to conquer it.

Any attack on the city would have to wait until after the harvest. It had failed for the past two years and large swathes of the land were in the grip of a devastating famine. Food remained plentiful in the harem, our sole privation being the rationing of water. For once I agreed with Ahinoam who, when Maacah raged at the loss of her daily bath, pointed out that, in Reuben and Gad, people were starving.

'In Geshur,' Maacah said, 'the comfort of the princess counts for more than the stomachs of the people.'

'No wonder they were too weak to repel our troops,' Ahinoam replied, to the delight of Haggith and Eglah.

As the drought worsened, David offered sacrifices in Nob and Gibeon as well as Hebron, but still the Lord was not propitiated. The people grew restive and there were rumours that several agitators had been executed. As always, my own fears were fixed on Manasseh where, even in wet summers, our well was at risk of running dry and it was half a day's walk to the nearest spring. By suborning the harem servants, I received occasional news from Paltiel and gave thanks for his foresight in teaching me to read and write. He leavened his account of the parched land, withered crops and slaughtered beasts with stories of the boys: the excitement of Malkiel and Shealtiel, who felt vindicated in their disdain for washing, and the misery of Hillel, whom we had named the little Levite for his hatred of dirt. I laughed and cried, pressing the scrolls and committing the words to my heart.

The scarcities increased and David, as discouraged as my father by the Lord's refusal to speak to him directly, was said to spend day after day with Abiathar, casting the sacred stones in a bid to discover the cause of the Lord's displeasure. In accordance with those who imputed it not to their own crimes but to his, I could have told him that it was for lying with his wife after she had lain with another man, and, worse, violating his wife's mother and murdering her son, but, chafing at my childlessness, he summoned me less and less at night. I saw him only when, along with the rest of the harem, I was required to attend the reception of foreign envoys or tribal chiefs.

Then came the news that confounded me. Whether in obedience to the Lord or acknowledgement of his misdeeds I neither knew nor cared, but David gave orders for my boys to be brought to Hebron. Abigail informed me and, at first, I failed to grasp the significance of her words, which felt as slippery as stones on a riverbed. Step by step, I allowed myself to trust them. I was filled with such ecstasy that, had David taken me to his bed that night, I would have opened my heart to him... I would even have beseeched the Lord to open my womb. My one worry was Abigail, whose sombre tone surprised me until I realised that she must be thinking of her own son, Chileab, who would never be restored to her. I resolved to ask one of the boys – either Shealtiel or Adriel, the closest to Chileab in age – to make her his special favourite.

I hastened to tell Mother, but the prospect of seeing her grandchildren meant little to one who had returned to her own childhood. Rizpah, however, shared my delight and, as she kissed my hand, I lamented once again that my pleas for her sons had held no sway with David, who'd threatened to hang them the next time I mentioned their names. Even that memory couldn't cloud my happiness and I prepared for the boys' arrival, wearing my brightest robe and asking Ahinoam to fashion my hair: not braided as I wore it in the harem but loose as it had been in Manasseh. At Ahitophel's instruction, I waited in the main courtyard and, although I would have preferred somewhere private, I was grateful not to have to explain the harem to the boys.

I sat and stood and paced the courtyard, watching in mounting dread as the evening shadows crept up the walls. I was less afraid that some disaster had befallen them along the way than that David had set out to trick me. Was this his punishment for my failure to conceive? Had his indifference turned to hatred as surely as my love? Abigail sought to calm me, but she was blind to his cruelty. Then, just when I expected Ahitophel or even David himself to admit to the subterfuge, a guard announced that the boys had arrived at the gate. Dishevelled, bedraggled and dragging their feet, they entered more like captives than princes. 'Mother!' Hillel cried in a cracked voice and tottered towards me. The others followed and I clasped them in my tightest embrace, first one by one and then all at once, struggling to make sense of the changes in them, from Penuel and Hillel's broad shoulders and Malkiel's whiskery chin to Shealtiel's long legs and

Adriel's missing teeth. As I breathed in their pungent scents, I prayed that I might stay like this forever, locked in a heaving mass of cheeks and chests and elbows and backs. Then Adriel rasped that he was thirsty and, appalled by my thoughtlessness, I ordered a bondwoman to bring water, which the boys fell on as if they hadn't drunk for days.

I ordered a second bondwoman to bring them a meal. But, in a voice as smooth as the clay with which he sealed his scrolls, Ahitophel declared that he would take them to eat in their chamber.

'No!' I exclaimed, chiding myself for startling Adriel. 'No,' I repeated, forcing my voice to a lower pitch. 'They've just arrived. They have so much to tell me. I want to hear everything,' I said, rumpling Shealtiel's hair.

'They're exhausted, my lady. They have been travelling for days. Would you put your needs before theirs?'

'Of course not,' I said, fearing that in two years I had forgotten how to care for children. 'I'll come with you.'

'We're not exhausted,' Penuel interjected. 'Don't let him take us away.'

'Where are they going?' I asked, as four guards approached in response to Ahitophel's signal.

'They'll be safe with their uncles.'

'What uncles?' I asked, as Jonathan and the twins' faces flashed through my mind and Ishbaal's severed head stuck there.

'The sons of your father's courtesan.'

'In the gatehouse?' I asked, my horror transmitting itself to Malkiel and Shealtiel, whose favourite story had been Joseph in Pharaoh's prison.

'I want to stay with you, Mother,' Shealtiel said, clinging to my waist.

'It's just for one night, till they find us somewhere together,' I said, unclasping his hands as if it were a game. 'Now make sure to get some sleep; we have so much to do in the morning.'

As they were led away, I felt that I was drowning but in air not water, having fallen into a pit deeper than Sheol. It was only when Abigail held out her arms to steady me that I realised I was falling in earnest.

'What's happening, Abigail? Tell me! I know that you know.'

'Not here. Let's go back inside.'

'I won't take a step until you tell me the truth.'

'I should have told you before, but I didn't want to alarm you.'

'I'm calm now. See how calm I am.' I gripped my left wrist with my right hand to stop it trembling.

'The Lord has revealed the reason for the drought.'

'When? How?'

'Through the sacred stones. I know that this will be hard for you, but it's because your father killed the Gibeonites.'

'My father vanquished many of the nation's enemies; I don't remember them all. Why should the Lord object?'

'Because they're not our enemies – at least they shouldn't be. When Joshua conquered Canaan, he promised them eternal protection in the Lord's name. The Lord now stands with the Gibeonites against his own people.'

'My father has been dead for nine years. Why should the Lord punish him – no, us – now?'

'I can't answer for the Lord any more than you can. It just is. Please, let's go back to your chamber.'

'You still haven't said what this has to do with my boys.'

'Only the Gibeonites can entreat the Lord to lift the drought. The king summoned the elders to hear their demands. They insisted that Saul's blood guilt be requited.'

'How? No!' Not needing an answer, I ran through the gateway to the inner courtyard, up the stairs and into David's chamber, where he sat eating with Joab and Abishai. As I entered, Joab jumped up and brandished his sword. 'Yes, go ahead,' I said. 'If my father's blood guilt must fall on anyone, let it be me.' I approached the blade, allowing its cold tip to scratch my throat. Joab looked shocked at the bead of blood, lowering his sword even before David gave the order.

'Michal… oh Michal,' David said evenly. 'Must you always be the one to disturb my peace?'

'Yes,' I replied. 'Even when we're dead and descended to Sheol, unless you tell me why you've brought my children – '

'Your sister's children – '

'To Hebron.'

'Have you forgotten how your father slaughtered the innocent priests of Nob?'

'No, of course not. Never. But who was it who drove him to it? Who was it who lied to the priests and ate their consecrated bread? Who was it who brought my father's wrath down on them?'

'I am not to blame for his sacrilege!'

'Besides, the priests were Levites, not Gibeonites.'

'The Gibeonites served them. And Saul's man killed seven of them. Now the Gibeonites demand that seven of his descendants be executed in exchange.'

'Which seven? There are only five boys.'

'And two by your father's concubine.'

'Whom you've kept locked up for years. Why? Were you waiting for just this moment?'

'Don't sneer at me! It's not my will but the Lord's.'

'How convenient that the two should coincide!'

'On the contrary, it is to be expected since he chose me to rule his people.'

'The truth is that you want all of my father's heirs dead.'

'Give me a son!'

'Never! I'd rather take hellebore; I'd rather take silphium; I'd seek out every wise woman the length and breadth of the land to cleanse the infection from my womb.'

'Shall I carry her back to the harem?' asked Abishai.

'Or throw her out in the street?' asked Joab.

'No, she's my wife. The world will see how David honours her, no matter the provocation.'

'You say that my father broke an oath, an oath made all those years ago. But what of your oath to my brother, to protect his house? Don't my sons – Merab's sons – belong to his house? Wouldn't he wish you to protect his orphaned nephews?'

'I've kept my oath,' he replied, his blush showing that my reproof had stung him. 'Jonathan has a son, Meribaal.'

'He's dead. Captured by Amorites along with his mother.'

'No, he's alive. Cared for by his nurse's nephew. I've received regular reports from one of your father's old servants. Do you think you can deceive me that easily?'

'He's lame. Please let him live. He can do you no harm.'

'And I can do none to him. I made an oath to my brother Jonathan.'

'My brother; your...' I lacked the word to complete the charge.

'But if the Lord required it, I would yield him to the Gibeonites. An oath made in the Lord's name supersedes all others. That's what your father failed to understand when he spared the Amalekite king. Mercy is meaningless when it defies the Lord.'

I walked through the palace, unable to feel the ground beneath my feet; unable to feel my feet; unable to feel my feelings. Sheol wasn't the only kingdom of the dead: I was dead and I returned to the harem; I was dead and I entered the chamber where Rizpah sat, haggard, alongside Mother; I was dead and I listened to Mother gabbling gaily as she fed the air between her fingers to the children in her mind; I was dead and I fell asleep, waking the next morning to find Rizpah wearing sackcloth, smearing ash on her face. I was angry at her show of mourning. What was her loss compared to mine? She had two sons; I had five. She had seen her sons grow to manhood; Penuel, my eldest, was just eighteen and Adriel, my youngest, not yet ten. But my anger was misplaced. Grief wasn't a well from which the more she drew, the less there would be for me, but an ocean in which both of us could drown. I clasped her to me and felt her heart thrashing in her chest like a bird in a snare. An ash caught in my eye, mocking my tears.

'I went to see Ahitophel,' she said.

'When?'

'You were asleep.'

'You should have woken me.'

'I didn't want to wake you. I begged him to allow me to accompany my sons on their journey. He spoke to the king who, to my astonishment, said yes.'

'Accompany them where? Are they leaving?'

'For Gibeah.'

'Why?'

'Saul's guilt is to be expiated in the heart of his kingdom,' she said quietly. 'David wants there to be no confusion.'

Was Saul's daughter to do less than his concubine? I knew that I had to go with her, and with them. I had to derive my courage from my father and brothers; I had to derive my dignity from Merab, when, as the last member – the last able-bodied member – of our house, I bore witness to its destruction. But all I wanted was to seal myself within a tomb and never set eyes on another human face. If Paltiel himself were summoned to comfort me, I would refuse to see him – unless it were to denounce him as a coward. Why hadn't he slit the boys' throats and spared them the shame of their public deaths? Why hadn't he drowned them in the well and spared them the need to atone for the guilt of a grandfather they had never known?

Yet I was the real coward. When I appealed to Ahitophel for the same permission as Rizpah, there was a part of me that was relieved when he refused, explaining that David was afraid that my presence in the Benjamite capital would provoke insurrection. He warned me that the convoy was to leave for Gibeah within the hour and, in a remark so inapposite that I must have misheard, reminded me of his promise that the boys would spend no more than one night in the gatehouse. He assured me that they had no inkling of their fate, having been told only that they were to return to their grandfather's house. One of them – whom he didn't name but I knew must be Penuel – had thanked him for restoring their birthright.

'He would have made a fine soldier,' he said pensively.

I heard myself shriek and saw myself claw out his eyes. But when my senses cleared, he was sitting at his table, with the same mirthless smile, and I was standing stupefied in front of him.

I rejected his offer of a final visit to the boys. How could I accept minutes when I had expected years? How could I pretend that we would meet again soon, as I had when I left for Hebron? Even if I found the words, I would never find the expression. My welling eyes and quivering lips would reveal their destination. I would fill their last days with such terror that, as they marched through the parched countryside, the drought that had blighted the crops would shrivel their hearts.

I left Ahitophel and returned to the harem. None of the women spoke, but Abital's son, Shephatiah, toddled up to me and clasped my hand. Too young to know the truth, he must have sensed the horror that his elders were afraid to acknowledge. I kissed his brow and pushed him away before he was splashed by the tears that his touch had triggered. I lay on my bed and, although the heavy door muffled all but the loudest sounds, I heard the boys being led out of the gatehouse and into the street. For two days, I heard the heavy tread as they tramped across the land (no donkey provided, even for Adriel). On the third day, when the footfall died, I knew that they had too.

I ran out into the courtyard, indifferent to the effect of my wild eyes and puffy cheeks on the playing children. While their mothers comforted them, I called for Abigail, who ushered me back to my chamber, where she promised to glean what she could from David in return for my eating the soup that I'd hitherto spurned. Anxious not to antagonize her, I took a few spoonfuls, only to vomit. As she wiped my face, I felt a flicker of hope that my body would rebel against all sustenance and I would die alongside my boys, albeit a more protracted and painful death as befitted a mother. But it was not to be. In the evening, she brought me another bowl of soup, which I stomached, evidence that, no matter the cause, my body refused to let me starve it and my punishment for living on after my sons would be to live on after my sons. For three days, Abigail had nothing to tell me. Then, in a tone whose studied softness made words redundant, she confessed that the boys were dead.

I waited for Rizpah to return. I knew that no detail would be too small for a mother's notice and trusted her not to spare me. My one fear was that her sons had been killed before mine, clouding her eyes for the aftermath. But when days passed with no sign of her, I suspected that she too was dead, either of grief or by her own hand. Abigail swore that she had heard nothing but I sensed her unease and, when I threatened to confront David, she relented.

'Remember that this was the Lord's will and not the king's,' she said. I nodded, lest my scorn silence her. 'The Gibeonites didn't stone them but hanged them from trees. They died quickly, but the Gibeonites refused to cut their bodies down.'

'It's the Law!'

'I'm sorry. So sorry.'

'How long did they... were they left?'

'They're still there.'

'After two weeks!'

'That's why I didn't want to tell you. The Gibeonites insist that they're kept there as a testament to your father's offence.'

'So they've not been buried?'

'No.'

'No prayers said over them?'

'No.'

'But left for every vulture and crow to swoop down on… every jackal and hyena to leap up on, tearing the flesh from their faces and arms, pecking out their eyes and tongues, picking their bones clean.' I felt myself choke and put my hands to my throat. The nooses still tied around their necks were crushing mine.

'No, not at all,' Abigail said, clasping my hands in hers. 'Rizpah has stayed there. She's turned her sackcloth into a shield against the sun. She watches day and night over the bodies of her sons – and yours. Should any predator approach, she springs up, hollering and brandishing a stick to drive it away. The people are in awe of her. They bring her food and wine and fresh linen, but she takes only bread and water and new sackcloth to replace the old.'

'She puts me to shame.'

'She puts us all to shame. Ahitophel warned the king that she's creating a scandal and urged him to have her removed.'

'Maybe he'll hang her too?'

'What? Why do you say that? He admires her fortitude… her devotion.' I snorted. 'It's true! And he's afraid of creating a worse scandal by expelling her.'

'No doubt. So how long is she to remain? She can save the bodies from the ravening beasts but not from the blaze of the sun.'

'Until the king receives a sign that the drought has been lifted.'

'It's summer! Unless the Lord works a miracle, it'll be dry for another three or four months.'

'Then that's how long it will take.'

Her prediction was borne out. As the summer dragged on and the heat seeped into the thick walls of the harem, making the women sullen and the children fractious, I thought of

Rizpah enduring a hundred times worse, her sons' festering corpses constantly before her. And if the sight were not cruel enough, what of the stench? I recalled the reek of my own body, unwashed during a week of mourning, and multiplied it by seven during three... four... five months of decay. Then, just when it seemed that her vigil would never end, the sky turned grey as swiftly as if it had been dipped in a bowl of dye. The clouds burst as if we were back in the days of Noah. I watched the children splash through the courtyard and echoed their delight. Surely this was proof that the Lord was appeased? Surely David could now give the order to take down the bodies of my sons and my father's sons... no, henceforth I would think of them as Rizpah's sons, since they were honoured as much by her blood as his.

David, ever wary of offending the Lord, summoned Abiathar to cast the sacred stones, which confirmed that the drought had broken. He ordered that the bodies be recovered and prepared for burial in my grandfather's tomb, and that the remains of my father and brothers be brought from Jabesh and placed alongside them. To my surprise, he invited me to attend the obsequies. Since my sons' murder, he had taken pains to avoid me and, when we met at the city gate, he looked relieved to see me wearing jewels and fine linen, rather than sackcloth and ashes. Once again he had failed to understand me. I was no longer the bereaved mother lamenting the cruelty of the Lord and his anointed, but King Saul's daughter returning to her birthplace to honour her dead.

My father's house looked exactly as I remembered it, but so small and unimposing after the palace. My cousin Keziah was living there and, seeing her for the first time since I married Paltiel, I was seized by a longing for the safety and surety of my childhood, far stronger than when I'd first seen Abner or Ahitophel or even Mother, since, unlike them, she belonged solely to that childhood, a world away from where I was now. With David eager to proceed, we had little opportunity to talk and, after she'd feasted us on all that the depleted storeroom had to offer, we set off for the hills and the tomb I'd last visited to venerate my grandparents fifteen years ago. The sepulchre stone had been rolled away and Rizpah stood beside it. As we approached, I stepped forward to kneel and kiss her hand. 'No, please, my lady,' she said, pulling me up. 'It's honour enough for me that my sons will be laid to rest with your brothers... with theirs.'

I entered the tomb with Rizpah, David and Abiathar. Both larger and lower than I remembered, it exuded a fragrance of frankincense and balsam, as well as something cloying, which was either an oil that I had failed to identify or else the odour that the others were designed to hide. As my eyes grew accustomed to the gloom, I made out the bodies of my ancestors laid out on ledges: some covered; others mounds of bare bones, where both the flesh and the winding sheets had rotted. Oil lamps marked the seven new arrivals, mercifully shrouded from view. Fear of a lifetime of broken sleep prevented my lifting the cloths; instead, I knelt and kissed one of the ledges. Shocked by the cold, clammy stone, I turned to see David standing in front of four jars, much like those I'd used to preserve fruit. With a jolt, I realised that they were all that survived of my father and brothers. I gazed at David. Was he thinking of Jonathan, whose warm flesh he had once embraced, reduced to the contents of a storage jar? Or was he wondering what kind of death awaited him?

He placed two swords beside the jars: a gesture that exalted himself as much as them, since it was thanks to his mastering the methods of the Philistine foundries that such precious weapons could be spared. I, in turn, placed a rattle beside the smallest of the shrouds, which I took to be Adriel's. Abital had pressed it in my hand as we set off and, although he had long outgrown it, I trusted that it might give Adriel some comfort as he passed into Sheol. Rizpah and Abiathar brought bowls of food and jugs of wine, which we distributed evenly. Then, with a final glance at the boys to whom I could offer nothing but tears, I followed the others out. Four men sweated to roll the stone against the entrance. Abiathar recited a set of prayers and lamentations, after which we each in turn poured libations and invoked blessings on the dead. I had hoped for some time for reflection, but David was impatient to return to Hebron. So I took my leave of Rizpah who, released from the harem, was to remain in Gibeah. I wasn't altogether sorry, since, despite my respect for her vigil, too much had passed between us for us to become friends.

We rode back through the driving rain, which David welcomed as though it were almond blossom heralding spring. Conversation, even had we wished it, was impossible but, when we stopped for the night in a cave outside Adullam, I seized the chance to ask him the question that perplexed me.

'Why did you wait so long to have my father and brothers brought back to Gibeah? Was it because with the murder of my sons, there was no one of our house left to claim the land on which his ancestors were buried?'

'Michal,' he said with a sigh, 'why must you always think the worst of me?' Forestalling my answer, he asked: 'Have you forgotten Meribaal?'

'He's crippled. He can claim nothing.'

'His claim is to my heart. You charged me with breaking my oath to Jonathan. On the contrary, I mean to honour it and honour his son. Tomorrow, when we're back in Hebron, I shall order that he be brought to the palace.'

True to his word, he sent Ziba, the servant of dubious loyalty, to fetch Meribaal from Lodebar. A week later, he arrived in Hebron to be welcomed with full pomp. Joining the royal wives, their children and the palace officials in the courtyard, I was both nervous and excited to meet a boy... a man (he was just a few months younger than Penuel), whom I had last seen aged four. He emerged, bent double and leaning on two sticks. After catching his breath, he advanced, half-escorted, half-dragged by Ahitophel and Ziba. While there was nothing of Jonathan in his gait, I found traces in his eyes and nose enveloped in a layer of fat. He hobbled forward, as if each step were a stab of pain, while the assembled company watched in trepidation, apart from Absalom, whose peal of laughter was cut short by his father's rebuke. Having reached within three cubits of David, he fell to his knees and crawled the remaining distance to kiss his feet. My disgust at the alien practice had never been stronger and I glowered at Ahitophel, who had evidently tutored him. Even David was uneasy, since he hastened to raise him, straightening his back and inadvertently revealing his height – at least the equal of my father's, whereupon, with a gesture midway between affection and anger, he pushed him down again, leant over and kissed him on both cheeks.

'A chair for Prince Meribaal,' he shouted to a servant, who ran to fetch one. Unsure where to put it, he hovered awkwardly, until David grabbed it from him and slammed it down. 'I call on all present to bear witness. This is the son of my brother Jonathan, who is to be as my own sons in Hebron, sitting at my table and enjoying the honours due to his father.'

Meribaal grinned abjectly, and I longed to tell him how fortunate he was to be crippled. Had my five boys been dropped in infancy, they might still have been alive.

'Amnon, Absalom, come to your father.' David called for his two eldest sons. The first ran towards him; the second shuffled shyly. 'How are my brave boys?' he asked, grabbing one under each arm and hurtling around the courtyard, as they screamed with terror and delight. To a burst of applause, he set Absalom down and threw Amnon up in the air, catching him moments before he hit the ground. Gentler with his second son, he slung him behind his back, manoeuvred him over his shoulder and under first one arm and then the other, before depositing him beside the hearth, where he lurched in a daze, his puckered face threatening tears. Maacah snatched him back, half-comforting and half-scolding him for his failure to match his brother. While Meribaal looked bemused, I wondered at David's need for such an overt display of his sons' robustness. It was as if he were competing with Jonathan even now.

His primacy affirmed, David returned to his quarters and the company dispersed. I hurried to greet Meribaal before Ziba led him to his chamber. He didn't remember me but appeared reassured by the word *aunt* and even more by that of *grandmother*, whom, brooking no objection from the self-serving servant, I took him to meet. I had tried to prepare her for seeing her one surviving grandchild, but her eyes had grown as clouded as her mind. For a time she'd known me by my voice and then by my touch, but now she knew me only in her memory, where I mingled with her dead parents, sisters and children, so that her entire life seemed to be taking place at once. My reference to Jonathan created a predictable confusion and, with a gulp of joy, she clasped Meribaal so abruptly that, frail as she was, she knocked him over. I stooped to help him, but he pushed me away with a look both of fury and desolation. He charged Ziba to take him straight to his chamber and, over the next few weeks, refused all my requests to return. Not until I told him that she was dying – vowing on his father's memory that it wasn't a ploy – would he agree to come. He sat by her side, wiping the spittle off her chin and gazing intently into her vacant eyes as if searching for a link to the noble lineage of which he was both the remnant and the ruin.

Two days later my mother died. Abiathar and Ahitophel accompanied me to Gibeah to bury her beside her husband and sons. The fields along the way gleamed silver with oats, golden with wheat and amber with barley, the ripening grain fed as much by my sons' blood as the spring rains. We returned to find the palace astir. David, assured of an abundant harvest, had resolved to mount his long-awaited assault on Jerusalem. He gave orders that as soon as the crops were gathered, the Israelites should muster in the Hinnom valley. He himself set out to rally the Judahites. While the other wives lamented his absence, I relished the respite. With my mother dead and Rizpah freed, I sought out Meribaal, now a familiar figure as he lumbered about the palace, inspiring both affection and mockery. His crippled limbs afforded him entry to the harem, and we would sit conversing in the courtyard, our peace shattered by the shrieks and thwacks of David's sons who, ignorant of the protracted siege, enacted their father's imminent victory. Fraternal rivalries were reinforced as Amnon, always assuming his father's role, defeated the wicked Jebusites, namely Absalom, Adonijah and Shephatiah.

David himself was less fortunate. The city's walls proved as inviolable as ever and, as the weeks went by, I entertained the hope, treacherous but thrilling, that he would be forced to retreat, prompting the tribes to renounce him. Then Jonadab brought the news that Joab had led a raiding party through an underground water shaft, catching the guards unawares and opening the gates to David's troops. After gaining control of the streets, they had stormed the palace, putting the king, his sons and all the men of his house to death, whereupon the Jebusite elders surrendered.

Leaving Joab to stamp out pockets of resistance, David returned to Hebron in triumph. After making thanksgiving offerings in the sanctuary, he came to the harem, where he embraced his children with a tenderness that would once have touched me. Bursting with pride, he informed us that Jerusalem, where our forefather Adam first worshipped the Lord, where Noah rebuilt his altar after the Flood, and where the Lord sent Abraham a ram to sacrifice in place of Isaac (a substitution, I thought bitterly, that he hadn't chosen to repeat), was to be the kingdom's new capital and renamed the City of David. As soon as preparations had been made, we were to move there. But our departure was delayed when the

Philistine kings, learning of David's conquest, set aside their differences and invaded the valley of Rephaim. Even though his forces were depleted, with half his men serving under Joab and others having returned home for the grape harvest, David won a resounding victory, slaying four of the kings and capturing their idols. With the Philistine threat removed, his peoples' loyalty was ensured.

Rather than return to Hebron, David went straight to Jerusalem, where a month later we joined him. As we rode through a valley arid even in winter, trudged up a gravelly slope and approached the stepped stone walls, my first impression of the city was grim. Jonadab, buttery as ever, greeted us at the gate and steered us through a warren of eerily empty streets to our quarters at the palace. There we found the late king's widow, bereft of both husband and honour after David had publicly violated her. Abigail insisted once again that he was staking his claim to the crown, but it smacked more of branding his sheep. The makeshift harem was cramped and I shared a chamber with Maacah and her children, Absalom, Tamar and Nechama, an arrangement that Jonadab assured me was temporary, since David had already begun to build a new palace. Eager to outshine the pharaohs, he had summoned the finest craftsmen from Sidon and Tyre and set the vanquished Jebusites to labour under them. The foundations were swiftly laid and, although some people denounced David's vanity, most saluted his ambition. They had asked for a king like other nations; they now had one who surpassed them.

David then embarked on his most cherished project: to house the Ark of the Lord in his city. For more than fifty years after its capture by the Philistines, it had languished in the town of Kiriath-Jearim and, in spite of its pre-eminent place in the story of the nation, few of us had ever seen it. David accused my father of having neglected it, thereby doubly insulting the Lord, since it not only served as his throne but contained the tablets of his covenant with Moses. That was a calumny, as he well knew, having often heard Father speak of his desire to bring it to Gibeah. But although the Philistines, punished with plagues and boils, had returned the Ark, Kiriath-Jearim was surrounded by their territory and to enter it would have led to war. Unlike David, Father took up arms only to remove threats and repel invaders, refusing to risk his soldiers' lives in any other cause. With the Philistines vanquished, David faced no such obstacle.

Rigorous arrangements were made for the Ark's transport, with David, Abiathar and a hundred priests escorting it from Kiriath-Jearim. Messengers kept Ahitophel apprised of their progress and, when they reached Nacon, he instructed the royal wives to join the Israelite chiefs and Jebusite elders at the city gate to await their arrival. Either from sympathy for my recent loss or residual loyalty to my house, the crowd greeted me with marked enthusiasm, as I took my place between a jealous Ahinoam and a wretched Meribaal, already flagging in the blistering heat. Overruling Jonadab, I ordered a guard to bring him a chair.

One… two… three hours passed, with no movement other than a herd of goats grazing at the edge of the valley. Maacah slipped away to nurse Nechama, leaving Absalom more vulnerable than ever to Amnon's taunts. Only Abigail's timely intervention averted a brawl. Then, offering no explanation, a grim-faced Ahitophel ordered everyone to disperse. As I led Meribaal through the gate, I heard two Jebusite women muttering that the Israelite god had refused to enter their city, and my heart soared. We returned to the harem, where we ate a modest meal, leaving the celebratory feast untouched. By the late afternoon, David and the Ark had still to appear. While the rest of us pondered in silence, Ahinoam voiced her fanciful conjectures, ranging from ravines cracking and rivers flooding to an attack by the Amalekites she abhorred. Finally, Jonadab arrived, eager as ever to be first with the news.

'The Ark was set on a specially built cart, drawn by a team

of oxen,' he said. 'But one of them stumbled, and Uzzah, son of the Levite who'd housed the Ark in Kiriath-Jearim, reached out to stop it falling – the Ark, not the ox, that is. So the Lord struck him dead.'

'Why did he do that?' Absalom asked, open-mouthed.

'Because the Ark mustn't be touched by anyone, stupid!' Amnon said.

'Then how did they put it on the cart?'

Amnon looked baffled and was about to answer with his fists, when Jonadab, less concerned to prevent a scuffle than to resume his story, explained. 'Their hands were covered. When he saw what had happened, the king was shocked and afraid to bring the Ark into the city in case the Lord reproached him for moving it or else Uzzah's touch had left it defiled.'

'My father's not afraid of anything,' Amnon said.

'Mine too,' Absalom said.

'He's the same one, stupid!'

'Your father is afraid of no man,' Abigail interjected hastily, 'but even the greatest king must be afraid of the Lord.'

'Especially one who has sinned as greatly as David,' I added. The children looked at me in surprise, their mothers in alarm. 'Perhaps the Lord doesn't wish to reside in his city?'

'That's what the king intends to find out,' Jonadab said. 'So he has left the Ark in the care of another Levite, Obededom.' Tamar giggled at the name. 'He begged to be spared such an honour, but the king was adamant.'

I pictured Uzzah crushed beneath the cart-wheels and asked myself what sort of god would destroy a man who had sought to protect his throne. The answer was clear: a god who had withdrawn his favour from my father on the slimmest of pretexts; a god who had rewarded David, not in spite of but because of his faults, strengthening his position with every rape, theft and murder; a god stamped by ingratitude and perversity. David might regard the events of the day as a temporary reversal, but for me the reversal was permanent. I finally had the measure of my adversary. No wonder Samuel told Father that his successor would be a man after the Lord's own heart.

David waited three months to discover whether disaster would strike the Levite. When he found that, on the contrary, the man and his whole household had prospered, he revived his plan to install the Ark in the heart of the city. On the day of its removal, the women of the harem, including the Jebusite queen, were once again summoned to greet it. To my surprise, Ahitophel informed me that I wasn't to join them. He conducted me instead to the top of the gatehouse, insisting that I would have a better view of proceedings from the window. Politic as ever, he declared that David was concerned that I might be crushed in the crowd, already five or six deep. I thanked him, well aware that someone – most likely Ahinoam, whose honeyed smile concealed a sting – had told him of my reception last time, and he would countenance no rival.

From my vantage point, I watched as the Ark emerged from the house, no longer drawn by oxen but carried on poles. After a mere six paces, the procession halted and an ox and a calf were sacrificed at a provisional altar. The ritual was repeated after another six paces and then another, and I realised that the priests were to slaughter two beasts every six paces until they reached the tabernacle. The path ran with blood, and the air was thick with smoke and the stench of burning fat (from this distance, it was impossible to tell whether the spectators were cheering or choking). The musicians blew trumpets, shook timbrels and beat drums, and David began to dance, twisting and turning ever faster. As the priests offered a further sacrifice, David tore off his mantle, robe and tunic and, naked but for a loincloth, whirled like a prophet in ecstasy. To my dismay, I felt a flutter of attraction towards him. It was as though the past twenty years had been swept away and he was once again the youth who had cured my father, except that he had become one with his music. The songs he'd composed on his lyre he now played on his flesh. I gazed transfixed as he soared and spun, sweat spraying from his hair and glistening on his skin, until his loincloth fell loose and he exposed himself in a state fit only for his private chamber. Was he in a trance, conscious of no one but the Lord? Or had he contrived the accident with his usual care, eager to display the member in which he took such pride?

I shrank back in disgust: with David, but also with myself or, more precisely, the tremor in my loins. I left the gatehouse and waited in the street for the procession to arrive, before accompanying it into the tabernacle courtyard, where the priests performed a final sacrifice. They then carried the Ark into the holy place, while David remained outside to bestow the Lord's blessing on the people. To a roar of approval, he announced that his servants were to give everyone present a loaf of bread, a draught of wine and a portion of the thanksgiving offering. Leaving Joab to oversee the distribution, he returned to the palace. I followed him into the courtyard, where Ahitophel handed him a fresh robe, which he brushed aside. Regardless of the consequences, I knew that I must speak out.

'David!' I called, trembling as he turned to me, his face red, hair matted and eyes blazing.

'What is it? I must go and bless my children.'

'No, you'll shame them, just as you've shamed yourself and the crown you stole from my father. You've made yourself the sport of every slave and bondwoman in the city.'

'Enough, my lady,' Ahitophel interjected, grabbing my arm.

'What?' David glared at him. 'Do you suppose that she intimidates me or else that I cannot answer?'

'Not at all, my lord,' he replied, recoiling.

David drew close enough to bite me. I felt his hot breath on my cheeks and prayed that they wouldn't flush; I sniffed the heavy musk of his skin.

'It was your father who shamed himself!' he said. 'Your father, abandoned by the Lord and assailed by evil spirits. True, before the people I am the king; but before the Lord I am no more than those bondwomen. I am the meanest wretch, the humblest servant, for I am the Lord's own servant. It's you who shame yourself! You who have failed as a woman, who have failed as a wife. And you'll carry your failure to the tomb. Let all here bear witness – ' he faltered on finding only Ahitophel, 'that I disown you. Never again shall I lie with you. You'll live among women who bask in the favour of their king and the love of their children. You'll watch the triumph of the house of David and know that you have no place in it.'

He walked away. Ahitophel followed. I forced a smile but there was nobody to see.

FOUR

Bathsheba

Just as the Law says that a bird must be free of blood before it can be eaten, so a woman must be free of blood before she can be touched. Until then she is unclean but not dirty, although no one has yet explained the difference to me. So once a month I climb on to the roof and cleanse myself of my stain. I would prefer to bathe indoors, especially in winter, but Uriah insists that to fulfil the Law, the water must flow freely from its source. As I have no wish to walk to the Gihon spring, with everyone in the district knowing the reason, I rely on rain-water gathered in the cistern. The prickling cold makes me feel purer than the ritual itself.

My husband Uriah, while not an Israelite by birth, has studied the Law more closely than many who are. When he came to the land, he gave up the worship of his Hittite gods: Wurusema, the sun-goddess, Teshub, the weather-god, and their children with names like tickles in the throat, and devoted himself to the Lord. He even changed his own name from Muttallu to Uriah, which means God is Light, a far more auspicious name than Bathsheba, which merely means Daughter of an Oath.

Uriah is a captain in King David's guard. No sooner had he founded his city than the king set up our first permanent army. Although the troops are drawn from all the tribes, his personal guard consists entirely of foreigners such as Uriah, whom he hired to command his charioteers. He had been impressed by the weaponry when he lived in Philistia, an episode of which it's wisest not to speak. Nathan, the prophet who is chronicling the king's story, maintains that he risked his life, ingratiating himself with the enemy so as to bring back the secrets of the iron swords, spears and chariots without which he would never have vanquished the Philistines, along with our other adversaries. But behind closed doors and in hushed voices, the elders who visited my grandfather spoke of his fleeing there from King Saul, fighting in the Philistine army, and even swearing allegiance to the King of Gath. How was a young girl, for whom the outside world was hearsay, to know what to believe?

The official reason for the king's employing foreigners is that they have skills that the Israelites lack. The Hittites are expert horsemen, whereas few of our men even ride donkeys. But according to my grandfather, the real reason is that the king fears that the Israelites owe their ultimate loyalty to their tribal chiefs rather than to him. He was holding forth to two fellow counsellors while I played with my doll in the courtyard. I paid them more attention than they did me, not because their conversation was interesting but because it was the only one there was. 'Surely that's wrong?' I interposed. 'The king should trust his own people more than strangers.' Grandfather looked as shocked as if I had aimed a rock at him rather than a question. He sent me upstairs with orders to forget what I'd heard, which was the surest way to make me remember.

My grandfather raised me after the death of my parents. My father was killed, fighting in one of King David's campaigns. I recall nothing of it, except that it was a great victory and the king himself led the procession to his tomb. My mother was pregnant and, in her grief, she gave birth to my sister in her sixth month. They both died, my sister living long enough only to be given a name, Amalya. But I wasn't allowed to say it out loud because it upset my grandmother. So I gave the name to my doll and for years it was a way both to keep Amalya's memory alive and to stave off loneliness. Then I lost the doll and it felt as if Amalya had died over again.

After Mother's death, my grandmother grew to hate me. She found fault with everything I did, never spoke to me unprompted and froze whenever I approached. Grandfather said it was because I reminded her of Mother, although if she had loved her as much as he claimed, surely she would have welcomed the reminder? Then she died too, and with Grandfather busy at the palace, I spent years alone in the house with no one but servants. As I grew up – too young to be sequestered from men but old enough to be admired by them – Grandfather liked me beside him when he received guests. He warned me against young men, but it was the old men who petted and pinched me, running their hands through my hair and even insinuating them inside my robe. When I complained to him, Grandfather replied that they had known me since I was a child and asked if I wanted to hurt their feelings. 'Of course not,' I said and apologised. Later, I wished that I'd asked why he'd allowed them to hurt mine.

My complaints must nonetheless have shaken him, for one day, after telling me that I was attracting too many glances in a tone that implied it was my own fault, he asked if I would like a husband. 'I've never thought about it,' I replied, which was both true and false: true because I had never met a man or a boy I could contemplate marrying; false because I frequently pictured myself married to one of the heroes from the ancient stories, especially Joseph and Samson. They had little in common except for the Lord's favour and my esteem. With Joseph, I would linger in bed all day, stroking his smooth chest and kissing his downy cheeks, as we regaled each other with our dreams. With Samson, I would sink into his sinewy arms and run my fingers through his lustrous hair, taking care not to snap a single lock.

Grandfather looked relieved that there were no illicit attachments to hamper his choice. 'His name is Uriah,' he said. 'A Hittite by birth; an Israelite by adoption.'

I was surprised that Grandfather, so jealous of his standing as the king's principal adviser, wished to marry me to a foreigner rather than the son of a tribal chief. Uriah, who treated me as an equal despite my age and sex, explained. 'Ahitophel is a very cunning man. He knows that he will benefit from an alliance with one of the king's most respected captains – one, moreover, who will someday command the entire army,' he said with a twinkle. 'And who isn't party to any of the deep-seated rivalries between the tribes.'

'He told me that was the reason the king employed you,' I said. 'Doesn't anyone in the palace trust anyone else?'

'We trust our wives,' he said and, in a rare display of affection (rare, I was coming to see because he loathed display and not because he lacked affection), he lifted me off my feet and whirled me round, before setting me down, deliriously dizzy.

The marriage contract was signed and the elders of the clan and the city attended the feast. Uriah brought several of his fellow soldiers, led by Joab, the king's great commander and our guest of honour. He kissed me with sump-like breath, the result, I later learnt, of a stomach wound that refused to heal. His heavily scarred arms looked as if children had used them to tally scores. Despite the sweep of his shoulders and the men at his command, he seemed lonely, which made me pity as well as fear him. No sooner had the cakes been served than Uriah and two of his friends rose to leave, prompting raucous comments from the men's tables and knowing smiles at ours. I had never missed my mother more, now that my only guidance for married life came from my grandfather, a list of 'dos' and 'don'ts,' much like the ones he used to give me as a child. He led me through the winding streets to a small house in the shadow of the palace. Seeing my new husband waiting at the gate, I realised for the first time that the steps I was taking could never be retraced. I would be Uriah's wife, the mother of Uriah's children, and one day, most likely, Uriah's widow. Yet I had never hoped for anything more, not least because my grandfather made it clear that there was nothing more for me to hope. 'Don't think you're special,' he would say, as he upbraided me for my latest misdemeanour. I didn't... I don't; I am happy with what I have.

Uriah smiled at me as though he were saluting; his two friends, whose duties ended at the threshold, greeted me more casually. I tried to ignore the pomegranate in my path, fearing that one of them had secreted it in his robe and dropped it without noticing. All was made plain when Grandfather borrowed Uriah's sword, handed it to me and, in a voice designed to carry (although there was no one but us to hear) declared: 'May you be as fruitful as the seeds of this pomegranate!' He told me to slice it open, but I miscalculated, striking the fruit on the side and knocking it down the street. Uriah's friends looked alarmed and Grandfather annoyed, but Uriah reassured them, saying: 'Among my people it's seen as a good sign: that our children will be born without pain.' Whether or not that were true, I loved him for it.

The pain of childbirth was a distant threat; that of the wedding night was imminent. Uriah was twenty years my senior and, unlike me, not obliged to prove his purity. Whereas my meagre knowledge of what lay beneath his tunic sprang from sneaked glimpses of goats in the meadows or, more ignobly, a trussed-up ram in the tabernacle, he was well acquainted with what lay beneath mine. My fear of disappointing him was almost as strong as my fear of his hurting me. Both proved to be groundless. While I expected him to take me with as little prelude as a goat, he showed himself charmed by every contour of my body. He tickled and touched and tongued until I shrieked and squirmed in delight. Who would have thought that the crook of my arm and the back of my knee would be so tingly or that my breasts would thrill to a mouth other than a child's? Ecstasy surged through me as he removed my under-tunic, exposing the part permitted only to him. He pulled off his loincloth and entered me, both celebrating and dissolving the distinctions that had ruled my life ever since I'd learnt about Adam and Eve. Any soreness was lost in a welter of sensations so intoxicating that the stains on the bedsheet the next morning might as well have been wine. What's more, when he hung it over the gate like a victory banner, I felt no shame.

Straight afterwards, he left for the palace as though we had been married for ten or even twenty years. I asked him lightly if he put his duty to the king before his duty to his wife. 'Of course,' he said, and I assumed that he was joking, only to discover that Hittites don't joke. Israelites do, of course, and he told me that the king had teased him about his wedding night, which he clearly found distasteful, although he wouldn't admit it. I was eager to meet the man who inspired such devotion and Uriah promised to take me to one of the palace feasts. Grandfather, whose unease at the prospect showed how little he trusted me to foster the links that were his life's work, reminded me that I had met the king already, when he attended my father's entombment. But I had been so daunted by the stories of his punishing disobedient children that I hadn't raised my eyes above his knees.

Uriah had no family and I knew none of his comrades' wives, so my grandfather was my only visitor, although his visits felt more like a tithe collector's than a guest's. For the rest, I was left to my own devices and those of Matred, our Edomite bond-woman, who, I was astounded to learn, had been a priestess in the service of their god, Qaus. I was horrified, then intrigued, then horrified again when she told me that they venerated Qaus not with animal blood but with human seed and their means of extracting it were those of a harlot.

'Did you use them on Uriah?' I asked, wondering if that were why he insisted I treat her with respect.

'No!' she replied, outraged. 'The master is a good man, the best I've ever known. When your troops vanquished ours, they came into the grove that was our sanctuary and violated the women, as if our bodies were dedicated to the worshippers rather than the god. The master put an end to it, although some of the men were so crazed that they challenged him. He would never do anything dishonourable.'

I see this for myself when he lies with me each night, no matter how far he has ridden during the day. While careful to show my gratitude, I assure him that I shan't be offended if one night he wishes to rest, whereupon he explains that the same Law that requires a wife to be clean for her husband requires a husband to satisfy his wife.

'So it's your duty?' I ask, as evenly as possible.

'Which I discharge with pleasure,' he says, smiling. Such a mixture of duty and pleasure is his precept for happiness.

I shall fulfil that precept when I bear a child. I am seventeen years old and have been married for almost a year. How much longer must I wait? Each night as he withdraws from me, I pray that he has filled me with new life, but I bleed as regularly as if my body were a calendar. My frustration is set to continue, since he is leaving to fight the Ammonites, whose king, Hanun, has dishonoured our emissaries in a manner too obscene for Uriah to describe. The king is sending Joab with an army to avenge them. On the eve of their departure, I join the many women making offerings to the Lord but, while I pray for the men's safe return, my foremost prayer is that he will use this last evening to make me fruitful. My hopes are dashed when Uriah sleeps alone, explaining that he and his men also went to the tabernacle, where they swore to abstain from lying with their wives until they achieve victory.

I resign myself to weeks – perhaps months – of loneliness, with nothing to divert me but my loom. I have promised to make Uriah a new mantle but leave most of the work to Matred, whose fingers are more nimble and mind less abstracted than mine. When my monthly blood flows, I am tempted to avoid the weary climb and jet of chilly water but, for all our shared secrets, I'm aware that Matred's first loyalty is to Uriah and fear that she might betray me. So I make my way to the roof. Cleansed, I return to my chamber and have scarcely finished dressing when I'm startled by an insistent knocking at the gate.

No casual caller would come so late and, as Matred hurries

downstairs, I'm tortured by the thought that Uriah has been wounded – or worse. But she returns with a spidery man whose imperious smile, otherwise so disconcerting, cannot herald bad news. He announces himself as Jonadab, the king's nephew and steward of the palace. I bow low, which he seems to expect. Looking up, I see his lean cheeks, as pink as a child's, and the trim beard confined to his chin, but the lamp is too dim to make out his eyes. He presses his thumbs under his arms like a bat's wings.

'What is it that they call you, my lady?'

I laugh with relief. If he doesn't know me, he can't have news for me and must be visiting the neighbourhood.

'Forgive me. I am Bathsheba bat Eliam. My husband, Uriah, is a captain in the king's guard. My grandfather, Ahitophel, is his chief counsellor.'

'I know them well,' he says, although the acquaintance seems to perturb him. 'But what of you? Do you also wish to serve the king?'

'I am a woman.'

'Nonetheless. The king has sent me to summon you.'

'Why?' My fears return. 'Has something happened to Uriah?'

'Possibly.' He shrugs. 'News travels slowly.'

'Then why?'

'No need to play the innocent with me!' He moves close. Now I see his eyes and shrink from their malice. 'Come!'

'At this hour?'

'To the king, all hours are equal. Woman, fetch your mistress's mantle!'

Matred does as he bids. I look to her for an explanation, but she refuses to meet my gaze. As I follow Jonadab, I realise that I have only ever ventured out this late in dreams. We enter the palace courtyard and I'm heartened by the soldiers standing guard, who remind me of Uriah. I long to explore and round out his all-too-terse descriptions, but Jonadab beckons me forward. We climb two sets of stairs, the first wide and shallow, the second narrow and steep. Once again I find myself on the roof, although this one is higher and, while it may be my imagination, the air feels fresher. I fill my lungs and forget the peremptory summons as I survey the city below me, glittering in the starlight. Suddenly, a voice, hitherto reserved for crowds, addresses me.

'He found you. That's good. Very good.' Jonadab falls to his knees and, with a tug of my robe, pulls me down beside him. 'Up, up!' the voice says testily. I know that it is the king's but I am anxious not to acknowledge it too soon.

'Bathsheba, wife of Uriah, captain of the guard, my lord,' Jonadab says.

'Uriah? So your husband is at war?'

'Yes, my lord. I trust that no harm has come to him.'

'What? No, of course not.' He advances on me and grips my chin. It smarts. I close my eyes and sense that he's appraising me much as my grandmother did a prospective servant. 'Good, good.' He moves away and I seize the opportunity to study him. Except for my father's obsequies, I have seen him only in parades and processions and presumed that the distance made him seem small. His chest and belly are round and firm. His hair is thin and grey and his scalp flaky, but his face, although heavily lined, remains handsome. For all that, his looks are less imposing than his presence. He exudes gravity and power, even splendour. 'Why are you still here? Go, go!' he says to Jonadab, who bows and leaves with an unbroken grin, as if inured to such rebukes, after which the king walks back to me. The night is so still that I hear his breath, which comes faster than his steady gait might suggest.

'I have longed to see you again.'

'My lord must be mistaken. He hasn't seen me since I was a girl.'

'There's no need to be coy.' He takes my arm and pulls me towards the parapet. My heart pounds in terror that he intends to throw me off. 'Look!' He points to a house two streets away, its roof in full view. How can I have been so blind? Like a child who shuts her eyes and imagines that she can't be seen, I have assumed that because I can't look up to the palace roof, no one on the palace roof can look down on me.

'I was walking here earlier this evening and I saw you bathe. I thought I must be dreaming. Then I saw you dry yourself and knew that I was awake.'

'I'm so ashamed, my lord. I had no idea that I could be overseen.'

'Really? Everyone in the city knows that I come up here in the evenings. When an easterly wind blows, the palace is stifling. This is the only cool spot. I've had the servants make up a bed.'

I follow his hand to the bed, its rumpled sheets as indecorous as my unemptied tub. 'Forgive me, my lord. While my husband's away, I live quietly. I hear no news from outside. I didn't know that it was your custom.'

'And I say you did!' His abrupt roar makes me quake, but more frightening than his fury is his certitude. 'Why else would you bathe in the open?'

'To obey the Law, my lord,' I reply, keen to remind him of an authority higher than his own. 'I was purifying myself after my monthly flow.'

'Must you?' he asks, flinching. I'm surprised that a man who has shed so much blood should recoil from that which issues naturally. 'So now you're free to lie with a man again?'

'But Uriah is away.'

'Yes, of course. Is he a good husband?'

'He's the only one I have.'

He laughs as if I've made a joke. 'He has done me worthy service. If all goes well, he should advance.'

I glimpse his meaning but blot it out, in case he sees the horror in my eyes. 'If all goes well in the campaign, my lord?' I ask.

'There and elsewhere,' he says, with another laugh. 'I long to be with them, outside the walls of Rabbah, instead of stuck at home. At least I did until tonight.'

'You should be there, my lord,' I say, desperate to distract him. 'The city could be taken in half – a quarter – of the time.' I recall Uriah's reverence for him. 'The men would fight twice as hard with their king at their head.'

'My nephew Joab and his generals think otherwise. They claim that my presence in the field is too great a risk. What would happen if I were to be injured or even killed? It's true that I have sons, but the oldest is only eighteen. I have yet to settle – ' He breaks off. 'The real reason of course is that they consider me too old… no longer the man I was. So what does that make Joab, who's three years older? How old would you say I am?'

'Sixty,' I reply hesitantly.

'Sixty!'

'I was about to say that you are as wise as a man of sixty, although you look no more than forty.'

He smiles and I breathe again, whereupon he lunges at me, stinging my lips with a kiss. 'You're right. I'll show you I'm a match for men twenty years younger.' He grabs me with one hand, while with the other he wrenches the mantle off my back. I try both to resist and shame him, thrusting him away and shouting: 'No, my lord, please! Think of your honour… Uriah… your daughters… the Lord!' My words have no effect as he grips the top of my robe, tearing Matred's delicate embroidery. My nail catches his neck and draws blood. At once he smacks me across the cheek. I am startled and hurt but above all relieved to have halted his attack. I know that I must pay for my defiance. He will banish me to the wastes of the Negeb, but Uriah will join me and we shall be free.

'Make no mistake,' he says. 'I am not a man who likes to fight for his pleasures. I fought for the kingdom. The rest I take as my right.'

'Am I my lord's subject or my lord's slave?'

'Both, if I wish it.' He stares at me coldly, but the coldness in his heart hasn't quenched the fire in his loins. He clutches my mantle, now hanging off one shoulder, pulling it to the ground.

'I shall scream.'

'Go ahead. This is a palace; people are accustomed to screams.'

Trapped and silenced, I know that I am lost. He rips off my robe so brutally that I suspect he is picturing it as my flesh. I am overwhelmed by his odour: not the heavy smell of a day's exertion but the reek of a stew left too long on the hearth. His mouth catches mine and our teeth clack. His hands squeeze my breasts so tightly that he seems intent on making them one. He drags me to the bed, cursing as he trips on my trailing robe. He sprawls over me, sweating and salivating, and his wetness is as loathsome as his weight. I pretend that I am a doll, telling myself that I've been wicked and must be punished, as if this violence – this violation – were my own choice. He presses his hand over my mouth and I wonder if I have spoken my reproach out loud or if the very quiver of my lips offends him. I bite his palm but, with my mouth crushed, it's a mere peck. I look up at the stars and try to work out which is Kimah and which Kezil, but his sweat blurs my vision. He rams into me as if he were storming a citadel. Then, croaking like a frog before rain, he topples forward and rolls across the bed. He grabs my under-tunic and covers his loins, less, I feel sure, to protect his modesty than his pride.

He claps his hands and the summons is answered with dismaying speed by Jonadab, who compounds my shame as he passes me my robe. Although I recognise it, I am uncertain what it's for, as though the injury I've suffered is to the head. 'Do you want help?' he asks, and the threat of his slithery fingers touching my skin rouses me. I snatch the robe from him and pull it on, its rips matching my own. I stand upright, aching even in parts of my body that the king hasn't mauled, and stoop for my mantle, drawing it around me like a shroud. Jonadab offers me his arm, which I slap away. Looking hurt, he steers me towards the stairs, his hand a palm's breadth from my shoulder. Before going down, I turn to take a last – what I trust will be my last – look at the king, who lies slumped on the bed, not acknowledging or seemingly aware of me. Jonadab leads me back through the courtyard, which is still lined with soldiers. I feel an intense urge to shriek out my story, enlightening them about the king they serve, but I doubt that they would be shocked. My life has changed more in two hours than in seventeen years, and I suspect that every man would be a David if he had the chance.

Quitting the palace, we enter a street that's unaccountably calm. The people may be asleep, but I wonder that the stones themselves don't cry out against the king's villainy. I swat a fly from my ear, only to discover that it is Jonadab's chatter.

'The king is an incomparable lover,' he says and, the next thing I know, he is carrying me into my courtyard. 'Don't be alarmed!' he tells Matred. 'Your mistress swooned in the street, overawed by her good fortune.'

'I'll take care of her,' Matred says. 'You may go, my lord.'

Jonadab looks aggrieved. 'Of course. But first…' He shakes down his sleeve to reveal a whorl of gold bands. He removes one and gives it to me.

'For you.'

'From you?' I ask in confusion.

'From the king,' he says, and I wonder whether he hands them out like a foreman's pim stones.

'I don't want it,' I say, giving it back.

'You will,' he says, dropping it at my feet. He then turns and leaves, as though discarding me with equal ease.

Matred helps me up the stairs and bathes me with the rose water I was saving for Uriah's return. Uriah! But I mustn't think of him. I clasp her wrist as she wipes the fluids cruelly mingled on my loins.

'You'll say nothing to the master,' I order or ask or plead, her loyalty to Uriah now my prime concern.

'What is there to say? My lady is well. She is young and healthy. She may be bruised but bruises fade.'

I want to kiss her but my lips are tainted, so I squeeze her hand.

Loneliness is my salvation as, with so few visitors, I have little call to lie. My wounds mend and my pains diminish, but my eyes remain raw, welling with tears even when I'm not feeling sad. The news from Rabbah is disheartening. The Ammonites have mounted a vigorous defence, receiving support from their old allies, the Arameans. Matred returns from the well with reports that the king of Damascus has sent twenty thousand reinforcements (a figure that my grandfather derides). Having longed for Uriah's return, I'm now grateful for the delay, since I am not yet ready to face him. I can talk without stuttering; I can even smile when Matred prompts me; but my body needs time to accept that Uriah isn't David. Until then, I'm afraid of pushing him away.

Matred, whose body was a conduit for her god's worship, exhorts me to forget my violation, as if the darkness and the hour enable me to dismiss it as a dream. But I wrestle with it night and day. Why did the king want me when he is rumoured to keep a harem of a hundred women – wives, concubines and slave-girls – to satisfy his every desire? Was he prowling the roof, bitter at being kept from the field? Was he so hungry for conquest that any woman would have served his purpose, or did something in me arouse him? Was I enjoying the sensation of the water on my skin... the soap on my skin... my skin itself... too much? I vow that, no matter how vehemently Uriah protests, I shall never bathe in the open again.

Six weeks later, I discover that the need for such bathing has passed. At first I think... I hope... I lie to myself that the shock of the violation has disrupted my monthly cycle. Never before have I yearned for the nagging cramps in my belly and thighs. In their place I endure a queasiness the moment I wake, which returns whenever I eat or drink, smell or even see food. Matred tempts me with simple dishes of butter-milk, lentil cakes and porridge, but I reason that if I starve myself, the new life – the living death – inside me will wither. I implore her to obtain some of the purgative herbs that her fellow priestesses took on falling pregnant, but she claims that they only grow in Edom. When I challenge her, she adds that they're poisonous and several of the women died. In desperation, I consider confiding in my grandfather but, when the occasion arises, I'm too ashamed. So I take the one course left to me and appeal to the man I had hoped never to see again, not even leading a victory parade.

My grandmother urged my grandfather not to teach me to write, arguing that nothing good would come of it. Had I had a brother, I've no doubt that he would have agreed, but he was determined to pass on his learning to his only grandchild. Never have I been more indebted to him than now, when I write to the king, begging him for a private audience. On the appointed day I take the petition to the palace and wait at the door of the great chamber with one other woman in a huddle of men. She informs me that her husband died last year and his brother has laid claim to his land. She's appealing to the king to protect her sons' inheritance.

'What about you?' she asks indifferently.

'My husband is in the army at Rabbah. His mother is dying and I'm requesting that he be granted leave to see her.'

Never before have I lied so easily, but then never before have I had such cause. I enter the chamber and, after giving my name, hear the official announce 'Bathsheba, wife of Uriah, captain of the king's guard.' I steel myself to stare at the king but, if he feels any remorse, he hides it as well as I do my repugnance. Emulating the widow, I fall to my knees and crawl forward to kiss his feet, which threaten to sicken me more than the greasiest stew, but I've reckoned without my grandfather. How can I have forgotten that he would be here, indeed standing beside the throne? He leans over and whispers to the king who nods and, before I can reach him, Grandfather grabs me and hauls me out of the chamber. We linger in the passage while he catches his breath.

'Why must you try to cause trouble for me?'

'I don't! Why would you think that?'

'Coming here, disturbing the king! He knows full well that you're my granddaughter.'

'He does?' Since when? Did he make the connection when I mentioned Uriah? Did it add to his excitement? If so, his offence is even more odious.

'If you have a problem, why didn't you ask me?'

I cannot repeat the lie I told the widow to a man who knows that Uriah's mother is long dead. Yet nor can I tell the truth to a man who cradled me as a baby.

'Speak to Jonadab,' I say quietly.

He frowns, as though aware of Jonadab's services to the king. 'Why? What do you have to do with him?'

'He came to the house at night six weeks ago. He brought me here.'

Even the oblique admission consoles me. But I'm forgetting Grandfather's age and, as he stands immobile, I fear that my words may have brought on a seizure. He fails to respond when I stroke or shake him, so I call for help. But before any arrives, he recovers, grasps my hand and marches me through the palace. We reach a door guarded by a soldier, who reddens as he bars the way.

'This is the harem, my lord. You must not enter.'

'It's not I who must not enter but my granddaughter. And I intend to make sure that she never does,' he says fiercely. 'Is Jonadab here?'

'I think so, my lord.'

'Call him.'

'This is the harem?' I ask, as the guard bangs on the door. Grandfather nods grimly. I long to step into the courtyard, which has fired my imagination ever since I watched the palace being built, but I know better than to betray my interest. 'And no man can enter?'

'Not if he values his life.'

'Except for Jonadab?'

'A shepherd who eats no mutton.'

His lip remains curled as the man in question opens the door.

'My lord, a pleasure but – ' Seeing me, he breaks off, a less practised dissembler than his uncle.

'Ask him what you need to know, Grandfather. I can't speak for shame, but it's the king's shame, not mine.'

'What's that?' Jonadab asks, regaining his composure. 'The king's only shame comes from unscrupulous subjects who traduce him.'

'Ask him, Grandfather. Ask how he came to the house in the dead of night and brought me here. Ask him!'

'You should curb your granddaughter's tongue,' Jonadab says. 'If it weren't for my respect for you, I'd – '

'You'd what?' Grandfather asks, with a cold fury that makes Jonadab cower.

'Do you know how many women claim to have lain with the king? An Asherite even swore recently that he impregnated her in a dream. I repeat, out of respect for you, I shall say nothing of this to the king.' He makes to go back into the harem. Grandfather grips his shoulder.

'My granddaughter is with child.'

I gasp. Jonadab turns and slowly removes the hand. 'Then it's a blessing that she has a husband.' He slips back into the harem. Grandfather stares at the door as if weighing up whether to follow him but, as the guard stiffens, he ushers me away. We walk back in silence and I wonder how he knew about the child. Am I putting on flesh already? Or is it the one thing that would have compelled me to act? We return home where he sits and broods, dismissing everything Matred brings him except for a cup of water.

'I've served him faithfully for twenty years,' he says at last. 'When King Saul died, I could have offered my allegiance to Ishbaal. With both Abner and me by his side, who knows what he might have achieved? And this is how David repays me! This is how he dishonours me!'

I expect him to chastise me, as he has for so many other transgressions, however unwitting. But while I am grateful that he's directing his anger at the king, I fear that he's ignoring the urgency of my predicament. 'I'm six weeks with child. Uriah has been away for twelve. What are we to do?'

'That snake, Jonadab, was right. You have a husband.'

'But when will he come home?'

'At once. We still have time. The baby will be born two months early. It will be his.'

'You want me to deceive him?' This isn't leaving a sack of grain outside and blaming it on Matred; this is giving him a firstborn not of his blood. Even if, like Rebecca, I one day contrive an exchange of birthright, I will have grossly abused his trust.

'Would you rather be stoned? That's the penalty for adulterers. Not for the king of course. He may not even know when the sentence is carried out.'

I feel the rocks raining down on me, the breath seeping out of me, and know that I must acquiesce. 'But how can we arrange for Uriah to return?'

'We can't; the king can.'

'And will he?'

'Oh yes. Not for my honour and certainly not for yours, but for his own. He sleeps in comfort while his soldiers snatch what rest they can on the rough ground. Would they be so loyal if they knew that, while they're fighting his wars, he's bedding their wives?'

Grandfather leaves to confront the king. The next morning, an unusually subdued Jonadab escorts me to the palace, where I find Grandfather alone with the king in his private chamber. From his expression, it's clear that they have reached an agreement, and I fall to my knees in both obeisance and relief.

The king commands me to take a seat. 'I've done you a grave injustice and I ask your pardon,' he says, with such studied humility that I'm convinced he is picturing penitence rather than feeling it. 'I have insulted you and, worse, I have insulted your grandfather, who's served me so steadfastly.' I bridle at that *worse*, although Grandfather seems to accept it as his due. 'The child you bear must be your husband's. I have sons from wives whose first husbands are dead. And a wife whom I married twice and yet bore me no son.' From his ill-concealed rancour, I know that he is speaking of Princess Michal, whose plight is whispered throughout the city. 'But I can have no son from the wife of one of my captains. So I've summoned Uriah to report on the progress of the campaign. The moment that's done, I will send him home and you will conceive your child. He will be born two months early but lusty and strong as befits such a father.'

'Thank you, my lord,' Grandfather says. I glimpse a new jewel gleaming on his finger and swallow a wave of nausea stronger than any from my womb.

'No, it won't work,' I interject, seized once again by panic. 'Forgive me, my lord, but Uriah has taken the soldier's oath not to lie with me until the war is won.' I wonder at his forgetting it, since he professed to have made just such an oath when he begged for the consecrated bread at Nob.

'Surely you can find a way to make him break it?' he says, much to my disgust. Doesn't he care that his army consists of men who have taken the selfsame oath and that the Lord's favour depends on their keeping it? 'How can any man resist your charms? Why, even I...' He has the grace to fall silent.

Grandfather takes me home. 'Didn't I tell you that I would

settle things? And remember, it's the king who has betrayed Uriah, not you. But I'll never forgive him,' he says bitterly. 'I'll continue to serve him, but I'll never forgive him, not even once you've borne Uriah a host of sons.'

Rabbah is two days' journey from the city, so three days pass before Grandfather sends word that Uriah has arrived at the palace. I immediately prepare for his return, bathing – in my chamber – and scenting myself with calamus and spikenard, braiding my hair and painting my cheeks and lips. Matred cooks her master's favourite stew of pigeon, lentils, leeks and onions. Night falls; the pot simmers on the hearth, yet he still hasn't come home. At Matred's insistence I lie down, but I refuse to take off my clothes or scrub my face and, when I wake the next morning, my robe is crumpled and my pillow smeared with ochre. In a torment of uncertainty, I send Matred to the palace for news.

She returns two hours later, her measured breath mocking my impatience. 'Well?' I ask, suppressing the urge to shake her.

'I saw the master.'

'He's still at the palace?'

'Yes. At the end of last night's feast, the king gave him leave to come home, but he slept at the gatehouse.'

'Why? Does he suspect me? Have Jonadab or my grandfather let something slip? Have you?'

'How can you even ask?' I stroke her arm in remorse. 'He told me that he couldn't sleep in a clean bed while his men lie in the open or in airless tents, assailed by flies and locusts.'

'That sounds like him,' I say, despairing of the decency I once admired. 'Did you tell him how much I ache to see him?'

'Of course.'

'And it didn't sway him?'

'He said that he's writing to you.'

'Writing! What use is that? I can't conceive from a scroll!'

'Hush, my lady. As soon as I left him, I went to see Lord

Ahitophel. He told me that the king is to keep the master here another day. Tonight, he'll order him to visit you.'

'There was a time when he didn't need to be ordered. But no matter, so long as he comes.'

Once again he fails to appear. Once again I primp myself and Matred prepares a meal. My grandfather even orders one of the palace musicians to play for us, but his plangent chords heighten my misery and I send him away at midnight. Once again I dispatch Matred to the palace at daybreak, but she returns minutes later with my grandfather, who informs me that Uriah has already left for Rabbah.

'What? Why? Why didn't you stop him?'

'How could I challenge the king? I was present when he summoned Uriah to a second meeting. Having heard his account of the battle the day before, he asked for his assessment of the various commanders. Afterwards Uriah spoke to me, worried that the king wanted him to denounce his fellow officers. I did my best to reassure him, but I could tell that he wasn't convinced. Then at dinner, the king plied him with wine, trying to get him so drunk that he would forget his oath. I thought he'd succeeded when Uriah staggered out of the chamber amid gales of laughter. But he collapsed in the courtyard and the guard, knowing no better, carried him to the gatehouse where he spent another night. The king has only just found out and, in a fury, he's sent him straight back to the front.'

'No, he can't! He must recall him. What am I to do?'

'Don't worry. The king has a new plan.'

'What plan?'

'A plan. That's all you need know.'

'But – '

'No buts. Meanwhile, Uriah wrote you this letter, which I forgot to give you yesterday.'

Grandfather has barely quit the chamber when I tear open the seal as if the clay were butter. I skim through the message and finding no word of reproof, read it closely: To Bathsheba, wife of Uriah. You will have heard that I'm in the city. I long to visit you, but I must stay away. The king is behaving most strangely. He assures me that I am one of his finest captains, so he must know that my place is in the field. Yet he calls me back for a report that he might have obtained from any messenger. From the questions he asks, I fear that he suspects my loyalty. He's testing me by suggesting that I spend the night with you, since he knows that, were I to do so, I'd break my oath to the Lord, who would withdraw his favour not just from me but from the men under my command. I trust you'll understand that I must forbear from seeing you until the campaign is won and we can lie together with the Lord's blessing.

Six days later, Grandfather brings me the news that Uriah is dead. 'He died the very day that he returned to the field.'

'How? Who killed him? Was that the king's plan?'

'No,' Grandfather says forcibly. 'You mustn't think that. And most of all, you mustn't say it. It was a coincidence, a happy one.'

'Not for Uriah!' I am flooded with memories of his goodness, his gentleness, his strength, and the stories he told of his life before he came to the land. I long to mourn the man with whom I was expecting to spend the rest of my life, but the cramps in my belly distract me and all I can think of is what his death means for my child. Desperate to focus my mind, I ask Grandfather how he died.

'As a hero,' he says. 'The messenger made that clear. With the siege dragging on, Joab tried to break the deadlock by sending a unit to attack the gates. After a brief foray, they were to pretend to fall back, drawing the enemy into the open, where a second unit would ambush them. At which point the main body of troops would storm the city.'

'But at the gates, wouldn't they be exposed to arrows and stones and every other sort of missile fired from the ramparts?'

'No doubt, which is why they were ordered to advance with all speed and retreat before the casualties grew too heavy. But things didn't go according to plan.'

'Did the ambush succeed?'

'I have no idea. Uriah's dead. What does it matter?'

'I'd like to think that he didn't die in vain.'

Joab himself brings Uriah's body back from Rabbah. Grandfather arranges to bury him in the new tomb he has built on the Mount of Olives. I am touched by the number of mourners who accompany the bier across the valley. I recognise a few of them: Abiathar the high priest and Nathan the prophet, who have come to honour my grandfather as much as Uriah; a group of Uriah's fellow officers, led by Joab. The rest are strangers, among them several women beating their breasts and wailing who, I presume, have either been paid by my grandfather or else owe him a service. It grieves me that Uriah must go to his tomb amid the same dissimulation that he went to his death.

Abiathar leads the lamentations and he, my grandfather and Joab follow the corpse into the tomb. Despite my grandfather's pointed gaze, I refuse to join them. The sepulchre stone is replaced and we return to the city, where Joab and Abiathar take their leave. The rest of the mourners come back to the house for the feast. No one speaks to me and I feel as though I have been buried alongside Uriah. In the evening, after the company has left and while Matred is clearing the debris, Joab arrives unexpectedly.

'I've come to pay my respects,' he says, as if to an enemy with whom he wishes to fight but has been obliged to parlay. 'Uriah was one of my most valued officers.'

'Thank you. You may go; I'll take care of that,' I say to Matred, who hands Joab a dish of fig cakes. He puts one in his mouth and swallows it whole.

'Besides, I wanted to see if you were worth it.'

'Worth what?'

'Uriah's death. The king's shame. The army's first defeat in years.'

'No, stay,' I say to Matred, who is halfway to the storeroom. I struggle to stop shaking and turn back to Joab. 'The king told you?'

'Give me some credit! When one of my best captains hands me a sealed scroll from the king, ordering me to put him at the forefront of the next attack and leave him unprotected, I know that it isn't a matter of strategy. Either the man has offended against the king or the king against the man. Given the persons involved, I opt for the latter. "So how can the king have offended?" I ask myself and make an informed guess.' Abandoning all semblance of courtesy, he moves towards me and presses his hand to my stomach. 'No, not big-bellied yet.' I gasp and see Matred running up behind him, clasping a knife, but he turns and effortlessly knocks first the weapon and then the woman to the ground. She crawls away, groaning and clutching her mouth. I long to go to her aid, but Joab's brutality has stunned me. 'Don't make the mistake of thinking me as noble as Uriah. Where was I? Oh yes. More than one hundred men died in the attack. There are wives and mothers and daughters across the land mourning their husbands and sons and fathers.'

'I knew nothing of it, I swear.'

'Of course not; you women never do. I only wish that when the king decided to betray one of my officers, he'd chosen one who was more expendable... Go ahead, cry all you like; I'm not stopping you. But ask yourself who you're crying for: your husband, his men, or yourself now you find that you're not who you thought you were, now your hands are sticky with more than mutton fat and olive oil.'

'What about you?' I sniff away my tears and confront him. 'If you supposed the order so wrong, why did you uphold it?'

'Would you have me defy my king? Believe me, I considered it. But then I realised the consequences of what David had done. My troops have been camped outside Rabbah for months, sweltering in the heat, gagging on the dust and staving off boredom. The one thing that sustains them is their love for the king: the king who has led them to so many glorious victories; the king who, when three of his soldiers risked their lives to bring him water, refused to drink it but poured it as a libation to the Lord in thanksgiving for his having protected them. What would it do to their resolve to learn that, while they were suffering in the field, the king was making free with their wives?'

'My grandfather asked the same question.'

'With good reason.'

'But how would they have found out?'

'Because Uriah did.'

'No, that's not true!'

'He told me so himself. And I admired his constancy more than ever. He came back to the city two weeks ago.'

'The king summoned him.'

'He slept at the palace. The guards told him what had occurred. One – or maybe more of them – saw you leave late at night, hair and robe awry. They thought it only right that he should know.'

'All he told me was that he feared the king suspected his loyalty.'

'He showed the king more loyalty than he deserved. As he did me. When I gave the order to charge the gates, an order that he knew meant certain death – unless, of course, there were a miracle, and David saves those for himself – he told me that he knew why. He'd worked out that he'd brought his own death warrant. How could David have been so rash? What if Uriah had opened it along the way?'

'He trusted him not to.'

'You're right. He reckoned on his sense of honour: honour he displayed to the very end, when he promised me that he'd say nothing to his men. He'd carry out my order as if it had been issued in good faith.'

'Did he mention me?'

'You? No. The man was living his last moments; why would he waste them? But my concern isn't Uriah; it's David. Because of you, he has behaved with cruelty, ingratitude and gross stupidity.' He shakes his head in bewilderment and I'm convinced that he – a man as dry as the desert – is about to cry. 'And there's worse. Because of you, I can never look at him in the same way again: the king I've served for more than thirty years, whose life I value more than my own, is tainted forever.'

He leaves me and I feel as crushed as if I had endured the full weight of the Law. I should have confessed what happened and accepted my punishment, thereby saving the lives of Uriah and his men. No stone could wound me more deeply than Joab's charges... I break off, appalled at my callousness. Here I am unscathed while Uriah lies in his tomb, covered in myrrh and honey, food for flies. He knew; Uriah knew! He went to his death willingly and wittingly. But why? Was it to free me or to indict me? Did he wish my unborn child to inherit his honour or my shame? Matred moans, and I turn to see her lips speckled with blood and foam. She smiles wanly – at least I think she does since, when she opens her mouth, I see that Joab has knocked out two of her front teeth.

Determined to observe the law of mourning if of nothing else, I attend the tabernacle first three days and then seven days after the obsequies, to be cleansed of the defilement of Uriah's corpse. But nothing can cleanse me of the defilement of my own skin. Meanwhile, Grandfather sets his mind to securing my future. Uriah's death may have removed the threat to my life, but what of my house? It is reserved for a captain of the guard, with no guarantee that the king will allow me to stay. When Grandfather tackles him, his response is to offer me a place in his harem.

'What's worse is that he thinks he's being magnanimous,' Grandfather says, unable to contain his outrage.

'So what did you tell him?'

'That no granddaughter of mine will be a concubine and, unless he consents to marry you, I shall trumpet his offence throughout the kingdom: not just what he did to you but what he did to Uriah.'

'How did he react?' I ask, astounded by his temerity.

'Exactly as you'd expect. He blustered that he was the king, that he'd hang me and throw my corpse on to the city dung-hill. But I stood my ground. I'm sixty-three years old; I owe the Lord a death. And the king backed down.' I am dumb-struck. 'He has issued a proclamation that he will honour the dead warrior, Uriah, by taking his widow as his wife.'

By rights we should wait ninety days until we marry. The reason, which would be comical if it weren't so sad, is to ensure that any child I might bear him isn't Uriah's. But, as he proved by remarrying Princess Michal while her second husband lived, he reads the Law from a tattered scroll. So I have scarcely taken off my mourning when I must put on my finest linen. It is the same robe that I wore to marry Uriah, to whom I remain wedded in my heart. Jonadab comes to fetch me, as sinisterly smug as ever. He peels off a bracelet, as he did once before, and hands it to me; I long to fling it back in his face or, better still, thrust it down his throat, but with a grateful smile, I slip it like a fetter on my wrist. He leads me through the main gate of the palace and, if he reg-isters the contrast to our previous visit, he shows no sign. We enter the harem, where twenty or so women stand, sit and loll, in clusters and alone. I cannot work out which of them are wives, which concubines and which slaves: distinc-tions that, I suspect, are blurred at night. A heavily jewelled woman in a purple robe walks up to me. Her face is kindly but so blotched and wrinkled that I take her for the king's sister, since no man would want her in his bed. I discover my mistake when she introduces herself as Abigail, the king's first wife.

'Forgive me, but I understood that was Princess Michal. Is she dead?'

'She might as well be,' a second woman interjects. She is younger than Abigail and plumply pretty, as though her features were fashioned in dough.

'She offended the king. She lives in the harem but secluded,' Abigail says.

'Imprisoned?' I ask.

'Secluded,' she says firmly, before introducing the plump woman as Ahinoam, mother of the king's eldest son, whom I have seen strutting through the city as if waiting for the day when he can rename it *The City of Amnon*. She then presents me to a group of women sitting around an ornamental pond, all of whom are wives. Several others, from whom if I am to preserve my status I must keep my distance, are concubines. But I am most intrigued to meet two of the king's daughters. His eldest, Tamar, who is about my age, hurries over to greet me and asks whether I will be her friend with the candour of someone whose trust has never been betrayed. She leads me to her younger sister, Nechama, who sits strumming a lyre, a skill she informs me that she learnt from their father. They are both unhappy because their mother, Maacah, is in disgrace and, like Princess Michal, confined to her chamber.

'What for?' I ask.

'Nothing,' Tamar says. 'At least nothing she's done. Her father, our grandfather, the king of Geshur, tore up his treaty with Father and sent troops to assist the Ammonites in Rabbah. It's so unfair. It's not her fault yet she's the one being punished.'

The wives all know my story but no one condemns me. 'It will be our first child since Eliphelet four years ago. It's good to know he can still function,' Ahinoam says, with welcome if shocking irreverence.

'It's like drawing water from a dried-up well,' Huldath, Eliphelet's mother, interjects, showing that the irreverence is shared.

'That's enough now,' Abigail says, although her smile gives her away.

'I think you're all horrid,' Tamar says, putting her fingers in her ears. 'I shan't listen.'

'Very wise, my dear,' Abigail replies.

'She doesn't get that from her mother,' Ahinoam says.

'Honestly, what will Bathsheba think of us?' asks another woman whose name I fail to catch.

'I love you all already,' I reply, although the truth is that I love being part of them; I doubt I shall love any one of them for herself, except Tamar.

A bondwoman – I have far too many names in my head to trouble with hers – takes me to my chamber, which is small but cooler than my chamber at home… what used to be home. I rest until Jonadab arrives to escort me to the main court-yard, where I watch the king and my grandfather sign the marriage contract. The king barely acknowledges me, except to glance with relief at my flat belly, which makes me wonder how closely he followed the births of his many children. His four eldest sons attend him, led by Prince Amnon, who studies me with all the interest that his father lacked. I force myself to return his smile. Not even the greatest king lives forever and my child's fate may hang on his successor's goodwill. The ceremony over, the women bring me to the feast. Much of the talk, far freer than I would have expected, concerns the king's capriciousness. I'm unsure whether they're trying to caution me or to intimidate me, but either way it's too late. Although I have assigned our first encounter to another Bathsheba, a Bathsheba who lies buried with Uriah, I cannot ignore his veiled threat that the palace is accustomed to screams. I can fight him and end up in seclusion like Princess Michal, or I can submit to him and live in comfort like ancient Abigail and plump Ahinoam.

Silence descends as the king leaves the courtyard. I feel a stab of revulsion at seeing him accompanied neither by Joab

nor by one of his sons but by Jonadab. After several minutes
and further ribald remarks, my grandfather collects me and
conducts me to the private chamber where the king waits with
Jonadab. There is no pomegranate on the threshold, but then
I suppose I am already too fruitful. Grandfather and Jonadab
return downstairs, the one with an encouraging smile and the
other with his customary leer, and the king leads me inside. I
am grateful that my violation took place on the roof, so that
there's nothing here to remind me of it – apart, that is, from
the man himself. I wonder how much of what he did he recalls
or whether it has merged with the memory of other similar
assaults, albeit ones with fewer consequences. After offering
me a cup of wine and telling me to lay my robe on the chest,
he undresses as guilelessly as a child.

My courage falters when he turns to face me, naked but for
his loincloth and, in the lamplight, I scrutinize him as I failed
to do before: the hard, heavy stomach; the pouches of fat on
his chest like a budding girl; the patches of hair on his mottled
skin like a hastily scythed field. I take off my clothes and fold
them more carefully than usual, before following him to the
bed.

'I'm very tired,' he says, and I recall Ahinoam and Huldath's comments on his waning powers.

'Then you must rest, my lord.'

'It's my duty to pleasure you.'

'And you have, my lord. What greater pleasure can any
woman ask than to bear the king's son?' I screw up my eyes to
obscure the image of Uriah but, when I open them, it is still
there.

'You think that it will be a son?'

'I know it.' I place his right hand on my belly and trace
the baby's shape. Then I slip off my under-tunic and draw the
hand towards my loins. I sense his resistance. 'My lord must
think of nothing but himself. His servant is here to fulfil his
every desire.' Matred has taught me the practices that she

and her fellow priestesses employed to exact the tribute that their gods required: practices that disgust me but which, she insisted, worked on even the most modest of men. And as my belly attests, the king is far from that. This may be my one chance to secure his favour and my child's future. I shudder as I comprehend how much is at stake.

'You're trembling.'

'With longing, my lord.'

I slip down the bed and stroke his member, while letting my hair ripple across his thighs. I roll the member between my breasts and feel the strength seep into it. I take it in my mouth like an impure sea creature. Banishing the fear that such practices might be unique to the Edomites, I slowly slide my finger inside him. I wait for him to spring up and even strike me but, to my relief, he pushes down, wriggling and gasping with delight. When he spills his seed, I follow Matred's advice and swallow it, in tribute not to her gods but to his potency.

For several minutes, he lies in a stupor. His eyes water, although I'm not sure if it is a sign of gratitude or age. 'Who taught you those tricks?' he asks.

'Uriah,' I say. He blanches and then smiles.

'I haven't known such bliss since I was a youth with… in King Saul's palace.' His hatred for her is so intense that he won't even speak the princess's name.

He takes a ring from his finger and places it on mine before sending me back to the harem with Jonadab, whose brow is beaded with sweat. He summons me night after night and, with hardened deceit, I thank him for the honour. My dread that he might consider my conduct depraved or resent my taking the lead proves to be groundless. As he puts himself in my hands, I understand that his private chamber is the one place where he doesn't have to be the king. From time to time he displays – or affects – concern about me and I assure him that his pleasure is all that I crave. I squeeze, caress and excite him; then, when he's ready to spill his seed, I draw him inside me to fortify our unborn child.

The more I bolster my position with the king, the more I breed resentment in the other wives. Even Abigail, who adopts a pose of wry amusement towards intimacies that she has long abandoned (or that have abandoned her), looks jealously at the jewels the king lavishes on me. Eglah, the mother of thirteen-year-old Ithream and the gentlest of my rivals, tells me that the women are all amazed since, as soon as their bellies swelled, the king shunned them. So, even though I am nearing the end of my term, with the baby pinching my breath, pressing on my loins and weighing me down as if he were made not of flesh and blood but of stone, I answer the king's summons with a smile.

I enjoy a week's repose when he journeys to Rabbah, where Joab has broken through the Ammonite defences. Rather than take the city himself, he delays the final assault, leaving the king to claim the victory. The day after his return, the king sends for me but, instead of his usual display of affection, he greets me coldly. I drop to my knees. He beckons me to rise but so peremptorily that, braving his anger, I crawl towards him, rubbing my hands and face on his thighs, which smell of his mule.

'No,' he says, recoiling and leaving me sprawled on the floor. 'You don't understand; Nathan has spoken.' I feel a tremor of unease as he cites the one man in the kingdom with the power to chide him: Nathan, the wandering prophet whom my grandfather brought to the palace; Nathan, to whom the Lord speaks in dreams and visions, filling the king, to whom the Lord speaks only through the sacred stones, with both envy and awe.

'What did he say?' I ask, as I haul myself up.

'You are the poor man's lamb.'

'I don't follow.'

'And I'm the rich man who stole you.'

I beg him to explain, which he does with none of his usual precision. I gradually piece together the tale that Nathan has told him of a rich man with a flock of sheep and a poor man with a single lamb. A visitor arrives at the rich man's house and, instead of slaughtering one of his own sheep to feed him, he steals the poor man's lamb. The king was outraged and declared that the rich man should die – not that he should replace the stolen lamb with two or even three or four more, which would have recompensed the victim, but die. Whereupon, Nathan spelt out that he was the rich man and Uriah the poor man. He had no need to identify the lamb.

My immediate reaction is that he merits the rebuke, not just for his treatment of Uriah but for his obtuseness. Only a man so blind to his own faults could have failed to grasp Nathan's meaning. Prophets don't concern themselves with livestock for no reason.

'We shall atone, my lord,' I say, fondling his hand. 'We shall sacrifice a hundred sheep to the Lord. We shall dedicate our son to his service: a son who will be the strength and shield of his father.' I bite back *in his old age*. I place his hand on my belly, but he snatches it away as if from a corpse.

'The child will die. Nathan told me.'

'No! That's a lie! Feel it! How can he know?'

'He speaks with the voice of the Lord. Your belly is the cradle of death.' As if to refute the charge, the child kicks me.

'But he's blameless.'

'He won't survive a week from birth. He will be taken as my sin offering.'

Every muscle in my body stiffens with loathing for him, which is all that keeps me from collapse. The child for whom I have fattened and sickened and sprouted hair on my belly will die. The child for whom I have lain awake all night with no solace but thoughts of his future will die. The child who has revived my love for a world that I'd wished to see engulfed by a second Flood will die. I have been violated twice over, first by the king and now by the child who is the living – the dying – embodiment of his guilt. But I shall say nothing. I shall make myself the embodiment of my revenge.

'My lord mustn't brood. If I had a hundred sons, I would gladly surrender them all to reconcile you to the Lord.' So monstrous is his vanity that he believes me.

From that moment on, I resolve to feel nothing. I allow myself to be mauled by the other women, their faces flushed with excitement as my imminent confinement brings back memories of their own. But to me, their interest means nothing more than if they were fingering the weave of my robe. To me, the child has no more substance than a shadow on the water, its kicks those of a soldier whose legs have been cut off at the knees. It has been given out that the child was conceived on our wedding night and even my fellow wives, who know the truth, connive in the deception. When my pains start, they express alarm at their coming so soon before my time. They crowd into my chamber and gather around the birthing stool: Eglah and Matred clutching me under the arms; Huldath pressing damp cloths to my face; Ahinoam rubbing my neck and shoulders. The pains tear through me like bolts of lightning. Eglah insists that I'll forget them as soon as I hold my baby in my arms, but I shout her down. I intend to remember every last one, to offset the pain of my loss.

He is born, and my resolution flounders. Matred cleans him, rubbing his body with salt and wine and wiping his eyes with olive oil, before giving him back to me. I sniff his warm, fresh scent and stroke his whorl of soft red hair (just like his father's, according to Ahinoam, who knew him when he was young). He is so perfect – so complete – that I cherish the hope that the Lord has relented. But it swiftly wanes. When I cradle him in my arms, he makes no sound; when I press him to my breast, he has no suck. His indifference, not just to me but to life itself, is chilling. Huldath, still nursing Eliphelet, offers to feed him. 'He may sense your anxiety,' she says softly. After a moment's hesitation, I hand him over, but he remains inert. While the women fuss and fret around us, I plead with the Lord. He once spared the entire wicked nation at Moses's entreaty; surely he can do as much for an innocent child?

Jonadab, displaying more delicacy during the child's birth than during his conception, waits outside to take him to the great chamber where, according to custom, the king will present him to the elders. Abigail, however, declares that, first, he should see him alone and has us taken to his private chamber. Even when the chair jolts against the steps and I cannot keep from crying out, the baby stays silent. The king greets us and guides us to his bed, before kneeling beside it. I ask if he wants to hold his son, but he declines. I expect him to leave as soon as we're settled, but he doesn't stir, first for one day, then two, and then three, refusing both succour and sustenance. Ahinoam who maintains a constant vigil, whispers that he has shown no such solicitude for any of his other sons, not even Amnon, when he fell down the ramparts and lay insensible for two days. At different times and with differing emphasis, Grandfather, Abiathar and Joab plead with him to sit and sleep and eat and, at the very least, to drink a cup of water, but he rebuffs them all. Is his display of devotion designed to stir the Lord's compassion or to regain his favour? Are his tears for his dying child or for himself?

On the fourth day he gives his son a name but I shut my ears to it, since it betrays the fear that he won't survive until his circumcision. Sometimes when my mind strays, I think him already dead, only for the faintest of breaths to offer a reprieve. My breasts ache with the milk he doesn't drink; my loins sting where he has ripped them. Nevertheless, I resist Abigail's exhortation to rest, convinced that, if I close my eyes for an instant, he will close his forever. I lose every sense but touch and become one with him as if he were back inside me. Then, after minutes or hours or even days, sight returns and I glimpse Nathan hovering by the bed. I scream and Eglah and Matred rush over.

'What is it?' Eglah asks. 'You were sleeping so peacefully.'

I look round and Nathan has disappeared. I look down and the child is dead.

All at once the chamber is bustling. Abigail snatches my baby from me before I have a chance to protest. David stands and calls for food, water and fresh linen.

'Surely you require sackcloth and ash, my lord?' Grandfather says pointedly.

'You understand so little, Ahitophel,' he replies. 'So far I've clung to the hope that the Lord would accept my penitence and spare the child. Now that he's dead, I can do no more for him. I have neglected my duties long enough.' Through cloudy eyes, I watch him head for the door.

'Bathsheba, my lord!' Abigail calls, stopping him short. He walks back to the foot of the bed.

'Take heart,' he says, as if to a dying soldier. 'The Lord's will has been done.' Then, with ominous reserve, he lifts my hand to his lips and leaves.

I return to the harem, where the women's kindness compounds my pain. Eglah makes me cakes, which taste of the sweetness I have lost; Tamar brings me flowers, which bloom with the beauty that has withered; Nechama plays me tunes, whose plaintive chords echo my sobs. Only Matred gives me comfort, draining my curdled breasts and singing as if to a child who suckles them.

I resist repeated entreaties to quit my chamber. My fear of seclusion fades since all the life I either want or need can be found within these walls. Then one night, while Matred lies on the floor beside me, the door opens and a figure enters, silvered by moonlight. Although we have never met, I recognise her at once and hasten to kiss her hand, which is weightless and cold.

'My lady,' I say, 'how have you left your chamber?'

'It's only my body that's confined,' she replies. 'My mind is free to wander.'

'My body is free to wander,' I say, 'it's my mind that's immured here.'

'Then you'll let David and his god win.'

'They have won. My child is dead.'

'I have no child. I had children who were dearer to me than my own flesh, although they weren't of my flesh. But you will have more sons.'

'Will the king lie with me again?'

'The thing that David most abhors is failure – his own, that is; he thrives on other people's. No, I'm wrong; there's something else: that another man should possess what once was his.' She blenches. 'Unless you wish to spend the rest of your life in here, while the maidservant's son becomes king, you must find a way to win back his trust.' She turns to go.

'Wait!' I grab her robe and am gripped by a sense of unease. 'Why are you telling me this? Why do you care about me? We've never even spoken.'

'But I've listened. I know that on your account the Lord has finally turned against David. And if he can do so once, he can do so again.'

She goes out and I return to bed, my blood racing for the first time since the birthing stool. The next morning I ask Matred if she saw my visitor. She insists that there was no one, her voice choked with dread that grief has unhinged me. I reassure her. Whether she came to me in person or just in a dream, Princess Michal has revived me. Her words remain with me as I bathe and dress and ask Matred to brush and scent my hair. I venture into the courtyard, where Tamar runs up as if she has been keeping watch, flings her arms around my neck and, tender to a fault, bursts into tears. Abigail scolds her, but I hug her close. I realise that I am strong enough to console those who seek to console me. She takes my hand and leads me to a group of the younger children, who are building a tower of sticks. As

I watch them laugh and play, quarrel and make peace, without wishing them dead, I know that I am healed.

My forty days of impurity pass, and Eglah and Abital take me to cleanse myself at the Gihon spring. So much has changed in a single year that I scarcely recognise the Bathsheba who refused to make the journey for fear that the women would smile and the men mock when they discerned my purpose. Three days later, the king summons me to his private chamber.

'I am glad to see you well again,' he says distantly.

'All that has ailed me has been my absence from my lord.'

'I've been considering your future. I have spoken to your grandfather and decided to release you from the harem and return you to his house.'

'My lord is most gracious,' I say, struggling to quell my panic, 'but this is my house now.'

'Not in the city, of course,' he adds, 'his house in Ephraim.'

'No, my lord, please!' I see myself dwindling into my grandmother, and at the age of eighteen, not forty. I shall be trapped as if I were in my tomb. 'How can I ever be happy away from the king?'

'Thousands of people are.'

'But they haven't known you as I have. I beg you: don't send me away! Give me another son, one who'll find favour with the Lord and bless our union.'

'When I look at you, I see death: Eliada's death – ' I start. He has spoken his name, which can never now be unspoken – 'Uriah's death, and a hundred unidentified corpses at the gates of Rabbah.'

'Then don't look at me. Close your eyes and pretend that it's night.' I move to him and, before he can protest, slip first my hand and then my head under his robe. I take him in my mouth; I use my fingers and tongue in ways that delight him as much as they did the Edomite gods. I swallow the salty-sweetness and, although not even the finest wine will banish the taste, I am content.

His passion sated, I thank him as if he had pleasured me and ask whether he would like me to return later. He nods, as though afraid that speech will betray him. To the surprise of my fellow wives – except perhaps for one, but, since her door remains locked, I can't be sure – I find myself summoned back to his chamber night after night. To achieve my ends, I engage in acts ostensibly at odds with them, until he is powerless to resist and I slide him inside me to spill his seed. Then one night, I put his hand to my belly and he realises that it's not the prelude to a new enticement. He leans over and replaces his hand with his ear. I don't know whether he is being sincere or mocking his own sentiment, nevertheless the gesture charms me.

'Do you dream for our baby, Bathsheba?'

'All the time. That one day he will be as great a king as his father.'

'Indeed he will,' he says, supposing that he is humouring me.

FIVE

Abigail

We live in peace. For the first time since Moses led the people back to the land that the Lord promised us, we are safe within its borders. In the north, David has driven back the Arameans and, in the south, the Edomites. In the west, he has driven back the Philistines beyond the shores of the Great Sea and, in the east, the Ammonites behind the Jabbok river. To the south east, he has driven back the Moabites deep into the Arnon valley. Their fate was particularly grim, since he refused to ransom the captives, instead, ordering his captains to lay them on the ground in three lines of equal length, even providing them with a measuring cord. He put two of the lines to death, while keeping the third alive to pay him tribute.

Joab described the scene to me, his relish of the details almost as hard to comprehend as David's ruthlessness. Is it that after so many years at war, the pleasure of killing men has palled and the pleasure of shocking women is all that remains? Or am I right to detect his growing disillusion with David, which, after a lifetime devoted to his service, he is unable to acknowledge? It's as if he has finally developed scruples and is as ashamed of them as other men are of carbuncles. Yet he cannot ignore them. After all, he saw his grandparents flee to Moab and, though they may be long dead, the memory of their welcome remains, rendering David's vengeance all the more unjust. Meanwhile, I too have an interest in keeping faith with the man to whom I have given my heart.

We live in peace. Across the land, people have built houses, dug wells, cut paths and ploughed meadows. In his own city, David has extended and embellished his palace with treasures abandoned by the Philistines when they set sail. Yet nothing consoles him for his failure to erect the building closest to his heart: a temple to house the Ark. Ever since he brought it here, it has stood in the tabernacle as if it were still with Moses in the desert. It grieves him that his throne is in a palace while the Lord's is in a tent. But Nathan has warned him that the Lord will never consent to live in a temple built by a man with bloodstained hands. And even though he promised that his successor will build the temple and his house endure forever, David is filled with despair.

Despite that promise, David has yet to announce which of his sons is to succeed him. He has sixteen and Bathsheba is pregnant again (sons may be a blessing, but I doubt that I am alone in hoping for a girl). He indulges them all, the older ones whom he neglected during his lengthy campaigns when they were young and the younger ones who are the solace of his old age. He appointed the three eldest, Amnon, Absalom and Adonijah, to his council at twenty and, presumably, the two nineteen-year-olds, Shephatiah and Ithream, will soon join them. It is said that he heeds their callow opinions as much as the guidance of Ahitophel and Hushai, his chief advisers. He has given both Amnon and Absalom their own households, and Adonijah is currently pressing for the same. Whereas Absalom is lavish in his expenditure but restrained in his habits, Amnon and his followers lead a life of riot, sparking rumour and resentment throughout the city. Nevertheless, David refuses to reproach him, maintaining that he himself was prone to youthful high spirits – which is quite unlike the disciplined, dedicated warrior I recall.

As a boy, he must have seen young rams locking horns even when there were no ewes for them to tup. Yet, when his sons quarrel and vie for position, creating discord that threatens the stability of the kingdom, he makes no attempt to intervene. For the first time I fail in my duty towards him, neglecting to point out his inadequacies as a father for fear that he will regard it as the bitterness of a woman whose only child died in infancy. I sometimes wonder if he even remembers him. When Meribaal tottered into the courtyard, I thought that I perceived a flicker of recognition, tinged with relief. But does that extend to his name? Nathan showed me the scroll in which he had recorded David's reign in Hebron. Among the list of his sons was Daniel. 'It's Chileab,' I said, as dismayed as if thieves had ransacked his tomb. He promised to correct the mistake, but who could have prompted it if not David?

I sat at the birthing stool for two days, while Chileab hung back as if he knew what life held in store for him. The women rubbed my belly with rose water and oil and gave me potions of fenugreek and cinnamon, to no avail. The pain was so acute that I longed as much for my own death as for his birth. However grave Eve's sin, the punishment was dispro-portionate. In Carmel, my sisters-in-law both claimed that they forgot their travail the moment that they put their babies to the breast, which may have been true when the babies were sound, but, with his shell-like shoulders and a head that emerged straight from his chest, Chileab looked more like a turtle than a boy. Reflecting on the transgression that had caused his deformity, I decided that it must have been my murderous hatred of Nabal. All that bitterness and loathing had festered in my womb and I had nourished my baby on gall.

David held him only once, at his circumcision. After per-forming the rite, he tucked the foreskin in his loincloth as he had done Amnon's a month earlier, but it was obvious to anyone who saw the mewling, misshapen baby that his strength would scarcely sustain himself, let alone his father. He confounded us all by living to the age of three, finally suc-cumbing to a fever caught from Amnon, who had shaken it off within days. Ahinoam was distraught, blaming herself for failing to keep the boys apart. She mourned him more tear-fully than I, who had wept for him every day since his birth. I reassured her that it was the death he would have chosen since he idolised his elder brother, who treated him with surprising tenderness, which I try to remember now that his customary mode is contempt. Absalom, on the other hand, used to taunt him. An uncommonly pretty child, he viewed anything ugly as a personal affront, an attitude that he maintained years later when he led his brothers in their mockery of Meribaal. Yet such is his charm that the slightest hint of contrition secures his pardon, whereas Amnon could sacrifice a drove of bullocks and still appear impenitent.

Like the acrobats in Gath, who spun across the palace courtyard, first one and then the other to the fore, so Amnon and Absalom are interlinked as they compete for their father's favour and, although it remains unspoken, for his crown. They grew up together, sometimes the closest of friends and sometimes the fiercest of rivals. No stranger would take them for brothers: Absalom has inherited his mother's fair skin and his father's reddish-gold hair, which he grows to his shoulders, to the envy of half the harem; Amnon is dark, in both complexion and manner. Whereas Absalom courts the people, Amnon cows them. He has yet to learn that humility befits those of high rank as much as those of low. His conduct is so overbearing that David permits only Judahites to serve him, fearful of the resentment he might stir up in the Jebusites or the other Israelite tribes. Yet, in spite of his contention with her brother, he holds Tamar in the greatest esteem. She was born a month after Chileab died and, while it may be fanciful, I like to think that something of his gentle spirit passed to her. For years, she was not only the mediator between Amnon and Absalom but at the heart of all their games. Then childhood ended, and nature and propriety drove them apart.

Although Absalom's charm has won the hearts of the harem, I favour Amnon. Regardless of my friendship with his mother and his kindness to my son, I trust him more. His failings are all too apparent, whereas Absalom's are like the errors in a sealed scroll. So when Jonadab sends word to

Ahinoam that Amnon is ill, I am happy to accompany her to his bedside. She claims to want my support in case the sight of his suffering distresses her, but it's clear that, as ever, she is afraid of him. It's as if Absalom's jibes about his superior ancestry have stung him and he blames her that her father wasn't a king. At least if I am with her, he'll bridle his tongue. I can't vouch for his sincerity, but he treats me with respect, even calling me his second mother. I remind myself that it's only a phrase.

Having obtained permission from Ahitophel and wearing the heavy veils that David has ordained for all his women outside the palace, we cross the city to Amnon's house. Jonadab's muted greeting shows that his banishment from the harem is still raw. While thankful that his singular blend of subservience and presumption has been replaced by the chary reserve of Hiempsal, the eunuch presented to David by Hiram of Tyre, I would have preferred his departure to have been instigated by anyone but Bathsheba. She has never forgiven him for his part in procuring her for David, which is harsh given that it's the bedrock of her power. Although the worst offence with which she could charge him was laxity, she persuaded David to dismiss him. Like all his brothers, Amnon scorned him, but he saw the benefit of employing his father's former go-between, the keeper of his darkest secrets. Just how Jonadab, a man with no small opinion of his worth, truckles to his cousin, twenty years his junior and inferior to him in every respect but birth, is a mystery. But then Amnon, like his father, parades his passions and, having no passions of his own – or at least none that he sees fit to disclose – Jonadab feeds on those of others.

'I'm deeply concerned for the prince,' he says. 'For days he has neither slept nor eaten.'

'Nor washed,' I say, as we enter the chamber where Amnon lies in bed. He turns his flushed and clammy face towards us.

'What are you doing here? Go away and leave me in peace.'

'What is it, my dear. You can tell your mother,' Ahinoam says, approaching him warily.

'Leave me alone!' Amnon buries his head in the pillow.

'I've brought your favourite honey cakes.' She waves the dish over his chest in a manner guaranteed to infuriate him and, without looking up, he knocks it to the ground.

'Why did you do that?' Ahinoam asks, kneeling to pick them up. She blows the dust off one. 'Don't worry, they're not spoilt.'

'Useless! You're absolutely useless!' Ahinoam moans, but when Amnon raises his head, he turns out to be addressing Jonadab. 'I told you to bring Tamar. Her cakes are the only ones I can stomach.'

'But I taught her to make them,' Ahinoam says. 'The way we used to in Carmel.'

'Who cares?' He grabs a cake from the dish she has placed on his pillow and flings it across the chamber. 'I wouldn't feed that to my mule.'

As Ahinoam moves to mop his forehead, he pushes her away so hard that she trips and falls. 'Stop this nonsense now, Amnon!' I say, finally intervening. 'Show some consideration for your mother.'

'Don't pretend that you never hit her when she was your maidservant!'

'Of course I didn't,' I reply, struggling to help her up.

'Maybe you should have. It might have knocked some sense into her. Why won't anyone listen to me?' he asks, as querulous as three-year-old Nathan. 'I want Tamar.'

'Act your age!' I say bluntly. 'You know very well that your father is negotiating her marriage to the prince of Hamath.'

'Why?'

'To seal the alliance.'

'We have an army. Isn't that enough?'

'So she can't come and go as she pleases, visiting unmarried men.'

'I'm her brother!'

'Half-brother.'

'Yes, rub it in, why don't you! Absalom is loved by two sisters, whereas I have no one. No one.' He turns to his mother. 'You couldn't even do that for me.'

'You're loved by many women,' I say, as Ahinoam tries vainly to hide her tears. 'You're notorious for it.'

'Is that all you'll allow me, Aunt? Bedchamber love? Can I never hope for the sweet companionship of a sister?'

'You'll marry and have the companionship of a wife.'

'When? Father hasn't found me one and I'm not permitted to choose for myself. Without my sister's voice, my sister's face, my sister's gentle presence, I shall lose my wits. Didn't Father lose his when he went to Philistia?'

'That was a cloak to protect himself.'

'I have no cloak. See!' He throws off his bedsheet to reveal the eruption of spots on his chest.

'My son, let me look.' Amnon pointedly turns his back on his mother. 'At least let me rub a salve on it.'

'No, the only salve I need you won't bring. Forget about me. Go away and leave me to die in peace.'

Jonadab, as ever lurking in the shadows, calls to us. 'It's wisest to do as he asks, my ladies.' With Amnon remaining intransigent, I lead Ahinoam out of the chamber.

'Don't worry. He'll be fine. Shall we take an offering to the tabernacle for his recovery?' I ask, back in the fresher air of the courtyard.

'An excellent idea, my lady,' Jonadab says, 'but, in my view, the only thing that will cure him is a visit from Tamar.'

'Why?' Ahinoam asks, both pained and perplexed. 'What can she do for him that I can't.'

'Nothing of course… and not as well,' Jonadab says. 'But a sick mind conceives strange fancies. And he has it fixed in his that she is what he needs.'

'Then I'll speak to the king,' I say. Although loath to subject

Tamar to such a foetid atmosphere, I am worried by the rash on Amnon's chest. Besides, twenty-five years of marriage to Nabal accustomed me to placating petulant men.

We return to the palace, where I'm granted an audience with David. Crossing courtyards lined with idling guards, I try not to think of the time when I walked this way every day. Now, as well as a council of advisers he has Bathsheba who, at the tender age of twenty-one, has secured an unrivalled place in his affections. Although the cause of his sin, she alone keeps him from dwelling on its consequences. The death of their son was just the first, for Nathan has prophesied that the Lord will take away his wives and concubines and give them to his kinsman. The only question is which of those kinsmen it will be: one of the brothers whom he has neglected; one of the nephews whom he has domineered; one of the sons whom he has allowed to run wild. I picture Bathsheba, undoubtedly a great beauty but no more so than most of the women in the harem, and wonder what it is that she does in the darkness to ease the pricking of his conscience. Maybe it's better not to know?

When I enter the chamber, she is sitting beside David, with Solomon at her breast. David, who previously evinced disgust at a woman's secretions, is happy to watch him suckling for hours on the gnawed, distended nipples she displays like battle scars. Solomon was born with teeth, yet she was determined to feed him herself. After Eliada's death I understood her vigilance, but that was the Lord's will and, besides, unlike his brother, Solomon was strong. But it became a point of honour with her to suffer the pain as if she were nourishing him not just on her milk but on her blood. Even when Nathan was born, barely ten months after his brother, prompting conjecture that he had been conceived on the very day of her purification, she continued to favour Solomon, handing the newborn to a nurse. Listening to her relentless praise of her son's every babbling word and doddering step, I fear that he will grow up as conceited as Amnon. Then I stop and remind myself that my judgement is coloured by my loss.

'That young man thinks of no one but himself,' David says, when I put Amnon's request to him. 'Today it's Tamar; tomorrow he'll want to see Nechama or Eglah or you, Bathsheba. Should I allow her to go? What do you advise?' I swallow my resentment as he appeals to her.

'If Abigail thinks it's for the best, it must be,' she replies artfully.

'Then I agree. Arrange for Tamar to go there in the morning,' he says to me. 'Make sure she discovers what's troubling him. If it's serious, we'll bring him back to the palace. If, as I suspect, he simply craves attention, we must impress on him that it's high time he faced up to his responsibilities.'

Ahinoam is waiting for me at the gate of the harem. After informing her of David's decision, I seek out Tamar in her chamber, where she sits with her mother and sister, embroidering the collar of a robe. I relay David's instructions and am amused by her excitement at a rare escape from the palace. Maacah scowls. Her rivalry with Ahinoam, although more discreet, is just as intense as that of their sons, and I discern her reluctance for any of her children to wait on the 'maidservant's boy'.

'Believe me, it's out of the utmost respect for Tamar that Amnon asks for her,' I say, in my most conciliatory tone.

'See, Mother,' Tamar says, her eyes welling with tears. 'If I don't go, he'll die.'

'Don't talk nonsense,' Maacah says. 'If your father wishes you to go, you have no choice. But you must take Nechama with you.'

'Oh no, Mother, please!' interjects Nechama, as reserved as Tamar is effusive. 'It's so hot. And I'd have to wear one of those hateful robes. Everyone will look at me.'

I share her apprehension. To protect his daughters from any charge of impropriety, David has ordered that they wear a long-sleeved, bright-coloured robe whenever they leave the palace.

'She's too sensitive,' Maacah says to me, before issuing Nechama with what I suspect is a daily reminder: 'You're the daughter and granddaughter of kings. Of course, common people will look at you. But I shan't force you. You must go on your own, Tamar. But don't linger. I want you back here in good time.'

The following morning Tamar puts on the designated robe as eagerly as if it were for her wedding. As she quits the harem, Ahinoam, who wisely left me to speak to Maacah alone, clasps her arm. 'Be kind to my boy. Find out what it is that's ailing him and what any of us can do. Make sure at least that he eats some of your cakes.'

'Don't worry,' Tamar says warmly, 'I promise I'll have him up and well in no time.' She plants a quick kiss on Ahinoam's cheek and hurries out.

'Most mothers have to defer to their sons' wives. I have to defer to his sister,' Ahinoam says to me sadly.

'She'll do everything she can. She's a good girl.'

'I know. It must be all that royal blood!' she replies, with a pointed glance at Maacah's chamber.

The day passes slowly, like most days in the harem, and it's not until sundown that the slowness starts to feel sinister. While Maacah frets about her daughter's absence and Abital, who has only sons, seeks to reassure her by condemning their timekeeping, I am summoned to David's chamber, where Bathsheba's absence, ordinarily a cause for relief, is now one for alarm. Jonadab, more flustered than I have ever seen him, is conversing with David, whose face is as grey as a pillar.

'Tell Lady Abigail what you've just told me,' he says grimly.

'All of it?' Jonadab asks, with a show of reluctance.

'All of it.'

'Princess Tamar came to visit Prince Amnon,' Jonadab

says, the titles adding to the gravity of his account. 'She'd brought a dish of dough and honey.'

'We thought he'd like to watch her make the cakes,' I say.

'Of course, of course. Nothing more natural. Amnon sent the servants away. I was surprised – '

'But you didn't think to question him?'

'It wasn't my place,' he replies, looking meekly at David. 'The smell of frying cakes was delicious. The sizzling oil. The bubbling honey. I can still smell it now. Though I don't think I'll ever be able to eat one again without thinking – '

'Enough!' David says.

'Yes, yes, of course. Amnon ordered me to leave too. I protested that it wasn't seemly. Brother and sister, yes, but with different mothers. So he leapt out of bed and pushed – '

'He leapt?' I interject. 'Yesterday, he could scarcely move. His chest was inflamed.'

'Nettles.'

'What?'

'I mean... I think...' He shuffles and stammers. 'I was as astounded as you. I couldn't believe that the sight of his sister... the smell of her cakes had revived him so fast. Then, as he was throwing me out of the chamber, I glimpsed a bunch of nettles beneath the bed.'

'Why bother us with trifles?' David says.

'Do you need me to tell you what happened next or can you guess?' Jonadab asks me.

'Tell me anyway,' I say, setting aside thoughts of the nettles. There will be time to consider his complicity later.

'As soon as I was outside, the prince bolted the door. I banged on it, frightened for the princess... frightened for him. Look!' He holds up his grazed knuckles like a child hoping for sympathy after falling from a tree he had been forbidden to climb. 'I pleaded, but he was deaf to my pleas. And to hers. I heard steps and scuffles, ripping and panting and screaming. And then moans – deep, contented moans.'

'Stop!' I shout, as he speaks words that no father should have to hear. David buries his face in his hands and I wonder whether the carnal detail is Jonadab's revenge for the years he spent pandering to his uncle's desires.

'Then everything went silent. I lay on the floor, trying to see under the door.'

'What on earth for?' I ask, extending my revulsion from the perpetrator to the witness.

'I was afraid that he'd murdered her, of course,' he says, affronted. 'I barely had time to scramble up when the door swung open and he flung her out, as if she were no better than a concubine.' David groans. 'She was naked. I looked away, from respect for her modesty – her lost modesty.'

'No, no, no!'

I watch helplessly as David punches himself in the chest.

'Forgetting my own safety, I pushed past him and fetched her robe and mantle (the tunic was too torn to be of use). I handed them to Tamar, who stared as though she had never seen them before. So I draped the mantle around her shoulders. She instantly shrugged it off, snatched the robe from my hands and scurried to the end of the passage, where she somehow managed to put it on. Struggling to make sense of what had occurred, I stared at Amnon. But his face was blank. No hint of tenderness or sorrow or contentment or disgust – with himself, I mean. All I saw was cruelty, but an inhuman cruelty like the idol of Dagon you brought back from Gath. Meanwhile, the princess had dressed and, wrapped in her mantle however tattered, she seemed to recollect who she was... where she was... perhaps both. "Do you mean to throw me out, brother?" she asked. The pain, the bewilderment, the quiet dignity of her voice would have melted any heart – even Dagon's – but Amnon was unyielding. He stared at her as at an insect he refused to swat in case it sullied his hand. "Where can I go? Who will have me? Don't leave me with this burden of shame. Marry me!" Yes, she was so desperate that she begged to marry her defiler. Can you credit it?' As he knew full well, the question was redundant, for we had the example of David's own marriage to Bathsheba. Notwithstanding the horror of his story, I had to acknowledge – even admire – the way he had expanded the circle of guilt to include David and that of perversity to include Bathsheba, his mortal enemy ever since the loss of his stewardship. 'A deaf man would have pitied her entreaties; a blind man would have pitied her tears. But Amnon walked back into the chamber and bolted the door. I asked Tamar if she wanted me to bring her back here. "You're very kind, Jonadab," she said, "I'll never forget how you've helped me."'

I cough to show that I see through what is at best an embellishment, but the grief-stricken king is grateful for any service to his ruined daughter. 'I thank you, Jonadab, for everything you did for her – everything you tried to do.'

'I only wish that it could have been more. She insisted on going to her brother's house.'

'Absalom's?' I ask.

'Yes, my lady. She gathered her mantle around her and dragged herself into the street, where she knelt and rubbed dust and filth into her tangled hair. She pulled on the rips in her robe – remember, she wore no tunic – so that streaks of her pallid flesh and the soft curve of her breasts could be clearly seen. And lower – '

'Enough!' David says. 'Were there people nearby?'

'Crowds,' Jonadab replies with unseemly relish. 'But, to my relief, they all looked away. Some faced the walls as she passed; others fixed their gaze on the ground. Only a few young children giggled and pointed until slapped into silence by their mothers. I followed her of course, to ensure her safety.' *Too late*, I think and for a moment fear that I have spoken out loud, but Jonadab continues unruffled. 'Others joined me, like a burial procession in which Tamar was both the chief mourner and the corpse. The news spread fast and Absalom ran out to meet us when we were still some distance from his house. The instant she saw him, Tamar fell to the ground and began to keen: a long, low wail ending with a screech, as if all the pain in her body had turned to sound. Absalom scooped her up and carried her home. I hurried after them and tried to explain. "Later," he shouted. "Later." But I'm sure that he already knew. So I came here, leaving the princess in the hands of her protector.'

'I am the princess's protector!' David says. 'She is my daughter. Absalom must return her to me at once. True, I can no longer expect Toi of Hamath to marry his son to her. But there will be some tributary king or troubled chief who'll be glad to gain my favour.'

'No matter the cost?' Jonadab asks.

'No matter. I'll send Ahitophel to Absalom. He knows him to be the wisest of my counsellors.' I hardly think that Bath-sheba's grandfather is the best choice for such a task, but now is not the time to say so. 'And you must return to Amnon,' he says to Jonadab. 'At the very least, persuade him to adopt an air of penitence.'

'Provided he'll listen. He may resent my helping Tamar and coming to you.'

'I'm sure you'll find a way,' I say, making it plain that, unlike his uncle, I harbour serious doubts about his sincerity. 'After all, you're a practised schemer.'

'Only in my lord's service,' Jonadab says. He leaves, bowing to David and ignoring me.

'You were too harsh with him,' David says.

'Perhaps. I hope so. But I trust that you'll take the same tone when you summon Amnon.'

'I can't bear to set eyes on him.'

'You have no choice. You can't disregard what he's done. The Law is unequivocal about the penalty for the violation of a betrothed woman. And Tamar was all but betrothed.'

'You want me to put him to death? I'm his father!'

'You're the king.'

'Would that I were the meanest slave! Leave me. I need to think. Besides you must tell his mother – and hers – before rumours start to circulate.'

'Not me, my lord. Let them hear it from someone more judicious: Ahitophel or Hushai.'

'Who better than you? My rock for all these years. No other woman means more to me… no other woman has done more for me. No, not even Bathsheba.'

'But I haven't given you a son… not one who lived.'

'After this you may count that a blessing.'

I return to the harem, which, though still in a state of ignorance, is full of foreboding. I gather the women around me and give them a condensed version of Jonadab's account, omitting as many of the shrieks and howls as I can without rendering it meaningless. Maacah supplies them in my place. Nechama, her eyes streaming, clings to her, both offering and seeking comfort. Ahinoam, mindful that Maacah's is the greater hurt, moans quietly in a corner. Not even Eglah and Haggith, her two closest allies, approach, as though blaming her for her son, a thought to which Maacah, breaking away from her daughter, gives voice. 'May the Lord's curse be on Amnon as it was on Cain. May the sons of David rise up and kill him as the sons of Jacob killed Shechem and all his people when he assaulted their sister, Dinah. Amnon is the dirt beneath my feet – no, a worm crawling in the dirt. But what can you expect from the son of such a baseborn mother?'

Ahinoam bridles and I fear that she may accuse Tamar of provoking or, worse, encouraging Amnon, when Michal, whose presence I had barely registered, chimes in. 'You mean *father*! After all David is no stranger to abduction and rape. Small wonder that his son follows suit.'

The women look shocked, as much by Michal's rare intervention as by her incendiary charge. I glance at Bathsheba who dandles Solomon and listens impassively, as though the remark had no pertinence to her. I have never understood why she used her influence with David to have Michal, then a stranger to her, released from her chamber – unless it were to flaunt the extent of that influence. No doubt she regrets it now.

Maacah, reassured to know that her daughter is in her son's care, is anxious to visit her but, when she asks permission, Ahitophel refuses. He explains that David has ordered Absalom to bring Tamar back to the palace but, in a direct rebuff to his father, he insists that she's safer with him. David could, of course, dispatch the guard to take her by force but he fears that it would be viewed as a second violation: a display of military might and moral weakness. For the moment he prefers to leave things as they are, basking in the sympathy of his people, as though he, rather than Tamar, were the true victim. Her body has been violated but his honour is stained.

Amnon returned to the palace to attend the council and, according to Bathsheba who heard it from Ahitophel (such is the roundabout way that information reaches the harem), he prostrated himself and kissed his father's feet in an obeisance that David ignored. As he took his seat, everyone present waited for David to pronounce his sentence, but he said nothing, any more than he has done since. I realise how hard it is for him to punish his son and, what's more, for a crime that he himself has committed, but it has to be done or else the injury will fester. Just as he or, rather, the baby Eliada paid the price for Bathsheba's rape, so Amnon must for Tamar's. The king's first duty is to uphold the Law.

Absalom comes to the council, sitting alongside Amnon but refusing to acknowledge him with so much as a glance. This time I receive an account not from Bathsheba but from David himself who, wilfully obtuse, sees it as the first sign of forgiveness. When I suggest otherwise, he retorts that he has spoken to Absalom and persuaded him not to seek retribution. His priority is to find Tamar a husband and, with their kingdom ravaged, his thoughts turn to one of the Moabite princes. When the prospect is raised, Maacah protests at her daughter living on a mountaintop and, incited by Michal, insists that David's sole concern is to send her away so that he no longer has to contemplate her shame. In the event, Tamar is in no state to marry anyone. When she finally visits her, Maacah reports that it's as if she has been possessed by an evil spirit in the shape of a wild beast. She doesn't speak but merely yelps and howls, wallows in her own filth, and lashes out at anyone who approaches – even her mother. When Absalom can no longer bear to have her in the house, he dispatches her to the farm that David has given him in Baal Hazor.

After the collapse of his son's betrothal, King Toi offers his daughter, Danatiya, to one of the royal princes and, in a show of gratitude for his support and his only public rebuke to Amnon, David bestows her on Absalom, permitting his second-born son to marry before his first. The wedding goes some way towards healing the divisions in the harem. Ahinoam congratulates Maacah and embroiders the bride's veil, its intricacy all the more remarkable given her stumpy fingers. Bathsheba gives Absalom a pearl the size of a plum that I first saw on the girdle of Achish's boy in Gath. I give Danatiya a comb of gold and bone that belonged to Shirah and which she immediately passes to Absalom, declaring – with reason – that he has the finer head of hair. I am relieved to see Amnon sitting beside Absalom at the first evening's feast, even though it's Adonijah and Shephatiah who escort him to his gate to await his bride. As they leave, Maacah draws her son aside for a private word. I am too far away to hear what is said, but his expression suggests that she isn't wishing him joy. Nevertheless, his reply appears to mollify her and she returns to the table with a broad smile.

Absalom's first child is born the following year. He names her Tamar, which I fear that David will take amiss but, on the contrary, he expresses delight at hearing the name again, spoken with love. Two months later, Bathsheba's fourth child – a son, of course – is born and named Shobab. She finally gives up nursing Solomon, although not in favour of the newborn, since she says, with calculated immodesty, that at twenty-three, she needs to preserve her breasts for the king. To mark both his daughter's birth and the annual sheep-shearing, Absalom invites his father and the entire household to a feast at Baal Hazor. I am excited. As the occasion for my first encounter with David, the festival holds a special place in my heart, but I haven't had a chance to celebrate it since we left Hebron. To my dismay, David declines to attend, claiming that such a large gathering will strain Absalom's resources and encourage his extravagance. I suspect that a more urgent consideration is his increasing discomfort in the saddle.

Disappointed by his father's refusal, Absalom urges him to send Amnon in his stead. David agrees. Amnon, still struggling to regain his favour, is loath to disobey but equally loath to journey to Baal Hazor. He offers several unconvincing excuses, when the obvious one is his fear of meeting Tamar. David, who has banished the thought of his ruined daughter, along with everything else beyond his control, asks him if he is deliberately trying to offend Absalom and perpetuate their feud.

'Not at all,' Amnon replies, 'but I hate the way that he seeks to impress you with his magnanimity.'

'That's perverse,' David says angrily, or so he relates to me later. Yet, while I share his hopes for the visit, I also share Amnon's misgivings. I refuse to believe that marriage and fatherhood have so changed Absalom that he will renounce their lifelong rivalry, let alone his outrage over Tamar. I propose that David send his other sons as a safeguard and, despite his concerns about Absalom's purse, he agrees. Enjoining Ibhar and Eliphelet to watch over him, Bathsheba even permits Solomon to go, her desire for him to associate with his brothers outweighing her fear of letting him out of her sight.

Jonadab arranges everything. Somehow he has convinced Absalom of his attempts to rescue Tamar and wormed his way into his favour. Meanwhile, he still serves Amnon. I suspect that he has promised each of the brothers to report on the other: reports carefully framed to his own advantage. He has even convinced David that his overriding ambition is to reconcile his two cousins, whereas I have no doubt – based, I admit, purely on instinct – that his true objective is to destroy them, if for no other reason than that they were born the king's sons and he his nephew. But I say nothing since, while David once respected my instincts, he now disdains them.

With the princes and their attendants in Baal Hazor, the palace feels as it did in the days when David was away on campaign. But the figure who flings open the harem door at dusk is no herald of victory. It is David himself and, though it may be a trick of the light, he appears to have aged twenty years. He tries to talk but the words stick in his throat and, after spluttering and choking, he disappears. No one speaks but the questions in everyone's eyes are the same: has there been news from the feast? has some fresh quarrel erupted between Amnon and Absalom? have their younger brothers been forced to take sides? Beyond that is the most pressing question of all: has anyone been hurt? Ahinoam leans against the wall and slowly slides to the ground. Maacah stands stunned, not so much as blinking when Nechama clasps her hand. The rest of us look from one to the other, unsure whether to offer comfort and, if so, to whom. Only Bathsheba moves. Leaping up from the pond where she has been dangling her feet, she rushes to her chamber and returns, dragging Nathan so fast that he stumbles and clutching Shobab so tightly that he screams.

She is followed by Michal, her gaunt face more vulturish than ever. 'Why are you all so quiet?' she asks. 'Has somebody died?'

One of the Jebusite concubines bursts into tears.

'We think...' Eglah says.

'We think there's been news,' Haggith elaborates.

'There's always news,' Michal says. 'If the great king shouts at one of his advisers or summons one of my supplanters, it's news.' She smiles in a bid to temper the insult. 'So what is it?'

'David was here a moment ago,' I reply. 'He didn't speak, but he looked as though he had borne witness to every murder since Cain slew Abel.'

'That's not news; it's justice,' she says sourly. She paces the courtyard, adding to the general agitation, but no one dares challenge her. Even disgraced, she exudes an authority that none of us can match. Time passes, and Shobab's cries and Nathan's protests are no longer a distraction but a cruel reminder of the sons who may never return. Footsteps can be heard outside but no one approaches the harem until, finally, Ahitophel enters, his mission granting him access that, age and rank notwithstanding, he has hitherto been denied.

'Ladies, I beg you to be strong,' he says, dispensing with a preamble. 'The king has had word from Baal Hazor. I can put this no other way; Absalom has killed all his brothers.'

There must be another way, since the one that he has chosen makes no sense.

'Absalom has killed Amnon?' Abital asks.

'Yes,' he replies gently. 'And all his brothers. Adonijah and Shephatiah and Ithream and Jerimoth and Ibhar and...'

The list is drowned in an outburst of shrieks and wails. Maacah alone stands silent, shocked and shuddering, even as Nechama, still gripping her hand, bends double. Some of the women tear their hair and their robes, adopting the tested patterns of grief as if to contain it. Bathsheba, dropping Nathan's hand but still cradling Shobab, flies at Maacah and claws her face, leaving two deep furrows in her right cheek. Matred, her maidservant, drags her off as she repeats: 'Solomon my king! Solomon my king!', while Nathan, bemused, totters behind them. Amid the cacophony of anguish comes the jarring sound of laughter. At first I ascribe it to a mind so distraught that its responses have gone awry, only to find, to my horror, that the glee is genuine. With no child of my own to mourn, I strike a blow for us all as I slap Michal hard across the face. She falls silent, panting like a beast glutted on its prey.

Too weak to lift Ahinoam up, I sink beside her, stroking her soggy cheek. I rock her as if she were my daughter and realise that David was right: for the first time I'm grateful that Chileab is dead and I wept for him privately, rather than in the mayhem of mass slaughter. Ghostly faces take shape before me: other mothers' sons whom I have watched grow, delighting in their accomplishments and commiserating on their sorrows, loving each for himself and them all for their kinship with David. So much youth... so much hope... so much life has been put to the sword. The Amalekites who murdered my family were strangers, but Absalom has bathed his hands in his own blood.

Ahitophel leaves the harem to its lamentations. Soon afterwards, Jonadab enters, as freely as if he had never been banished. 'My lady,' he says, walking towards Ahinoam and me. With his eyes respectfully lowered, I am at first uncertain which of us he's addressing, but his next remark makes it clear. 'I mourn with you. Amnon was more than my kinsman; he was my friend.'

'And Adonijah and Shephatiah,' I say. 'And Solomon,' I add, conscious of Bathsheba keening in the corner.

'What of them?' he asks, perplexed.

'They were your kinsmen too.'

'I would never deny it.'

'And dead.' I shriek at him, wishing that my words were blades.

'Of course they're not dead... Oh no! Has that rumour reached you too? Trust me, Amnon... Amnon alone is dead.'

Ahinoam howls.

'But Ahitophel has just been here,' I say.

'And I have just come from the king. When Absalom's men

struck Amnon, I bustled all the princes away. One of the servants, seeing them missing, thought that they had been taken out and killed. He rode straight back to the city, wanting to be the first to inform the king. He's paid a heavy price for his haste.'

'Dead?' I ask. Jonadab shrugs.

'Solomon is alive?' Bathsheba asks slowly.

'Yes, my lady,' he replies, resisting any impulse for revenge. 'Alive and well, like the rest of them. I rode at full pelt. They can't be far behind.'

Indeed, they are so close that he has scarcely finished speaking when Adonijah and Shephatiah enter. Haggith rushes to embrace her son, but Abital is rooted to the spot. Shephatiah moves towards her, but she holds him at arm's length, running her fingers over his face and chest.

'Has Jonadab told you what happened?' he asks.

'You're all safe?' she replies.

'Except Amnon,' he says reproachfully.

'The Lord be praised,' Bithiah says. 'I mean...' Everyone knows what she means.

'Tell us what happened,' Haggith says, as Adonijah finally escapes her grasp.

'The journey took four hours,' he replies. 'We reached Baal Hazor at noon, where we were greeted by Absalom and his men.'

'No,' I interject. 'That's for later. Tell us what happened to Amnon.'

'We were feasting,' Shephatiah says, intent on a hearing. 'Just the men, Danatiya and Tamar: the baby Tamar. Our sister was nowhere to be seen. There was so much food: pigeon stew; goat stew; fish freshly caught from the Jordan; duck; a goose.'

'Amnon's favourite,' Ahinoam says. I rub her hand.

'He enjoyed it,' Shephatiah says tenderly. 'He was seated on Absalom's right. The servants made sure that his cup and dish were always full.'

'That was kind,' Ahinoam says dully.

'But they killed him,' Adonijah says, fired with youthful indignation.

'Hush!' Haggith says. 'What happened next?'

'The servants brought in the fruit. They put a dish of peaches in front of Amnon and then two of them took out knives and held them to his throat.' Ahinoam whimpers. 'That's when Absalom gave the signal.'

'You don't know that,' Shephatiah interjects. 'No one saw.'

'He must have done,' Adonijah says. 'Tamar came down the stairs into the courtyard. Our sister Tamar, not the baby. At first I didn't recognise her – '

'No one did,' Shephatiah says. 'It was a shock.'

'She was completely bald. As bald as your eunuch,' Adonijah says, pointing to Hiempsal, who, devoid of purpose, stands silently against the wall. Maacah sobs and Nechama twists a hank of hair around her thumb. 'She walked towards Amnon slowly, solemnly, a knife in her hand like a priest preparing for a sacrifice. He didn't move a muscle but stared at her defiantly.'

'You didn't have a clear view,' Shephatiah says. 'He was resigned, not defiant. Smiling as if he were waiting for her to plunge in the knife herself.'

'She should have done. She should have stabbed you all,' Michal says.

Both boys start at the unfamiliar voice and one so deep that, anywhere else, it might pass for a man's.

'She stabbed no one,' Adonijah says, flustered. 'She stopped just short of the table, which was when Absalom gave the signal – ' Shephatiah makes as if to interrupt again. 'When we assume that Absalom gave the signal, and they slit his throat.'

'His head fell into the fruit,' Shephatiah says.

'"You are avenged," Absalom said to Tamar. "You are cleansed. You are at peace." But she didn't seem to hear or, at any rate, she didn't respond. She didn't laugh or look happy – '

'But she didn't scream or look sad. She stood – '

'She stood silently for a moment and then walked out of the courtyard and back up the stairs. No one spoke – not a sound – until Solomon started whooping and clapping. He actually clapped.'

The women shift their accusatory glances from Maacah to Bathsheba, who rises to her son's defence. 'He's not yet four. Death to him is a goat slaughtered in the tabernacle. I've told him that it makes the Lord happy.'

'This was his brother,' Haggith says sharply.

'He's not yet four,' Bathsheba repeats. 'Blood is what is offered to the Lord.'

'We were dazed,' Adonijah says. 'Some of the younger ones began to panic.' Shephetiah's harrumph indicates that some of the older ones did too. 'Absalom swore that he meant no harm to anyone else. We were his brothers and he loved us. He ordered the servants to take Amnon's body away. You were there – ' He points at Jonadab, whose silence compounds my misgivings. 'You urged us to carry on eating.'

'You did what?' I stare at him in disbelief.

'I didn't know what Absalom might do next. I thought the safest thing was to act as if nothing had happened,' he replies, contradicting his previous remark.

'But it had,' Adonijah says. 'Our brother was dead. So I told Absalom that we had to leave if we were to return to the palace by nightfall.'

'Adonijah managed it all,' Shephatiah says admiringly. 'He ordered the servants to saddle the mules. He even thanked Absalom for his hospitality.'

'He was half-crazed; he must have been to suppose that I was sincere.'

'We rode straight back, but somewhere outside Geba, Ibhar fell ill. He had a sort of fit.'

'What? Is he hurt?' Bithiah asks. 'I must go to him. Where is he?'

'Where are they all?' Eglah asks.

'He's fine. They're all fine. They're on their way. We took Ibhar into the town. He recovered at once, but we thought he should rest before riding back. We left Ithream in charge and came on ahead.'

'I must have come a different way,' Jonadab says, as if to explain his rapid arrival. 'I've been back and forth so often.'

'We wanted to bring the news to Father,' Shephatiah says.

'And to you,' Adonijah says to his mother, who covers his face with kisses, which for once he doesn't brush off.

The account concluded, I lead Ahinoam to her chamber. The women watch in silence as we pass, but the moment I close the door, they erupt in shouts of joy and thanksgiving, not vicious and vengeful like Michal's, but in their own way equally callous. Bathsheba's cry of 'Solomon my king!' continues to gnaw at my mind. Did I fail to catch the pause in what was 'Solomon! My king!', a plaint for both her murdered son and his bereaved father? Or was my initial suspicion correct and she was mourning not just the death of her own hopes but of the land's?

Absalom relinquishes Amnon's body to David, who buries it with every honour. Lamentations rend the air, as we process across the eastern valley to the tomb that David has lately built for himself. We return to the palace where he feasts the mourners, sitting on a stool lower than the least of them, ashes matted in his hair and beard and smeared on his face. Burnishing his son in his memory, he declares that not only has he lost one who was dearer to him than life itself but the people have lost their next king: it was Amnon who would have built the Lord his temple and secured his everlasting favour on the land. His words sadden me, not because he ignores Amnon's faults (his hands were also stained with innocent blood), but because he only named him as his heir once he was safely dead. Now that he has raised the issue of the succession, it will be a running sore. Adonijah and Shephatiah, flanking their father, are too artless to hide their excitement. Might one of them claim the crown or will the king pardon and endorse their elder brother? As if reading their minds, David repudiates Absalom.

'Let all here bear witness that I shall avenge my dead son. I have today sent a squad of guards to Baal Hazor to bring Absalom back to the city.'

His declaration meets with a murmur of approval, if only at his taking action after dithering over punishing Amnon. The one note of dissent comes from Ahitophel who, rather than waiting for a private audience, entreats him to show mercy to Absalom.

'Am I not due to punish my son's murderer?' David asks, furious at the public challenge.

'Are you not due to punish your daughter's violator?' Ahitophel asks. 'An eye for an eye and a tooth for a tooth, according to the Law.'

'But Tamar still has her eyes and her teeth, whereas Amnon is grinning in the grave.'

I would be more inclined to protest if I didn't suspect that, for all his love for his sister, Absalom felt his own dishonour more keenly than her pain. Wondering what penalty David will exact, I fear that if it is too harsh it will provoke resentment – even rebellion – across the kingdom. Absalom is the best-loved of his sons, having won the place in peoples' hearts with his charm and beauty that David had with his sling and sword. My fears prove to be unfounded, since the guards return from Baal Hazor without Absalom, who has fled to Geshur with his wife and daughter, leaving only his sister behind. Although he rants and curses, I sense that David is relieved.

Absalom remains in Geshur for three years. Maacah begs David to forgive him and summon him home. When he refuses, she begs to be allowed to visit him and, at the same time, say farewell to her aged father. But the man who set such store by Michal's gory bride-price will never sanction

Maacah's return to the father who sealed their alliance with her maiden blood. I fear that in denying her request, he punishes himself most of all. 'You've lost one son,' I say, 'why deprive yourself of another?' He insists that he has a 'quiverful of sons' to support him, but when he mistakes Ithream for Ibhar and pretends that it was a joke, his weakness is exposed. In desperation, I approach Bathsheba, trusting that her sway by night will exceed mine by day. She promises to assist in any way possible but, even as she speaks, I know that she will do nothing. My mind harks back to that 'Solomon my king!' How many of his elder brothers would have to die for her son to ascend the throne? Or does she plan to deny their birthright and subvert the succession?

To my surprise, Absalom's most persuasive advocate is Joab. I doubt that he has any great affection for a man whose easy charm is everything that he lacks in himself and mistrusts in others, but he sees the effect that his absence is having on David, to whom his loyalty is absolute, even if it is now that of subject and soldier rather than kinsman and friend. Like Nathan before him, he addresses David through a story although, unlike Nathan's, the story is not his own but that of a woman from Tekoa. I have no way of knowing whether her plight is genuine and happens to serve Joab's purposes or if she is playing a part that he has devised, but she is – or claims to be – a widow whose sole surviving son fears for his life after killing his brother in a quarrel. Moved by her plea, David pardons him, only to discover that, by implication, he has pardoned Absalom. I am amazed that he is so easily duped since the parallel is even more pronounced than it was with Nathan's stolen sheep and, as he berates Joab for his duplicity, I wonder whether he's colluding with him in order to bring Absalom home without losing face. Thirty years by his side may have made me unduly suspicious, but I can't help asking why, if he is as angry with Joab as he professes, he doesn't punish him, any more than he did for murdering Abner.

David permits Absalom to return but refuses to receive him, declaring that he doesn't trust himself not to forgive him at first sight. 'Then do it,' I say. 'Banish him or reinstate him but, whatever else, avoid half-measures. They'll simply make him bitter and you wretched.' It is, however, increasingly hard to tell him anything that he doesn't wish to hear. Whereas he once asked for advice, he now asks only for approval and I am forced to sneak my doubts into a stream of flattery like herbs into a sick child's soup. Absalom writes him letter after letter, expressing remorse and pleading to be restored to favour. David keeps them by his side to read over again, particularly proud of those that are smudged with tears – as though he has never sliced an onion! After two years of rebuffs, Absalom solicits help from Joab, but, either because David's mood has improved since his son's return or because he's tired of being an intermediary, he ignores him. In fury, Absalom sends his men to burn Joab's barley crop. I expect Joab, the most short-tempered man I've ever known, to wreak instant revenge. But, in a response that makes me question my own judgement, he offers to speak to David on Absalom's behalf.

David finally relents and agrees to welcome Absalom, ordering the entire household to witness their reunion. We assemble in the great chamber. David sits on his throne, surrounded by his younger sons and chief advisers; a unit of guards lining the walls in a show of strength that only emphasises Absalom's confidence in coming alone. He runs towards David like a prisoner into sunlight and kisses his feet. As David leans forward to lift him up, the contrast between father and son is stark: David, golden-crowned, heavy and hunched, with tears streaming down his face; Absalom, golden-haired, slender and straight, his eyes dry. After pressing him to his breast, David releases him and pronounces a formal pardon, to which Absalom replies with a profession of penitence, gratitude and lifelong loyalty. As we make our way down to the courtyard for the feast, I keep close watch on Ahinoam, fearful of how she will react to seeing her son's murderer, but she shows no sign of recognising him. In the years since Amnon's death, she has withdrawn into herself, rarely speaking and greeting every remark with the same vacant smile.

Absalom swiftly regains his place in David's affections and, if his younger brothers are disgruntled, they know better than to show it. Enchanted by his first grandsons, the three boys born to Danatiya in Geshur, David treats their father more indulgently than ever, even rebuking Bathsheba when she protests at his riding in a horse-drawn chariot while he himself makes do with a mule. He laughs it off as the ostentation of youth, when it's evident to anyone with half an eye that it's the presumption of a king-in-waiting.

While David hides away in the palace, increasingly unwilling to venture into his city, let alone to the far reaches of his kingdom, Absalom woos the people. After thirty years on the throne, David is showing that distaste for the routine of government he condemned in Saul. Even immured in the harem, we hear the clamour at the gates when the guards turn away petitioners. According to Haggith, whose reports from Adonijah are a useful corrective to those that Bathsheba and I receive from David, Absalom seeks out the spurned petitioners, inquiring about the nature of their grievances, sympathising with their frustration and insisting that if he were king, the case would be very different. I sense a growing threat of insurrection and put my fears to Ahitophel but, far from sharing them, he extols Absalom, describing him as the mainstay of David's old age. Bracing myself, I speak to Joab, who is equally dismissive, insisting that the issue is one for father and son to resolve between themselves. I finally pluck up courage to address David, whose response is both contemptuous and cruel. 'Are you trying to outdo Michal? Your own son is dead so you begrudge the love that I have for mine. I expected better.'

So I keep silent when David grants Absalom licence to visit the sanctuary in Hebron to give thanks for their reconciliation. It would be equally effective – and far easier – to do so in the tabernacle, but he claims to have vowed to perform the sacrifice in his birthplace. From the hubbub in the streets, he appears to be taking half the city with him. Chief among them is Ahitophel, whose presence reassures David since he is not only his longest-serving and most trusted adviser but Bathsheba's grandfather and therefore has a dual interest in preserving his crown. Yet in all these years, he has never shown particular concern for Bathsheba or her sons. It's as though, having brokered her marriage, he resents her independence and the influence she exerts on David.

Three days after Absalom's departure, Hiempsal assembles the women in the courtyard and, his voice quavering, orders us to get ready to vacate the palace. A chorus of 'Where's and 'Why's is underscored by the wailing of Shobab and Shammua, Bathsheba's two infant sons, instinctively sharing the alarm. I ask if the Moabites or Edomites, profiting from David's preoccupation, have regrouped and invaded, but Hiempsal insists that he knows nothing. Determined to find out for myself, I bundle up my jewels, to which I attach an importance I would once have scorned, and venture into the main courtyard, where a captain informs me that messengers have arrived from Hebron with news that Absalom has declared himself king. Disaffected men are flocking to him from across the land and he is preparing to march on David's city.

My outrage at Absalom's treachery gives way first to anger at David's sanctioning his visit and then pity at his deception. Eager to lend him my support, I hurry past the distracted guards, reaching the great chamber just as Joab is leaving. Ushering me away, he tells me that David is in council and not to be disturbed.

'Why are we fleeing rather than staying to fight?' I ask.

'Can't you see that I'm busy?' he replies. 'Besides, this isn't flight but a tactical withdrawal to give us time to marshal our forces. David is more concerned about the city – this palace, the tabernacle and everything that he's built – than he is about himself. When we attacked the Jebusites, the walls seemed unassailable. Then we found a way through the water shaft. Absalom knows the story well enough. What's to stop him doing the same?'

'Why don't you block it off?'

'Then what would you drink? Take it from me, this business won't last long. At the first reversal, Absalom's followers will desert him. You'll be back in your bed before the grape harvest.'

Joab heads to the gatehouse and I return to the harem, which is in turmoil. With the women reluctant to relinquish their treasures, the servants are adding packs and boxes to already overladen donkeys and carts. David has ordered all his wives to accompany him, but Michal refuses. To my amazement, he doesn't coerce her. It's as if he calculates that her presence on the journey would do more damage than the challenge to his authority. He is taking all the Jebusite concubines but leaving the foreigners, charging them to keep watch over the palace and prevent looting, an impossible task for any women, let alone those who can barely speak the language. Although Hiempsal maintains that there are too few donkeys to transport them, I am convinced that the real reason for abandoning them is David's fear that the sight of too large a harem, especially its more exotic members, would inflame the populace. What in a young man was admired as a sign of virility would in an old man be condemned as unbridled lust.

For the children, this is an adventure. Adonijah, Shepha-tiah and Ithream, who are old enough to fight, march boldly among the guards. Eager for their first taste of battle, they seem unperturbed that it's against their brother and fellow countrymen. Their younger brothers and sisters ride in the carts, except for Solomon, whom Bathsheba insists on keeping by her side. She claims that his presence makes her feel safe, but one glance at the callow youth with his scraggy chest, spindly arms and sloping shoulders suggests that it is the other way round. While David may have embellished his stories of grappling with the lions and bears that attacked his flock, I have no doubt that if any enemy, man or beast, threatened her eldest son, Bathsheba would tear it apart with her bare hands.

After a long delay, David appears, followed by Ibhar proudly bearing his shield, and we make our sluggish way out of the city, down the hillside and across the valley. As we begin the ascent of the Mount of Olives, we spy a second procession in our wake, led by four Levites carrying the Ark. My assumption that David, anxious to save the sacred throne from falling into Absalom's hands, has ordered them to join us, is confounded when, breathless and sweating, Abiathar, the high priest, and Zadok, his assistant, arrive.

'We have come to bring you the Lord's protection, my lord,' Abiathar says.

'I thank you for your concern,' David replies, 'but you must return the Ark to the city. We have given it a home. That matters more than whether the guardian of that home is David or Absalom.'

'Surely you wish to have the Lord with you?' Zadok asks.

'If the Lord is with me, he will restore me to my city. If not, I shall live in the wilderness once again.' He raises his voice to address the entire company. 'This isn't a fight between the Lord and the uncircumcised but a quarrel between father and son. Besides,' he adds to the priests, 'you must be my eyes and ears in the city, sending me word of all that goes on.'

'We are yours to command, my lord,' Abiathar says, before instructing the Levites to return. I tremble as they make their perilous descent but, despite the heavy load, steep slope and uneven ground, the bearers don't miss a step. At one point they risk colliding with Hushai, whose erratic advance stems as much from his own frailty as his donkey's obstinacy, although he veers aside just in time. The Ark continues on its way and the aged adviser heads towards us. He has dressed in sackcloth and ashes, a token of distress that smacks of despair. For a man of his years, the ride must be painful enough without the added chafing of the robe, and David, with a mixture of solicitude and shrewdness, sends him home, insisting that he will be more use to him if he stays in the city to counter Ahitophel and mislead Absalom. No sooner has Hushai turned back than Ziba, Meribaal's steward, arrives, leading two donkeys laden with bread, fruit and wineskins.

'What's this?' David asks. 'I forgot about your master yet he thinks to send us these rich supplies.'

'Not so, my lord,' Ziba replies. 'I'm here without his knowledge. I told him of your lordship's departure and he laughed. I asked if he wanted to follow you and he refused. He prefers to stay in the city and wait for the rebels to restore him to his grandfather's throne.'

'He imagines that Absalom is attacking me – breaking the sacred bonds of kinship – for his benefit?' David asks incredulously.

'Or else that the two of you will destroy each other like wild beasts and he will step into the breach.'

The notion strikes me as implausible. On the few occasions I have spoken to Meribaal, his one desire has been to live in peace – preferably, in obscurity – not to ascend a throne that he can only reach on his knees. But David, disposed to see treachery everywhere, believes it and grants Ziba the title to his master's lands, which I suspect that he has been plundering for years.

The last stragglers having arrived, we wind our way down the mountain towards the east. We must present a sorry spectacle to the many onlookers who leave their homes and fields to watch us pass. Even so, their reticence unnerves me. Time

was when David could not venture out of doors without eliciting a chorus of cheers. Now the deafening silence is broken
only by the odd shout, no doubt prompted as much by fear of
the heavily armed guards as by reverence for the king. Joab,
hot-headed as ever, proposes to order the guards to teach
the 'disrespectful curs' a lesson, but David overrules him,
refusing to compel his subjects' loyalty. Even when we enter
Bahurim and an old man loudly curses him for supplanting
the house of Saul, David refuses Abishai's demand to silence
him with his sword. 'How can I punish a stranger who reviles
me and wishes me dead when my own son does the same?' he
asks, in a response worthy of his crown. But when he turns
aside, he is white.

Bathsheba echoes Joab's sentiments. Her constant need
to proclaim her devotion to David is precisely what makes
me mistrust it. After all, if I can't forget her violation, how
much harder must it be for her? Nevertheless, I am careful
not to challenge her and nod politely when, quivering with
fury, she draws her donkey alongside mine. 'How dare these
people insult him? Don't they realise how much they owe
him? When have they or their forefathers ever enjoyed so long
a peace? Fifteen years! Fifteen years, when they've been able to
till their fields and tend their flocks: fifteen years when they've
been able to see their daughters married and their sons come
home at night, not marching off to war.'

'When did their forefathers ever pay such heavy tithes?' I
ask. She makes to reply but I forestall her. 'I'm not saying that
I agree with them. Far from it. But I understand them. They
sweat and toil to swell the king's coffers.'

'And his toil? He labours for them night and day.' I stifle a
laugh at the thought of his night-time labour, with which she
is more familiar than I. 'If they want peace and protection,
they have to pay for it.'

'But do they want the city that they've never seen? Rightly
or wrongly, it's said that he cares more for his buildings than

his subjects. You remember the Ephraimite who came from Shechem – only two days' journey away? He was so disappointed that the palace wasn't made of gold. How everyone laughed! But if such beliefs are widespread, peoples' resentment is understandable. What's more, they now find him travelling with thirty mysteriously veiled women, some wearing lavish jewels.' I gaze in reproof at her jacinth earhoops, gold nose-ring and emerald bracelets.

'Would you rather we sneaked through the land like thieves? The splendour of his women is the splendour of the king and the splendour of the king is the splendour of his people.'

'I yield to no one in my love and respect for David.' Even as I speak, I feel a flicker of doubt; although my love is as strong as ever, my respect has been shaken. 'But he has taken his people for granted.'

'What do they know of Absalom? How many victories has he won? How many laws has he framed? And, yes, how many cities has he built? What can he give them that David can't?'

'Youth? Hope? Or maybe just novelty? David has been king for more than thirty years. People with so little else in their lives need change to give them meaning.'

With a toss of her head, she draws back her donkey and calls Solomon. We ride on through increasingly barren terrain, finally reaching a sheltered ravine, where we pitch camp for the night. We share a simple meal of bread, cheese and olives, along with the dates brought by the newly enriched Ziba. As I crouch down behind a line of boulders, which provide a measure of privacy from the men, I'm amused to hear women young enough to be my granddaughters grumble about the dirt and discomfort. To my relief, Maacah, who would otherwise be the first to protest at privations no Geshurite princess should have to endure, is silent. Mindful that it's her son from whom we are fleeing, she moves a short distance from the rest of us, spreads out her mantle, lies down and squirms.

The night air is sharp and, while Ahinoam, cushioned by her own flesh, snores gently beside me, my old bones grate on the stony ground. From the far side of the ravine, above the snores and the chatter and the indeterminate groans and murmurs of man and beast and even the earth itself, comes a gentle strumming. Both moved and intrigued, I slip between the sleeping bodies to find David sitting by a waning fire, playing his lyre. Abishai, keeping watch beside him, nods to let me pass. I stand expectantly, knowing that David senses my presence, although it's a moment before he looks up.

'I thought it was you.'

'I heard you playing.'

'Do you remember?'

'It's my whole life.'

At a stroke he is no longer the careworn king, portly, jowly, his once-flaming hair a dying ember, but the young warrior falteringly confessing that he writes poems. Then he was too shy to sing them to me, even in private. But in later years they have been sung by the priests and Levites in the tabernacle and in sanctuaries across the land: poems of joy and thanksgiving when the Lord has showered him with blessings and of pain and perplexity when he has withdrawn his favour. He has made himself the voice of his people, king by dint of his words as much as his sword. But the poem he sings now is as desolate as the night itself, shot through with anguish as he chastises himself for the wickedness that has led the Lord to turn against him and his beloved son to rebel. I long to take him in my arms and comfort him as I did in Carmel, Gath and Hebron, but I find myself held back as if by an iron chain. It is not the years or the crown or the presence of younger, more beautiful women that constrains me but rather his impregnable sense of guilt.

I listen as he plays, repeating the same desperate phrases, until, unable to bear any more, I make my way back to the women. I don't think that I sleep, although in the wilderness the line between dream and reverie is blurred. We break camp before dawn, trekking through the arid, dusty hills; then in the late afternoon, we reach the Jordan. The water is low and Abital's donkey and baggage are the only casualties of the crossing, the drowning beast diverting the children. We reach the town of Succoth where the elders offer their homes to the king, his wives and generals, while the soldiers bed down outside the walls. Our stay is short, since the next morning we leave for Mahanaim, where we are to set up headquarters. It's a wise move since, by occupying what was once Ishbaal's capital, David reminds people not only of his past victories but that he is king of all Israel. And it's heartening that after the indifference shown to him in Judah, not only are the Gadites friendly but Joab's muster yields results. Eavesdropping on the new recruits, I find that Goliath has grown by two cubits and David's legend increased accordingly. For all my unease, I would never disabuse them since, in the battle against Absalom's youth and promise, that legend is the strongest weapon we possess.

Joab urges David to return to Judah and attack Absalom before he secures his position. David, as anxious to avoid fighting his son as endangering his city, holds back. Any hope that Absalom will acknowledge his perfidy and renounce the crown is dashed by Abiathar's son, Jonathan, who, as agreed, brings word from the palace. Hearing of his arrival, I hurry into David's chamber, which still reeks of the pelts that were stored there. Although he greets me warmly, it is clear that my presence disconcerts the young man.

'Forgive me, my lady, but what I have to report isn't fit for a woman's ears.'

'These ears have heard... these eyes have seen things unfit for anyone, man or woman,' I say.

'Lady Abigail has as strong a stomach as any soldier,' David interjects, to my consternation.

'Whatever you say, my lord,' Jonathan replies. 'The night

that he entered the palace, Absalom ordered a tent to be pitched on the roof. He had the concubines that my lord left there brought to him and he lay with them, one by one. I was among the crowd in the street below, watching the shadows play on the walls of the tent.'

'And the Princess Michal?' I ask, as David sits aghast.

'I couldn't see their faces,' Jonathan replies slowly.

'But he lay with all the women?'

'So I understand.'

'I wanted to bring her with me. You were there; you heard,' David says to me. 'She can't blame me for that.'

'She can't blame you for anything,' I reply. But even as I speak, the memory of his lying with her mother springs into my head. 'I tried to be gentle,' he said to me, 'but her body was clenched.' Now Absalom has done to his wife what he did to Saul's.

'I should have brought her by force. I should have brought them all. I should have heeded Nathan's prophecy, but it was too painful. Besides, sooner or later it had to be fulfilled. He never specified which of my kinsmen would rob me or which of my women he would take. It might have been Ahinoam or Abital or Bathsheba or even you. At least apart from Michal, they were women sent to me in tribute or won in war.'

'They are still people.' I am sickened by Absalom to whom the women were tokens, by David to whom they were trophies, but, equally, by myself to whom they were an embarrassment. In common with the other wives, I made no attempt to befriend them. Except for exchanging courtesies, they kept to themselves, speaking their own languages, which suited those of us who liked to pretend that we had chosen our fate.

Joab revels in the news, trusting that the conclusive evidence of his son's intentions will finally spur David to act. But he refuses to be rushed, preferring to wait for Absalom to make the first move, a tactic that is vindicated two days later when Abiathar's second emissary, Zadok's son Ahimaaz, brings word that his army is on the march. Just as David had hoped, Absalom ignored Ahitophel's advice to launch an immediate attack and swallowed Hushai's lie that, by waiting to mount a full-scale offensive, he would demonstrate his superior strategy. The rebuff drove Ahitophel to despair. He quit the palace for his house in Ephraim where, according to his steward, he examined the accounts and inspected the storeroom, arranged for the repair of a broken fence and gave instructions for his meal. Then, with no indication that anything was amiss, he went up to his chamber and hanged himself.

I am shocked. Despite his treachery, I retained my respect for the old man, who was a wise counsellor first to Saul and then to David. However hard he tried, he never displayed the same esteem for David after his violation of Bathsheba, but he continued to serve him – or, rather, the crown – until he thought that he had found a worthy successor. But, on discovering that the son was as obdurate as the father, he took the only course left to him. Even traitors can die with honour.

Claiming that he has to consult his generals, David charges me with breaking the news to Bathsheba, who is more distressed than I expected. Having lost no opportunity to denounce her grandfather since his defection to Absalom, she breaks down on hearing of his death.

'Forgive me,' she says, struggling to compose herself. 'Please don't mention this to the king.'

'He was your grandfather!'

'Yes. He disapproved of me all my life. He betrayed the king, so he deserved to die. And yet I can't stop thinking of how he went about it. No fuss, no mess. Methodical to the last. Even journeying to Ephraim.'

'Was it his favourite place?'

'Not at all. He disliked the quiet. He was always happiest in the palace, at the heart of great affairs. He'd built himself a tomb outside the city. It's where we buried Uriah. He must have feared that when Absalom was defeated, his body would be disinterred and defiled. Who'll take the trouble to travel to Ephraim?'

I seek out Solomon who, studying a scroll, shows little concern for his mother's grief, until I allege that his father has asked him to console her. Meanwhile, David prepares to encounter Absalom. So many men have rallied to his cause that he divides the army into three: a third under Joab; a third under Abishai; and a third under Ittai, a Philistine who was once Achish's representative in Hebron but has since aligned himself with us. David declares his resolve to take overall command himself, provoking a noisy confrontation with Joab, which, in the cramped confines of the house, I can't help overhearing.

'That's madness!' Joab says, adding a belated 'My lord', as if in response to David's glower. 'You're in no fit state. You're too slow. You'd be a liability.'

'I'm three years younger than you!'

'But I haven't spent half my life sitting on my backside, listening to petitions, feasting with emissaries.'

'More to the point, the enemy's chief objective will be to capture you,' Abishai, more politic than his brother, interjects. 'We'd have to employ so many men to protect you that we'd leave ourselves vulnerable elsewhere.'

David emits a mollified grunt. Although he later rails against Joab's insolence, I detect his relief at not having to face his son in the field.

He assembles the army at the city gate and makes them swear to capture Absalom alive. It is plain from Joab's expression as he takes the vow that he has no intention of keeping it. For the first time in years I find myself among a crowd of women waving off the departing troops. When the last man marches away, David orders a guard to bring a stool, on which he sits in the shadow of the gates. I approach, eager to comfort, support or merely distract him during his vigil, but he prefers to wait alone, dismissing me along with the guard. I return to the house, where time passes so slowly that it feels like the day when the sun stood still so that Joshua could destroy the Amorites. Now, however, there is no foreign enemy to defeat; it's Israelite against Israelite, father against son, and brother against brother, since Adonijah, Shephatiah, Ithream and Ibhar are ranged against Absalom.

Dusk finally falls, swiftly followed by word that the watchman has spied a messenger heading towards us. In company with Bathsheba, Solomon and Bithiah, I run down to the gates just as Ahimaaz arrives from the battlefield. Scarcely pausing for breath, he prostrates himself at David's feet.

'Praise to the Lord our God, who has delivered us from the hands of our enemies.'

While the bystanders echo his words, David darts forward and asks haltingly: 'And my sons, are they safe?'

'Quite safe, my lord. All four have fought valiantly.'

'Four? There are five. What of Absalom?'

'I can't say, my lord. I only know that the princes Ithream, Ibhar, Adonijah and Shephatiah have shown themselves worthy of their father. Your enemies are routed, praise be to the Lord.'

From his furtive expression, I sense that he could say more but that he is reluctant to break bad news to the king. He has scarcely finished speaking when a second messenger arrives, who, less aware of David's conflicted loyalties, greets him with a tally of enemy losses.

'And Absalom?' David asks, cutting him short.

'Dead, my lord. And may all the king's enemies lie beside him!'

'No, no, no!' David shrieks, leaping forward and grabbing him by the throat. Ahimaaz and two guards look on in horror but shrink from laying hands on their king.

'Stop! You'll kill him!' Solomon shouts, startling me as

much as David, since I have never before heard him address his father unprompted. His warning brings David back to his senses; he releases the man, who falls to the ground, his eyes red with blood, clutching his neck and fighting for breath.

'You lie!' David says.

'No, my lord, it's true,' Ahimaaz interjects. 'Joab told me to say nothing.'

'Why?' David asks harshly. 'Did he kill him himself in the field?'

'Not in the field, my lord, in the forest. When he saw that the day was lost, Absalom fled. He was caught in a thicket, his neck between two branches.'

'Why didn't the men cut him down? What about their vow to bring him back alive?'

'Come indoors, my lord,' Bathsheba says. 'You should rest. You can question him later.'

'No, now!' he says angrily, as if by curtailing the account, she is killing Absalom twice over.

'Joab shot him himself,' Ahimaaz says. 'With three arrows: the first to his belly; the second to his neck; the third between his eyes.'

'Joab!' David spits, as though his nephew's treachery surpassed his son's.

'But he still wasn't dead,' the second messenger rasps with relish. 'He squealed and squirmed until ten of Joab's men stabbed him, chopping him to pieces like a wild roe.'

'No, no, no!' David howls and runs back to the house. We women follow, only to find that he has bolted his chamber door. We stand outside, begging to be allowed in, as he sobs and sputters, the great poet struck dumb by anguish deeper even than that he felt for Jonathan. Then I stood with Ahinoam, listening as he composed his lament for his friend; now all I hear are the same words repeated over again: 'Oh my son Absalom! Oh Absalom my son, my son!'

The army returns to a silent city. In deference to David,

the women refrain from victory songs and dances, shutting themselves in their houses, to which the men slink back like deserters. Seething with rage, Joab strides up to David's chamber, pushes past us and pounds the door with his bloody fist.

'Stop this wickedness and come out now! You make me ashamed to be your general... ashamed to be your kinsman. Thousands of men have fought for you today and hundreds have fallen. Is this how you honour them: by locking yourself away and mourning the wretch who would have stolen your crown? You should be out there with them, greeting them and hailing their victory. And I tell you one thing: if you don't pull yourself together, not a man among them will be left by your side in the morning – and I will be the first to go!'

He waits with confidence for David to emerge, as if they were still boys and older, larger and more devious, he had him cornered. Sure enough, a few moments later David appears. I am unable to gauge his expression since he's staring at his feet, but the acrimony in his voice is unmistakable.

'You're right, of course: sons are easier to replace than generals. Gather the men at the gates and I'll address them. They shall have feasting and celebrations tomorrow and rich rewards when we return to the city.'

We remain in Mahanaim three more days before crossing back over the Jordan. To compound his grief, David is unable to recover Absalom's body, which Joab has buried in a forest pit, concealed beneath brushwood and stones. I too have cause to mourn, for Ahinoam, the servant and sister who has shared so many of my joys and sorrows since David's men first knocked at Nabal's gate, died the day after the battle, too crazed to appreciate the bittersweet victory, made so much sweeter for her by the death of the man who murdered her son.

SIX

Michal

I almost wanted him back. At least when he was in the palace, no matter how thick the walls between us, I had known where to direct my hatred but, once he crossed the Jordan, he might have been anywhere: in the mountains of Gilead or the plain of Madaba or the forests of Bashan. It had been six days since Absalom led his army in search of him, time enough for them to have met in the field, but there had been no word. No messengers had arrived for Nathan or Hushai; no wounded soldiers had limped home to their wives or corpses been delivered to their widows. For all I knew he was dead: slain by his son, as my father had been by order of his son-in-law. Had the Lord finally heeded my prayer?

Were it not for the uncertainty, I might have been content. I was less constrained than at any time since Abner abducted me. The harem was barely secured. Hiempsal, looking to prove his manhood, had been killed attempting to repel the invaders. Absalom had replaced him with Jonadab, the one man whom, like his father, he could trust to respect his rights. During the years that I was confined to my chamber, I saw more of him than of anybody else, which would have driven me to despair had I not elected to live among my dead: husband; father; sons and brothers. Sharing my ordeal, they sustained me in ways that Jonadab with his hollow deference would never understand. I had been wary of him ever since his boyhood visit to Gibeah, but it was not until Absalom's requisition of the harem that I had the true measure of the man. He was the one who led us up to the roof and, while the flickering torchlight obscured the other onlookers' faces, his displayed the same mixture of excitement and revulsion that I'd seen in Penuel and Malkiel when they disembowelled a hare.

Despite that glimpse of his night-time face, his daytime face remained guarded. But of late he had struggled to conceal his apprehension. When Absalom set off, his golden hair streaming behind him like his horse's mane, Jonadab insisted that he would soon return victorious. But as time passed, he was obliged to admit the possibility that the Lord had favoured the father over the son. Eager for allies, he permitted me to walk outside the palace. I wore my veil (not for modesty, which was lost after my reputed coupling with my husband's son), but for protection. No matter who won the battle, I was David's wife and a target for both the Jebusites, who deplored his transformation of their city, and the Judahites, who resented his increasing repression. But the handful of people out in the streets hurried past, heads lowered, as anxious as Jonadab to know which king they would be hailing on his return. So, after two desultory excursions, I kept to the eerily empty palace. My only companions were the concubines but, even had I been able to speak to them, I would have had nothing to say. They huddled in the courtyard for hours on end, lamenting their violation as if they were their own virgin daughters. How had they suffered? Their sole purpose was to serve a king's pleasure. What did it matter whether that king were Absalom or David?

They keened through the day only to rest at night, when, lying awake in a silence as deep as Sheol, I would have welcomed the occasional wail. On the third sleepless night, when the absence of news had become unendurable, I quit my chamber to consult Nathan who, as a prophet, had no need of messengers. I had expected him to take flight, preserving the scrolls that David valued almost as highly as the Ark itself. Indeed, there could be no surer sign of his vanity than his appointing Nathan to document his life, rather than trusting the elders to transmit the story as they had done those of all our leaders since Abraham. Hearing that Nathan had transcribed the accounts of David's brothers in Bethlehem;

the priests at Nob and Hebron; Joab, Abishai and other generals who had fought alongside him, I proposed that he talk to me, the sole surviving witness to events in Gibeah, but he declined, declaring that a woman's testimony was invalid.

Stung by Nathan's contempt, I had avoided him ever since, and I still feared that he would refuse to help, but the darkness emboldened me and, after hurrying through the bleak courtyard, I knocked firmly on his door to show that I had no qualms about intruding. When bidden, I entered a small, drab chamber, smelling of camphor and old skin. Nathan sat in bed, an oil lamp casting a faint glow on his heavy brows, sharp nose and the thick beard that put me in mind of the bush in which the Lord had appeared to Moses.

'It's very late, my lady,' he said, rising and throwing a mantle over his bony shoulders.

'Forgive me. I couldn't sleep. I'm desperate to have news of the king.'

'Which king? The one to whom you're married or the one to whom you're bound: King Absalom?'

'Have you transferred your allegiance?' I asked, both astonished and hopeful.

'Not I. But I saw you being led into the tent.'

'But did you see me inside it?' He fell silent. 'I thought not. Absalom afforded me the courtesy of dousing the torches.'

'Was that his only courtesy?'

'No. I almost wish that it were. The rape of ten thousand concubines would not have shamed David so much as the rape of his first – his true – wife.'

'So what stopped him? I doubt that it was compassion.'

'He felt the force of my argument. I told him: "I am your father's discarded wife. Would you disgrace yourself by lying with a woman your father scorned?"'

Nathan studied me intently, and I realised that equivocation might be a stronger weapon than truth. 'If you say so,' he replied at last. 'We must hope that King David believes you.'

'If he wins the battle.'

'He has won the battle.'

'The Lord has told you?'

'The Lord has willed it. I don't know if it has happened or is yet to come. All I know is that it is.'

Once again I was confronted with the Lord's perversity. All my life I had been told that he viewed things differently from us. Now I knew that it was not because he was clearer-sighted but because he was blind. How else could he favour David: a man who had lied, cheated, betrayed and murdered his way to the throne; a man so steeped in blood that he had devised new forms of butchery? 'The Lord you serve is an unjust god.'

'Take care what you say! He hears everything.'

'No, he is deaf to my cries, my pleas, my prayers! As a child, I could never understand why he rejected Cain's sacrifice and commended Abel's. Of course I was only a girl and so, unlike my brothers, I didn't have Samuel to explain the story. But when I grew up, I found that there was nothing to explain. The Lord is as cruel and capricious as Pharaoh.'

'Enough! You come to my chamber in this unseemly manner. You speak sacrilege – '

'Unseemly? You flatter yourself or you mock me or both. The only unseemly manner is the Lord's. As with Cain and Abel, so with Saul and David. You know better than anyone how the Lord forgave David his transgression with Bathsheba. You brought him his pardon.'

'And his punishment.'

'Wasn't my father punished? Tormented by an evil spirit, like a hornet trapped inside his head. And was he pardoned? No, he was tormented still further when the Lord turned against him and, in his confusion – in his pain, in his terror and his despair – he became the tyrant that the Lord – or, at any rate, your predecessor – accused him of being. Samuel did, however, speak one truth, when he declared that the Lord would replace him with a man after his own heart. A heart that's as hard as iron and as cold as stone.'

'You forget that I am King David's chronicler! Who was it who enabled him to escape Saul's wrath?' he asked, tearing my insides like a fisherman tugging a hook that had previously tickled.

'That's the one wrong for which I shall never forgive myself: the one for which I shall pay all the rest of my life, and in death it will weigh heavier on me than the rock in which I lie entombed.'

He fixed me with a look, which, had he not been bound to David, I might have taken for sympathy. 'My lady, it's time to cast off your bitterness and find peace.'

'Bitterness is my peace! It's the one thing that comforts and sustains me. And the best part is to know that David will never find it. Even this victory that the Lord has granted him will be a defeat. He will no longer trust his sons nor his counsellors nor his generals nor even his women. He'll yearn to speak to the Lord, but all he will hear is the clamour of his own entreaties. He can sacrifice every ox, every sheep and goat and dove in the kingdom but he'll know that the only blood that can atone for his sins is his own. He can – '

My prediction was cut short by a loud knock. A servant entered and I was amused at how swiftly Nathan drew away from me, wrapping his mantle around himself as if he feared that my visit might be misconstrued. The servant whispered in his ear and Nathan nodded, first to acknowledge his report and then to dismiss him.

'News from the battlefield?' I asked, as the servant left.

'Nearer to hand. Meribaal has tried to kill himself.'

'He's dead?'

'Tried!'

'I must go to him. Where? How? Are you sure?' I asked, keen to exonerate my one remaining kinsman. 'He's unsteady on his feet. He might have tripped on a sword.'

'He used a rope,' Nathan replied drily. 'He threw it around a beam, but he must have slipped from the stool when he reached for it. The servant found him flailing about on the floor. He helped him up and put him to bed.'

'I must go to him.'

I walked back through the palace, newly aware of the tangle of beams overhead. My anger at Meribaal's cravenness melted when the first thing I saw in his chamber was the noose quivering in a draught, and the second was his two sticks propped in a corner, confining him to bed. Unabashed, he greeted me with a bleary smile. 'My aunt!' he exclaimed, waving his cup, as if introducing me to a group of strangers.

'Are you hurt?' I asked, more coldly than I had intended.

'Just here,' he said, placing the cup on his heart and spilling wine on his tunic, as if to lend credence to his words.

'What were you thinking?' I asked, staring pointedly at the noose.

'What do you care?' he replied, with a sharpness that seemed to sober him.

'Of course I care. You're my brother's son. The last of our house.'

'The house, yes! You care that I'm not worthy of my father and my grandfather. But what about me? I care that I'm not worthy of myself. Myself! When Absalom's troops rounded up all the men left in the palace, they didn't spare me a second glance. Even the eunuch fought back.'

'He was killed.'

'He died honourably, defending the harem. But I could do nothing. I sat here while Absalom took you up to the roof; I sat here while he defiled you.'

I gazed at him in amazement, in guilt and in gratitude. 'You tried to end your life because you failed to protect me?'

'Do you remember how Absalom taunted me as a boy?' he asked, deflecting my question with his own. 'I could see how he was teaching his sons to do the same. He summoned me to do him obeisance. I crawled the length of the chamber to the throne and kissed his foot, which was as leathery as a sandal. He lifted it and rubbed it on my cheek – it wasn't painful, at least not to the cheek – and his sons laughed. Then he lifted me up and pulled me by the ear so that I stumbled forward, more stooped than ever, my whole weight resting on my sticks. "Look, boys," he said, "is he a man or a sheep? A sheep with two human legs and two wooden ones?" "A sheep," the eldest boy shouted. He must be six or seven, the same age as Absalom when I came here. And I saw it happening all over again.'

'Not necessarily,' I said, as ashamed of my failure to protect him as he of his to protect me. 'Absalom may already be defeated. As for his sons, who knows what will happen to them if... when David wins?' For the first time I considered the effect of David's victory on somebody other than myself. 'David has always been kind to you.'

'Oh yes, he kept his oath to my father, but I've paid for it and not just in derision.' He drained his cup, which seemed to fuel his resentment. 'Ziba gives him the revenues from my lands – those same lands that he granted me – to cover the cost of my quarters. But, as you say, the king is kind. Who else would seat at his table a man whose crippled legs prevent him from entering the tabernacle?'

'Nonsense! Who's preventing you?'

'Moses... the Law. Ask Abiathar! But the king is kind. Hasn't he kept me alive when, at the first whisper of famine, he could have slaughtered me as he did my cousins? Oh yes, the king is kind.'

He fell back on his pillow, which was worn so thin that a reed poked through the weave. I laid my hand on his cold, clammy forehead. 'You're tired. You will have forgotten all this by morning.'

'Perhaps. But then I'll remember it afresh.' He began to garble. 'You're right, Aunt, the king is kind. Whatever else he takes from me, he allows me my wine.'

He slumped and I moved away. I glanced at the noose, which I longed to rip down while he slept, turning the memory into a bad dream, but the beam was too high and I didn't trust myself on the stool. As I walked back to my chamber through the mockery of another dawn, my anger at his cowardice threatened to reignite. So he felt unmanned by his deformity, cheated by David and humiliated by Absalom: what was his grievance compared to mine? Married to a man I loved but who favoured my brother; married to a man I grew to love, from whom I was snatched away; mother to five murdered sons. How gladly I might have found comfort in death! But I lived on as a permanent reproach to David and a reminder of the Lord's malice towards our house. Why else would a prince so avid for the crown that he would have lain with his father's stable as well as his harem, have spared me?

I reached the harem's unguarded gate and entered the courtyard, where Tamar rushed up to greet me. Meeting her feverish gaze, I had the uneasy sense that she'd sought the same release in madness that Meribaal had in wine. On taking the city, Absalom had summoned her from Baal Hazor where she lived in seclusion, neither honoured daughter, lawful wife nor respected widow. Given her condition, it was clear that he had brought her not to grace his household but to rally support. For months he had promised disaffected suppliants that, if he were king, he would grant them the justice that David neglected. What better way to win round any waverers than by parading the most notorious victim of that neglect?

By the time of her arrival, Danatiya had moved into the harem, claiming Abigail's chamber for herself and her daughter and Ahinoam's for her three young sons. Far from welcoming Tamar, she kept her distance from her. Was she ashamed to acknowledge a madwoman as her sister-in-law? Or did she fear that a similar fate might befall her or, worse, her own Tamar, whom I noticed that she never addressed by name? Such unease must have been compounded by her daily encounters with the concubines ravished by Absalom. Poor woman! Whatever happiness she'd enjoyed with him had vanished the moment that he seized the throne. The future was fraught with uncertainty. If Absalom defeated his father, would she share her bed not only with the resident concubines but with those who returned as captives – to say nothing of all the others whom he would gain as trophies in years to come? If David defeated his son, would he seek to reassert his legitimacy by lying with his son's wife as he once had with his wife's mother?

By petting Tamar like a child, I could avoid engaging with her as a woman. Despite the general belief that she had lost her wits, I was convinced that she had renounced them, choosing or, at the very least, allowing herself to become her rape. She no longer washed or changed her linen but exuded a thick, salty odour as if she were still trapped in Amnon's bed. She no longer spoke but grunted and groaned as if she were the embodiment of his beastliness. But Amnon was dead and the people she hurt were those who would have cherished her given the chance. I too had turned away from her until her maidservant let slip that she had borne Amnon's child. When pressed, she insisted that I had misunderstood, but her terrified stare betrayed her. The more I pondered, the more certain I grew that it was less the child itself that she was seeking to conceal than its subsequent murder. Was it a boy or a girl: a son killed in order that he would never know his mother's shame or a daughter in order that she would never know such shame herself?

So I curbed my revulsion at her reek, her dirt and dishevelment, and led her into my chamber, which, to her mother's dismay, had been her refuge as a girl. She sat beside me on the bed and laid her head in my lap. As I stroked her straggling hair, I felt unusually close to her. For years the women of the harem had kept themselves and their children away from me as though afraid that I might infect them – with what? My sadness? My sterility? But she, who hissed and hit at anybody who approached, sought me out. I longed for one of Nathan's scrolls on which to rewrite the story of our lives. She would be not Maacah's daughter but mine. She would marry the prince of Hamath and Amnon would treat her with respect. I brushed a tear from my eye and a lock from hers and was thankful that there was no one to see.

Nathan was right, as I had known that he must be, and David won the battle. He set off at once for home, and a succession of messengers arrived, first from Mahanaim, then from Succoth and Abel Shittim, to inform Hushai and Abiathar of his progress. Jonadab, desperate to save himself, went to meet him in Geba, so I slipped out, unhindered, and joined the crowd at the city gate hailing his triumphant return. Grateful for his victory (or fearful of his vengeance), they cheered him more fervently than they had done in years, but David barely acknowledged them. His face was fixed and his body slumped in an expression of grief that would have delighted me had Adonijah, Shephatiah, Ithream and Ibhar not been riding behind him. I wouldn't rest until they lay alongside Chileab, Amnon and Absalom and the tally of his dead sons exceeded mine.

While Joab and Abishai greeted the crowd, David and his entourage headed straight for the palace. I hurried back to the harem and waited for the women to return, take off their dusty robes, wash and give me a report. For more than an hour nobody came, unnerving the concubines, who clung together, looking as lost as when they had first arrived in the city. Finally, Jonadab appeared, his smug smile a sign that he had made his peace with David, convincing him that Absalom had forced his hand and his loyalty never wavered.

'You're to put on your veils and come at once to the great chamber. Quick, quick!' he said, clapping his hands as if we were geese.

'Veils?' I asked. 'Within the palace?'

'The king wishes to cover your shame.'

'Since when?'

'Since you lay with the traitor Absalom.'

'And what of your shame? You who took us up to the tent and watched us with eyes like brands.'

'I had no choice. Absalom compelled me to bear witness.'

'And did you witness him lying with me?'

'It was dark. The guards put out the torches. I couldn't see.'

'But what did you see in here?' I asked, prodding his forehead. 'What do you still see?'

'Stop!' he shrieked, as I repeated the gesture. 'You have no right. I am the king's kinsman.' He pushed me away and smoothed his hair as if that alone had been ruffled, before turning to the concubines, several of whom were smiling at his discomfiture.

'Veils, now!' he said, drawing his hand in front of his face. As they hurried to obey him, he went to collect Danatiya, who emerged dressed in sackcloth, although I wondered whether the ashes smeared on her cheeks were as much to conceal her beauty from David as to mourn Absalom. She clutched her youngest son by the hand, while ten-year-old Tamar walked behind with his two older brothers. Even I, who sought nothing more ardently than the downfall of David's house, pitied their plight and was sure that their grandfather would feel the same. Determined to mar their reconciliation, I went to fetch Tamar, my Tamar, or rather David's Tamar, whom he had not set eyes on since her rape. She was unusually docile, even allowing me to fasten her veil. Jonadab, eager to make haste, either failed to register her clinging to my arm or else presumed that, after years of keeping aloof, I was consoling a concubine.

We entered the great chamber, where David sat in state, but, despite his victory, he looked diminished: his shoulders sagging; his belly swollen; his skin pallid against the golden throne. He was flanked by his wives, sons and counsellors, and those fortunate concubines whose sole afflictions were to be travel-stained and saddle-sore. Given no order to proceed, Danatiya and her children fell to their knees, swiftly followed by the concubines. I alone stood fast, clasping Tamar to me. David's darting glance missed neither the reverence nor the defiance, but he ignored both, instead summoning Meribaal before him. I had visited my nephew twice since the failed hanging, but on each occasion he had been too befuddled to converse. Loath to deny him his one solace, I wished now that I had kept him sober for David's return. He staggered towards the throne where he stood, propped up by Ziba and a servant. His speech as disjointed as his legs, he spluttered and snickered until Ziba, noting David's glare, interrupted, declaring that he'd tried to persuade him to leave the city but he had remained in the hope of seizing the crown. On hearing the news of David's victory, he'd attempted to kill himself but had even bungled that.

'That's not true!' I cried out, to general consternation. Detaching myself from Tamar, I strode forward and lifted my veil. 'My lord, will you allow a steward to slander one of royal blood? Jonathan's son... Jonathan's son,' I repeated so emphatically that even those born long after my brother's death must have perceived a hidden meaning. 'He stayed here so as not to hold you back.' Meribaal emitted a timely gurgle. 'Even if the king – may the Lord preserve him – had been killed alongside Absalom, he would have had many worthy sons to succeed him. I see them standing before me.' I bit my tongue. 'Look at this man, a helpless cripple. How could he sit on the throne? He'd slide straight off it.' My attempt at levity fell as flat as Meribaal himself, now lying prostrate on the floor.

'Then why should he fear my return?' David asked.

'Not yours but Absalom's. Absalom who had treated him with cruelty and contempt from their first meeting. Ziba lies; we'd received no news of your victory. We hoped for it; we prayed for it; but we knew nothing of it.'

David gazed from Meribaal to Ziba to me and back again. 'How can I know which of you is speaking the truth?' he asked, a startling admission from one who prided himself on his judgement. 'So I must believe both of you – or neither. When you took flight with me, Ziba, I granted you all your master's lands.'

'You did, my lord, and I hope to share their bounty with my benefactor.'

'Quite,' David said quickly. 'But now I am mindful to return half to my brother's son.'

'Whatever my lord wishes,' Ziba replied. 'My one desire is to serve you.'

'And mine is for your safe return,' Meribaal interjected, in a moment of semi-lucidity.

'Come forward, Prince Meribaal, to make obeisance.'

With Meribaal immobile, Ziba and the servant dragged him up and deposited him at David's feet but, rather than kiss them, he sank back on the floor and snored.

The strained silence was broken by David's laughter. He turned to me. 'Jonathan's son, did you say?' I bowed my head and drew back. Then, with rare delicacy, he tapped Meribaal on the cheek with his toes, before signalling to Ziba and the servants to carry him out.

'You, my lady,' he said, looking past me to Danatiya, 'who, I am assured, played no part in your husband's schemes; with whom I'm united in grief, wife and... father.' His voice faltered. 'You are to return to Baal Hazor, raising my grandsons, until I see fit to summon them here.'

'I thank my gracious lord,' Danatiya said, moving forward to pay him homage, but David waved her back before she had time to kneel.

'And Jonadab, you shall accompany her as her steward.'

'But my lord!' he exclaimed, his face contorted with horror.

'Hushai has informed me of your service – your painstaking service – to Absalom; I trust you to extend it to his widow and fatherless children. Besides, after so many years in the tumult of the city, you deserve the seclusion of the countryside.'

He thrust out his foot and, for a moment, I wondered whether Jonadab would break the habit of a lifetime and rebel, but, swallowing his outrage, he knelt and kissed it. Then, just as he was set to rise, Joab stepped forward and, with both burly hands, pressed his face back on the foot. Several of the women laughed openly at his abasement. I even caught a flutter of the veils by my side, which ceased when, after Jonadab quit the chamber, David addressed the concubines.

'You women, who shame me by your very being: what am I to do with you?' It was a question few of them could understand, let alone answer. 'Do you expect to live here in luxury, enjoying the king's favour, after lying with his son? No, of course not! You shall be taken from here and confined in the gatehouse, never again to see the light of day.'

Although the faces flanking him were studiously vacant, it was clear to everyone that his leniency to Jonadab had been an exception and he was once again bending the Law to his will. The only ones who failed to detect it were the concubines themselves, granted a few moments' grace before the prison gates closed on them forever... unless Adonijah or Shephatiah or whichever of his sons succeeded him were to denounce his father's cruelty and set them free.

A guard, mistaking Tamar for a concubine, approached us but I pushed him away. 'What fresh device of yours is this?' David asked.

'Not mine, yours. She is your daughter.' David looked at the girls standing close to him. 'Your daughter, Tamar.' The shock in the chamber was as palpable as if I had brought her back to life. Maacah moaned and buried her head on Nechama's shoulder. David rose slowly and walked towards us. He lifted Tamar's veil and gaped, as if expecting another idol of Ashtoreth. Tamar leant forward and kissed him full on the lips. He recoiled and she grabbed his hand, pressing it to her breast. He slapped her face, but before he could remove his hand, she sank her teeth into the palm. He howled, shook her off roughly and returned to the throne, licking his wound. Tamar leapt about, shrieking and giggling and rubbing her hands up and down her thighs. She stopped short in front of her mother and sister; Maacah turned aside but Nechama reached out to her. Tamar stared at her for a moment with no sign of recognition before scuttling away. To one who had observed her closely, her movements looked forced, even feigned, unless the large crowd of onlookers had disturbed her.

'What is this?' David asked, clawing at the arms of the throne.

'She's distracted, my lord,' Hushai said. 'Prince Absalom brought her to the palace.' He pointed at me. 'This lady has been kind to her.'

'Take her away! Take her at once!' David said to a guard, who advanced on her, but his failure to secure her hands left her free to grab his member. A second guard seized her, pinioning her arms. 'Should we return her to the women's quarters?' he asked.

'No, to the gatehouse, along with the others.'

'But Father... my lord – ' Nechama interposed.

'Not one word!' David said, flushed and panting as if it were he who had been attacked. 'Unless you and your mother wish to accompany her.'

Nechama made to reply, but Maacah cupped her mouth. David, meanwhile, turned to me.

'And you, my lady, what am I to do with you, the principal witness to my shame?'

'I've witnessed so much of your shame; I'm inured to it.'

'Even in his hunger for my throne, Absalom couldn't bring himself to lie with you. My other women were sacrificed to his ambition, but you were like an offering left out too long to be lawfully consumed.'

'Is that what you think?' His scorn fired me; his smugness strengthened me. 'How can you be so certain?'

'You told Nathan.'

'But did I tell him the truth?'

'Would you lie to the prophet?'

'I have no love for prophets, as you well know. Yes, I lied. And I lay with Absalom. He held me in arms that should have wrenched the crown from your head. He clasped me to a chest like adamant. And he entered me with a member that would have fathered an army of kings. A member so potent that coupling with him was the greatest pleasure of my life.'

Glancing at the women, I caught Abigail's look of dismay and Bathsheba's of admiration, but I had no chance to reflect on either for David rose from the throne. 'You lie!' he spat.

I refused to back down, although I knew that I was sealing my doom. 'Lead me to your chamber and I'll show you the bruises. A month old and they've still not faded! You should be proud to have engendered such a son. A second Samson.'

'What kind of woman are you? The others bore their infamy in silence; you boast of it.'

'I revel in it! Not infamy but pride. Pride to have been possessed by such a man!'

'Guards!' David shouted, and two seized me without waiting for a further order. He turned to me, his face now white with fury. 'You pollute the palace; you pollute the throne. You shall be locked in the gatehouse with the others: left there to rot, disgraced and forgotten.'

'But not by you. How will you ever forget me?'

'Take her away!'

The guards dragged me out. For all their savagery, I rejoiced to know that my life with David was over and I would be united with my daughter, Tamar.

SEVEN

Bathsheba

For such an impetuous man, the king is taking a long time to die. Absalom's death shot an arrow into his heart as lethal as those that Joab shot into the prince's body. Yet whereas Absalom died in an instant, his father clings to life, as though the wound itself has healed but the barb was dipped in venom, which has been seeping into him for the past three years.

Despite his infirmity, he refuses to name a successor. After a lifetime spent strengthening the kingdom, he is jeopardizing its future. Loath to acknowledge his own mortality, he fears that others will anticipate it by looking east while he sinks slowly in the west. Abigail, ever loyal, maintains that he prevaricates because there's no obvious heir, incensing Haggith, whose son Adonijah is next in line. He is as arrogant as Absalom, whose excesses he appears to be emulating. He has even appropriated his chariot, in which he careers around the city, through streets so narrow that it can barely pass. He curries favour both with his younger brothers and the tribal elders and has won over Joab and Abiathar, gaining footholds in the army and the tabernacle. He takes care not to criticise his father in public and insists that everything he does is in his name, but he's as shallow as his mother and is sure to slip up soon.

Even so, there are eleven princes standing between him and Solomon: Shephatiah; Ithream; Ibhar; Elishua; Elpelet; Nogah; Nepheg; Japhia; Jerimoth; Eliada and Eliphelet. Sometimes their names pound my head so violently that I fear it will crack. I dream of their dying all at once, buried in a rockslide or drowned in a flood or killed in a battle – no, not a battle, which would reflect badly on Solomon. Although, by law, the eldest son has the greatest claim to his father's lands, must it be the same with the crown? After all, the king was the youngest of Jesse's sons.

The longer his father lingers, the greater Solomon's chances of outflanking his older brothers and ascending the throne. Although his cheeks remain dismayingly smooth, it is harder for his rivals to dismiss him as a callow youth now that he has a wife and child. He has me to thank for that – not that he does, of course. My power over the king may have waned now that I am no longer pressed into night-time service – as I struggled to squeeze the sap from his withered stump, my ministrations came to humiliate rather than comfort him – but with kohl to enhance my eyes and almond oil to moisten my skin, I can still beguile him. So, when he proposed last year to marry one of his sons to the Ammonite princess, Naamah, I cajoled him into choosing Solomon. It caused uproar in the harem, with Eglah and Bithiah protesting that Solomon was only sixteen and their sons remained unwed, but I felt no remorse. Unlike his older brothers, as hot-blooded as their father, Solomon is cold... no, not cold, circumspect; apt to question even his most intimate feelings. He needs his mother to safeguard his interests.

Quiet and unassuming, with small breasts and wide hips better suited to slaking desire than to arousing it, Naamah is the perfect wife for Solomon. As if to confirm it, their son Rehoboam was born almost nine months to the day after their wedding. I dote on him and console his mother when she complains of Solomon's indifference. How strange, given the passion that first drove and then bound his father to me, that Solomon should be so aloof! Is it possible that we expended so much heat in his begetting that there was too little left for his life? Or is it that, having heard how the king's lust drove him to sin, he has determined to quash not only all carnal instincts but any hint of affection? I am accustomed to his stiffness towards me, kissing my cheek in the same way that he kisses Abigail's or Maacah's hands, but I long for him to be more demonstrative towards Naamah, a foreigner and still a girl.

I understand her need for tenderness. After my firstborn

son was taken from me, my one thought was to conceive a second. Choking back my revulsion, I gave myself to the man responsible for the deaths of both my husband and my child. Who would have thought that so much love could spring from so much hate? Since the day he was born, I have felt an attachment to Solomon that nothing – not even the birth of his three younger brothers – could shake. His childhood filled me with constant anxiety. Rooms that had been places of refuge became fraught with danger. Every knife, every vessel, every flame was his enemy. Then he grew up and became, as he put it, his own man, able to do without my protection. The truth is that he needs it more than ever, now that the threat comes wrapped in a brother's smile.

Adonijah may have Joab and Abiathar behind him, but we have Nathan. Even a prophet is susceptible to charm and, over the years, I have turned my former adversary into my foremost ally. Despite his unjust claim that I was a party to my own seduction and therefore scarcely less culpable than the king, he has found no fault with either my piety or my care for my children, the second of whom I named after him. I prevailed on him to teach them the stories of the tribes, to the consternation of the other wives, whose sons learnt little more than to read, write and make weapons. Huldath sent an outraged Eliphelet back to his lessons, even though, at twelve, his sole ambition was to prove himself in the field. His younger brothers were plodding scholars, but Solomon excelled. He devoured Nathan's stories, filling scrolls of his own with copies and notes. At times I fear that his studies will distract him from his destiny, but I take heart from Nathan's avowal that Solomon is the worthiest of the king's sons to succeed him. He promises to do all that he can to advance his cause, which he promptly disproves by refusing to bend – or, rather, to bolster – the truth.

'Has the Lord ever told you that he favours Solomon?' I ask hesitantly.

'No.'

'Might he have spoken when you failed to apprehend it?'

'A prophet always apprehends the Lord's meaning!'

'Since you believe that Solomon should inherit – that he must inherit – the crown, couldn't you say – or at least hint – that the Lord does too?'

'Take care, my lady. Your son may be worthy to succeed, but you may not be worthy to stand behind him.'

'Forgive me. It's not my will but the king's. He has told me often – so often I've lost count – that Solomon is his chosen heir.'

'Are you sure that he wasn't indulging you?'

'He swore it before the altar. "May the Lord strike me down if I don't name him," he said.' I curse myself for picking a form of words that I've never heard him use.

'Then he must proclaim him at once.'

'But he's grown old. His mind is muddied. Who knows how much he remembers?'

'It's up to you to remind him.' He looks at me so intently that I blush.

There is no time to lose. Every day Adonijah consolidates his position. His latest move has been to present the king with Abishag, a twelve-year-old Shunammite from his mother's clan, to be his bedmate. Although barely ripe, she fulfils his needs. Despite the fires kept constantly lit in his chamber, he complains of feeling cold, but he no longer summons any of his concubines, let alone his wives, to warm him. It's as if he fears that, with his gross, bristly body, reeking as after a week in the saddle, and the rotting teeth that he refuses to rub with tuber root, he will disgust as much as disappoint us. But Abishag brings neither experience nor expectations, so he has nothing to prove. She attends him day and night, too young even for a monthly respite. I approach her when, on a brief escape to the harem, she sits sobbing among the concubines. I dismiss them and dry her tears, but I cannot afford to pity her.

'What is it? Tell me what's wrong? I promise you'll feel better,' I say, as she struggles to speak.

'It's horrible,' she says at last. 'Once my brothers put a badger – a dead one – in my bed. I felt it on my feet, all furry and flabby, and when I kicked it out, its juices spurted over my legs. But this is worse.'

'This is the king.'

'He smells worse than the badger. His breath... his body. I can still smell him on me now.'

Her words are drowned in a flood of tears. I summon Matred to wash and scent her with my finest oils, while I braid her hair. Lowering her guard, she recounts her daily ordeal. It is almost touching to learn that he wants nothing more than to lie beside her, clinging to her like a second skin. The closest he has come to defiling her is when he lost control of his bowels.

I discover, too late, that Adonijah is using her to spy on the king. Having obtained proof of his impotence, he is preparing to act. It's Shobab, more alert to palace intrigue than Solomon, who reports the discussions that Adonijah has had with several of their brothers. 'What kind of man turns his back on a fresh young virgin?' he asked, a view with which my fourteen-year-old son clearly concurs. I curb my irritation in the need to find out more. Learning from Absalom's mistakes, Adonijah rejects open rebellion, preferring to reason his way to the throne. 'As with the girl, so with the kingdom,' he declared. 'Our father is old; he neglects his duties. No one loves or honours him more than me. My utmost desire is that he should live out his days in peace and not in the turmoil of war, which is bound to break out when our enemies hear of his weakness and launch an attack.'

Shobab is not expecting the slap he receives at the end of his account, but his flagrant support for Adonijah's argument enrages me. It is true that a younger man is needed as king, but that man isn't Adonijah, and I shall spare no effort to thwart him. I swiftly repent my sharpness with Shobab who, rubbing his cheek and glowering, shows no inclination to tell me more. Abjectly apologising, I slap my own hand, as I did when he was a child, and coax him into revealing that Adonijah is hosting a feast, which all his younger brothers (apart from my four sons), Joab, Abiathar, and various of the elders are due to attend. With the blindness of youth, Shobab's sole concern is his exclusion from the gathering. I, on the other hand, am desperate to ascertain its purpose. Is it a council of war or a coronation meal?

I hurry to Nathan's chamber, where Solomon sits alone, studying a scroll, on which I vent my fury, sweeping it from his hands, to my immediate regret. He looks at me quizzically and picks it off the floor, blowing away a speck of dust with a casualness calculated to exasperate me.

'While you sit here reading… reading,' I repeat, as if it were a crime, 'Adonijah is making his bid for the crown. He has invited all your brothers – your half-brothers, that is – to a feast. But not you and Nathan and Shobab and Shammua. Why do you suppose that is? Because he knows that we'll oppose him.'

'Because he knows that you'll oppose him, Mother. I'm quite sure that neither Shobab nor Shammua has given it a thought.'

'And you? Don't you care that everything I've hoped for – everything I've worked for – all these years will be lost?'

'Which is what?'

'You. You! Don't pretend you don't know! You were born to be king, and not just because you're your father's son – they're all your father's sons – but because you're mine. And what do you do?'

'I put myself in your hands, Mother.'

I stare at him. 'That's very wise.'

Leaving word for Nathan to join me the moment he returns, I walk to the king's chamber. I consider taking Solomon but fear that his reserve would antagonise his father and, besides, I can make a better case for him when he isn't there. Despite the urgency, I must keep calm and avoid provoking the king; in the past I reported so many of his sons' misdemeanours that he accused me of sowing discord. I enter the chamber to find him propped up in bed, his mouth gaping like a stranded fish. Abishag sits beside him, so close to the edge that she is in danger of falling off. I wonder if the two guards at the door, who can be little older than Abishag herself, have been chosen because, like her, they don't unsettle the king or because their youth makes any secrets that they might disclose easier to discredit.

I move to the bed and try to ignore Abishag's trembling. Determined to secure the king's endorsement of Solomon, even if I have to fabricate it myself, I wonder whether her dread of me would trump her loyalty to her kinsman should I call on her to corroborate my account. I bow, more for her sake than the king's, to demonstrate my respect for authority, even if it is no longer embodied in the torpid figure who turns to me with eyes that scarcely register my presence.

'My lord,' I say, hoping that he will be more responsive to my voice. 'While you lie here, your crown is being wrested from you.' He raises a listless hand to quiet me. 'Don't you care that your kingdom will be torn apart?' As I wait for him to reply, I catch sight of Abishag trying to creep out of bed and plant myself in front of her. 'Don't you care that I and my sons will be at the mercy of Haggith, who hates me?'

'Wine,' he says, gasping. Abishag reaches for a cup, which I snatch from her.

'Have you forgotten your promise to make Solomon your heir?' Frustrated by his silence, I slap his face. He starts; Abishag screams; the guards rush in. 'No cause for alarm,' I tell them. 'The king rolled on to the girl's arm. He's heavy.' She sits tight-lipped and, after a cursory glance at the chamber, the guards return to their posts. Pushing Abishag off the bed,

I take her place and hand the cup to the king. 'Here, my lord, drink!' A steady gulp appears to revive him.

'Is that you, Bathsheba?'

'Always, my lord.' His chest heaves in silent sobs. I lay his head on my breast and stroke his matted hair. 'I thank you, my lord.'

'For what?'

'What you said just now – what you said all those years ago – that you choose Solomon to sit on your throne.'

'I did?' He searches my face as if to find the words inscribed on it.

'In your wisdom, my lord. And Abishag can vouch for it.' I turn to her, sprawled on the floor, and flash her my most dangerous smile, like a scorpion in a basket of figs. 'You repeated what you swore at the altar that Solomon should be king after you.'

'I did?' He looks at me dazed and I feel a sliver of shame. To play on his bewilderment is a kind of violation, which makes us equal.

'Don't you remember, my lord?' I ask, in a voice raw with pain.

'Maybe… yes… I think so.'

'There, I was sure you would. That's why you're the wisest and most revered of kings.'

Nathan's entrance cuts short my flummery. I inform him that the king has bestowed the succession on Solomon. I look expectantly at Abishag, who gives a tentative nod. Nathan reports that Adonijah and his supporters have ridden out to Ein Rogel, the sacred rock of the Jebusites, where Abiathar has sacrificed oxen, sheep and calves in a blatant attempt to sanctify Adonijah's claim, away from the scrutiny of the tabernacle. He exhorts the king to summon a council and publish his son's treason. Looking at him, slumped on the pillows, I fear that he won't be able to stand, but Nathan calls the guards, who lift him up, with only a passing grimace at his loincloth. I fetch a maidservant who wipes his face and chest, while he swipes at her as at an insistent fly.

Wide-eyed, Abishag tugs at my robe.

'What is it?'

'What about me?'

'What about you?' I ask, impatiently. 'You're a fire by his bedside, which has died out. Shall we throw away the ashes?' She whimpers; I relent. 'You're to say nothing to anyone, do you understand?' She nods repeatedly. 'Very well then, go to the harem and wait. Wait. That's what we do in the harem: we wait.' Nathan looks at me in reproof and I fear that I have spoken out of turn. Abishag leaves, and Nathan and the servant start to dress the king, who protests as if the linen were sackcloth. As he once again assumes the mantle of royalty, I seek out Solomon and his brothers and prepare them for the council.

In spite of the haste and the defection of several of the elders to Adonijah, the great chamber is packed by the time we arrive. I spot Hushai, his hair and beard as wispy as a spider's web, and Zadok, dressed in a pure white robe and headdress, his feet unshod as if he has come straight from officiating in the tabernacle. More welcome than either is Benaiah, the captain of the king's guard, in full armour as though poised to attack the rebels. Joab may command peoples' memories but Benaiah commands the only standing force in the city. Was it arrogance or recklessness that led Adonijah to dispense with his support? I glance at Solomon, who studies everything with his usual detachment. When I ran to his chamber and gave him the news, he thanked me as if I were fetching him for a meal. Is it any wonder that people find him inscrutable when his own mother struggles to know what goes on inside his head?

David enters, supported by the two guards, who half-drag half-lift him as though he were Meribaal. Seized by an intense if unfounded fear that he'll collapse before he reaches the throne, I hold my breath until he sinks on to the seat. Nathan, whose sense of urgency matches mine, enjoins him to speak.

'I call on all present to bear witness that I confer the succession on my son, Solomon,' he declares. The effort of speaking any sentence, let alone that one, exhausts him. He kicks out his foot and, although I am not sure whether it's a summons or a spasm, I thrust Solomon forward to pay him homage, which he does impassively, neither acknowledging the honour nor recoiling from the foot.

'Praise to King David! Praise to King Solomon!' Nathan exclaims, a cry that is picked up throughout the chamber. Rather than the expected relief, I am filled with apprehension, which won't be assuaged until Solomon is crowned.

'Where's Bathsheba?' the king asks.

'Here, my lord,' I reply, kneeling before him. He looks over my head as if unable to locate my voice. I stand and take his hand.

'Didn't I promise you that Solomon would be king?' he says. 'So he shall be this very day.'

'May the king live for ever!' I reply, and for a moment I mean him.

'Where is the priest? Abiathar...?' he asks, looking around.

'No, Zadok, my lord,' Nathan says.

'Zadok, come forward.'

'I'm here, my lord.'

'You and Samuel – '

'Nathan, my lord,' the prophet interposes.

'That's what I said. You and Nathan – Nathan – are to conduct Solomon to the sacred spring, anoint him and proclaim him king over all Israel. Then bring him back here so that my sons and my counsellors and my whole household may swear allegiance.'

The gathering disperses. Zadok goes to the tabernacle to collect the horn of sacred oil and Benaiah to the gatehouse to muster the guards. Nathan dispatches a servant to fetch the king's mule. I accompany Nathan, Shobab and Shammua to the city gate before deciding to turn back. The ceremony is the fulfilment of my every dream, but now that it's taking place, I have no wish to be there. I don't know why. Perhaps, having imagined it for so long, I am afraid of being disappointed? Or else I am worried that witnessing it will leave me with nothing left to dream? So I send for Naamah, who arrives, cradling Rehoboam, blissfully unaware of the great events occurring around him. We walk up the ramparts and watch Solomon ride out of the city. Even I wouldn't claim that he is the most handsome of the king's sons but, robed in white, mounted on the milk-white mule and gilded by the midday son, he dazzles the eye. He is followed by the priests and Levites and, by my count, at least fifty armed guards. As word of the ceremony spreads, the people, first in dribs and drabs and then in droves, join the procession to Gihon.

The spring is obscured by the rockface but, from the blast of the ram's horn and the distinct if dissonant cries of 'Long live King Solomon', I am able to picture the proceedings. Then an insolent jibe of 'Which one is Solomon?' rises from the street below, shattering my concentration. I bridle, before reminding myself that anyone still in ignorance will learn the answer soon enough. I turn to Naamah, whose eyes are moist, and reach for Rehoboam, whom she grudgingly yields up. 'Listen to that, little one,' I say, lifting him high in the air, 'one day it's your name they'll be cheering.' He squalls and grasps at his mother's sleeve.

The procession snakes back through the valley and Naamah and I hasten to the palace, eager to be the first to pay homage to Solomon on his return. As he rides through the gates, we fall to our knees, where he leaves us while he dismounts. I know that he is the king, with more pressing concerns than greeting his mother, but it still smarts. He heads straight to the great chamber, while Nathan remains to report the confusion in Adonijah's camp.

'The princes have rushed back from Ein Rogel to the city, which is rife with rumours that Solomon plans to kill them all.'

'Nonsense!' I say, horrified.

'Rumours,' Nathan replies, 'not edicts.'

Later in the afternoon, the rumours are discounted when we gather in the great chamber to acclaim the newly crowned king. He summons Naamah and me to take our places to the left and right of his throne. As I approach, he kisses me; that is I feel his breath on my cheek.

'So you need me by your side,' I say.

'I need to keep you close, Mother,' he replies, with the ghost of a smile.

His brothers, their mothers, Joab, Abiathar, and the elders who threw in their lot with Adonijah, crowd into the chamber. My hope that he will begin his reign with an act of clemency is realised when he promises not to punish them for past misdeeds but, rather, to honour all those who honour him.

They line up to do him obeisance. Shammua giggles as he sees his older brothers kiss toes that he used to tickle, but I silence him with a frown. The princes are succeeded by the royal wives, led by Abigail, whose age and frailty should exempt her from kneeling, but Solomon extends his foot, which, with an effort almost as painful for us to watch as for her to make, she brushes with her lips. She struggles to rise and Ibhar and Nepheg step forward to help her, while Solomon stares straight ahead. She is followed first by Maacah and then by Haggith, whom Solomon addresses.

'Where is your son, my lady?'

'In the tabernacle, my lord. He seeks sanctuary until he has word that your lordship pardons him.'

'Tell him to quit the Lord's house and return to his own. Provided that he's contrite and pledges loyalty, I shan't hurt him.' With a low bow, Haggith backs out of the chamber. 'Now I too must go to the tabernacle to make a thanksgiving offering. This evening, I invite you all to a feast... that is, all who are not sated from eating with Adonijah.'

As he leaves, I am struck by how painlessly his accession has been accomplished. Unlike his father, Solomon has been crowned without spilling a single drop of blood. The sole transgression has been mine. Not that I am the only mother to have dissembled on her son's behalf. If Rebecca could deceive Isaac to secure Jacob's inheritance, surely I can deceive David to secure Solomon's throne? Just as her deceit was justified when Jacob engendered the twelve tribes, so shall mine be when Solomon proves to be a wise and virtuous king.

Two hours later, Solomon returns and, despite his distaste for such revelry, hosts the feast. I preside in the harem, with Abigail to my left and Naamah to my right. The meal is lavish, but nobody pays much attention to the food. Abigail declares that she has no appetite and when I look at her, pinched and cloudy-eyed, pale and toothless, I wonder if her final act of devotion will be to accompany the old king to the tomb. The other women study me with varying degrees of apprehension. Bathsheba, whom they once disdained, is now mistress of their fates. Are they recalling all the slights and sneers, the lewd laughter when the king summoned me and the resentful glances when I returned festooned with jewels, and wondering how I will be revenged? They needn't worry. Like my son, I intend to be gracious. In token of which I summon a maidservant.

'Take the leftover food to the women confined in the gate-house and make sure that they all – especially Princess Michal – know that it comes from Bathsheba,' I tell her. Meanwhile, I trust that Solomon has thought to send some of the choicest dishes to his father, even if he can do little more than smell them.

With Solomon ruling in his own right, receiving envoys, resolving disputes and drawing up plans for the temple, it is easy to forget that the old king remains alive. Solomon has doubled the guard at his chamber door, replaced all his former servants and forbidden him any visitors but me. Defying their derision, I inform the other wives that he is too weak to receive them. Abishag remains his constant companion, squashed in his bed as though she were trapped beneath an overturned cart.

She no longer returns to the harem, but one night, to my amazement, she bursts into my chamber, her hair as tousled, eyes as wild and robe as besmirched as if she had fled from a captured city. I'm about to reproach her for abandoning the king, when she blurts out: 'He's dead.' My mind goes blank and my body numb. For a moment – how long a moment I'm not sure – I stare into the void of a world without David. I slowly regain my thoughts, my senses and my bearings.

'What did he say?' I ask. 'I need to know his last words.'

'He didn't speak; he couldn't… not since early morning. And then it wasn't anything I could understand, just a name.'

'Which?' I ask. Was it Michal or Abigail? Did first loves triumph at the end? Might it even have been Bathsheba? Or was it one of his sons? Absalom? Amnon? I daren't hope that it was Solomon.

'Did he have a son called Jonathan?'

'No, why? The only Jonathan I know of was King Saul's son.' She looks perplexed. 'Princess Michal's brother.'

'He kept muttering: "Jonathan, Jonathan".'

'No, you were distressed; you must have misheard.' My relief that he hasn't shown a deathbed preference for one of his other wives, let alone their sons, gives way to resentment that his final thought should have been of a friend. 'What he said was: "Solomon, Solomon".'

'But I'm sure – ' As she starts to contradict me, I remind myself that she's only twelve.

'Think carefully, my dear. Think of your future, and I'm sure you'll remember that his mind was fixed on Solomon, giving him his blessing and predicting that his reign would be even more glorious than his own.'

'Yes, yes, I remember,' she stammers. '"Even more glorious".'

A few hours later, his dying words are on everyone's lips.

We bury him the next morning. The day is dull, neither bathed in the glow of the Lord's love for his servant nor battered by storms of grief at his loss. With the rest of the women, I put on sackcloth, smearing my face and arms with ashes, and process through the valley to the tomb. Solomon leads the way, accompanied by the royal princes; Joab, eyes darting back and forth, follows with Abishai and Ittai; the elders of nine of the tribes come next, those of Dan and Asher having failed to arrive in time. I lead the women, with Maacah and Abital on either side. Away from the harem, I am struck by how they've aged (Abigail, the oldest of us all, is too weak to leave her bed). We assemble at the tomb where the Levites sing lamentations, many of which were written by the king himself. Abiathar, looking almost as uneasy as Joab, and Zadok pour libations.

While Solomon, Nathan and the priests escort the king's body into the tomb, I study the mourners, spotting Abishag among the concubines. Even the ash on her cheeks cannot taint her beauty. I speculate on her fate. To my immense relief, Solomon has renounced his claim to his father's harem, since the prospect of his lying with Maacah or Haggith or any of my rivals revolts me. On the other hand, no one who has lived in such intimacy with the king as Abishag can be allowed to return to her clan. With Matred grown clumsy and neglectful, I might take her as my maidservant. But, turning back, I find her exchanging glances with Adonijah, which are manifestly not those of condolence.

It was I who persuaded Solomon that it would be a noble gesture, appreciated by all his brothers, to invite Adonijah to their father's obsequies. I assumed, however, that he would show more tact than to attend the feast. Not only does he come, but he makes straight for me.

'May I beg a kindness, my lady?' he asks.

'Of course,' I reply coldly, excusing myself from a Reubenite who served with Uriah.

'You are the only one who can speak to Solomon – to the
king – on my behalf.'

'Isn't it enough that he has pardoned you? What more do
you want?'

'No, it's not for myself… well, not only. It's for Abishag.'

'What about her?' My chest constricts.

'I am the one who brought her to my father.'

'I'm quite aware of that.'

'She's my mother's kinswoman. I've known her – I've loved
her – since she was a girl.'

'She's still only twelve!'

'That's why I've waited until now. I lent her to my father
because I knew she would please him. But I was sure that he
couldn't please her.'

'And you blazoned his failure to the world!'

'It was wrong, I know. I've repented and made a sin offering. But my desire for Abishag hasn't changed. I want to
marry her.'

I look at him in consternation. To ask this, which would be
widely interpreted as an act of rebellion, and, what's more, to
ask for my help, is the height of folly. Then again, no one could
be that foolish without being sincere. 'What are you thinking
of?' I ask, in the motherly tone that Solomon so resents. 'Don't
you realise what it means to take one of the dead king's concubines? Have you forgotten your brother Absalom?'

'But Abishag wasn't his concubine. He lay beside her but
only as I might lie beside Shephatiah or Elishua. He didn't
couple with her. What a thought!' He winces. 'She's a virgin.
Marrying her is no different to marrying one of the maidser-
vants who washed my father's linen.'

I am moved by his candour. He has lost so much; what harm
would it do for Solomon to grant his wish? Not only would his
magnanimity win him credit, but Adonijah's gratitude would

ensure his support. 'I can't promise anything,' I say, 'but I'll do what I can for you... for you both.'

'My lady,' he replies, bowing and kissing my hand.

I wait for the next council meeting to put his request. Solomon has summoned me to attend, along with those of his brothers – Adonijah himself, Shephetiah, Ithream and Ibhar – who were counsellors to his father. Even if Shobab and Shammua are too young, I urge him to find a place for sixteen-year-old Nathan, but he refuses, telling me bluntly to solicit no more favours for my sons. Wounded, I take my seat.

Before opening the proceedings, Solomon surveys the chamber with an air of surprise. 'I ordered Joab and Abiathar to appear. Who can tell me where they are?'

'In the tabernacle, my lord,' Zadok says.

'Together?'

'Abiathar is performing the daily censing and Joab has sought sanctuary. Both of them fear that they've offended you.'

'Not me but my father,' Solomon says solemnly. 'Days before he died, he called me to his bedside and told me that, if I wanted to secure my throne, I must rid myself of my enemies. I should put to death his kinsman Joab, who slew Abner, King Saul's great general, in cold blood. Abiathar had been no less treacherous but, given his service to the Ark, I should simply banish him to his lands at Anathoth.' He turns to Benaiah. 'My father's judgement is mine. Take your men and go at once to the tabernacle to see it carried out.'

'But my lord, if Joab has sought sanctuary...' Benaiah says.

'His guilt debars him. Drag him away and, if he resists, kill him on the spot. Even at the foot of the altar. It's not you who defile it with his blood, but he who defiles it with his presence.'

'As you command, my lord!' Benaiah leaves, and I gaze at Solomon in disbelief. I begged him repeatedly to visit his father in the last weeks of his life but he refused, claiming that it would be both painful and pointless since he was unable to utter an intelligible sentence, let alone offer advice. Despite my dismay, I trust that, after such severe rulings, he will be disposed to look more kindly on Adonijah's request, which I kneel to put to him.

'Mother, what is this?' he asks harshly. 'Stand up!'

'Not until you've agreed to grant my petition.'

'Not until I know what it is.'

'I speak on behalf of your brother, Adonijah.'

'Stand up!' Solomon steps down from the throne and wrenches my arm. 'Whatever it is, say it to my face, not to my feet.'

'Your brother entreats that you allow him to marry your father's maidservant, Abishag.'

'What? Am I hearing you correctly? Are you Bathsheba, who professes to devote her every waking thought to my welfare?' I feel the eyes of the entire council boring into my skull. 'Don't you see what he's asking? Why did Absalom lie with all ten of my father's abandoned concubines? Ten!' He shudders. 'Why did my father court the lifelong hatred of Princess Michal by lying with her mother?'

'But Abishag wasn't the king's concubine, let alone his wife. She sat with him, sang for him and soothed his distress.'

'So? What matters isn't what is but what is seen to be. Who taught me that, Mother?'

'I was wrong.'

'I'm amazed… no, I'm ashamed. I thought you were strong-willed, deaf to blandishments, but you're as weak as every woman. You've allowed this false brother – this traitor to my father and myself – to beguile you. Benaiah!' He scans the chamber. 'No, of course. Guards, take this man outside' – he points to Adonijah – 'and hang him.' The guards advance on Adonijah as if they were bringing a wild roe to bay. He cowers behind Ibhar and Ithream, using them as shields, while they stand stock-still, looking as horrified by one brother's cravenness as the other's cruelty. The guards prise Adonijah's fingers from their belts and drag him out, screaming and pleading.

'Do you understand now?' Solomon asks, drawing his face close to mine. 'No more meddling; no more entreating. You take charge of the women's quarters and leave me to take charge of the kingdom.' Meeting his gaze, I detect a cold fury – almost a hatred – and wonder whether everything I have done has been in vain and he would have been content for Adonijah or any of his brothers to wear the crown while he worked on the scrolls with Nathan. Banishing the thought, I watch while he returns to the throne and orders the steward to pitch a tent on the roof.

'Then at nightfall, bring Abishag the Shunammite to me. Let the torches be lit so that the whole city can see us. She is my goods, my chattel. She is as much my flesh as the beasts in my stables... as the meat in my dish. I am King David's son and all that he possessed is mine. Tonight I shall lie with his woman. Tomorrow I shall lay the cornerstone of the temple.'

Write name
note ruthlessness & family routine
Writy 88.